Age of Legend © 2019 by Michael J. Sullivan
Theft of Swords excerpt © 2011 by Michael J. Sullivan
Cover illustration © 2019 by Marc Simonetti
Cover design © 2019 Michael J. Sullivan
Map © 2016 by David Lindroth
Interior design © 2019 Robin Sullivan
978-1944145293
All rights reserved.

Published in the United States by Riyria Enterprises, LLC and distributed through Grim Oak Press.

Learn more about Michael's writings at www.riyria.com
To contact Michael, email him at michael@michaelsullivan-author.com

MICHAEL'S NOVELS INCLUDE:
The First Empire Series: Age of Myth • Age of Swords • Age of War • Age of Legend • Age of Death • Age of Empyre
The Riyria Revelations: Theft of Swords • Rise of Empire • Heir of Novron
The Riyria Chronicles: The Crown Tower • The Rose and the Thorn • The Death of Dulgath • The Disappearance of Winter's Daughter
Standalone Titles: Hollow World

First Edition
Printed in the United States of America

2 4 6 8 9 7 5 3 1

Published by

RIYRIA
ENTERPRISES

Distributed by:

GRIM
OAK

WORKS BY MICHAEL J. SULLIVAN

THE LEGENDS OF THE FIRST EMPIRE
Age of Myth • *Age of Swords* • *Age of War* • *Age of Legend*
Forthcoming: *Age of Death* • *Age of Empyre*

THE RISE AND THE FALL
Arrow of Death (Fall 2020) • *Farilane* (Spring 2021)
Untitled #3 (Fall 2021)

THE RIYRIA REVELATIONS
Theft of Swords (contains *The Crown Conspiracy* & *Avempartha*)
Rise of Empire (contains *Nyphron Rising* & *The Emerald Storm*)
Heir of Novron (contains *Wintertide* & *Percepliquis*)

THE RIYRIA CHRONICLES
The Crown Tower • *The Rose and the Thorn*
The Death of Dulgath • *The Disappearance of Winter's Daughter*
Forthcoming: *Drumindor*

STANDALONE NOVELS
Hollow World (Sci-fi Thriller)

SHORT STORY ANTHOLOGIES
Unfettered: "The Jester" (Fantasy: Riyria Chronicles)
Unbound: "The Game" (Fantasy: Contemporary)
Unfettered II: "Little Wren and the Big Forest" (Fantasy: Legends)
Blackguards: "Professional Integrity" (Fantasy: Riyria Chronicles)
The End: Visions of the Apocalypse: "Burning Alexandria" (Dystopian Sci-fi)
Triumph Over Tragedy: "Traditions" (Fantasy: Tales from Elan)
The Fantasy Faction Anthology: "Autumn Mist" (Fantasy: Contemporary)

Age OF Legend

Age of Legend

BOOK FOUR OF

The Legends of the First Empire

MICHAEL J. SULLIVAN

*This book is dedicated to Shawn Speakman for creating
Grim Oak Press and making a habit out of beating the odds.*

Contents

Contents

Author's Note

If you're reading this, I'm going to assume you've finished *Age of Myth, Age of Swords,* and *Age of War.* If you haven't, please stop now, go back, and do so. Otherwise, the story will not be nearly as entertaining. If you have read them but need a refresher on those books, you can find recaps for each at www.firstempireseries.com/book-recaps. You can also take a gander at the Glossary of Terms and Names section in the back of this book. It's written to be spoiler-free, and it's updated after each book to provide more detail when events change.

Okay, what can I tell you about this book? One of my goals for this series was to provide insight about the foundations of the world of Elan, and much of that has been explored in the first three books. But one day as I was just writing away, a character—who shall remain nameless—made a morbidly funny joke. They do that sometimes, but in this case my jaw dropped, and I stopped typing.

What if it wasn't a joke?

Just as the Big Bang was said to have given birth to the universe in less than an instant, a whole new direction for the story exploded in my head. *Can I really do that?* I thought excitedly. The answer was, *I have to at least try.* And that is how the second half of the series was born. In doing so, I went even deeper into the bedrock of Elan to create something I feel is truly special and unusual, and I hope you will agree.

Now, there are a few things in this second half that I've done differently than my other books, and I want to warn you about them in advance. The first involves the span of time. The war between elves and men lasted six years, but revealing all the events that occurred during this period is both unnecessary and actually counterproductive to the plot of the story being told. When I originally wrote *Age of Legend,* I opened it a full six years after *Age of War.* But when my alpha-reader wife, Robin, read the novel, she found I'd made a leap that was too far. Relationships had matured, discussions that should have taken place years before were only now being brought up, and there was too much of a gap between *Age of War* and *Age of Legend* to easily follow the events. In order to fix these problems, *Age of Legend* is now presented in three parts. The book opens immediately following *Age of War.* Part two occurs a year later, and part three jumps another five years into the future. Some readers, like those who'd prefer to see all the significant events in the lives of their beloved characters, will be disappointed with me skipping ahead, and for that I'm sorry. But I believe I owe you the best story I can produce, and doing otherwise would have resulted in a meandering plot that would likely drag the story off focus. The best way to solve this was to cut out the fluff and touch only on those events needed to move the plot, so that's what I did.

Okay, so that's the first thing. The second is that this book is not self-contained as all my previous works have been. Yes, it does have a beginning, middle, and end, but when you get to the last page you really have only completed act one of a three-act play. The fact of the matter is that the entire second half of the series takes us in a whole new direction, and it'll require three full-length novels to tell the story the way it needs to be told, and each of these tales has a very defined climax that wraps up each book. Bottom line, this novel ends much in the same way as Tolkien's *Fellowship of the Ring* concluded the "fellowship" portion of that tale, and as with that book, when you finish, you will find the story is far from over.

Now, I know this will cause some distress for some readers. Few alive today were forced to wait for Tolkien to publish the second book in his series, and while I regret the delay you will face, the good news is that this series is complete, and we'll have an accelerated release schedule for the next two volumes. For those wondering why I don't just release them all at once, there are two reasons. First, a completed manuscript does not a final book make. While almost all of my work is finished (barring some minor rewrites), my editors, beta readers, gamma readers, publicists, cover artists, designers, and so on have to do their magic to make the novels the best they can be, and that takes time. Rest assured, we'll get the books out just as soon as possible, and we'll even offer early copies to Kickstarter backers just as we did with this book.

That's really all you need to know going into the start of the second half of the series. So I'll repeat something I've said in other author's notes: I have greatly appreciated receiving all the amazing emails, so please keep them coming to michael@michaelsullivan-author.com. It's never a bother hearing from readers—it's an honor and a privilege.

Now, as this preamble is over, let's all gather in a circle around the lodge's cozy eternal flame and listen as I invite you back to an age of myths and legends, to a time when humans were known as Rhunes and elves were once believed to be gods. In this particular case, allow me to take you to the *Age of Legend*.

Michael J. Sullivan

April 2019

Age of Legend

PART I

CHAPTER ONE

Innocence Lost

*What a strange treasure is innocence, a virtue to the old and a curse
to the young, so highly prized but eagerly parted with—the riches
of beautiful skin traded for the wisdom of calluses.*

— THE BOOK OF BRIN

Suri sat alone with a sword across her lap, staring at what most would call
a dragon, but which the onetime mystic of Dahl Rhen saw as a fragment of
her broken heart. Having been shattered several times, her heart had left
pieces strewn across two continents. But the part she watched that morning
was both physically huge and the only one visible.

For days, she had monitored the dragon-like creature lying atop the
hill. Being the one who had created the thing, Suri felt responsible for
whatever it might do. She'd kept a vigilant eye on her handiwork, but after
it had saved the inhabitants of Alon Rhist by slaughtering half an army,
her creation hadn't moved. It hadn't so much as twitch its tail. This came
as both a comfort and a concern to nearly everyone. Most hoped that the
once miraculous—now unsettling—dragon lying on their doorstep would
just fly away. They wanted their monster-savior to go back to whatever
mysterious place it had come from. Few knew of the creature's origin,
although news of Suri's involvement had spread. The mystic imagined that

the gilarabrywn remained a disturbing fixture to most, sort of like a wasp's nest on the porch—if wasps could tear through stone and breathe fire. The beast remained curled up, still as a stone, like an enormous sculpture or an unusual rock formation. A quiet, sleeping dragon, while not ideal, was better than the alternative.

From where Suri sat, with the rising sun casting her subject in silhouette, the gilarabrywn blended into the craggy outline of Wolf's Head, and some effort was required to make sense of its shape. Suri struggled to remember where the head and tail were, but the wings were unmistakable. Even folded, they stood up from the hilltop—two sharp points like listing flagpoles. Suri felt the weight of the black-bronze blade on her lap and considered going closer. She would have to release the creature eventually, but tomorrow always seemed better than today. Instead, she sat on a rock, beside a dead tree, at the bottom of a sea of guilt.

If I go up there, its eyes will open. Suri was certain of that. Those giant orbs would narrow on her, staring with . . . *what? Hatred, fear, pity?* Suri wasn't sure and wasn't confident she'd recognize the difference. *The worst thing about a gilarabrywn is I have to kill them twice.*

Despite several days of pouring rain, the Grandford battlefield remained stained. The beige rock and dirt had a rusty tinge, and the air smelled foul, especially when it blew from the west. Not all of the bodies were buried; many Fhrey had been left to rot. There was too much to do, too few people to do it, and burying the enemy was low on everyone's list of priorities.

"This is a horrid place," she said, looking at the beast, "but you always knew that, didn't you?"

She had felt the bleakness of the plains of Dureya even before the day when the premonition of Raithe's death had threatened to overwhelm her. The Art granted a second sight, a sixth sense. Arion sometimes called it a third eye, but that wasn't right. The sensation had nothing to do with vision. What it granted were feelings, impressions, and usually they came in a jumbled, tangled mess. The closest and strongest perception usually stood out from the background noise, but here the clamor was deafening. Generations of men had fought and died on this land.

And nothing has changed.

In her hands, Suri held Arion's knit cap. She rubbed her thumbs over the little holes in the open weave of thick wool yarn, and she recalled Arion's voice. *Still, I feel it, this little string that stretches between you and peace. When I look at you, I sense hope. You're like this light in the darkness, and you get brighter every day.* Arion had said that just a few days ago, but that seemed like another lifetime. Suri didn't feel brighter.

Sounds of movement came from behind her. Someone was walking from the ruins of the fortress across the bloodstained clay. Malcolm. She didn't need to look or use the Art to know who it was. He was the only one who wasn't frightened of the wasp's nest on the porch or the mystic who had summoned it, and she had been expecting his visit.

Since Raithe's and Arion's funerals, Suri had spent most of her time at this exact spot. She and the gilarabrywn were a pair of unlikely twins tethered together. Suri occasionally left in search of food, but she was careful to avoid others. She didn't want to talk to anyone, answer questions, or face looks of pity—or, more likely, fear. She didn't want to talk to Malcolm, either. While he had nothing to do with Arion's death, he had pushed her into killing Raithe and creating the gilarabrywn.

"Strange, isn't it?" he said, approaching. "How with time, simple things, silly little things like knit hats, can become so important. Magical, in a way."

Suri looked down at the hat and nodded. "She only wore it for a short while, said it itched. But I remember her best that way."

He sat down beside her, his big knees sticking up like a grasshopper's.

"Are you . . ." Suri was about to say *Miralyith*, but even as she spoke, she realized he wasn't. Miralyith gave off a signal, a hot spot, a light. Malcolm seemed like everyone else, except more so. She'd never noticed before, but if he were a tree, he wouldn't be any old one. Malcolm would be the perfectly shaped, full-leafed oak that everyone imagined when thinking of a tree. He wasn't ordinary, that was certain, and he also wasn't easy to comprehend. Looking at him was like trying to make sense of a cloud. She gave up on the possibility of understanding Malcolm. Not every puzzle needed to be solved, and some things were more trouble than they were worth. She guessed he was like that.

"Am I what?"

"Nothing." She shook her head. "Never mind."

"How are you doing? You okay?"

"No."

They sat in silence as a dry wind failed to convince brittle grass to dance.

"Tell me something. Is this it? Was that all?" Suri asked. Malcolm had revealed he could see the future, and she didn't know how much more she could take.

"You'll have to be a little more specific."

Suri expected he would know what she was referring to, that he could read her mind, but maybe that was unfair—people thought she could read minds, too. "Arion believed that if the fane knew a Rhune was capable of the Art it would result in peace between our peoples." She nodded in the direction of the gilarabrywn. "Well, the fane saw with his own eyes, so the war should be over. Is it?"

Malcolm sorrowfully shook his head. "No, it's not."

"Then why did you . . ." Suri's eyes teared up. "If you knew it wouldn't be enough, then why sacrifice Raithe?"

"You already know the answer to that. The fane's forces would have overwhelmed us, and everyone would have died. Raithe saved us. *You* saved us. *And* . . ."

"And?"

"It was necessary for what's yet to come."

"So, what about me? Is my part in all this over? I mean, I did what Arion wanted, and what you needed, so I'm done, right?"

Suri didn't care about the future, having been shattered by the past. She had reached record levels of self-loathing after killing two of her best friends and failing to save a third. These were not the actions of a virtuous person. As it turned out, butterflies weren't beautiful. They, like pieces of a broken heart, were monsters. Innocence hadn't just been lost, but crushed to death without mercy, and Suri didn't feel so much lonely as left behind. She planned to return to the Hawthorn Glen, bury herself in the forest, and never come near people again.

Malcolm frowned. "You're thinking of running away?"

Oh, sure, now *he can read minds.*

"You can't. Not yet. I'm sorry to say you've only taken a few steps in the role you'll need to play." He sighed. "I wish I could tell you everything will be all right from now on, or that the worst is over—"

"It gets worse?" Suri's eyes grew big in disbelief.

Malcolm frowned again. "The point is—"

"How can it possibly get worse?"

"What you need to focus on is that in the end everything will be—"

"Worth it?" she said hotly. "*Nothing* can make up for what's already happened—nothing!" Suri was standing without realizing she'd gotten up. "Minna is dead. Arion is dead. Raithe is dead. And I killed all of them!"

"You didn't kill Arion, she—"

"She was in Alon Rhist because of me!"

"Suri, you need to calm down," Malcolm said softly.

"I don't want to calm down! I'm not going to calm down! I—"

"Suri!" Malcolm said sharply and pointed toward the hill.

The gilarabrywn had its head up, eyes open and glaring. While she found it hard to interpret the facial features of an enchanted creature, Suri was pretty sure the gilarabrywn wasn't pleased.

The mystic took several deep breaths, wiped tears from her eyes, and sat back down.

"I never asked for any of this," she whispered.

"I know, but it was given to you just the same. We have but the roads that lie before our feet, and all too often our choices are limited to walking or standing still. And standing still gets us nowhere."

"What about going back?"

Malcolm shook his head. "What you think of as a retreat is merely going forward in a different direction. Both paths are equally fraught with peril."

"So, what am I supposed to do?"

"Well, not running away will suffice for now." He looked over at the gilarabrywn, who settled back down. "And don't release that yet."

"No?" Suri had dreaded the idea of plunging the sword into her creation. Doing so wouldn't be murder, not really, but it would feel like it. Convincing her to put it off wouldn't take much.

Malcolm shook his head. "Like you, it still has more to do. The good news is you don't have to do the deed. Give me the sword. When the time comes, I'll see he's put to rest."

She handed him the black-bronze blade with Raithe's true name etched along the weapon's flat side.

"So, if I can't go to the Hawthorn Glen, what should I do?"

"You'll discover your new path when you reach it. That's the beauty of roads, they all lead someplace."

As if to illustrate the point, Malcolm stood up. He smiled at her—a good smile, the perfect smile for that moment—and it did make her feel better. He started back toward the ruins of the Rhist, then he stopped and focused once more on the gilarabrywn. "Did Arion teach you how to make that?"

This puzzled Suri, as she assumed Malcolm was already familiar with everything related to the creation of a gilarabrywn. He had certainly seemed well educated that night in the smithy when Raithe was transformed. "The weave I used was etched on the Agave tablets."

Malcolm's eyes narrowed, and confusion filled them as if he and Suri no longer shared the same language. "Agave tablets?"

Suri nodded. "Slabs of stone deep inside Neith with markings on them. Brin did the translation."

"Where did these tablets come from?"

Suri shrugged. "The Ancient One carved them." Now it was Suri's turn to be confused, and her brow furrowed. "How come you don't know about this? I thought you knew everything."

Malcolm was no longer displaying that perfect smile. "So did I."

Brin sat at the little desk in the pigeon loft, her back against the stone wall. Around her, a dozen birds cooed from individual coops. Persephone had asked her to keep watch for any reply from the fane, and since the loft was one of the few spots untouched by the devastation of the battle, Brin had decided to move in. The place was perfect for working on her book. It already had a tiny desk that had been used to compose messages to Fhrey outposts.

Being so engrossed in her work, she didn't notice Malcolm's arrival until he cleared his throat and asked, "How's the book coming?"

How did he know I was up here? She looked over, dumbfounded.

"That's what you call it, right? A *book*?" he asked.

"Yes, *The Book of Brin*."

Malcolm nodded. "Roan and Persephone mention it often, and with a great deal of pride, I might add. It sounds wonderful, this idea of making a permanent record of everything that's happened. But you need to be careful. Don't allow personal opinion to distort facts."

Brin leaned forward on her stool, planting her elbows securely on the surface of the desk. "Are you referring to Gronbach? Because that vile mole has earned every negative thing I wrote about him."

"The dwarf?" Malcolm paused and thought a moment. "Well, I wasn't referring to him specifically. But now that you bring it up, I should point out that you run the risk of painting a whole race with the same ugly brush, which could have unexpected consequences in the future. My point is, you need to be as accurate as possible because *your* account may well be *the* account."

This wasn't news to Brin. The whole reason she'd started her project was to make a single permanent record of all past events, a common resource to be used and added to by subsequent Keepers. "I'd never lie. Keepers are honor-bound to be exact and precise."

Malcolm nodded but exhibited a pained smile. "And yet, they *have* frequently failed to preserve the past accurately."

"What are you—"

"Let's take Gath of Odeon, for example. He's a legend among your clan, isn't he?"

Feeling that Malcolm's visit had shifted from brief to prolonged, she covered her ink cup and sat back. "Yes."

"So, what *is* a legend?"

Brin found the question bewildering. Malcolm was trying to make a point, one she instinctively felt she wouldn't like. He was looking for something in particular, but she had no idea what that might be. Giving up, she offered the obvious answer, but with a noncommittal shrug. "An important story or person, I guess."

Malcolm sighed. Apparently, that wasn't the answer he was looking for. "You do understand that not all stories are true, right?"

"I know some people lie, yes. But I told you, I'd never—"

Malcolm held up his hand to stop her, then pointed at the other stool in the room. "Do you mind?"

Brin gestured an invitation, finding it odd that he'd asked. This wasn't her bird loft.

He pulled the stool over and sat across the desk from her, leaning forward, elbows on knees. "Brin," he began gently, "there are times when people can say something happened that didn't, *without* lying. They believe it to be the truth, even when it isn't. Sometimes it's a simple mistake. Other times it's because someone lied to them, perhaps even out of kindness. And then there are instances when a story changes over time. Keepers might add a little flair to make their tales seem more exciting." He thought a moment. "Or to illustrate a point."

Brin offered only a confused expression.

"Okay, let's go back to Gath. He's regarded as a wise and heroic person, right? He's the one that led the Ten Clans out of the east when the great flood came. Gath is seen as a savior of the Rhunes, and rightly so. But the stories about him are bigger than that. He isn't known as just some average fellow who in a time of crisis found the courage and determination to push everyone into leaving, is he? The stories make him out to be more than that."

"You mean like how when he was a kid, he solved so many riddles?"

"Exactly. Maybe he *was* unusually bright, but perhaps that part of *his story* was added later by people just trying to show him as wise. It's entirely possible he wasn't smart at all. When you think about it, making him appear special actually gives the wrong impression. The truth is that everyone can achieve greatness, but many don't try because they think of themselves as merely ordinary."

This made Brin remember a day long ago when Konniger held his first lodge meeting. Persephone had tried to persuade him to move the clan, but Maeve, the Keeper at the time, had killed the idea by saying, "Gath of Odeon was renowned even before the flood. Heroes like him no longer walk among us."

And yet they did—or maybe, as Malcolm suggested, heroes aren't born, they're made, grown from ordinary stock and fertilized by crisis.

Malcolm continued, "*The Book of Brin* solves the problems of forgetfulness and embellishment, which might just make it the most important thing ever created by mankind. But if it isn't accurate, it could create other issues. Your book will be seen as an authority, like an eyewitness, and as such it won't be easily disputed. With so much responsibility, you need to be careful about what you write. Wouldn't you agree?"

Brin nodded, feeling altogether frightened. What had begun as a way to make Keepers' jobs easier had morphed into something potentially dangerous. She felt like a child who'd brought home a bear cub because it was cute. She looked at the pages of her book spread out on the desk and worried what might happen when the cub became a grown bear.

Malcolm looked at the parchments as well. "So, how far have you gotten?"

"Not nearly as far as before." A rush of frustration threatened to make her cry. With all that had happened, her emotions were like milk in a too-full bucket—they spilled over easily. "I had a lot more done, but it was destroyed during the Miralyith attack. I worked so hard, and now"—she gestured at the pages on the desk—"this is all I have. I had to start over."

"I see." He nodded solemnly, then offered a positive smile. "But second attempts are usually better than firsts."

She frowned at him, then reconsidered. "I'm working on the Battle of Rhen right now and . . ." She shrugged. "It's coming out pretty good. I guess it *might* be better than the first time."

"Have you finished the part about your time in Neith?" His eyes went to the largest stack of pages.

She sighed. "Not yet."

"But you still remember?"

"I'm a Keeper—that's my job."

"Of course." Malcolm nodded. "Would you mind telling me a bit of it? About Neith, I mean. In particular, about the stone tablets."

Brin nodded. "Okay."

Malcolm smiled and settled back on his stool.

"We found slabs of rock with markings on them." Brin showed a self-conscious smile. "You see, I didn't really invent this thing Arion calls *writing*. I tried to, but I hadn't worked it all out. Well, not until I found the tablets, that is. Almost everything I'm doing now is based on what I found there."

"How were you able to understand the markings on the stones?"

"It wasn't hard. The tablet on top of the stack was a guide. It showed the list of symbols arranged in groups by the sounds they corresponded to. Once I understood each mark, it was simple to do the substitutions."

Malcolm looked confused. "I still don't understand. I look at what you've done here, and it's beautiful, but I can't tell you what it says. How can you?"

"Well, of course you can't. You didn't study the guide. I have it memorized, so it's easy for me. Let me show you." She pointed at the page she was working on. "See here, this mark makes a *wa* sound like *water* or *want,* and this one sounds like *all,* as in *ball.* Put them together and you get *wall.*" She patted the stone behind her.

He nodded. "Well, yes, that makes sense, but how do you know"—he pointed at one of the markings—"that this one sounds like *wa?*"

"Well, it's obvious, isn't it? The symbols are universal." She pointed at her page again. "When I first wrote sun, I used a circle to represent the *sss* sound. Anyone would do that, right? So, the circle is a universal symbol for *sss.* Once I went through the guide, I knew I was on the right track."

Malcolm shook his head. "That only makes sense if everyone in the world speaks Rhunic. In Fhrey, the sun is called *arkum,* and in Belgriclungreian it's *halan.* The goblins call it *rivik.* So, why isn't the circle an *ar, ha,* or *ri* sound?"

Brin paused, considering this. "I don't know, but I must have been correct because it worked. After I performed the substitutions, the words made sense. Even the names were right."

"Names?"

"Yeah. The tablets told of the world's creation. They mentioned Ferrol, Drome, and even Mari. So, I must have gotten the sounds correct. I suppose the writer must have spoken Rhunic."

Malcolm shook his head. "Actually, those names are the same in every language, even Ghazel, but that doesn't explain the other words. You're right. The fact that you deciphered them correctly is undeniable. So . . ." Malcolm rotated a page in order to view it right-side up. Brin had no idea what he hoped to see. To him it would be nothing but rows of indistinguishable markings. "There's only one explanation," he said. "These tablets were created for *you.*"

"*Me?* That's not possible."

"Of course it is. Before Gifford was born, Tura told Padera he would one day win a race to save humanity. He—well, everyone really—thought this was preposterous, and yet he did exactly that. The proof of the prophecy is self-evident because it was fulfilled. Since you read the tablets, my hypothesis is a sound one."

"But it doesn't mean *me* specifically, right?" Brin didn't like the idea that an ancient being who was capable of creating a monster like Balgargarath had left her a personal note. That was as scary as Tet. "Anyone who speaks Rhunic could have deciphered them. It didn't *have* to be me."

"Have you taught anyone else your symbols? Does anyone but you know the correlations between these markings and their sounds?"

"Well, no, but—"

"Then whoever wrote these was certain you'd find them. That, or . . ." He tapped a finger thoughtfully to his lips.

"Or what?"

"Or they knew your markings would be so widely known that anyone could read the tablets. This would suggest your symbols really *will* become universal. Either way, the writer clearly had the gift of future-sight. But because it was *you* who read them, and given that this is far too unlikely to be mere coincidence, I'll stay with my first conclusion: These were intended for you, and you alone."

Brin began to wish Malcolm hadn't visited that morning. He'd only been there a few minutes, and she was terrified of her book and frightened that some ancient powerful being knew her name.

"Suri mentioned something called the Agave. What's that?" Malcolm asked.

"Ah . . . It's a chamber deep, deep below Neith. Rain said it was like the world ended down there, and he's a digger, you know? It's where the Ancient One was trapped. He's the one who wrote the tablets. He taught the dwarfs how to make bronze and iron, secrets he gave them in exchange for his freedom. But the dwarfs didn't keep their word. I'm pretty sure that's a *thing* with them. Anyway, he eventually offered them a seed from the First Tree, and he told them if they ate its fruit, they'd live forever. When they opened a hole to get the seed, the Ancient One escaped and left Balgargarath behind to punish the dwarfs and stop anyone from entering Neith."

Malcolm looked concerned, like a father who'd lost track of his children and heard the distant howl of a wolf.

"Malcolm, is something wrong?"

"Yes, I think so. You've just answered a great many questions I've wondered about for a very long time, but you've also created a long list of new ones. I'm going to have to leave for a while."

"Leave? Are you going to Neith?"

He nodded. "To start with, yes. I'm going to see if I can recover those tablets. If I do, can you translate them for me?"

"Of course!" Brin's face blossomed into a wide grin. The thought of reading all the tablets made her giddy with excitement. "Before you leave, go see Roan. She can give you charcoal and vellum and show you how to make rubbings from the tablets. There are too many of them to carry. They'd be too heavy anyway—" Reality hit, and the grin faded. "But you can't reach them! Suri collapsed the mountain. There's no way to get in."

"Maybe, but I'm going to try anyway."

"Why?"

Malcolm laughed, shaking his head. "That would take too long to explain, and I—we—don't have that kind of time."

"Well, if you get to Caric, watch out for Gronbach. Don't trust him. That dwarf is an evil liar."

Malcolm flashed an amused smile. "I'll be careful, and you should, too. Right now, you are the only one capable of reading those tablets, as well as your book. You'll need to change that, or what's the point? While I'm gone, teach others so that your symbols really will become universal."

"Will you be gone long?"

"I suspect so. After I visit Neith, if I can't—as you say—get in, I may need to go looking for the Ancient One."

"Search for him? But he has to be dead, right? Or do you think he was telling the truth about immortality?"

"We've just learned that someone who has lived for thousands of years at the bottom of the world left you a message, one that you received. I don't think it's wise to rule anything out."

"Would it help to know his name?"

"You mean besides the Ancient One?"

"That's just what the dwarfs called him, but in the tablets, he referred to himself as The Three."

Once more, Malcolm's eyes widened. "I *really* do have to go."

CHAPTER TWO

Exodus

In the beginning, our clans were nomads. Then we settled on dahls, and for generations we did not move. The war made wanderers of us once again.

— THE BOOK OF BRIN

Persephone insisted she'd be able to walk, but Moya declared that wasn't going to happen. The keenig's Shield spoke with both hands on her hips, reinforcing her seriousness with the same glare she had used on Udgar just before putting an arrow through his throat. For such a beautiful woman, Moya could be as scary as the Tetlin Witch.

"I've ordered a wagon for you," Moya said, as if this would make any further debate pointless.

"Everyone else is walking. I can't ride in a cart like some privileged—"

"Seph, you can't walk. It's been less than a week since you were gutted. You can barely stand up straight, and you're still as pale as a goose egg. You'll be lucky to get down to the gate without help." Moya sighed and softened. "I know you're all about image and putting up a good front, but imagine how it will look if everyone sees you fall on your face. You're the keenig, our fearless leader. Let's not ruin everyone's screwed-up fantasy by giving the dirt a big kiss. Besides, it's a nice wagon. I picked it out myself and arranged for everything. There are plenty of pillows and blankets, plus wine, cheese, a girl to hold your cup and wipe your brow, a boy to fan you, a piper to play music, and two muscular, handsome, shirtless men who will stand on either side. They'll protect you not only from harm but also from the sun, as they hold a canopy to provide shade while you roll along in style."

Persephone looked at her, horrified.

"I'm joking. Relax. By Mari, when did you lose your sense of humor?"

Persephone knew exactly when, and Moya would have, too, if she'd thought about it. But she didn't. Everyone was doing their best not to think, ponder, or reflect—plenty of time for that later. For now, they kept busy: working, digging, gathering, packing, moving, always moving. The horror of the battle remained fresh; stopping would give their sorrows the opportunity to catch up. As long as everyone had something to do, they could delay facing the loss of their homes and loved ones and pretend life could continue like on any ordinary day. Well, maybe not ordinary, but close enough.

Confined to her bed, Persephone had no such luxury. All she could do was reflect on mistakes made, lives lost, and her mountain of regrets.

Moya tapped a finger against her lips. "Although now that I think about it"—a wicked smile rose—"the part about men holding a canopy is kind of tempting. I wish I *had* arranged for that." Focusing her glare once more on Persephone, Moya added a pointed finger. "But I'm serious about you traveling in a wagon."

Persephone had been sequestered in what she assumed to be the best remaining room in the once-upon-a-time fortress that, after three days of battle, had become a devastated ruin. Moya had insisted on the finest accommodations possible for her wounded keenig. As Persephone lay in one of the tiny prison cells beneath the imploded Verenthenon, she knew the destruction of Alon Rhist was all but total.

Hastily cleaned and decorated with drapes, the room was so small there wasn't room for anything except the bed, which forced Moya to stand in the hallway. For several days, the labyrinthine warren of prison cells known as the *duryngon* had served as living quarters and administrative center of the *Forces of the West*. Persephone had invented the name out of necessity. She couldn't refer to those she led as the Ten Clans or the Rhune Horde because that would leave out their Fhrey allies and the three dwarfs. Besides, Forces of the West had the benefit of sounding powerful and inclusive.

"How are things coming?" Persephone asked.

"Fine," Moya said, but Persephone wondered how much of that one-word report was born of not wanting to add to her stress. Perhaps sensing that her keenig expected more, Moya added, "Where are we going anyway?"

"Merredydd, I suspect, but I'll need to speak to Nyphron first. I've only visited Alon Rhist, and I don't know which of the other Fhrey fortresses might suit our needs best. I'm told Merredydd is closest. But can it support all of us? Alon Rhist was the primary Instarya fortress, so I'm assuming it was the biggest, but with all the added Gula, even it would be too small. If no other outposts can handle the army, Rhen might be a better option."

"No walls left in Rhen," Moya pointed out. "Not anymore."

"Not at the moment, but we can rebuild."

"Do we have that kind of time? And how good will wooden walls be?"

"I was thinking Frost, Flood, and Suri could assist with that."

"Suri doesn't like walls."

"True, but I think she'll help just the same. The important thing is that Rhen isn't too far, and it has plenty of room, wood, water, game in the forest, and cultivated fields. Who knows what we'll find at the other Instarya settlements."

"Shouldn't we just stay here? Can't Suri put everything back the way it was?"

"I doubt it. I don't know how the Art works, but I'm certain it's easier to destroy than to rebuild. Would you know where every rock and splinter goes? Do you think she does? I suppose she could do something: clear the rubble, put up new walls perhaps, but if we're going to that much effort, we might as well start fresh somewhere else—someplace that doesn't have corpses for a foundation. No, we can't stay here. I want to get moving the moment Nyphron gets back."

Moya's brows rose. "He returned yesterday."

"He did?"

Moya made a sour face. "Doesn't bode well, does it? Your not knowing, I mean."

"What are you talking about?"

"I heard you two are getting married." Moya cringed, as if expecting a slap.

"Where did you hear that?" Persephone asked, shocked.

"Nyphron." Moya looked a little confused. "He made it sound like it's something you two have been discussing."

"We've been *talking,* sure, for about a year, but I haven't said yes."

"Oh, well, I can see why. He comes back and doesn't even stop by to say hello? If Tekchin did that, I'd—"

"How's that going?" Persephone wanted to change the subject, avoid talk of marriage, but given that she was contemplating a similar arrangement with Nyphron, she was genuinely curious.

"What? Tekchin and me?"

Persephone nodded. As far as she knew, Moya and Tekchin were the only Rhune–Fhrey pairing in history. In many ways, it made no sense that an arrogant, eleven-hundred-year-old Fhrey warrior would find a twenty-six-year-old Rhune mate-worthy, but in others, it was perfectly logical. They were both wild things: passionate, aggressive, and competitive. The two were so much the same—reflections born in different realities. As unlikely as it seemed, they somehow fit each other perfectly.

Persephone saw similarities between their affair and her relationship with Nyphron. She and Nyphron both viewed themselves as leaders first and individuals second. They focused on the roles they played in shaping the future rather than any personal comfort or desires. Even the fact that he hadn't visited her right away made sense. Upon returning, Nyphron's priority would be hearing reports from the defense forces he'd left behind, not checking up on her.

A Rhune fiancé might have rushed to her out of an emotional desire, a need to reassure himself she was safe. Such sentimentality would take unwarranted hold of his judgment. There was no reason to fear for her well-being. She was adequately protected, and any concerns he might have would be immature and irrational compared with the many real concerns left in the wake of such a devastating battle. Nyphron was neither childish nor illogical.

Raithe was both, and I loved him for it.

What Persephone wanted to know from Moya was whether a relationship between Fhrey and humans could work. *Is such a pairing plausible?*

"We're good." Moya effortlessly rolled her shoulders. Then she paused and narrowed her eyes. A new smile appeared on her lips, this one hinting at self-satisfaction. "Are you asking about how we——"

"By the Grand Mother, no!" Persephone threw up both hands, warding her off.

Moya's grin only grew more mischievous. "I think you'll be pleasantly surprised to discover that Fhrey are even more——"

"Stop! Stop it! I don't want to know anything about *that*. I was just thinking, well, it's a completely different culture. I was only curious if ah . . . ah . . ."

Moya folded her arms and watched in amusement as Persephone struggled.

"I mean, Fhrey women are so . . ."

"Boring?" Moya supplied. "That's what they are, you know? Or at least that is how the Fhrey see them."

"I actually meant——"

"No, seriously. Tekchin says it all the time. Sure, Fhrey women are gorgeous, but they're also dull. We lowly Rhunes have short lives, so we don't have time to be tedious. I know I don't. And to me, Tekchin is so much more than a man, *especially* in bed. He's . . . he's, ah . . . well, he really is sort of like a god—and don't you ever tell him I said that."

Moya looked so suddenly concerned that Persephone found herself smiling. She realized it was the first time since—

"You're going to marry Nyphron, aren't you?" Now it was Moya's turn to change the subject, and suddenly their conversation felt like a game of Truth or Dare.

"Yes, I suppose, as soon as we get settled again."

"Wonderful." Nyphron's voice echoed from down the corridor.

"Shush." Persephone put a finger to her lips. A moment later, the Galantian leader appeared at the threshold, sidling up to Moya, who inched over to share the doorway.

"How much did your Fhrey ears hear?" Persephone asked, concerned.

Nyphron grinned. "Enough to know that Tekchin is godlike in bed. He's gonna love that."

Moya's mouth dropped open, her expression aghast. Nyphron gave her a moment to retort, but the keenig's Shield said nothing.

"And"—Nyphron looked at Persephone—"that I'll need to arrange a feast following the pitching of the new camp in the High Spear Valley. That's how we do such things in Fhrey society. We publicly announce our association, and then the attendees eat and drink themselves stupid."

"Our *association?*"

"Association, marriage, same thing."

Persephone looked at Moya, appalled. "See what I have to put up with?"

"Tekchin is worse. He won't have a ceremony and refuses to say he loves me. He's always going on about how actions are more important than words."

"And for once, he's right," Nyphron declared. "Pronouncements are a foolish frivolity. But in this case, a public display is unavoidable."

"How come?" Moya asked.

"Politics," Nyphron stated. "She's the keenig, and I'm commander of the Instarya, so it's important for everyone to witness our joining. The people need to *see* the two of us as a unified team and *hear* our pledges to each other and the cause."

"Romantic, isn't he?" Persephone said.

Despite his keen ears, Nyphron didn't seem to hear that. He hooked a thumb back over his shoulder. "I noticed a number of carts being lashed to horses outside. What's that all about?"

Persephone wanted to think he'd switched subjects because the talk of romance had made him uncomfortable, but Nyphron was never uneasy. He was merely his usual focused self and had spent enough time on small talk.

"Roan had the idea of having a horse pull them," Persephone replied. "A single animal can haul heavier loads than a team of men."

"Will horses do that? My experience is that they are skittish things, stupid animals that are best avoided. Won't they end up kicking the cart? They'll probably bust it and break a leg in the process."

"Roan and Gifford have been working with the animals that survived. I heard they're having good results." She looked to Moya. "Isn't that so?"

"They had a little trouble at first, but they've worked things out. Oh, I forgot to tell you." Moya's face lit up with excitement. "Gifford took me for a ride yesterday in this little two-wheeled cart Roan and the dwarfs built. He hooked it up to Naraspur and, sweet Mari, we flew across that plain so fast my eyes watered. We chased a group of deer! If I'd had Audrey with me, we could've filled the storehouse."

"Really?" Nyphron appeared intrigued. "You think you could down a deer with your bow while riding in a cart?"

"I can shoot anything, anywhere." Moya smiled at him. Now it was her turn to wait for a retort, but just as before, none came. Maybe the two were figuring out ways to coexist.

"Moya, I need to speak to Nyphron privately. Can you go spread the word that we'll be leaving soon?"

"As you wish, *Madam Keenig*." Moya smiled and bowed to Persephone, who rolled her eyes in response as her Shield retreated.

Nyphron stared after her. If he were anyone else, Persephone might think he was appraising the view, but Nyphron's mind was working on something, and it had nothing to do with watching Moya walk away.

"So, what happened?" Persephone asked.

It took a moment before he responded. "Hmm? Sorry, what?"

"The fane? What happened when you caught up to him?"

Nyphron ran a hand through his helmet-crushed hair. "Oh, that. We didn't. The troops he left behind offered little resistance but provided enough time for the fane to escape. To be honest, I hadn't planned for such a significant victory. For him to be routed like that . . ." He shook his head. "I left soldiers in the High Spear Valley, and we'll consolidate all our forces there for the next stage."

"And what will that be?"

"Preparing for the advance. The Gula came the moment they saw the signal fires, and most didn't pack so much as a blanket. It'll take months to organize a supply chain capable of supporting our combined forces as we shift to an offensive stance, and by the time it's in place, winter will arrive, and that's no time for war. If we do this right, we can take the fight to Lothian by next spring. By then, we ought to be in good shape."

"Shouldn't we get behind walls? Isn't that why we came to Alon Rhist in the first place?"

He clapped the stone of the cell. "The old girl served her purpose, but beyond all reason, the tide has turned, and now *we* are the hunters. The fane is the one who needs to hide in a fortress. Now comes the time for us to press forward and bring the fight to him. That's why we're moving up to the High Spear."

"Isn't being in the open dangerous?"

"No. The fane can't mount an assault no matter where we are. He has lost most of his warriors and has only a few remaining Miralyith. And the best news is that it'll take more than three seasons to significantly improve his situation. We, on the other hand, have more than enough men and will be well supplied and well armed by then. And let's not forget the dragon. Did you know that girl, Suri, made it?"

"I told you about her. Didn't you believe me?"

He frowned. "It's not that I thought you lied, but rather she doesn't look capable of such a feat. At first, I thought Malcolm had something to do with it, but it turned out to be the mystic. I would never have thought such a thing was possible. Over the winter, we'll have her make more. The war will very likely be over by this time next year."

The first gilarabrywn had required Minna's life. Raithe had paid the price for the second. But the real cost had landed on Suri's shoulders. Persephone was confident that nothing would convince the mystic to make a third. She considered explaining this to Nyphron, but now wasn't the time, especially since he'd opened the door to a discussion she'd been waiting to have since he'd left. "I've been thinking about that . . . about the end of the war, I mean. You said yourself that we did exceptionally well. And the fane ran, didn't he? He must be scared, right?"

"'Terrified' is the word I'd use. He knows his remaining days are few."

"Agreed." She nodded. "So, wouldn't that make him receptive to a peace treaty?"

Nyphron laughed. "A what?"

"It's something Arion once said. She thought if we could prove ourselves to be capable . . . if the other Fhrey understood we aren't mindless animals, we could win their respect and learn to coexist. During the attack, when I thought we'd lost, I sent a message about peace talks. I haven't heard back but—"

"You did what? How?"

"I sent a bird to Estramnadon. I knew the fane wasn't there, but if he made it back, especially after seeing how we held our own, it might open a door. And now our position is even stronger. We've made him run, and he'll—"

"You are right about that. We've beaten the fane. He's running to Erivan with his tail between his legs. He's got nothing. But you're wrong about negotiating. We don't have to. We've won. What's the point in talking? We have no reason to grant concessions and settle for compromises. All we have to do is march across the Nidwalden and set fire to the Forest Throne. I plan to execute Lothian in his arena with a full audience in attendance. Conquering armies don't negotiate. Peace is what we'll have when Lothian and all his Miralyith are dead."

Persephone shouldn't have been shocked. Nyphron was a warrior, and violent men like him saw things in simple terms. "Kill them so they can't kill you" was the creed they followed. He was espousing a concept difficult to deny, fueled by cruelty and fraught with unforeseen consequences. Persephone had learned that making friends of enemies was far superior to a campaign of scorched earth. "But we don't need to kill—"

"Yes. We do. Trust me. I know Lothian. Do you think the fane will pardon me after the part I've played? I wouldn't. I know what's in his heart and mind because he and I are alike when it comes to those who have wronged us. If we let him live, we'll regret it."

"But Arion wanted both our peoples to—"

"Arion is dead."

The way he said it, so cold and unfeeling, silenced her. She wasn't yet up for a major battle. Moya was right about Persephone's lingering wounds: They still hurt, and in more ways than just her physical lacerations. Nyphron was moving to a posture of preparation, so there would be a suspension in the fighting. There was time to bring him around. "I'm sorry. You're right. We have a lot to do, and it's best to focus on the preparations for the move."

"Good." He straightened and looked once more down the corridor in the direction Moya had headed. "Do you think she was telling the truth about using a bow while riding in a horse-drawn cart?"

"I thought you were starting to understand Moya. That woman has only a vague notion of what shame is, and she doesn't need words to manipulate men. She's not one to exaggerate."

"Fascinating." Nyphron nodded, once more lost in thought.

"What?"

"I'm remembering that wagon with your stone god rolling down the hill and crashing through the gate of Dahl Tirre. It crushed everyone and everything in its path."

"Don't remind me. Lately, I feel as if I'm—"

"Excuse me," Nyphron said, and with that, he left her alone.

"I'm glad to see you, too, dear," she muttered while listening to his footfalls fade away.

Gifford stood in the street, dumbfounded, staring at one of fate's fascinating acts of irony. Only Hopeless House had been spared the devastation that had visited the rest of the buildings in Little Rhen. Almost every single one of the pretty houses had been reduced to a pile of rubble, and many were gone completely, burned to ash. But the hideous eyesore that had been home to the local misfits Gifford, Habet, Mathias, and Gelston had somehow survived untouched.

"You know what gets me the most, Woan?" he asked while shaking his head in disbelief. "I don't have a single thing inside that I need. Ev-we-one lost so much, but"—he gestured at the perfectly preserved stone cottage—"I've got nothing to pack."

All around them, survivors filled carts with what little they could salvage from the wreckage. Clothes, plates, plants, and rugs were piled by people with tears in their eyes. Most of them were Fhrey.

We humans have one advantage: We're more experienced at loss.

Everyone was preparing or waiting to leave. Many of the civilians of Alon Rhist would be going to Merredydd, but the Rhunes and the Instarya were heading east to Gula country. East was the way to the High Spear Valley; east was the direction of war.

Gifford and Roan were making a final walk-through of the city, or what was left of it. She had spent much of the last few days arranging for the creation of dozens of wagons. They'd reclaimed most of the timber from the wreckage of those pretty little homes, and as they walked, Roan's eyes were scanning the area for any remaining useful items.

She hasn't changed. Then he looked down at his hand clasped in hers, swinging comfortably between them, and reconsidered. *Well, maybe a little.* The thought made him grin so wide it hurt his cheeks.

From the moment he'd pulled her up onto Naraspur's back, and she'd hugged him for the first time, they hadn't been apart, and almost always they held hands. Since then, they'd slept under a single blanket, Roan pulling his arms around her. That first night, they'd both cried. It seemed like everyone had. Gifford didn't know what caused Roan's tears. So many things could have been the source: remorse, relief, guilt, exhaustion. But Gifford knew exactly what had made him weep. Until that night, he'd never known tears of joy.

He hadn't tried to kiss her, not yet. Gifford, who was now officially the Fastest Man Alive, advanced at a snail's pace for fear of breaking this fragile and yet wonderful dream he'd stumbled into. He wasn't sure how much Roan had changed, or what she could bear. He only knew he could touch her now without making her freeze up or pull away. Holding her hand had been his first foray into a glorious new world. Somehow, being dressed in Roan's armor, shining in a rising sun, had made all things possible.

I should have kissed her then. Everything seemed so clear in hindsight. *She would have let me. It would have been so easy, but now . . .*

Gifford looked once more at their joined hands as if witnessing a miracle.

This is more than I ever dreamed possible, and if this is all—it's enough for a lifetime.

"There you are," Nyphron said while climbing through the fallen rocks near the southern stair that led from the upper courtyard to the city.

He was focused on Roan, which didn't surprise Gifford. Most people ignored him, but to the Fhrey, it was as if he didn't exist.

"Moya tells me you've found a way for a horse to pull a cart. Is that true?"

Roan shook her head. "Gifford did it." She looked at the potter. "I only worked out a means of attaching them. He's the one with the gift for horses."

"*Him?*" Nyphron appeared confused as he looked at the cripple's twisted body. "*You're* Gifford? You can't be the guy Plymerath keeps going on about, his Night Hero who rode through the fane's camp?"

Roan nodded enthusiastically, and while smiling at Gifford, she recited the lines from Brin's account of the battle:

> *"The Night Hero, in armor shining,*
> *Did vanquish fear, in truth providing,*
> *Hope for all, and silver lining,*
> *To a night so dark and uninviting."*

Nyphron stared at her for a moment as if she'd gone insane. He shook it off and turned to Gifford. "You're the first Rhune to ride a horse." Once more, the Galantian surveyed Gifford's twisted body. "Never would've guessed that." He turned his attention back to Roan. "Moya said you made a small cart, a fast one. I was wondering if such a thing could be used in combat."

"What do you mean?"

"She said yours could hold two people. I was thinking that if one person handled the horses and the other used a bow or javelins, it could prove deadly. But it would need to be covered in Orinfar symbols. Can you make more like the one Moya rode in?"

Roan nodded.

Turning to Gifford, he asked, "And do you think a horse could be controlled in the chaos of battle?"

"I guided Naw-as-pa while being attacked by both javelins and magic. She didn't like being out in that, but she did it. Animals may be a lot like people. With twaining it could be possible."

Nyphron grinned. "This war is going to be easier than I ever imagined. It's like a god is pointing at me and saying, *It's your time.*"

Gifford looked back at his fingers still intertwined with Roan's and nodded. "Yes, I know exactly what you mean."

Along with everyone else, Tressa carried the entirety of her belongings across one of the seven bridges that spanned the Bern River chasm. She chose the southernmost one because it was the least crowded. Her worldly belongings weren't much: a few sacks of food, a too-thin blanket, and her ratty breckon mor, so threadbare it could no longer be considered decent. Tressa also carried a gourd of water and what remained of Gelston's possessions. Gelston came with her, and she coaxed him across the bridge like a goat being put out to graze. The old shepherd had never recovered from being hit by Miralyith lightning, and he followed her without saying a word.

Tressa made a point of staying at the end of the procession and toward the center of the bridge. She didn't want anyone sneaking up from behind and pushing her off. She knew good old Gelston wouldn't help. He'd merely stand by, looking on stupidly.

Tressa could name more than a dozen who might do the deed. Moya, the keenig's Shield, would be number one on that list. Back in Dahl Rhen, Tressa had tried to force her to marry The Stump. Moya had already disliked Tressa, but that failed plan had hardened Moya's feelings, causing her to trade enmity for outright hate. It shouldn't have mattered. Moya was a nobody. A loudmouthed pretty face with no family, but Persephone was supposed to have been a nobody as well.

This whole situation is an impossible nightmare. No way a woman could ever be keenig, and who would imagine Moya as a Shield? Just goes to show the absurdity of life when the gods put those two in charge.

Tressa had always known life wasn't fair, but only recently had she realized the game was stacked against her in particular. *Almost enough for me to feel flattered by all the attention . . . almost. If I disappeared, no one would even notice, not even Gelston. It's like I don't exist.*

She'd made it across the bridge without incident. Moya, Nyphron, and Persephone—whose privilege allowed her to ride in a wagon—led the parade east. By the time Tressa had crossed the bridge, the front of the line was a quarter mile ahead. She hung back while the procession continued its march across the plateau of the Dureyan high plains, a dusty, irregular, flat surface of rock, mud, and clay. Far ahead, the old hag Padera sat beside Persephone, and since Gifford now traveled everywhere by horse, Tressa and her clueless turtle Gelston were at the very back of the column. With each minute, the gap grew wider as they lost a bit more ground to the mass of people marching east. She made no effort to catch up. Didn't want to. She preferred not to breathe their dust.

When the front of the line reached Wolf's Head, the parade stopped. They had come to where the dragon lay. The line of people curved away from the beast, and there appeared to be a discussion happening at the front.

"Nyphron wants to be certain the dragon will come along," someone from behind said.

Tressa nearly jumped out of her skin. She'd thought she and Gelston were alone. The shepherd hadn't reacted at all. His eyes continued following the course of a bumblebee. This was at least safer than staring at the sun—something he'd done often enough for her to worry about him going blind. Whirling around, Tressa was stunned to find Malcolm. If it had been anyone else, Tressa might have unleashed an insult to cover up her startled reaction; instead, she collapsed to her knees.

"What are you doing?" Malcolm asked, sounding a little annoyed.

She didn't look up, focusing on his feet. "I know who you are."

"Of course you do, you've known me for over a year."

"Let me rephrase . . . I know *what* you are."

A silence extended between them, and Tressa thought Malcolm would try to insist he was just an ordinary man. If he did, she didn't know how she would respond. She wasn't about to call *him* a liar.

"I see," Malcolm replied.

These two words came as a relief but also stopped her heart. Tressa had spent nearly every waking hour mulling over the events that had occurred in the smithy the night Raithe was killed and the gilarabrywn made. She had come to the conclusion that Malcolm was a god posing as a man. He never said so, but it was clear he knew the past, present, and future of everyone there. She also had felt something that night—something profound. The moment she'd given up her ring, which had fulfilled his earlier prophecy, she'd felt something she'd never experienced before. When he smiled his approval, Tressa discovered a warmth of pride that stunned her. She was proud of herself; not the sort of pride that came from achieving a goal, but rather the kind that came by doing something right, something good. She'd felt heroic.

All I did was hand over a stupid ring that didn't belong to me, and yet somehow Malcolm made it into an act of virtue.

She still didn't know why or how. The whole thing seemed like a magic trick, a gift: one that made her feel less alone and, for the first time, virtuous. Except she wasn't. Tressa still thought of herself as a horrible person. Everyone else did as well, which was why she watched her back when crossing the bridge. That moment in the smithy was but a spark in the darkness of her existence, a flash that showed a glimpse of another world, a place she didn't belong.

A mere man couldn't make her feel that way.

Malcolm nodded as if he'd been holding a conversation with himself and was pleased with the outcome. "That should make this easier, then," he said.

This terrified her. Being pushed off the bridge seemed appealing compared to the frightening promise of that comment.

Tressa braced herself, and as she clenched her fists and jaw, Malcolm looked amused and a bit sad.

"I'm not going to hurt you, Tressa. I've chosen you for something important."

"I'm not a good person," she replied quickly, not knowing why. Even though it was the truth, it was also something she had never expected to say out loud.

Again, Malcolm smiled—not a smirk, not a grin, but a look of sympathy. "Do you suspect you're unique in that assessment?"

Tressa thought of her husband Konniger and ticked through a list of others. "I suppose not, but why pick me?"

"If I only worked with the truly virtuous, I'd have few choices. You see, when you want to build a wall, it's best to ask a mason."

Tressa knew he was saying more than she understood, likely more than she ever could understand, but that was to be expected. "What do you want me to do?"

"At the moment . . . nothing."

"But you *will* want something?"

"Yes, but not for several years."

"So why come to me now?"

"Because I'm leaving and I'm not sure when I'll be back. I have to make certain you know what to do when the time comes."

Once more, Tressa stiffened for bad news. "Will it be . . . will it be awful?"

"I can see you have a profoundly negative opinion of yourself."

She shrugged. "A lot of people hate me."

"A lot of people hate me, too."

This admission surprised her.

Malcolm sighed, sadness once more filled his face. "But I'm afraid to say that what I will ask of you will not be pleasant."

She bit her lip and nodded. "Can't be as bad as Raithe. At least there's no chance of me being turned into a dragon, right? I mean, it wouldn't work because no one loves me the way Suri loved him."

Malcolm's voice grew dark and cold. "No, it won't be that—it will be worse. As I said, when you need a wall built, you ask a mason."

She still didn't understand what that meant, but it frightened her.

He pulled a delicate chain from around his neck. On it was hooked a small bit of irregularly cut metal not much more than an inch long. "Take this." He held it out.

"What is it?" she asked, accepting the odd token.

Malcolm smiled bitterly. "Perhaps the most valuable thing in the world, so you'll need to keep it safe."

Tressa studied the bit of metal at the end of the chain, captivated by the phrase *most valuable thing in the world.* If anyone else had said it, Tressa would have laughed, but because it was Malcolm, she felt a tremendous weight of responsibility. A weight she felt in her heart would be too heavy to bear.

And what will be the consequences if that proves to be true?

"It's a key. Do you know what that is, Tressa?"

She shook her head, but committed the word to memory: *key.*

"There are places that are forbidden, doors that won't open, *locked* doors. A key is used to *unlock* them. What you hold in your hand is not just any key—it's the Master Key, a very special thing that will open *any* door."

"Am I going someplace I'm not allowed? Not that doing so would be a problem. I've never been the sort to follow rules."

"If you agree, then yes, I need you to travel someplace where even I can't go."

She nodded solemnly, as if taking a vow.

"And you'll have to take others with you—seven, to be exact."

"Seven?" She looked at the key, then back at him. "How can I—I can barely get Gelston to follow me. I'm hated. Nobody will—"

"Trust me. When the time comes, it'll all make sense. You won't have to do much because the pieces will naturally fall into their places. I've already seen to that. In the autumn, several years from now, when everything has gone poorly, Tesh will bring news about the cage, and no one will know what to do. That's when you'll need to step forward. Will you do that for me?"

She nodded, even though she still had no idea what he wanted her to do.

"Before I leave, there are two things I have to tell you. Two things you need to know. Have you ever heard the song 'Beyond the Woodland Hills'?"

"I don't think so."

"It starts like this . . .

"Far beyond the woodland hills, beyond the mountains vile,
Hidden in a mist-soaked swamp upon an awful isle.
She haunts the lapping blackened pools and creeping ivy ways,
And there awaits with hair of brown and eyes of greenish-gray."

"Doesn't sound like a happy tune," Tressa said nervously. "Not the sort you'd clap and dance to, I mean."

"No, it's not. Do you know it? It's very old."

She shook her head.

"I'll teach it to you, then. And you'll have to remember it. All of it, word for word."

"I need to know a song?"

He nodded in the way a healer might when a mother asked after her dead child. The solemn look on his face left Tressa with but a single word in her vocabulary: "Okay."

"The second thing you need to know, Tressa, is that in Estramnadon there is a door . . ."

CHAPTER THREE

Return of the Fane

Pride is a high and slippery cliff, and when you fall from such a height, the drop can crush you.

— THE BOOK OF BRIN

Imaly sat in her dayroom, staring out the window at the trees in the garden. The buds were starting to open, or as her great-grandmother used to put it, "The trees are stretching." The grand old lady had been a little nutty that way. She'd have to be—no sane person could have become the first fane.

As a descendant of Gylindora Fane, Imaly had inherited her great-grandmother's home. The surprisingly humble bungalow, while located in the heart of the city of Estramnadon, enjoyed a luxurious degree of isolation because of the private garden surrounding it.

If Gylindora were alive, she'd be out there right now, making a basket.

That's what the first fane had done before ruling the six tribes and what she'd continued to do during stressful times. She had said it calmed her. Imaly never learned how to make a basket but wished she had.

I'd have a whole stack of them by now.

Imaly heard the faint sound of tentative shuffling. The home wasn't large, but Makareta was slow to learn her way around. More noise indicated she'd entered the kitchen. There was a pause, and then after a good deal more shuffling, Makareta peeked into the dayroom. The young Fhrey wore a scarf tightly wrapped around her head—her denial kerchief. She'd worn it night and day, wrapped as tightly as she could manage, with every strand of hair tucked deep inside.

A week before, Imaly had agreed to harbor the girl, who had rebelled against the fane and killed several Fhrey during the short-lived Gray Cloak Insurrection. Upon arriving at Imaly's house, and even before asking for food, Makareta had begged for a razor.

"Why would you want such a thing?" Imaly asked, thinking the girl might harm herself.

"To get rid of this!" Makareta hissed while holding up a lock of her hair as if it were a parasite attached to her scalp.

"Couldn't you just use magic to . . ." Imaly pointed to her head and made a vague twirling motion.

"Use of the Art can be detected, and sometimes traced. I can't risk even the smallest of weaves. Each day this mop gets longer, and I don't have anything to cut it with. I tried ripping it out, but that hurt too much."

Imaly grimaced, picturing Makareta crying in the forest as she struggled to tear the hair from her head.

"Just please get it off," Makareta begged.

"No," Imaly replied. "You need to keep it."

"But . . . I promised to do whatever you ask, and I will."

Imaly took hold of the girl's hand. "It's not a punishment. It's for your own good. A bald head on a young lady means just one thing: Miralyith. Anyone seeing you—even a glimpse through one of these windows—could get us executed. Do you want that?"

The girl had shaken her head, then gritted her teeth and shuddered as her hair swung with the movement.

After that, Imaly laid down the law: The hair stayed, windows were to be avoided, Makareta couldn't leave the house, and under no circumstances could she use the Art. Given how dependent Miralyith were on their magic and assuming the assertion about its use being traceable was true, Imaly saw this last rule as the most crucial to protect them.

Makareta had agreed, and as far as Imaly could tell, she'd kept her promises. Imaly had purchased some cheap Gwydry-style clothing; rough, tough, and simple, the working tribe's attire was as far as one could get from a Miralyith's asica. Dressed in a tunic and trousers that looked to be made from the same material as tents, Makareta was completely disguised.

"Could I have some tea?" Makareta asked after sitting on the settee in the corner, the seat farthest from the bay window that looked out on the garden.

Imaly sighed. "Certainly, if you make it yourself."

Initially, Imaly had treated the destitute Fhrey like a guest. But Imaly's generosity was wearing thin, and she wasn't about to be a Miralyith's servant.

Makareta stared at her, baffled. "I—I don't know how."

"Boil water and run it through leaves. It's not complicated."

Makareta looked toward the kitchen as if her worst nightmare had come true.

Imaly rose and led the way to the stove. "I'll show you."

Imaly went through the process, and when she'd finished, she said, "Now the next time you want some, you can make it yourself."

Makareta didn't look confident, but she gladly accepted the hot cup and sipped.

"Honestly, this experience might be good for you. Your reliance on magic has made you an invalid. It's a wonder you can feed yourself."

"Not *magic*," Makareta said. "It's called the *Art*."

"Whatever." Imaly waved dismissively. "Look, I know how boring it's been for you. Why don't we find something to help pass the time? What is it you like to do?"

Makareta shrugged.

"Didn't you . . . I seem to recall that you painted."

Makareta nodded. "And created sculptures, but that was before—"

"Before you conspired against the fane and launched an overthrow of our whole way of life?" Imaly frowned. "Yes, I can see that painting landscapes and bowls of fruit might not have the same allure as inciting insurrection. But let's say we try it, shall we? I'll get you some supplies, clay and paint. You can set up in the parlor, make it a studio. I'd like some nice pictures and statuettes. You can do that. Okay?"

Makareta nodded, but there was no enthusiasm in her eyes. She was merely placating her host.

The girl is still in shock.

Makareta had spent a year in hiding before coming to Imaly. How she'd managed to elude the searchers was a mystery. Imaly was certain of one thing: It had taken a toll. Every day, the girl must have woken anticipating a gruesome death. The stress would have been incredible.

I shouldn't expect her to recover overnight. I only hope she gets her head on straight soon. I need a powerful Miralyith, not a skittish girl.

Imaly made a mental note to pick up some strips of river grass when she went to the market. Given the situation, she might just want to take up basket weaving after all.

News of the fane's return had arrived several hours before he did, and Imaly had given orders for everyone to present themselves along the streets. They did so in fine fashion. All of Estramnadon lined up, the old and young, in their finest clothes. They were there to cheer the return of their victorious army and the ruler who had led the charge. Imaly and Lothian had had their differences, but she felt the fane deserved to be welcomed home in all his glory.

Imaly stood on the palace steps, shoulder to shoulder with the other members of the Aquila. She had a fine view of the plaza and avenue, but because of the buildings and trees blocking the start of the route, she heard the fane's arrival long before seeing it. First came the drums and then the horns of triumph, two additional preparations she had arranged. Following them came the cheers of anticipation. Then the shouts and fanfare fell silent. It was so quiet, Imaly could hear the fane's footfalls even before she saw him round the corner.

Volhoric, who stood beside her, gasped. "Oh, dear lord Ferrol!"

Two thousand proud Fhrey warriors dressed in shining bronze armor and fifty asica-draped Miralyith had set out to teach the Rhunes a lesson; what Imaly now saw was a handful of limping, filthy, bloodstained Fhrey. The once grand army of Fane Lothian dragged itself home to the hush of all those who had come out to celebrate their victory.

Imaly could've used that moment of failure to publicly highlight Lothian's foolish arrogance and overconfidence. She could've humiliated him and his tribe. But as the fane climbed the steps toward her, she didn't have the heart to utter a word—didn't even know what to say.

Imaly expected the fane to stop at the top of the steps, face the gathered crowd, and speak. He needed to explain. He needed to calm fears and help everyone understand what had happened. Instead, Lothian didn't so much as pause, and he might have continued to walk right into the palace if she hadn't stopped him.

"My fane," she said quietly, respectfully, and with far more compassion than she had ever used in the past, "you must say something. The people, they are—"

He stopped and looked at her. His eyes were tired, his shoulders slumped, and his face hung as if weighted. "You speak to them. You've always been better at that than I."

"What shall I tell them?"

"That we are in this for our lives now. We must kill all of them, or they will surely kill all of us."

Behind the defeated fane, his son, Mawyndulë, offered her a sheepish glance and shook his head in disgust as he reached the top step. Imaly couldn't tell what the prince was thinking, but she would find out. She needed to know all she could because she sensed everything had changed. Most important, the message sent by the self-declared Rhune ruler had just transformed from politically advantageous to a potential deliverance from annihilation.

She turned back to Lothian and caught his attention once more. Moving in close, she lowered her voice. "My fane, I've received a message from Alon Rhist, from the Rhune leader. They are seeking peace."

Lothian shook his head. "A message of that sort would have been sent before the last battle, when we held the upper hand. No one offers peace to the defeated." He said this so quietly that she barely heard, and then he continued his trek into the Talwara.

As the fane and the prince entered the palace and the doors closed on a stunned crowd, Imaly realized that she, too, had underestimated the Rhunes—a mistake she vowed never to make again.

PART II

CHAPTER FOUR

Battle of the High Plains

I have always found it amazing that in the vast expanse of eternity, several significant yet unrelated events can occur simultaneously. Such things make me wonder what the gods know that I do not.

— The Book of Brin

"Brin?"

The Keeper of Ways was digging out the first of several pegs holding up the tent where she and Padera had lived for a year. At the sound of her name, she looked up.

Panting for air, his face glossy with sweat, Habet beamed his familiar smile. As far back as Brin could recall, he'd been the Keeper of the Eternal Flame for Clan Rhen. It meant he was responsible for ensuring that the lodge's fire remained lit, an important job because everyone in the dahl used the eternal flame to light their lamps and cook fires. The tedious but simple task suited Habet because he was similarly simple. Some, like Sackett and Heath Coswall, had called him stupid. Likewise, Krier, who had also tormented Gifford, made fun of Habet. But all the taunting was pointless since the man never noticed the slights. Brin didn't think Habet was dumb, just slow; and like Gifford, his limitations were more obvious than his talents.

"Padera wants you," he said in his quiet, slow manner, which often sounded like he was on the verge of falling asleep.

"I'm in the middle of taking down our tent. I can't do two things at once. Tell her I'll come when I'm done," Brin explained in frustration. She and Padera had lived together for the last year and a half, sharing first the little cottage in Alon Rhist and now this tiny tent. Brin took care of the old woman, a considerable task that she felt no one gave her credit for—least of all Padera.

"Padera wants you," Habet repeated.

"She always wants me, and I'm already working on this job for her."

Brin and the others from Alon Rhist had suffered the winter in the High Spear Valley, sheltering on the southern bank of the eastern branch of the Bern River. Thin canvas had made a weak defense against the bitter winds, and Brin had shivered herself to sleep on far too many nights. She was happy to welcome the return of spring, but with it came the resumption of war.

The army was marching north that morning, and with it went Tesh, but Brin was stuck packing, and after that, more demands from Padera would keep the two apart. Brin held no illusions about her future with Tesh. The man she hoped to marry was one of the best warriors on the field, but war was a fickle and dangerous thing. Skill certainly helped, but she feared that would be inadequate protection against fate.

Everyone's hopes, except hers, had risen since the Battle of Grandford because there hadn't been any sign of the fane's forces. People tried to assure her that the Rhune army was merely going to stroll northward across fifteen miles of open meadow without finding any resistance. The rest of the camp was supposed to follow after the uneventful advance. Within a few days, the whole camp would be resettled at the eaves of the Harwood Forest.

The majority were excited to move, eager to find a new spot to pitch their tents. Brin couldn't care less. Her only desire was for Tesh to live to see another day. Anxious and sick with worry, she wanted to see him off, to watch, and to know without question that he would be safe. Instead, she was stuck packing while the old woman was off to who knew where. Everything had been left to Brin, and she wasn't entirely certain how she would manage. She felt overwhelmed, angry, and frustrated. The stubborn stakes holding up her tent made matters worse, and now Habet was here with another edict from the grand, exalted Padera, who wanted something else of her.

"Padera wants you," Habet said for the third time. He hadn't so much as changed his tone.

"Why?" she shouted. "What does she want?"

The outburst made Habet blink and take a step back. "Needs help . . ."

"She always needs help," Brin said more to herself than him.

" . . . help with baby."

"Baby?" Brin's eyes widened. "Oh for the love of Mari! Why didn't you say so?"

Brin ran down the bank to the river.

Suri had created a bridge out of dirt and sod so that the span was a lush green causeway dotted with wildflowers. Normally, the causeway was more than ample, but that morning, with everyone getting an early start and hauling heavy loads, it was jammed with people. Brin, thin and small as she was, still couldn't hope to fit through the cracks in that crowd.

This day! she screamed in her head. *Can nothing go right?*

In front of her, a Gula woman with a massive basket on her head waited with five children. They were hemmed in on one side by a wagon stacked dangerously high with barrels and on the other by a half-dozen sheep being driven across by a Menahan shepherd. No one was moving.

Padera needs help with the baby. Persephone is having her baby!

"Where's your shield?" Grevious asked Tesh as they stood outside, buckling on armor. All around, men moved and metal weapons clanked.

"Don't use one."

"You've used it in practice."

Tesh clapped his dual short swords. "Shields are for defense."

Grevious put a friendly arm around Tesh's neck and glanced at Edgar, who smiled at Atkins and shook his head. "Look, kid, I know you think you're the god of war and all, but out there"—he indicated the meadow they were about to cross—"if we run into resistance, it won't be like practice."

Grevious, Edgar, and Atkins were veterans of the Battle of Grandford. Each had survived the fight of Wolf's Head, as well as the final combat when the fortress of Alon Rhist had been overrun. Atkins was a bearded redhead from Warric; Edgar had been Harkon's Shield until the chieftain died, but Grevious was the most famous of the three. He had won glory, and a nasty scar across his face, while defending the city gate. Legend held that he'd single-handedly killed two Fhrey warriors before being blown aside by a Miralyith. Along with Brigham—the youngest of the Killian brood—they were all members of the First Cohort, First Spear. In addition, they were shoulder-brothers of the First File, meaning they were the elite of the elite, and would be front and center at the start of any action.

Tesh had trained with them daily, and they had become like uncles—all except Brigham, who was his same age. While Tesh was giddy with the possibility of seeing action, Brigham didn't look very confident. The Killian lad, the last surviving male member of his family, looked positively sick.

"There aren't any enemies out there," Eres assured them as he passed by, checking on his troops. "We're just going for a hike this morning."

"I'm sure you're right," Tesh replied with a good-humored smile. Then, once Eres had moved on, he told Grevious, "Too bad because you're also right about it not being like practice. If there were any elves, I'd get to kill some."

Grevious looked confused for a moment, then chuckled and once more spoke to Edgar and Atkins. "When we do eventually clash with the Fhrey, this guy will either die in the first few seconds, or he'll become a legend."

Tesh finished strapping on his breastplate, then noticed the carts forming up near the eastern tents. "What's with them?" He nodded in that direction.

"Looks like Lord Nyphron is planning on trying them out," Atkins said.

"For what? Hauling back the wounded?"

Grevious shrugged. "Dunno. Maybe. Look a little small for that, though."

"Aren't you the optimistic one!" Atkins shook his head.

"Can't see what else they'd be good for," Tesh said.

"Must be good for something," Brigham added. "He's made a lot of them."

A horn sounded and all the men trotted through the rows of canvas tents toward the newly raised black flag. Tesh was glad to leave the High Spear Valley, where generations of Dureyan and Gula warriors had died fighting each other at the behest of the Fhrey. Now, with the start of the new season, he hoped to spill a different kind of blood. The fact that they were still mainly commanded by Galantians was not only frustrating, but actually the one cloud raining on Tesh's sunny day.

Persephone had married Nyphron the previous summer in a disgraceful ceremony that doomed the human race to continued servitude just as they were starting to breathe free air. Nyphron continued his role as commander of the army and put his Galantians in charge of each cohort. Eres led Tesh's, and, like all Fhrey, he did so from the rear.

They formed up on the north bank in perfect lines, just as they had been taught. Tesh had never understood the point. Combat was a chaotic dance; lines had no place in that celebration of death, but Tesh would obey the rules if it meant he got to kill elves. He took his place between Grevious and Edgar on the front line. Grevious had the honor of the exact center because Eres felt that experience was more important than aptitude. Tesh's skill in practice was renowned, but no one knew how well he'd do in a *real* fight. *Blood makes a difference, especially when yours is on the line* was a commonly repeated phrase.

"We'll see how the whelp does when blood is spilled," Eres had said, believing, incorrectly, that Tesh had never killed.

The bulk of Alon Rhist's surviving civilians, most of whom were Fhrey, had gone to Merredydd. The few Rhunes not in the army or providing military support had returned to the villages of Rhen. Those in the High Spear were soldiers, healers, smiths, huntsmen, or cooks. This was a fighting community. The whole camp was preparing to move north, but some had paused in their packing to witness the army's march. Eres had them all facing north, which meant Tesh couldn't see Brin, but he knew she was watching. She'd be trying to pick him out of the thousands of men under the bright morning sun.

"Forward!" Eres shouted, and the line advanced in unison.

They trudged onto the plain. Off to the right was Mount Mador, whose snowy cap was the source of many rivers and whose perfectly symmetrical shape betrayed its artificial nature. The mountain had been made by magic—a spell that had killed thousands of dwarfs. Mador was beautiful, and it was also the biggest, most infamous grave marker in the world—a monument to the majesty of warfare.

Up and to the left lay the dragon, who had saved them during the Battle of Grandford. It had lain motionless in the same spot for nearly a year. Grass had grown around it as if it were an abandoned house. Some thought it might be dead. Tesh had been told that Raithe, his chieftain and mentor, had sacrificed himself to create it. Raithe had been like a second father to Tesh, pointing out that the best way to kill elves was to learn how they fought and use that knowledge against them. Then, just before dying, Raithe made Tesh promise to get married and raise a family, rather than wage war. Tesh intended to make good on that vow, but not yet. He had a prior commitment to fulfill. The one he'd made to his real father, his mother, and whole clan after they were slaughtered by the Fhrey.

"Nice weather for a war, don't you think?" Atkins said from four shoulders down.

"It'll be hot later," Edgar replied. "Once the sun gets high, our armor will act like ovens."

"Then I hope the beer barrels are brought up quickly. This will be a thirsty day."

Tesh was inclined to agree about the nice weather. Even if there wasn't a fight, the hike across the field of flowers beneath a blue sky was pleasant; the only downside came from wet patches where melted snow hadn't fully dried. When they got closer to the Harwood, he'd look for a nice spot to have a picnic with Brin, someplace level and dry.

Ahead, something shifted in the tall, swaying grass.

A bird? A quail, perhaps?

Tesh heard excited voices from down the line. Looking, he saw a gap in the row, then more than one as his brothers-in-arms collapsed.

"Scatter!" Eres shouted.

This wasn't one of the usual commands. The whole point of the line was to make an impenetrable barrier. At no point had any of them been trained to *scatter.* Splitting up ruined everything.

They did it anyway, managing as well as one might expect for a previously unattempted maneuver. Tesh and Edgar bumped chest plates, laughed, then ran in opposite directions. Tesh barely managed to get more than a couple of yards when he heard a whistle and felt a gust of air. At first, he thought it was a rising breeze; then he recognized the sound and dived behind a large rock.

An instant later, he heard a pattering sound like rain. Men screamed as the arrows fell.

"Arrows? How do the Fhrey have arrows?" Grevious shouted. He had jumped behind the same rock. The two of them crouched with their shoulders to the stone.

The entire cohort was in disarray. Everyone ran in random directions while, in the middle of the field, two dozen men lay dead, still in neat rows.

A second wave of arrows fell, killing or wounding a dozen more. With a *pfft* sound, one struck an inch from Tesh's foot. The series of high-arching flights stopped. That's when target practice began. Individual archers picked off runners and those trying to hide in the tall grass.

"Most are up there," Grevious said while pointing. "See them on that rise?"

"Over here, too," Tesh announced, spotting blue and gold on a mound. He watched as they popped up, fired, then disappeared.

Men continued to scream. The noisy wounded received a second volley to shut them up. When Tesh peeked out, an arrow pinged off the stone just inches from his face.

"Tet!" he shouted, jerking back.

"Stay down. They can't hit us here," Grevious assured him.

"They're working on that," Tesh said, watching two elves running low, loping like wolves as they circled around. "They're flanking us, moving to a better position."

Grevious looked at Tesh with a mix of frustration and fear. "We can't do a damn thing."

"I didn't even get close enough to swing at one," Tesh growled. "I'm gonna rush 'em!"

"Don't be a fool. They'll cut you down in a second. You don't even have a shield, and my little buckler isn't big enough to block arrows."

That's when they heard the thunder.

"Oh great." Grevious shook his head. "Now what?"

Tesh heard it, too, and he looked for the clouds, but the sky was clear. "Miralyith?"

Grevious shook his head. "Not that kind of thunder."

The sound wasn't coming from the sky, but from the camp. "Horses!"

"It's those little carts," Grevious confirmed. "They—" He never finished his words. An arrow punctured his throat and made a dull crack when the metal tip collided with the rock.

~

"Faster!" Moya shouted as Gifford slapped the reins, driving the horse across the open plain.

The little carts with the big wheels rumbled across the flat land as Moya readied her bow. In a staggered line, the other carts raced into battle behind her. She led the charge, acting like the tip of a fast-flung spear. She didn't have orders to do so; this wasn't part of any plan. The carts had been assembled and manned with the intent of trying an experiment. No one expected even to see the enemy that day, much less to encounter resistance. The idea was for Moya and a few others to ride out and determine if the horses would tolerate rushing past the advancing soldiers. That was before the Fhrey appeared, before the arrows, before the First Cohort had been devastated.

After witnessing the slaughter and hearing the screams, Moya had shouted, "Go! Now!" And the potter-turned-war-hero jerked the brake lever free and launched them forward so quickly that Moya nearly fell out.

The others saw them go and must have thought the green flag to advance had been waved because every cart with a horse soon took to the field. The sound of those combined thundering hooves was astounding.

"Don't hit the bodies!" Moya shouted at Gifford.

"Twying not to! Not easy to get it to go exactly the way I want. We moving weal fast!"

Gifford wasn't kidding. The ground was a blur, and even small bumps in the sod caused the cart to bounce, jarring Moya's teeth.

"Uh-oh!" Gifford exclaimed as another cloud of arrows took flight. The haze of gray went up in a typical arc, and it was obvious who the target was. The archers didn't care about the warriors anymore. They were now aiming for the carts.

Moya cringed in anticipation, but when the arrows landed, they hit the ground several yards behind them. Gifford grinned at Moya, who grinned back.

"Faster!" she shouted. "Run them down."

Gifford pulled hard on a leather strap, causing the horse to curve right. They swung dangerously close to an outcrop of rock.

"By Mari, Gifford, at least let the elves have a chance to kill us before you do!"

"Sow-wee. It's like dwiving an avalanche," he offered, his mangled lips unable to pronounce the *rrr* sound in *sorry* and *driving*.

"There they are!" Moya shouted against the wind after spotting the gold-and-blue uniforms in the high grass of a hill just ahead. She lifted her bow as three Fhrey released their arrows—not at Moya or Gifford, but at the horse.

The animal collapsed, and the cart flipped, throwing its passengers like atlatls. Not being spears, Moya and Gifford didn't go far. They hit the turf and rolled to a stop in front of the Fhrey archers.

Dazed, bruised, and shaken, Moya discovered she no longer held Audrey. The bow landed in the grass several feet away, and the arrows were scattered.

She heard the creak of Fhrey bows.

Moya heard Gifford roll forward and felt him press his back against hers, shielding her body. She flinched in anticipation after hearing the arrows release. Even with Gifford in front of her, she expected death. What she got instead was a drumroll on metal as the Fhrey arrows bounced harmlessly off Gifford's armor.

"Thank you, Woan," Gifford whispered.

"Gifford, look out!" Moya shouted as the Fhrey dropped their bows and charged.

Moya scrambled for Audrey but knew she'd never reach it in time.

Gah! Brin bounced on her feet, forced to stand still behind a wall of stagnant travelers. *The one time that Padera really needs me and—*

"Forget this," she said aloud, shaking her head in disgust. She pushed through the crowd to the edge of the bridge. A foot below, the river was just a few feet deep, and the current didn't look too strong. Still, Brin's eyes followed the river's track to its source—the snowcapped Mount Mador. *It's going to be cold.* She gritted her teeth and jumped.

When she hit the water, several people on the bridge gasped, and one shouted, "Are you all right?"

Brin took a moment before responding. She had to. She'd been correct about the water's temperature, and for a few seconds, it took her breath away. Brin had also been right about the depth and current. The water only came up to her waist, and she was able to keep her position by digging her feet into the gravel at the bottom.

"Yeah, I'm fine," she lied.

The water was bitterly cold, and when she lifted a foot to take a step, the river pushed her back. Bending over, she used her cupped hands like oars to pull on the water and draw herself forward. Half of her was still dry, but it was no use trying to stay that way. This was an all-or-nothing gambit.

This is gonna hurt, she thought, and with a deep breath, taken more in defense against the expected shock than for air, she dived into the water. Using her arms to stroke and her feet to push hard against the riverbed, she half swam, half ran across the bottom. The water grew deeper before it became shallower, and at one point she was truly swimming. As a result, Brin was pushed downriver.

She emerged on all fours: soaked, freezing, and exhausted. But none of that deterred her, and she got up and ran. The movement-generated wind exacerbated the chill, but the exertion promised to warm her eventually. On the northern bank, she had no problem finding Persephone. Hers was the largest tent on that side of the river.

Brin entered to find Persephone on the ground, covered in a grass-stained blanket. The keenig was soaked in sweat. She lay on her back, eyes squeezed shut, panting through clenched teeth. The Fhrey physician, the same one who had treated Persephone after the attack from the raow, was rolling up his sleeves as if preparing to wash pots. Justine, a pretty young woman and orphan from Menahan, was there, too. She was the one Colin Highland's mother had secretly picked to be her son's wife shortly before all the Highland boys were killed in the Battle of Grandford.

"There you are, girl!" Padera grabbed Brin by the elbow. "Where have you been? Go find Roan and tell her to bring her bag. Then fetch a bucket of water. Make it warm but not hot. And get a bunch of clean cloths."

"You called me just to get Roan?" she asked dumbfounded. "Why didn't you just—"

"Do it. Now!"

Persephone cried out, and Brin burst back through the tent's flap and into the sunlight.

Everyone was rushing. There were shouts and hurried feet. Brin assumed the commotion was due to the camp breaking, but when she found Roan, the woman was standing on a stack of crates peering north with a look of terror on her face.

"Roan! Roan!" she called. "Persephone needs you! She's having her baby!"

Roan looked down at Brin, then back out at the meadow as if trying to decide something.

"Roan, hurry, and bring your bag!"

When Roan nodded such that Brin was certain she'd understood, Brin rushed off in search of water.

A few fires still had pots on. She picked the closest one.

"What are you doing?" a Gula man complained when she grabbed up his steaming container.

"Taking this by order of the keenig," she said. This was a lie, her second of the day. She grabbed a bucket and filled it with river water, then mixed the two until the temperature became warm but not hot. Then she stole a handful of rags from a basket, cloth that she was fairly certain was meant to serve as bandages for the wounded.

I've become a liar and a thief, and it's not even midday.

As she returned to the tent, she heard Padera yelling, "Push!"

The moment Brin stepped inside, Padera took the rags and water. "Get a blanket—a *nice* one."

"How am I going to—"

"Go!"

Brin couldn't find any. Her blanket was on the far side of the river. She paused in frustration trying to think where she might—

Distant screams of men caught her attention.

Looking north, Brin saw that the meadow's grass had been trampled in a wide swath, revealing the path the army had taken. She could see them, weapons glinting in the sun, perhaps just half a mile away.

They're fighting!

The neat lines had been broken, the formation forgotten. On the ground lay motionless bodies.

Tesh!

છ

The spectacle of the flipping cart surprised Tesh. He watched in shock as Gifford and Moya flew, then hit the turf. They tumbled and grunted but were all right. Then the archers shot, but the arrows did nothing.

When Tesh saw the Fhrey drop their bows and pull swords, he gave a glance to the sky and whispered, "Thank you, Mari!"

Tesh drew both his swords and sprinted from behind the rock. He was only a few strides away, but elves were wickedly fast, and they were closing on Gifford.

"*Egat, eyn mer Tetlin, brideeth!*" Tesh shouted as loud as he could. He didn't actually know what it meant, but he knew that the elven curse was insulting. The Fhrey clearly understood and looked up in surprise, gifting Tesh the extra seconds to close the distance.

Tesh led with his left, a weak backhand. This had been a Sebek technique, the old Thunder and Lightning move. The first blade was blocked; the second blade killed. Elves were soft compared to iron.

Like cutting cheese. The idea just popped into his head, making him smile.

Before the second elf saw the threat, perhaps before he even knew he was going to swing, Tesh dropped to one knee, ducked, and thrust his blade under the elf's layered armor, lacerating his stomach. As that one fell, another volunteered to be Tesh's third kill of the day. Already down on one knee, Tesh pushed up hard, leaping off the ground to avoid his opponent's low stroke, and while still in the air, he twisted, swung, and severed the third elf's head from his neck.

Three! That's one more than Grevious.

But there were more. They came at him in a wonderfully accommodating single line, a full five heartbeats separating one's arrival from the next. Tesh only required three beats. These elves weren't Galantians. They weren't even Instarya. The Fhrey that came at him appeared to have less training with a blade than the men who made up the water bucket brigade. They had Fhrey speed and balance, but nothing else, and as their bodies began to cover the ground, fear gnawed away even those few assets.

His arms, chest, and hands were slick with blood, and he was just warming up. With the heat of the sun on the back of his neck and the smell of the gore-scented air in his nostrils, he felt good. Better than good; he felt great. Then everything stopped. The flow of elves held back, frustrating him. Tesh had had a nice rhythm going. He didn't want it to stop, but his enemy refused to advance. They didn't run away, either, which he sensed was odd. They seemed to be waiting for—

"Tesh!" Gifford shouted.

Surprised that the crippled potter was still alive, Tesh turned just in time to see a Fhrey in the high grass loose an arrow in his direction.

Moya reached her bow.

She grabbed it up, along with a few strands of grass. Finding the bow's string still taut, Audrey was ready if only—

She found an arrow sticking up, its point buried in the dirt. Not one of hers, this was a Fhrey arrow. *Any puddle in a drought,* she thought as she jerked it from the turf and fitted it to her string.

Spinning around, she found Tesh standing in a ring of dead Fhrey. The rest stayed back as an archer took aim at him. Moya drew Audrey's string, but knew she would be too late. She could hit the Fhrey, but the archer's arrow would kill Tesh.

She didn't think about what she did next. There was no pondering, no evaluation, no decision made. Like most things Moya faced in her life, she merely reacted. If she had thought about it, she likely would have chosen differently, but in that fractured moment when thoughts were too slow, Moya did the only thing she could. She simply didn't have time to realize it was impossible.

Both bows launched arrows at the same time. The Fhrey loosed his at Tesh, and by all accounts it was a fine shot. It likely would have caught him in the exposed hollow just above his collarbone. But it never landed. In mid-flight, halfway between string and neck, the two arrows collided. The sound of the impact cracked like lake ice during a spring thaw, and echoed across the battlefield.

Tesh and the Fhrey looked at her in wonder.

When the Fhrey reached for another arrow, Tesh ran at him. At that same moment, Moya spotted a cache of her arrows a few feet away and jumped for them. The race was won by the most unlikely of all. Gifford, still on the ground and near the Fhrey archer, swung his frighteningly brilliant blade. He missed his opponent but destroyed the bow.

A moment later, the attacker was killed by both a thrust from Tesh and an arrow from Moya.

The remaining Fhrey ran. Moya wanted to think the three of them caused the rout, but it was impossible to ignore the arrival of the remaining carts, the reformation of the soldiers . . . and one more thing.

The dragon had gotten to its feet.

Rising up, the gilarabrywn had extended its massive wings, spreading them out and casting part of the field in shadow. When the beast was lying down, it was frightening. On its feet with wings extended, the monster was shocking in its size and magnitude. This made even Moya nervous, but it utterly terrified the Fhrey. Moya expected the dragon to take flight, breathe fire, and indiscriminately kill them all. Instead, the monster merely watched the rout.

"Gifford! Are you all right?" Moya rushed to his side.

He pulled off his helmet to look at her. "I think I got a bwuise on my knee," he told her.

"A bruise? Are you joking?"

"No." He reached down, grabbed his brace-covered leg, and winced. "I think I landed on it when we flipped."

The Fhrey retreated. The battle was over, and with its conclusion, Brin spotted a bit of neatly folded blue cloth. She grabbed it and ran back. By the time she returned to Persephone's tent, she heard crying—the sound of a baby.

All Brin saw when she entered was the child. Tinier than she would have imagined, it was a boy, a very little, rosy boy. Padera was washing the infant in a basin. Roan took Brin's cloth and wrapped the baby, then handed it to an exhausted-looking Persephone, propped up on sacks of grain. But the new mother was smiling, and her eyes grew bright as the infant was placed on her chest.

"Isn't that a Galantian cape?" Roan asked.

Only then did Brin notice the shimmer of the fabric. She shrugged.

The keenig stared at the tiny bundle with the bald head, and for a moment Brin saw sadness cross her face. "Dear Mari," she whispered as she cupped it to her breast. "Grant me this one thing. Let this one outlive me."

ॐ

The night was filled with dung fires.

As far as Tesh could see, which in the dark wasn't far at all, scores of campfires flickered. The north bank of the Bern, nearly as barren as the south, allowed little fuel for victory parties, but the soldiers made do.

What had started as toasts to fallen men-at-arms had, with the news of Persephone's successful delivery, become a celebration. Nyphron had ordered barrels cracked and cups distributed.

"To Grevious!" Edgar shouted, lifting his dented and dripping cup. "A fine warrior and good friend." This was Edgar's fifth toast to a man who, until the Battle of Grandford, couldn't have been described as popular. War had given him fame beyond his merits. The accolades had lasted less than a year.

"May he swim the river to Phyre," Trent of Clan Nadak declared. "And find the gates to Rel open and welcoming."

"Bah!" Atkins shouted. "Grevious is on his way to Alysin!"

This was followed by a series of agreeable grunts and a solid nod from Pliny, who was an absolute fool and had no idea what they were talking about. The man merely wanted to be seen as part of the group.

Pliny of Clan Melen, a farmer of oats and barley, had joined the camp in the months after the Battle of Grandford when Nyphron had marshaled all able-bodied men. He and Trent had flittered around Tesh ever since the fighting ended, pleading to be trained.

Tonight, Tesh was noncommittal and a bit curt. He was in a surprisingly bad mood, considering that he'd been named one of the Heroes of the Battle of the High Plains, a title he shared with Moya and Gifford. All three had garnered prodigious praise: Gifford for demonstrating the deadly power of the horse-drawn cart; Moya for the spectacular arrow-to-arrow shot that saved Tesh's life; and Tesh for his lethal performance, proving beyond any doubt that Rhunes were more than a match for the Fhrey.

"Although," Atkins added, "if there is a different place in the afterlife for a prophet, Grevious might well go there, for it looks like the man who became famous for killing two Fhrey also had foresight." He sloshed his drink in the direction of Tesh. "The poor bastard was right about him, wasn't he?"

Edgar stepped up beside Atkins and put an arm around his neck. Neither man was too steady on their feet. "To be fair, he made two predictions about Tesh, and only one proved to be true."

"Well, he ain't dead." Atkins slapped Edgar on the back. "So I guess we're in the presence of a legend, eh, boys?"

"Tell us again how many you killed?" Edgar called to Tesh.

Tesh stood a bit apart from the rest, deeper in the night. He, too, had a cup of what was probably beer, but he hadn't tried it. He just held it, shifting the drink from one hand to the other.

"How many?" Edgar demanded in a louder voice.

"I told you, I don't know. I lost count."

This caused Edgar and Atkins to explode into fits of laughter.

"The lad doesn't remember!" Edgar said.

" 'Lost count,' he says!" Atkins managed while doubled over, eyes watering.

"I don't understand," Brigham said, looking from Edgar, to Atkins, to Tesh. "What's so funny?"

Brigham Killian, whom Tesh genuinely liked, had only recently joined their little group. He was seventeen—the same age as Tesh—and they were often the butt of the older men's jokes. Tesh had grown up in Dureya and was used to worse, but Brigham was from the more genteel world of Clan Rhen and didn't understand playful ribbing when he saw it.

Edgar walked over and good-naturedly put an arm around Brigham's shoulders. "That man there is a legend because during his first-ever battle, he slaughtered fifteen Fhrey all by himself," he said, then laughed again.

"I know that," Brigham said. "I was there. But why is that funny?"

"What you're missing is that Tesh isn't failing to tell us the number because he can't remember or because he's too humble—it's 'cause he just can't count that high!"

Edgar and Atkins erupted once more into fits of laughter, and this time they pulled almost everyone else with them.

It was true. Tesh refused to count higher than twelve. The way he saw it, beyond that, there weren't any more *real* numbers—at least not any with their own names. What followed were those queer *ten* numbers that were repeats: four-ten, five-ten, six-ten. And everyone mispronounced them like Edgar just had. Instead of five and ten, he called it *fifteen*. As far as Tesh was concerned, *thirteen* was the most dangerous number because it was the first one that went beyond the acceptable range. Almost as bad were the stranger sets like the two-tens and three-tens that everyone gave nicknames to like *twenty* and *thirty*. The whole system was a ridiculous mess of terms that had no practical purpose. No one needed to count higher than twelve anyway. Anything more than that was best summed up as a Tet-load. Tesh might have pointed this out, probably would have if he'd been drinking along with the rest, but he had only been holding the cup.

"What's wrong? Why aren't you drinking?"

Tesh turned to find that Brin had appeared at his elbow. Her face, revealed by the dim firelight, showed concern.

He half considered explaining the trouble with numbers, nicknames, and the unnecessary complications found in them, but that wasn't what she was asking about.

In their eagerness to anoint Tesh as the new Grevious, Edgar and Atkins had failed to notice that Tesh had never needed a refill. Brin had only just arrived, but she immediately saw what no one else did.

Is that the way with all women? Or is it just her?

"Hey, Keeper!" Atkins shouted her way with a big drunken grin. "You need to remember what that lad did today. Fifteen, that's what. *Fifteen!* That's a record that won't soon be broken, and the kid doesn't even know what *fifteen* means. Do you know what *fifteen* means, Keeper?"

Brin narrowed her eyes at Atkins as if she thought him insane.

"Come on." Tesh took her hand and led her aside, farther from the fire, deeper into the night.

"What was all that about?" she asked.

"The number of Fhrey I killed."

"Oh." Brin nodded as he brought her to a little bluff.

"Ignore them. What about you? I heard you had a big day. You were there? At the keenig's tent?"

"During the birth?" Brin nodded as a big smile filled her face. "Beautiful baby. She named him Nolyn."

Tesh puzzled on this a moment. "Odd name, Nolyn." He wasn't well educated, but he'd picked up some of the Fhrey language. "*Lyn* means 'land' in Fhrey, right?"

Brin smiled and nodded.

"For a man who doesn't understand the term *fifteen*, that's quite impressive, isn't it?" Tesh said while poking her in the side and making her giggle.

"Yes, yes, you're right!" She slapped his finger aside. When she was convinced he had stopped, she took a breath. "His name is a combination of Rhunic and Fhrey. Persephone borrowed from both cultures, but since he really isn't from either, she's making a statement."

"No land!" Tesh pieced the riddle together.

"Yes." She nodded.

"Doesn't sound too promising, does it? To be born into isolation? To belong nowhere."

"He's unique," she said. "In a way we all are, right? Everyone has to find their own place."

"How does he look?"

"I told you. He's beautiful."

"That's not what I meant. What about his eyes, ears, and hair?"

Brin sighed. "You hate them so much, don't you?"

"You didn't answer the question."

"His ears are round, and he has too little hair to tell."

"And his eyes? Are they blue?"

"No. Actually, they're . . ." She hesitated.

"What? They're brown, right?"

She shook her head. "They're green."

"Green? I've never seen green eyes."

She shrugged. "I told you, he's unique, and wonderful, and I wish you didn't hate the Fhrey so much."

"You're saying you don't? Hate them, I mean?"

"Honestly, no. I *was* scared of them, still am a bit, but not so much now."

"They murdered thousands of us. They wiped out my entire clan, nearly did the same to Nadak. Brin, I watched them murder my mother and father, my uncles and aunts, friends and neighbors."

"Do you think you are the only one? I lost my parents when the Fhrey attacked Dahl Rhen. And you've seen what happened to Gelston; he's my uncle."

"Then you should understand. How is it that you *don't* hate them?"

"Because of Arion, Nyphron, and Anyval. He's the healer who saved Persephone after the raow attack, and today he helped Padera deliver Nolyn. Our old chieftain Konniger tried to kill Persephone, but I don't hate all men or chieftains."

"That isn't even close to the same thing." Tesh frowned and shook his head. He didn't want to argue with her. He'd had enough fighting for one day.

"Well, if you hate them so much, why aren't you happy with your *fifteen* kills?"

Tesh sighed and plopped down on the brittle turf.

"Well?" Brin looked concerned again and knelt beside him.

"I don't know. You're right. I should be, but I'm not." He looked back at the dung fire where Edgar and Atkins were hooting loudly. "I should be drunk and laughing with them." He let his head rest against the turf and looked up at the stars that wrapped the world with sparkling brilliance, one of the few beautiful things to be seen in Dureya and Gula. "I should be dancing with you. I should be shouting to Raithe that his death has been avenged. I should feel full, and satisfied, and . . . happy."

"But you don't?"

Tesh shook his head. "I feel empty. Even more than before, and I don't know why."

"*They* seem to think you're a hero." She tilted her head toward the men at the fire.

Tesh nodded. "*They* want me to teach them how I did it: Trent, Pliny, even Atkins and Edgar. Brigham, too. He's the last Killian, you know."

Brin nodded. "I grew up with them. Had a crush on Brigham and his older brother Hanson."

"You didn't."

"I did." She lay down beside him. "But that was before I met you."

Tesh pulled her close, letting his hand run up the back of her neck and fill the valleys between his fingers with her hair. "If I had been killed today instead of Grevious, would you have missed me? Would you have cried?"

"That depends. In this what-if scenario, does *Brigham* survive?" She flashed Tesh a wicked smile and, turning her head, pretended to search for Brigham.

"You're horrible, you know that?"

She turned back to him. "No, I'm not." She kissed him, softly and gently. "And you're not bad, either."

Tesh would have fallen in love with her at that moment if he hadn't already plunged off that cliff.

"You *are* going to marry me, right?" she asked.

"I have to. I gave Raithe my word, and I will as soon as this war is over."

"Well then, you'd best keep that promise." She nuzzled him. "You don't want Raithe coming back from the dead and stalking you as a manes."

"What's that?"

"The walking dead, usually someone who refuses to enter Phyre"— she poked him in the chest—"because they have a gripe against a loved one who wronged them."

"Ah, I see. Well, if that's how it works, then you'd best steer clear of Brigham Killian, or you'll both be hearing from me after *I* die."

She smiled up at him. "I have a better idea—don't die."

"I won't if you won't."

"Agreed." Brin nodded. "The two of us will live forever."

"Sounds like a fine plan. Do you know I love you?"

"I heard a rumor," she said skeptically. "Wasn't sure whether I should believe it or not."

Tesh pulled Brin tight and kissed her. When at last he let her breathe again, she whispered, "So the rumor is true."

CHAPTER FIVE

A Change of Plans

Language is one of mankind's greatest virtues, but also one of its biggest tragedies; it almost lets us understand each other.

— THE BOOK OF BRIN

Mawyndulë sat at the magnificently crafted table in the fane's council chambers. Long and elegant, with tapered sides and curved edges, the table was beautiful. Not only did Fhrey not kill Fhrey, they also frowned on butchering trees. So some old Eilywin had probably wandered the forest for months in search of just the right wood: a tree that had been knocked down by a storm and caught by its brothers so it didn't rot in the dirt. Suspended, it would have dried. Likely, the woodworker took days to cut and haul the perfect pieces back to his shop. Many months would have been required to shape them properly. Then came the fitting and joining, aligning the grains and colors. At last came the sanding and finishing. Multiple coats of varnish gave it both protection and a luxurious sheen.

Mawyndulë ran his hands over the silky-smooth surface, where he found no discernible gaps between the pieces that formed a perfect herringbone pattern. The table was indeed a work of art that had demanded centuries of training, a millennium of know-how, and years to make.

I could have done better in three minutes—four, tops.

That was the difference between art and the Art.

One of the differences, he reminded himself.

No matter how much training or skill the Eilywin had, or how long they labored, they still couldn't make it rain, raise a mountain from a field, or—

"Nothing? Nothing!" his father shouted at the room of dignitaries. "You've had a whole year, and you come to me without answers?"

Mawyndulë hated when his father got this way, when he resorted to shouting at people who had perfectly good hearing.

The fane glared, holding out his hands toward his staff, generals, and members of the Aquila.

What did he expect? Mawyndulë wondered. *It wasn't like they would say, "Oh, I'm sorry, my fane! What were we thinking? Here, we forgot to present you with this magic stone. Rubbing it will make all your problems disappear. It has unlimited wishes, so please take a moment and grant us eternal life as well as little pink bunnies to wash our clothes while reciting poetry."*

Everyone of note was in the room, clustered around that wooden table. Everyone except Jerydd, of course. He couldn't leave Avempartha, not even for a minute. They all bowed their heads. No one was ever happy when the fane lost his temper, and it spilled over like a boiling pot.

"We did our best." Metis spoke up, surprising Mawyndulë. The First Minister—Gryndal's inferior replacement—had never impressed the prince as being brave. She certainly wasn't smart.

"Best?" the fane erupted.

Hundreds of tiny figurines, which had been painstakingly set out on the table to create a miniature reproduction of the war's landscape, took flight, making everyone flinch. Pops and pings rang out as they shattered against walls.

"Don't talk about *your best* when you come to me with news of defeat!" the fane screamed.

The newly appointed commanders, who'd replaced those that died at Grandford, fared better in that they'd survived their first taste of combat.

They'd also managed to preserve the majority of their forces by ordering a hasty retreat. The fane saw it differently.

"You had bows! Did you use them?"

"Yes, my fane," one of the commanders replied weakly. "And while we did kill many Rhunes, I'm afraid we did little to diminish their threat. Their numbers are simply too great."

Mawyndulë didn't know the speaker's name. He had the narrow eyes of someone from the outer villages. In his father's need for replacements, he had recruited from every corner of Erivan.

"And the Rhunes had a new weapon," the nameless commander went on, "carts pulled by horses. The contraptions were fast and carried archers of their own. Perhaps in the Harwood—if we can bring the fight to the forest—we'll stand a better chance. The dense trees will make those carts useless. Then we can—"

"Carts? You complain about carts?" Lothian erupted.

"And . . . there's the dragon, sir."

"It's alive? I thought it hasn't moved in a year."

"It didn't until we attacked. It's still guarding their camp."

The fane couldn't say much against that. He, too, had found himself impotent against the beast, a fact that did nothing to ease his mood.

Mawyndulë spotted the little chair in the corner beside the table with the water pitcher and was instantly awash in regret and irony. He was still unimaginably young but was no longer relegated to that humiliating sideline, no longer a mere spectator in his father's war room. He'd survived the Battle of Grandford, killed the traitor Arion, and saved his father's life from that murderous dragon. Mawyndulë was no longer merely the privileged prince; he had the respect he deserved. And yet . . .

What a wonderful place that little chair had been. I just didn't realize it at the time. What a lovely thing it had been to believe in the supremacy of the Fhrey and the permanence of Erivan.

For the last hour, he—like the fane—had listened to a dozen people speak, and one fact became quite clear: The Rhunes were coming, and the Fhrey were powerless against them.

"There must be something that can stop that abominable dragon!" The fane stood up, leaned across the table, and focused on Mawyndulë. "Ask him again."

The fane didn't need to say who. Everyone knew.

During the Battle of Grandford, Mawyndulë revealed his ability to speak long distances with Jerydd, the kel of Avempartha. This was the reason Mawyndulë hadn't been forced into the tutelage of Jerydd, why he hadn't been exiled to Avempartha—he was too important now. His father liked having instant communication with the kel. Mawyndulë wasn't certain why Jerydd hadn't been forced to teach Lothian the trick, except maybe the fane didn't want anyone poking into his private conversations. Jerydd was known to do that. The old Miralyith had a problem respecting privacy, but as Mawyndulë had no life to speak of, the intrusions didn't turn out to be too much of a problem. These days, the old kel rarely bothered Mawyndulë except for war meetings. He always established contact for those.

"Jerydd can hear," Mawyndulë told his father. "What do you want to ask?"

"How do we kill that dragon?" The fane sounded strangely feminine the way his voice was reaching up into the high-pitched girlish register that did nothing to assuage fears or squelch rumors that their leader had gone insane.

Again, Mawyndulë had to clench his jaw to keep from showing emotion.

Tell him the answer hasn't changed, Jerydd said in his head. *The dragon can't be killed.*

"Jerydd still has no answer for that."

The fane's face crumpled up like a wrung washcloth.

"Unacceptable! Unacceptable!" Like the figurines of a moment before, the untouched wine goblets took flight as stemware and a spray of crimson liquid decorated the room. Then with both hands fisted, the fane screamed—a genuine screech, high and harsh, the sort little owls made at night, a sound that had always scared the piss out of the prince.

The fane's outburst had the same effect on everyone in the room. Those assembled stood still and stiff, waiting for the tantrum to pass—hoping it would. Mawyndulë noticed Imaly shift her eyes in his direction. She, who was always so vocal in the Airenthenon, hadn't spoken a word in the war room.

"We are Miralyith!" the fane cried. "We are gods. Gryndal would have been able to do something. Where is the bastard now?"

Lothian happened to be looking at Vasek when he said this, and the Master of Secrets was clearly torn between offering the obvious—and dangerously insulting—answer or ignoring a direct question. He opened his mouth but was saved by the fane's next outburst.

"He abandoned me, you know?" Lothian leaned heavily on the table with both hands, staring out at his landscape of broken glass and splattered wine. "Started the whole wretched thing and then got himself killed. Did it on purpose, I imagine. Both Arion and Gryndal betrayed then abandoned me."

Mawyndulë was appalled. To lump Gryndal with The Traitor was inconceivable. He started to open his mouth, but Imaly gave him the tiniest of headshakes.

She knows what I'm thinking.

Making a pact with Jerydd that granted the kel potential access to every word Mawyndulë uttered was bad enough. Now Imaly appeared to be able to read his thoughts.

"Everyone has lost faith. Faith in the Miralyith, in Ferrol, in me." His father turned around and faced the window. "Get out. Everyone leave . . . except Imaly. You wait here."

Synne stepped forward then. She waved with both arms at those gathered, shooing them out as if they were a flock of birds. Under different circumstances, being ushered out by a glorified bodyguard might have ruffled such an illustrious flock's feathers, but this day everyone wanted to get away.

As Mawyndulë exited with the rest, he caught sight of Imaly. She didn't look honored to be singled out.

⫰

Imaly remained seated at the table, waiting. She didn't know what for. Lothian certainly wasn't going to offer tea and crumb cakes. The two weren't friends. *Adversaries* was a more accurate assessment of their relationship. She had made a point of embarrassing Lothian whenever he set foot in the Airenthenon. She saw it as her responsibility to keep him humble. Everyone else treated him like a god. Being Miralyith only made that worse, deepening the divide between the fane's tribe and the other Fhrey. Her responsibility was to keep his feet grounded, take him down a peg or two, and she had done a good job.

Maybe too good.

She watched the fane, who was gazing out the window, waiting for everyone to leave.

He's not going to kill me.

She felt surprisingly confident in this. Lothian wasn't shy about executions, just the opposite. He made a spectacle of them, wanted people to see *justice* doled out. If he planned to kill her, he would have insisted everyone remain, maybe even invited more to watch.

If he's not going to kill me, then what?

In the last year, the two hadn't spoken much. The fane had refused to attend any Aquila meetings. Rumors had leaked that Lothian had been in a dark depression all winter. It had finally lifted in the spring after a demonstration of the newly trained archery corps. Lothian had let his hopes rise with the warming temperatures, and now his spirit had been dashed from greater heights.

What if he's planning abdication? Ever since his ascension, all I've desired is for a non-Miralyith to rule. But what if that comes to pass? If we can't survive the Rhunes' assault with Lothian in charge, what chance will we have with someone else?

This thought was fresh in her mind as Synne closed the door to the council chambers and Fane Lothian came away from the window and stood next to her chair. He put the knuckles of his fists on the table in front of her and leaned in, speaking low. "We need to revisit the subject of the message you told me about when I returned from the Battle of Grandford."

"The one the Rhune leader sent?"

"Yes. Precisely."

"Are you saying you're willing to consider the Rhune leader's proposal for peace?"

The thought was almost too good to believe. Imaly had never even considered this a possibility.

Lothian crouched down so that his face came close to hers. His next words were close to a whisper. "The problem is we don't know if the message came before or after the last battle at Alon Rhist."

Does he expect me to know?

When he didn't say anything further, she assumed he was waiting for her, and she ventured to speak. "Given that I don't know exactly when the last battle was fought, and that I also am unaware how long it takes for a bird to cover that distance, all I can say with any certainty is that the bird arrived six days before you did."

Lothian stood up, moved away, and then sat in his own chair. He thought a moment, and she guessed he was trying to calculate the time. From the more-than-irritated but less-than-angry expression, she guessed he, too, was unable to solve the riddle.

"If they sent it before the last battle, it means nothing," Lothian said. "If they sent it after, it could mean everything. I need to know."

Lothian focused on her, a terrible desperation in his eyes. For the first time, she genuinely felt sympathy toward him. In that brief moment, she saw a leader trying to do his best for those he ruled. Lothian was willing to sacrifice his pride in return for the lives of the people of Erivan. Imaly wondered if she'd misjudged him. Up until then, she had believed the fane to be arrogant beyond the ability to adequately govern, the sort who felt the Fhrey existed for his benefit rather than the other way around.

"Might I suggest responding?" she offered. "You have pigeons, correct? You might inquire if the offer is still available."

"That could be dangerous. We'd appear weak." He rubbed his chin thoughtfully. "But if nothing changes soon, what choice will I have? And if that day comes, we might all consider joining the Umalyn tribe and pray for Ferrol's mercy."

℘

"A moment if I may, my prince." Vasek waited outside the war room for Mawyndulë and coaxed him aside.

The Master of Secrets looked older these days. His hair teetered on the threshold between blond and white, and the structure of his face was collapsing. His skin was starting to sag in that horrid way that afflicted the aged. He had to be in his second millennium. That was always when the ancient began to *look* old, but Mawyndulë had thought Vasek was twelve hundred at the most. Somehow, the Master of Secrets had managed to age a thousand years since Grandford. A lot of people had.

"I was wondering if you've had contact with, or have heard about any resurgence of, the Gray Cloaks."

"Gray Cloaks? No."

Vasek nodded, disappointment on his face.

The two began walking away from the closed doors, putting distance between themselves and the war room. "Why do you ask? Have *you* heard something?"

Together they moved down the grand stair that led to the front doors of the Talwara.

"Nothing specific, but I am charged with being suspicious."

"But something must have brought this to your mind."

Vasek shrugged as he moved down the steps, taking them one at a time, his sandals slapping the marble, his hands clasped before him. "This is a dangerous time. Our forces are stretched thin. The smaller villages have been depleted and many are—well, let's just say morale is quite low." He paused when they reached the bottom of the stairs, then stepped to one side.

Lowering his voice, he said, "Your father was quite accurate in his assessment that the esteem of the Miralyith has suffered. Fear of your tribe has been replaced by fear of the Rhunes. Some—more than some—*blame* this crisis on the Miralyith." He glanced back at the war room. "And I fear the fane is vulnerable, weakened by stress."

That was one way to put it. Mawyndulë would have gone with *driven mad to the point of ineptitude,* but he was the prince, and Vasek was the Master of Secrets.

"If someone were inclined to cause trouble, this would be a perfect opportunity. We are shorthanded here at the palace, and at this moment, there are only four known Miralyith in the city."

"Really?" Mawyndulë was certain Vasek was mistaken.

"Indeed. Your father, you, Vidar, and Synne."

"What of . . ." Mawyndulë paused to think. He had never been a social person and had known few people even before the war. He thought of Onya, but then he remembered she had died in the Battle of Grandford. Kasimer had died then, too. "Wait, what of Crymson?" Mawyndulë asked, recalling the name of a Miralyith who had shown up in the Talwara in the previous fall.

"Crymson was sent to the bank."

Sent to the bank was sure to be a new, and decidedly unpopular, phrase. As Mawyndulë understood it, the eastern bank of the Nidwalden River was lined with Miralyith under command of the kel, who had created a net to prevent any Rhune or Instarya from crossing. But he had no idea that matters had deteriorated to the point that *every* Miralyith had been sent to the new frontier.

Is Vasek asking about the Gray Cloaks to find more recruits? Are we really stretched so thin? If so, eventually a hole in the net can be found and exploited. How did the tide turn so substantially?

Mawyndulë was struck by the irony. The Miralyith had replaced the Instarya as the exiled protectors of Erivan. That was how the whole mess got started.

Can history repeat itself? It shouldn't be possible for the Miralyith to suffer the Instarya's fate while a Miralyith sits on the Forest Throne, but . . . wasn't Fane Alon Rhist a leader of the Instarya during the last war?

A moment before, Mawyndulë wouldn't have believed it possible—but a moment before, he didn't know he was one of only four Miralyith left in the entire city of Estramnadon.

"Do you really think a member of the Gray Cloaks would take their place on the line? Is that what this is about?"

"Desperation makes for strange alliances. I'm not exaggerating the danger. If anything, I'm understating it. Matters haven't been so grave since the war with the Dherg, and Makareta hasn't been found."

Mawyndulë stopped breathing at the sound of the name. Usually, Fane Lothian had a particularly grotesque penchant for publicly disposing of those who had opposed him, and Mawyndulë wondered whether his father had executed Makareta in secret to spare his son the pain of her death. *Probably not. My father has never cared enough to be concerned about my feelings.* Regardless, she might still be dead. Another Miralyith could have killed her in a way that left no remains and then died in the same battle, taking the knowledge to his grave.

Or maybe . . . can she still be alive?

"Have you heard anything about her?"

"No," Mawyndulë said.

"So she hasn't tried to contact you?"

He shook his head.

"Would you tell me if she did?"

Mawyndulë's brows rose. "Tread carefully. I am not the fane, so I'm not allowed to do to you what my father did to Cintra, but apparently I am but one of four Miralyith in the city, and Ferrol has no restrictions on causing pain."

Vasek frowned. "A reminder isn't necessary, my prince."

When Mawyndulë showed no understanding, Vasek pulled back his sleeves to his elbow, revealing burn marks that shriveled his skin. "They don't stop there."

The marks were too uniform, too even, to have been made by a natural fire.

"No, I haven't seen her," Mawyndulë said. "But if I had, you wouldn't need to ask. You'd know."

"How so?"

"Because I would make a great spectacle of her death."

Vasek stared at him for a long moment, then nodded. "In that case, let me provide a word of warning: Be on guard if you do encounter her. Makareta murdered at least five Miralyith that afternoon in the square. Several she caught off guard. One she did not."

The way he said it, Mawyndulë knew what he meant. "Synne."

"Yes," Vasek said. "Makareta would have succeeded in killing Lothian if not for Synne putting up what every Miralyith who was there has described as a *miraculous block*."

"So, that's how she got her job."

Vasek nodded. "Makareta may be young, but she *is* talented and exceedingly dangerous."

Mawyndulë smiled. "So am I."

CHAPTER SIX

The Dragon and the Pigeon

The wisdom of sacrificing one to save many appears obvious, but too often that depends on who is the one and who are the many.

— THE BOOK OF BRIN

Persephone held Nolyn tightly—too tightly. She could barely stand letting him go, given the deaths of her previous children. Nolyn was her fourth son. The first died so soon after birth that they hadn't had time to name him. Her second, Duncan, survived only to the age of three. He grew sick and never recovered. She'd named her third son Mahn, perhaps as a wish, a hope that he would live long enough to become one. He did, and she thought she'd escaped the curse of outliving those she'd given birth to— until the bear killed him. Nolyn was her last chance, and she was terrified of losing him, too.

And yet the boy needed rest, and Justine was waiting. During the feeding, he'd wriggled and thrust out his arms, tangling sticky fingers in Persephone's hair. Now his eyes were drooping as milk dribbled down his chin, but still his fists held on. "Let go, you little monster," Persephone said, gently pulling strands of hair from his clenched hands. She passed him over.

Justine grinned lovingly at the boy. "Did you hear what she called you?" she cooed. "I don't think you're a monster. No, I don't. Nuh-uh. You're not like that at all, are you?"

"That's because you didn't feed him. In addition to trying to turn me Miralyith-bald, I swear he's got teeth coming in. And he's only eight weeks!"

The three were in Persephone's tent, otherwise known as the Keenig's Lodge. Nyphron had his own quarters. Why he bothered, she didn't know. Her husband was never in camp long enough to use either. He and the army were three miles north at the edge of the Harwood, ensuring that it was once more safe to move the base camp. Over the last few months, steady advancements made by the Forces of the West had resulted in three relocations, making them efficient at moving. Persephone, by virtue of having a child to care for, remained behind with the support staff, those who were hauling water, creating bandages, sharpening weapons, cooking food, and waiting for word on whether to advance or evacuate.

Persephone could have employed a wet nurse, freeing her to lead the army as a proper keenig should, but doing so would merely be an exercise in vanity. She wasn't a warrior or military strategist. Such tasks were better suited to Nyphron, who had spent his whole life leading men into battle. Besides, Nolyn needed her, and she him.

In the past, those who led the Rhunes in times of crisis had always been men, and the emergency usually involved warfare. But what if the calamity was pestilence? Or famine? Or merely divisions between the clans? A keenig was still required, but they wouldn't need to be a warrior. Men of that sort were apt to seek conflict when none was necessary because people felt comfortable doing what they were best at. Persephone had come to realize that a good ruler needed more than a firm hand. They should be wise, compassionate, strong, self-sacrificing, and creative—less a father and more a *mother*.

"You're the baby keenig." Justine nuzzled Nolyn. "The keenigling."

"*Keenigling?*" Persephone chuckled.

"Can you say keenigling?" Justine asked the baby, who blew bubbles in reply. She held the boy to her chest as she paced and bounced around the open area in the center of the tent. Her footfalls were silenced by multiple wool carpets.

"That's a mouthful for anyone," Persephone said. "Sounds downright dwarven."

Justine turned and displayed an expression as if she'd just heard something profound. "What *do* dwarfs call their rulers? It's like *keenig*, isn't it?"

Persephone nodded. "They call them *king*. I suppose you can use kingling. That's a bit easier."

Justine frowned, then turned back to Nolyn. "We like keenigling better, don't we?"

Persephone felt she ought to get up and go out, if only to show the residents of the camp that she still lived. She didn't want to. She needed sleep, having gotten so little of it over the past two months. After an arduous delivery, Nolyn had awakened every few hours. Persephone didn't mind, but she had become so exhausted that she'd asked Justine to sleep in the lodge to provide more help. The young woman was both a gift from Mari and a source of Persephone's guilt. Justine was only available because her whole family, and her husband-to-be, had been killed in the Battle of Grandford. She became nursemaid to Nolyn because she had no one else.

There are far too many Justines made by this war. Being keenig is to be a mother to all, and to be a mother is to be—she frowned—*tired.*

Running footfalls approached, drawing attention from them both. The silhouette of a slender figure cast itself onto the canvas wall.

"Morning, Habet." A breathless voice came from just outside the tent. "Madam Keenig, may I—"

"Come in, Brin," Persephone said, then sighed after realizing that the Keeper also shared Justine's plight. Sarah and Delwin had been killed during the giants' attack on Dahl Rhen.

The girl ducked through the flap. It being midsummer, she was barefoot and dressed in a lightweight, Rhen-patterned breckon mor. Her face and shoulders were a healthy golden tan, just as always at this time of year. Persephone felt a dash of envy, knowing that she herself was pale as a patch of spring snow.

Brin spotted Justine holding Nolyn, and her face broke into a smile. Persephone was certain the girl had run to her tent for a reason, but like a dog catching a scent, the Keeper had made an abrupt turn and converged on nurse and baby.

"He's awake!" Brin exclaimed. "He's never up."

Justine's and Persephone's brows rose together in surprise.

"Well, never when *I'm* here," Brin clarified, then rubbed Nolyn's nose with her finger. "He's so cute."

"He's a monster," Justine divulged. "His mother just said so."

"He's not," Brin argued. "He's . . . he's a . . ."

"Keenigling?" Justine offered.

"A kingling," Persephone corrected.

Brin looked at both of them as if they were insane. "What are you talking about?"

"That's what the baby of a dwarven king is called, right?" Persephone asked.

"No," Brin replied. "The child of a king is a prince."

"Really?" Persephone said. "What is the child of a keenig called?"

Brin shook her head. "There has never been such a thing. We've only had a few keenigs and all were young, unmarried men. Their children came after they stepped down from the position. And certainly none have ever *given* birth."

"Prince?" Justine said, and looked at Nolyn as if mentally trying on the title to see how it fitted. "I like it."

"Can I hold him?" Brin asked.

Justine looked at Persephone, who nodded.

Brin clutched the child as if she held a giant egg. "He's growing so fast."

"Brin, are you here just to burp Nolyn and give us language lessons?"

"Oh, no." She looked mortified. "I forgot. Hamlin has just come from Alon Rhist."

"Who?"

"A rider. A pigeon from Estramnadon has arrived. The fane has sent word!"

When they'd left the remains of the Rhist to set up camp in the High Spear Valley, Persephone had left a small contingent behind, including Fhrey who had previously run the pigeon corps. As days stretched into months, and months into seasons, her hope of hearing a reply to the message sent during the height of the Battle of Grandford had all but vanished.

"A message?" Persephone sat up straight on her mattress of blankets and straw. "What did it say?"

Brin smiled at her. "The fane wants peace."

Suri stood in the meadow just outside the line of tents, watching Gifford trying to juggle three stones. She couldn't hold back the tears. He wasn't doing badly. For a man with a back as twisted as an ivy vine, he did quite well. Gifford wasn't managing anything fancy—no spins or behind-the-back catches—but despite his awkward stance from a nearly useless leg and a tilted set of shoulders, he hadn't missed a single toss. The problem wasn't him at all; it was the stones themselves. They had belonged to Arion.

Gifford stopped juggling. He caught the three smooth rocks and stared at her. He might have been frowning. Interpreting expressions on such a distorted face was a tricky business, but an apology was in his eyes. "I'm sow-wee I can't do this so well." He glanced down at the stones. "My body just isn't good fo' such things."

"You're doing fine." Suri took a moment to wipe the tears from her eyes and cheeks. "It's not you."

"Then what's wong?"

Suri didn't answer. She didn't know how. Words couldn't explain.

Arion had been dead for more than a year, but it felt like only yesterday that Suri had been the one juggling those stones while Arion watched with amused pride. A whole year and still little things—like the stones—flooded her with memories that spilled out in tears. Better than keeping them in and drowning, Suri figured. And it wasn't as if she thought about the dead often. Suri went whole weeks without remembering Arion, or Minna, or Tura, or Raithe. Well, a day at least. She was certain one full day had passed when she hadn't thought about any of them. Maybe not a *whole* day. Avoiding thoughts of Raithe while the gilarabrywn sat on the hill was impossible. And it was difficult to fall asleep without imagining her pillow breathing softly in and out. And of course, being summer, butterflies fluttered nearly everywhere—horrible, awful butterflies.

That day, however, it was the stones.

Suri forced a determined smile and slapped her hip. "Old war wound acting up." It sounded like a joke. She'd meant it to be. Suri had been rent by the war, but the pain wasn't in her hip.

Gifford nodded and put the stones back in the bag without a word.

Suri liked that about him. Maybe his perception of the Art was improving, and he could sense what she was feeling. That would be good because Gifford wasn't managing to do much else. He failed in all but the simplest of weaves. She urged him to touch the larger chords—tried to get him to make it rain. He hadn't managed a single drop. Suri could tell he really didn't want to, that he was scared. Chords could be dangerous in any number of ways. Suri sympathized, and the irony was too much—one more link to the past, to Arion. Teaching Gifford the Art was a bittersweet torture as she shadowboxed with a much-missed ghost.

Knowing that Arion had wanted to find and educate other Rhune Artists, Suri felt that continuing the project was a way she could busy herself and honor Arion's memory. She also had nothing else to do. She refused to aid in the war, wouldn't use the Art to kill people who were now defending themselves from an aggressor. Teaching Gifford gave her a more tangible reason to stay than the ominous conversation she'd had with Malcolm, who'd mysteriously disappeared around the time they left Alon Rhist.

Suri restricted her lessons to an hour and refused to see Gifford outside training sessions. Spending too much time with him was dangerous. Gifford was nice, just the sort of person she could be friends with, and butterflies, Suri determined, couldn't have any. Friendship, happiness, and contentment were for caterpillars.

Gifford held out the stones, but Suri shook her head. "You keep 'em. I think that's how it's supposed to work."

"How what is?"

Suri thought a moment, but once more words failed, and Gifford didn't press. Why Roan loved him was easy to see. The woman, whom Suri had once thought incapable of smiling, had learned how once she and Gifford started living under the same roof. The potter, it seemed, was a far better instructor than the mystic. Gifford and Roan's home was in the center of an ever-growing yard of oddities and raw materials acquired by the pair or given to them by well-meaning neighbors who wondered what she might make from the things they brought.

The army had moved ahead once again, advancing to the north, leaving the camp to its daily rituals of cooking, cleaning, repairing, and building. Summer had replaced spring and begun giving out stiflingly warm hugs to all. Everything was quiet, and even a bit lazy as things were apt to be in the hot season. Then Suri heard the thunder.

It wasn't a rain-producing roll, and even without using the Art, Suri could tell the difference. Having heard it many times now, she recognized the sound of horses on the plain. Looking north, she spotted a group of carts headed her way. They were calling this new invention *chariots*. Suri didn't know why. Maybe it was something to do with *chairs*, or *carts*, or perhaps it was a Fhrey or Dherg word. All she knew for certain was Roan, who had invented the contraption, hadn't named it. She would never give anything a moniker that Gifford would have trouble pronouncing.

While still a good distance away, Suri spotted the shining bronze armor and blue banner of Nyphron. When traversing the area between the base camp and the front line, he traveled with a squadron of chariots. The Art told Suri nothing terrible had happened, but apprehension was in the air.

Nyphron rolled up near Suri and Gifford. He pulled the horse to a stop just outside the line of tents.

"Something wong?" Gifford asked.

"No," Nyphron replied, then gave a glance to the north. "Well, nothing too serious, but we're encountering stronger resistance up in the swamp near the Harwood. The Miralyith have come out to play again. They're hiding the Fhrey archers, and yesterday morning they swallowed an entire squadron."

"Swallowed?" Gifford asked.

"In the muck," Nyphron replied. He turned his attention to Suri and gave her a knowing smile. "You must order your dragon forward. One look and every Miralyith will flee. They are a cowardly people."

"I can't do that," Suri said.

"Of course you can. You've done it three times already. Once we clear this nest, you can settle the beast on the eaves of the forest, and we'll move the camp again."

"It won't go," Suri said. "It's reached its limit. The weave restricts the distance it can travel from where it was created. And in this direction, this is it."

"Are you certain?"

Suri nodded.

Nyphron's face grew a scowl while he looked back and forth between the gilarabrywn and Suri as if one or both were conspiring against him. In a huff, he stepped off the chariot and advanced on the mystic. He was dressed in battle armor, sword at his side, shield on his back.

"Fine," he said with a tone that didn't sound the least bit satisfied. "Make another one. In fact, come with me. We'll go to the edge of the Harwood, and you can make it there. The Asendwayr are hiding in the trees. They have camps in the forest where our chariots can't travel. After you make another dragon, you can order it to set fire to the forest and flush them out."

"No!" Suri said, aghast.

Whatever quiet conversation had been going on around them stopped, and a hush spread.

Nyphron's scowl deepened. "What do you mean, *no?*"

She paused to get the words just right, so he couldn't possibly misunderstand. "Under no circumstances will I ever make another gilarabrywn."

Nyphron took a step toward her, opening his mouth. Then he stopped and reconsidered. After taking a calming breath, he asked, "Why not?"

Suri didn't answer. The complete explanation was quite personal and more than a little painful, and she couldn't ignore the weight of so many eyes on her. "Making one comes at a cost," she finally said.

Nyphron waved a dismissive hand. "This is war. There is always a price to be paid. Many men have done so with their lives, and a lot more will die before this is over."

"It requires a sacrifice," Suri quietly explained.

"Is that all?" Nyphron rolled his eyes and chuckled. "The Umalyn offer up lambs to Ferrol all the time, and He's never granted them a dragon to slay their enemies. Just tell me what you need, and I'll see you get it."

"Doesn't work that way. Death isn't enough. I would have to kill—" She stopped and glanced at Gifford. Suri felt suddenly sick and looked away, opting to stare at her own toes, and she found them dirty. Arion wouldn't have approved.

"What am I missing? What would you have to kill?" Nyphron pressed.

Gifford would've known not to ask that question.

Suri hesitated, wondering how to reply. She went with the simplest response. "Not what . . . *whom*. I have to destroy the life of someone dear to me."

"I've sent hundreds of men to their deaths, and there were many I've cared for. I lost Sebek at Grandford. Such is the nature of war. Every life is precious to someone, but one person is nothing when weighed against the hundreds—no, thousands—that will be saved." Nyphron spoke with all the compassion of a fist. He also seemed to think she was one of his soldiers, someone he could order around. She wasn't, and she didn't like him thinking that way.

"Are you volunteering, then?" she asked, lifting her eyes to meet his.

Nyphron smirked. "I doubt you think well enough of me for it to work."

"You're right about that."

Nyphron's eyes drifted toward Gifford, and Suri's face instantly hardened.

Just then, Persephone came out of her tent with Brin at her side. This was the first time since the birth that Suri had seen the keenig without a baby in her arms.

"What about Nolyn?" Suri quickly asked. "I think he might work. I'm quite fond of the lad. If you really want another gilarabrywn, we can do it right now. Fetch him, give me a sword, and hold your son down while I slit his throat."

"You forget yourself, mystic." Nyphron spoke in an icy tone. "Threatening the life of the keenig's son is treason."

"Then don't ask me to make a gilarabrywn, and no one will call you a traitor."

Nyphron clenched his teeth, his eyes hard. He took a menacing step toward her. Dressed in full armor, he would be protected by Orinfar markings engraved on the underside, but runes were easy to circumvent. Suri felt the air around her. A light breeze was blowing from the east. That current could be amplified, thrust between them if he—

"You live in this camp," Nyphron said, having taken no more than that single step. "You eat the food provided for those fighting this war, but you refuse to aid us?"

"I'd be happy to leave," Suri said, and she'd never meant something so sincerely in her life. She would have left sooner, if it hadn't been for Malcolm. But if he'd stopped her from leaving so she could create more gilarabrywns, he was gravely mistaken.

"You might as well. You're of no use to us."

"What's going on?" Persephone rushed forward and placed herself between the two.

"Nothing," Suri said. "I was just leaving."

వ

Persephone and Nyphron walked in silence back toward the Keenig's Lodge. Nyphron led the chariot's horse by the reins. Once they'd reached the tent, she asked, "So, are you going to tell me what that was all about?"

"The mystic refuses to make another dragon. She claims it requires taking a life, but her failure to do so will kill hundreds, maybe thousands."

"You didn't *really* ask her to do that, did you?" Persephone turned, but Suri had already disappeared into the maze of tents, Gifford slowly following her trail.

"Yes, after she told me the present one is broken."

"Pardon?"

"She says it can't advance, but I don't know if that's true or if she's just being obstinate." He pointed to the north. "Men are dying by the dozens. Rhunes. *Your* people, and she's whining about taking a single life?"

Nyphron didn't understand, couldn't, and Persephone felt guilty about not explaining sooner. She should have anticipated and preempted the whole affair. She hadn't done so because the idea of explaining how Raithe had died—and to Nyphron of all people—was too painful. "It's unfortunate you found out that way. I should have mentioned it before now, and I'm sorry you got so upset. You looked like you were going to hit her. Were you?"

Nyphron didn't respond, but the anger was still bright in his eyes. He wasn't accustomed to being told no, and certainly not by a teenage Rhune.

"Look, the next time you speak to Suri," Persephone said, "keep in mind that she has the power to level mountains, and while she's been forced to grow up much too quickly, she still has the emotions of a young girl—one who has suffered more than you know. Striking her wouldn't have been wise. Believe me. I've seen how *not wise* such a thing is."

"If she's dangerous, we should—"

"Suri's not dangerous! She just proved that, or weren't you paying attention?" Persephone sighed as she realized this wasn't a conversation they should be having in public. Luckily, her tent was far from the rest. Only Brin was there, standing at a distance, waiting for instructions about the fane's message. "And now that you know she has to kill someone, who should that be? I'll tell you who—me. I wouldn't allow anyone else. But she won't make another, and there's nothing anyone can do to force her."

Still angry, Nyphron tossed the reins over the horse's head, preparing to leave.

"Where are you going?" Persephone asked.

"Back," he said, now angry with her as well. "I came to get the dragon." He looked up at the hill where it lay. "Now I have to devise a new plan."

"Are we losing?" she asked.

"What? No." He looked at her as if she were insane. "Not at all. It's just . . . the battlefield is—I don't know—it's hard to express to someone who hasn't been there. I'm feeling uneasy."

He mounted his chariot, a pretty thing that someone had taken the time to paint, swirls of flames surrounding the wheels.

"Wait," she said to stop him. "I have news that could prove more valuable than another dragon. It could save the lives of thousands."

He studied her with interest. She liked that about him. All the men she had known in the past became deaf to reason once their blood was up, but not him. Nyphron dismounted, ready to hear more.

"We received a bird from the fane," she told him.

"A bird?"

"A response to the message I sent last year. A rider from Alon Rhist delivered it this morning."

"Slow bird."

"Lothian wishes to discuss a peaceful conclusion."

"Of course he does. He's losing, and he knows it."

"But we could end this war now. No one else needs to die. Isn't that why you asked Suri to make another dragon? To save lives?"

He scowled at her as if to suggest she didn't understand anything. "That's not the point. Why do you think it took the fane so long to reply? Don't you find it interesting that the bird arrived just as we are pushing him back to the eaves of the Harwood? It's the same reason you sent your message. Desperation. Lothian knows it's just a matter of time." Nyphron looked at the hill where the gilarabrywn lay and smiled. "I came for a dragon and got a pigeon instead, but perhaps that's better. Victory, it would seem, is closer than I thought. If you feel a need to reply, tell Lothian your offer has expired, and I plan to watch his head leave his shoulders. Better yet, deal with him in the same way he treated you. Ignore it. Leave the fane wondering in silence while we march on Estramnadon. He and his Miralyith think they're so smart. Let me tell you something: Clever are the Children of Ferrol, quick, certain, and dark their fate."

With that, he climbed back into his chariot, shook the reins, and raced north.

As he left, Brin trotted over. "Is everything all right? Did you two come up with a response for the fane?"

"No. Nyphron doesn't want peace; he doesn't want to save lives. He wants revenge, to bring Fane Lothian to his knees."

"Really? What did he say?"

"'Clever are the Children of Ferrol, quick, certain, and dark their fate.' You should put it in your book. That may have been the most eloquent thing he's ever said, and the stupidest. My husband appears to have forgotten that he, too, is Fhrey."

"What about the fane? Do you want to send a response?"

Persephone watched as Nyphron raced away. She couldn't help sharing his feeling that something about the battlefield wasn't right. And watching him diminish into the distance, she discovered she was worried. Not just about the progress of the war, but about him. "Don't send any word," she said. "Nyphron's right. The fane can wait just as we did. Besides . . . right now, I don't want to close any doors."

❧

Throwing herself on the bank of the nearby stream, Suri decided there was something horribly wrong with the world. She landed on a stone that jabbed her ankle. Digging it out, she threw it into the water with a frustrated cry. It answered with a tiny *plop!*

Not the world—people! she revised.

They were the problem, and it was why she'd avoided them for most of her life, an existence that was so much happier when it had been only her and Minna.

I'm tired of everyone making such ridiculous demands: Arion, Malcolm, and now Nyphron.

Before long, she heard the familiar, telltale *clip, drag, clop.* "Tough fo' me to keep up," Gifford said. "I almost lost you." Unable to simply sit, he crumpled to the grass with a muffled grunt.

"I'm going back to the Hawthorn Glen," Suri said, making her mind up as she said it. She was grateful that Gifford was there to hear, so he could tell others why she wasn't around anymore. "Nyphron's right. I have no reason to be here. I don't do anything. I'm just getting in the way."

"You been showing me magic."

"Yes, for a year, and without much success, just another thing I've failed at: teacher, sister, friend, and butterfly."

"Buttafly?"

"Something Arion used to say. She thought a Rhune who used the Art could stop the war and save the lives of humans and Fhrey. She kept telling me I'd have to be something I'm not. I was perfectly happy as a caterpillar, but she wanted me to fly."

"I know exactly how you feel." Gifford nodded as he adjusted the position of his bad leg with his hands. "Padewa did the same thing to me because Tu-wa said I would save mankind one day."

Suri raised her head and blinked at him. She'd never heard this story. Given that it involved Tura, she found it especially interesting, but mostly she was intrigued because she and Gifford apparently shared a remarkably similar curse: Someone demanding the impossible.

"Yep." Gifford nodded at her expression, as if to say, *Can you believe it?* "When I was still in my mom's stomach, Tu-wa said I'd be fast—the fastest—and my speed would save ev-we-one. But my mom would die giving me life. She could have stopped me fwom coming, but didn't. And just like Tu-wa said, my mom died. When I came out like I am, it seemed like Tu-wa didn't know what she was talking about."

Suri nodded, stunned by the revelation.

"Padewa loved my mom, so she hated me. Maybe she hated Tu-wa, too. She thought I'd killed my mom fo' nothing. I wouldn't have bet on me, but it wasn't as if I had any say in being like this." He gestured at his twisted leg.

"But Padera was wrong," Suri said. "You did go faster than any man ever has. That Instarya named Plymerath called you the Shining Hero of the Night or something like that. And you lit the fire at Perdif that brought the Gula, so you did save everyone."

Gifford nodded. "Didn't think I could, but yeah, I did. Funny how stuff happens—even when you don't think it will. So, maybe what Aw-we-on said will still come twue. Maybe the time fo' you to fly hasn't come yet."

Suri stared at him.

"But you should watch out. When it happens, it will be unexpected, likely in the middle of the night." He held up a finger and pointed it at her. "Want some good advice?"

Suri nodded.

"Take shoes. I didn't and wished I had."

"I don't wear any."

Gifford looked down at her feet, and, sticking out his lower lip, he added, "Good. One less thing to wo-wee about."

"You shouldn't be talking to me like this."

"Why not? I thought we was fwiends."

"No!" she snapped, jumping to her feet. "We are *not* friends! We are never going to be friends. Don't you understand? I can't have friends. Ever!" She began crying.

Gifford climbed to his feet and placed a gentle hand on her shoulder. "It's okay. We don't have to be fwiends. How about I be an Absolutely Lousy Enemy. I can do that." He paused a moment, then gave her a hopeful grin. "What do you say?"

Suri wiped her eyes. "I hate you."

"Good. That's what enemies ah . . ."

"Are for?" she provided.

Gifford nodded. "Still leaving?"

Suri sighed and shrugged. "Maybe tomorrow."

"Might have wain."

"You mean rain?"

"Yeah, that."

"Guess I'll see how it goes."

"Sounds like a plan."

Gifford gave her a hug; she squeezed him in return.

He took the first of his many awkward steps toward the camp but stopped partway. Turning, he waved and said, "I hate you, Su-wee."

She waved back. "I hate you, too, Gifford."

With that, the crippled hero continued his trek into the sea of tents.

CHAPTER SEVEN

The Battle of the Harwood

They came without warning. That was the problem with the Fhrey—they were quiet. In the fields that could be crossed by chariots, we had the advantage, but in the forest, our enemy became ghostly assassins.

—— THE BOOK OF BRIN

The days of marching in lines had ended. That tradition died along with the first thousand men who had entered the Harwood. Tesh liked to think of himself as the one thousand and first. He'd heard the screams of those who'd had the chance to cry out—few did. The long line that had been four men deep just sort of melted away. The elves had managed the feat with quiet bows and silent daggers. Some were in the trees, others hiding in the bushes, and then there were those who buried themselves so they could emerge behind the line. Before anyone knew what was happening, hundreds lay dead beneath the ferns.

Crouching in the thickets, Tesh didn't say a word, but he established eye contact with Edgar, Atkins, Brigham, Pliny, and Trent. He waved them over. The six gathered in a hollow as Eres shouted for a regrouping of the line.

"The commander wants us back shoulder to shoulder," Pliny whispered.

"Eres can kiss my ass," Tesh replied softly. "Lining up is suicide. We need another approach. They're all around us." He looked up at the trees where shafts of light shone like curtains hung among the dense boughs. He heard movement, the crunch of dry leaves.

Small animal? Friend? Murderous elf?

Tesh had both swords out. He held them low, trying to keep his profile small.

"You have a better idea?" Edgar asked hopefully.

"Seek and destroy. Pair up. Watch each other's backs. And don't trust sound."

"What do you mean?"

"Try to imagine being deaf. Act like it. Believe it because we won't hear them. Rely on your eyes, but don't trust them too much, either. My guess—we'll see them just heartbeats before their blades swing at our throats."

Pliny traced fingertips along his neck with a grimace.

"Trent, Pliny," Tesh said, "bring up the rear and keep a close eye behind us. I'll go first. Atkins, you watch my back." He pointed at Brigham. "You stick with Edgar, and remember what I taught you. And everyone stay low and quiet."

No one questioned him, even though Edgar was twice Tesh's age and had been the Shield to the chieftain of Clan Melen. Atkins, who was larger than Tesh and had fought in more battles, was no slouch, either. But after training with Tesh, and in light of his successes in the field, they all envied his skill and trusted his instincts. Then there was the fact that in times of dire peril, people were predisposed to follow anyone with confidence. Tesh had learned that little trick from Nyphron.

At that moment, whatever advance the elves were making was off to their left. To his right, Tesh could hear the crash of branches, as if a deer were darting through the brush. He lifted his head above the undergrowth and saw movement. A man in iron armor was racing blindly through the trees. Tesh was positive the man had no idea where he was going, which, unfortunately, was right toward them. As he got closer, Tesh recognized him as a Gula he'd had a meal with a few months ago. *Not a bad guy for someone from Clan Strom.* Tesh had no idea what the fool was thinking; he probably wasn't. *That's the face of panic.*

Then it happened. What had appeared to be nothing more than bushes launched an attack with incredible speed—Fhrey speed. One came from the left, another from the right. They converged on the running man, both stabbing deep. The first sword pierced the side of his neck above the guard and just below the helm; the other blade entered an armpit. Tesh's onetime meal partner dropped with a sound similar to a sigh.

Tesh didn't bother watching the Gula fall. His eyes stayed on the elves as they shrank back into the undergrowth. He marked their places and inched forward, trying to imitate a cat pursuing a mouse. Not a bad idea except for two problems: Tesh wasn't a cat, and elves weren't mice.

His little troop of men traveled through the forest, their heavy armor making them slow. They did have one small advantage: The elves were arrogant by nature. Not for a moment did they imagine Tesh could see them in their hiding spots. And for the most part they were *nearly* invisible. Each wore clothes the color of dirt and wood, and they had leaves attached to light leather armor covering their shoulders, backs, and heads. They sacrificed defense for offense, protection for stealth.

As Tesh inched forward, he occasionally lost sight of them, and a little panic fluttered in his stomach until he once more spotted a finger or shoulder. They stayed motionless until Tesh was just shy of sword's reach. Then everything happened at once. The two Tesh had been stalking lunged toward him. They were fast, but not nearly as quick as Sebek had been, and once metal crashed, Tesh relaxed. All tension and fear faded into routine. He'd done this a thousand times and against more skilled opponents. He easily killed the first, then in the same movement, he deflected an attack on Atkins, who was trying to cover Tesh's flank. His off-hand sword killed that second elf an instant later.

A quiet grunt delivered the news that the fight wasn't yet over. Spinning, he saw Trent fall to his knees as two more elves advanced from the rear.

They waylaid my ambush!

Tesh ran back to where Edgar and Pliny fought. As he did, he caught sight of a bright flash, a blade moving through a shaft of sunlight. Looking, or thinking, would have been fatal. Instead, Tesh instinctively stabbed out to his right with one blade while raising his second in defense. Both weapons encountered something, and he heard a high-pitched squeal. Tesh didn't bother to look. When fighting elves, time was measured not in seconds or even fractions of them, but in moments of incalculable brevity. Wasted movement or glances equaled death.

Trusting that he'd killed whoever had attacked, Tesh inserted himself into the fight between Edgar and Pliny and the two elves who had jumped them from behind.

Slower than Tesh, and lacking his muscle-memory instincts, Edgar was still the next-best Rhune warrior in the army. He'd already been good before Tesh started giving him pointers, and those skills showed as he killed his opponent with a well-placed slash.

Atkins came in third on Tesh's list of best fighters, with the late, great Grevious taking fourth. Pliny and Brigham had talent but lacked training. If they survived, Tesh would give them more than what Eres had. He'd teach them the secrets he'd stolen from the Galantians. He made this decision even as he killed the fourth elf, who nearly took Pliny's head off.

The noise of the fight, and that high, elvish squeal, drew more enemies to their position.

"Form a circle!" Tesh shouted, and without hesitation they put their backs to one another.

The elves came out of the forest like bees from a rapped hive. Their decision proved to be disastrous. With Tesh's men in a circle, their eyes watching all directions, the enemy couldn't hide. They broke upon the Rhune blades like waves upon granite.

This is it, Tesh thought. *This is how we'll win.* In past months, he'd focused on only training himself, but now he realized the massive advantage of a team. A single Tesh was dangerous, but a squadron of them would be invincible.

An arrow hit him in the back of the head, ringing his helmet. Another glanced off his shoulder plate. Tesh didn't have time to do anything about those and kept fighting as more elves charged. He killed another, and another, and his successes drew unwanted attention.

The ground turned to muck under his feet.

He felt it gather at his ankles, trapping him, restricting his movement. Sheathing his swords, Tesh grabbed a tree branch. The muck wasn't magical, just ordinary dirt infused with regular water, but the two had been mixed using the Art and churned by his own movements. Pulling on the limb, Tesh crawled to solid ground. Then it, too, began to liquefy. Everywhere his feet landed turned slick and soft. Tesh leaped to a log, which quickly became an island within a lake of goo.

Then the log burst into flame. He gasped as the fire ran up his body. Totally engulfed, Tesh could barely see because of the orange tongues licking up his face. In terror, he almost jumped off, but he took half a second to look for a clear spot to land. In that brief pause, he realized something— no heat, no pain.

Magic fire. Not real. They're just trying to scare me. Don't want me on the log.

A moment later, the fire went out, and the mud stopped liquefying.

"Help!" Atkins shouted, and Tesh found him knee-deep in the muck. He helped pull his friend free.

"What happened to the Miralyith?" Tesh asked.

"Brig got him." Atkins pointed to where the young Killian stood over the body of a robed elf.

An arrow hit Tesh in the shin but glanced off his greave. Looking up, he found the archer nested in a nearby tree. Pliny saw him, too, and threw his spear, just missing his target. Still, he'd been close enough to make the elf give up his perch and retreat.

"We need to bring bows," Tesh said. "If we had them, the Fhrey would be in real trouble."

"Be good to use this stuff, too." Atkins pulled on the shirt of a dead elf that was dyed in various shades of green and brown. "Hard to see them when they're dressed like this."

Tesh nodded, then looked around. No one was fighting. Edgar and Pliny were checking on Trent, who was prone and motionless. Pliny was bleeding from a head wound. The blood ran into his left eye, making him knuckle-wipe it.

"Don't you dare take off that helmet," Edgar said, vocalizing exactly what Tesh was thinking.

"What? You think I'm an idiot?" Pliny replied. "I just can't see out of this eye."

"So use the other," Atkins told him. "Imagine it's all you have, or it just might turn out that way."

"Great, I've got sweat in that one. And I'm already pretending to be deaf. Do I have to be blind, too?"

Brigham ran back and rejoined their circle. The kid's face was flushed red with excitement.

"Thanks," Tesh told him. "That *brideeth* was gonna kill me."

"Yeah, he didn't seem to like you very much." Brigham smiled. That expression said everything. They were all grinning. *We're alive—not just* still *alive, but more alive than ever.*

This wasn't their first battle, but the previous ones had been fought on the plain. Out there with the chariots, it was easier. Tesh hadn't felt seriously threatened until they entered the forest. Here, the enemy decided to make their stand. This was their first *real* fight.

Tesh felt hyperalert. He could spot the turn of every leaf and saw colors more vibrantly. He noticed the movement of light and the dust motes that seemed to hover in the angled shafts. *I'm on a higher plane right now.* His fights with Sebek had been learning exercises, and they came with a safety net. The combat in the High Spear Valley had been too easy to elicit this kind of rush, but here in the dense forest where Death held hands with the living, Tesh felt something had changed. By necessity he had stepped into another reality, a world with different rules. And it wasn't just him; he saw the same look of realization in each of those silly grins.

We are gods.

Tesh counted the dead. "Twelve to one; not bad," he reported.

"Day's still young," Edgar replied.

Worried to the point of nausea, Brin stood at Padera's side in the healing tent while the dead and wounded rolled in by the hundreds.

"Hold him down, girl!" Padera shouted as the soldier on the table began to writhe.

Gifford arrived just in time to pin the man's shoulders down. Although the potter's back was twisted and one of his legs nearly useless, his arms were powerful. The patient stilled as Padera went to work. The soldier's arm was dangling at the elbow by a few strands of muscle, and the wound was blackened with filth. Padera had to cut it clean above the joint, so she set the teeth of her saw to his skin. Most patients had passed out by this point, but not this one. He screamed so loudly that Brin started to cry. She felt foolish, weak, and stupid, but it was more than just the scream that got to her. Everything was a contributing factor: gallons of blood, the smells of urine and burnt flesh, and the weeping of once strong men. But more than just these foreign sights, the lack of familiar things contributed to her tears: missing arms, hands, and eyes. In some cases, the whole of a face was gone, as if a raow had gotten loose in the camp. More than anything, though, her tears sprang from the absolute knowledge that she would soon discover Tesh among the dead or dying. She was certain she'd need to hold him down as Padera cut off an arm or filled his empty eye sockets with clay.

Padera finished with the saw, and the man stopped screaming—he'd either gone unconscious or died. Brin couldn't tell anymore. The nightmare she was caught in felt random and senseless. Some lived, others died, and there seemed to be no telling which way the fates would decide. One man had looked fine. He'd walked into the healing tent on his own and calmly sat down, waiting his turn. When a lull came, Brin waved to him, but he didn't move. She went over and laid a hand on his shoulder. "What's wrong?" she had asked him.

He didn't answer.

"Have him hauled out to the pile," Padera told her.

"What?"

"He's dead."

Padera was right, but Brin had trouble believing it.

That's what had started sending Brin over the edge. Until then, she'd been doing well. After that, the blood, burning flesh, and lost limbs got to her in ways they hadn't before. Her shield had cracked, and she felt every blow from then on.

"Get some air," Padera told her. "And get your head back on. I need you."

Brin nodded and slipped through the flap.

Outside, the wounded were lined up across the field in absurdly neat rows. On the other side of the healing tents, the dead were heaped in piles where flies swarmed in a hideous, dark cloud. Their combined hum made so much noise they could have been cicadas.

The Battle of the Harwood had been a disaster—their first full-scale defeat. Nyphron had ordered the retreat at midday, and the dead and wounded continued to pour out long after sunset. Soldiers told tales of ghosts in the wood, invisible Fhrey. Most never saw their enemy. The days of easy victories were clearly over.

Brin walked to the edge of the camp and looked toward the distant forest, which formed a thick blue line on the horizon. Empty wagons rolled north, and another line of full ones traveled toward them, ragged soldiers walking alongside. Covered in blood, they stumbled and staggered.

The moon was rising, its yellow face already above the horizon. The day was over. The battle had been lost, and still she found no sign of Tesh.

The fresh air helped to clear her head, and Brin returned to Padera, who stood in a pool of blood, surrounded by a pile of arms and legs that were stacked like cordwood. Brin took over the searing of bloody stumps using a flat-iron paddle. Most of her patients were unconscious, but Gifford had to hold down a few for her. All of those screamed and begged her not to do it.

"That's it for now," Padera finally declared several hours later. The staff of healers, mostly pallid, exhausted women, dragged themselves out into the cool night air.

Brin tossed aside her bloodstained apron and walked across the camp. She got halfway to the little stream that ran behind it before realizing she had no idea where she was going. She looked up and was almost surprised to see stars. The world felt as if it had changed too much for such normal things to still exist.

Tesh is dead, she told herself. *They haven't brought his body back, probably can't find it.* She knew that Tesh would have rushed forward, driven ahead of the line, and gone too deep. She imagined him lying alone in the forest, his dead eyes still open, staring up but unable to see the stars.

Brin stood in the dry grass feeling empty and exhausted. *Those are the same stars I used to look at when I lived in my parents' little home that was filled with soft wool and the paintings I made on the walls. The same stars I used to see when roaming the hills around Dahl Rhen with my dog, Darby. The same stars I looked at just last week with Tesh. He pointed at that one—that bright one—and said it was his favorite.*

Brin had never known anyone with a favorite star before, but she'd never known anyone like Tesh. He had his training, she had her writing, but they always found time for each other—usually at night under a sparkling sky.

"Brin?" The sound of his voice nearly killed her.

Turning and seeing Tesh standing there, she cried out. Tesh looked concerned until she tackled him.

"By Mari! Where have you been?"

"Well, there was this war—"

"Everyone else has been back for hours! Are you all right?"

"Tired. Hungry."

"But . . ." She examined him with eyes and hands. Dirt mixed with blood stuck to his face. His hair was matted with sweat, and his armor looked nearly black with mud. "You're not hurt?"

Tesh shook his head.

"Is everyone else . . . Edgar and Atkins and Brigham, are they . . ."

"We lost Trent," he said, nodding grimly. "But everyone else is fine. Well, Pliny has a little cut on his forehead, but it's nothing."

Brin didn't know what to say. She had expected him to be dead, or at least coming back to her with pieces missing. But his eyes were light and a little smile had formed on his lips. Tesh didn't seem to have come from the same place as everyone else.

"Let's get you some food," she said, leading him to the last set of cook fires where pots still bubbled.

"You ought to be proud of that one, lassie," a man whom Brin didn't know said as he pointed at Tesh. He did so with his left hand, his right wrapped in bandages. "We lost today's battle, but he won his—he, and his little band, saved dozens of us."

"Eres was certainly no help," added a man with his head wrapped all the way around and down over one eye. "Ordering us back into a line made easy targets of those who listened."

"Shouldn't speak ill of the dead, Davy," the first man said.

"Eres is dead?" Brin asked.

All the battered men gathered around the bubbling pot scraped their bowls and nodded.

"One of the last to die, I think," Davy said. He gestured to the others around the fire. "He was back near the rear, close to the forest eaves."

"A Fhrey musta come up from behind," the fellow with a wrapped right arm said. "Probably hated Eres for turning traitor agin 'im."

"Makes sense," Davy agreed. "But I thought Fhrey can't kill Fhrey. So whoever took Eres out must have *really* hated him. Maybe there had been a history between them. I mean, he was the only one whose head had been cut off."

"Anyone else want more?" Tesh asked. "Or can I finish this?"

CHAPTER EIGHT

The Face of Evil

People always believe their problems are the worst and the rest of the world has it easier, but that cannot be true. Someone has to be wrong . . . right?

— THE BOOK OF BRIN

Imaly heard the familiar shuffling as Makareta entered the breakfast nook. The girl wore only an undertunic and was wrapped in a bedsheet that dragged across the floor. After a year, she'd become less emaciated but more destitute. Dark circles wreathed her eyes, and her hair, which had once been a major source of frustration, had grown into an epic disaster of stubborn rebellion. The kerchief no longer made an appearance. And while Imaly had provided a brush, the Miralyith refused to accept that she had hair. This unwillingness to acknowledge reality extended to just about everything. Makareta no longer cared.

The girl shuffled to the table, then stopped and peered skeptically at the teapot. "Is it still hot?"

Imaly rolled her eyes. "The teapot? Ferrol save me from the Miralyith. Just touch it."

Makareta placed fingers on the pot and quickly jerked them back with a startled cry. "What are you trying to do? Kill me?" She held out her hand. "Look, I'm burned!"

"You are not."

"It hurts!"

"Stop being so melodramatic."

The girl continued to pout as she poured a cup of tea, then sat down. She pulled out another chair and put her feet up, crossing them at the ankles. Makareta wore a pair of oversized slippers, the toe portions of which had been sewn to look like the faces of mice.

That's new, and a little disturbing.

"Are there any more seedcakes?" Makareta asked without bothering to look around.

Imaly slapped both hands on the table and sat up straight, glaring at Makareta.

"What?" the younger Fhrey asked.

"You're pathetic. You know that, don't you? If you want something, get it yourself. And don't try to pretend that you didn't expect me to fetch you one."

The wild-haired Miralyith cocked her head back and presented the sort of scowl that only the truly young and spoiled could conjure. "It's fine. I don't want one *that* badly." Makareta sipped more of her tea. "What storm cloud rained on your sugar pile this morning?"

"You."

"Me? Well, sorry for . . . what exactly? Living?"

Imaly frowned. "Not you, specifically, although sort of. I was actually referring to the Miralyith as a whole. You've made a mess of our society, and I resent being forced to clean up. It wasn't supposed to be this way. My job—my sacred duty—is to ensure that all tribes are equally represented and that the horn only gets into the hands of someone well suited to lead our people. After that, it's Ferrol's judgment that determines who rules, but none of that matters since it has become suicide for any non-Miralyith to blow the horn."

"So, this is one of those the-younger-generation-is-ruining-the-world tirades, is that it?" Makareta blew across her steaming cup and sighed.

"No, this has nothing to do with your age. It's about how the Art has warped you—you and all Miralyith. A person needs hardships. Overcoming trials through perseverance, self-reliance, and sacrifice is what you missed out on. Pain, fear, drudgery, boredom—lots of boredom— these are the things that build character. And you need to experience loss and remorse because falling down gives you the opportunity to rise once more. Overcoming challenges turns a self-centered infant into a caring adult. Empathy—the ability to understand and appreciate the feelings of others—is the cornerstone of civilization and the foundation of our relationships. Lack of it . . . well, lack of empathy is as close to a definition of evil that I can come up with."

"Then you must be quite wicked, Imaly, as I'm not sensing any empathy from you."

"Because I make you get your own seedcakes?"

"No!" Makareta burst out. "Is that what you think?"

"All right, Mak, why then? I've taken you in, given you food and clothes. Please educate me on how I'm lacking empathy for you. I'm listening."

Makareta didn't answer right away. She started to cry. "You don't know anything." In frustration and anger, she pulled at her hair as she sobbed over the cup.

Imaly got up and gave the girl a hug, rocking with her. "It's okay. You're safe here. I know it's been hard, but everything will be fine."

"No, it won't! Nothing will ever be *fine* again. I'm not an idiot. I know you're planning on using me, although I'm not sure how. And when you're done . . ." She cried again.

Imaly sat back down. She could lie. The old Curator was particularly good at that. She could convince Makareta—well, anyone really—of just about anything. That was her gift, *her* Art. Lying so often had become a habit, and after a while, Imaly discovered she couldn't stop. She even lied to herself.

"I'm sorry, Mak. I shouldn't have said it would be fine. It just came out. And yes, you're here for me, not you. But isn't this house better than the alternative? I know it's boring, and you feel confined, but do you remember what it was like when you didn't have a roof over your head or anyone to talk to? Maybe you should focus on what you have rather than what you've lost. Perhaps you can start sculpting again. That could cheer you up."

"You really don't understand anything, do you? I'm not depressed about being cooped up, bored, or cut off from using the Art. You think you're so smart, but you're really just as stupid as everyone else."

"Yes, yes, of course. No one can possibly understand the troubles you face." Imaly was being sarcastic, but Makareta nodded in complete agreement.

"No, Mak." Imaly shook her head. "Everyone feels this way when things go wrong. Don't you see? Right now, you're wallowing in self-pity, thinking no one in the entirety of history has had it worse than you. But that just isn't so."

"Yes, it is." Makareta fixed Imaly with a hard, vicious stare.

Imaly sighed.

Makareta's eyes blazed. "How can you stand there and say anyone else has ever had it worse than me? I killed Fhrey! I broke Ferrol's Law!"

"I know that, Mak, and the guilt of what you did, combined with the fear of what the fane might do to you, is no doubt adding to your depression, but—"

"I don't care about any of that!"

Imaly stared at Makareta, genuinely stumped. "Then I really don't know what—"

"The retribution for breaking Ferrol's Law isn't a myth! I can feel it." She slapped her chest with a palm. "The emptiness. I'm dead inside. I'll never enter Phyre. When I die, where will I go? What happens when a person can't enter the afterlife? Will I cease to exist entirely, or will I roam eternity lost and abandoned? The Umalyn never say. I think that's because they don't know." Makareta wiped her face and looked into her cup. "You speak of empathy and remorse, but those things are meaningless when you lack a soul. So yes, O Great Sage Imaly, no one is worse off than me. Or can you name another Fhrey who has broken Ferrol's Law?"

Imaly didn't answer.

"I don't wallow in depression because I'm spoiled and bored. I sit here because I'm soulless; and without a soul, nothing matters. My fate is forever sealed. No amount of good deeds or understanding will erase that stain. The fane himself can't absolve my crime. The rest of my life is pointless. It has no value because any future achievements I do or penance I perform won't matter. I've been disqualified. My only hope is that my torment will end with my life, but my greatest fear is that I'll not be granted even that small concession. Can you imagine what it would be like to be me for even a single day? How about for all of eternity? If a lack of empathy is truly the face of evil, Imaly, you should look in a mirror."

Dressed in her councilor robe, Imaly climbed the steps to the Airenthenon for a special meeting called by the fane. Given that he hadn't attended the Aquila in more than a year, she ought to be mentally hashing through the possible reasons to have a session now. Instead, Imaly was still pondering Makareta's bizarre announcement about her lost soul.

Why would she lie about such a thing?

Imaly wasn't the sort to believe in fairy tales. As an eminent member of the crafting tribe, she'd been groomed from a young age for leadership, a family tradition. Imaly exemplified the tenets of her people: practical, sensible, reasonable. This notion of having a soul, and being able to lose it, wasn't something she had ever seriously considered. She saw the notion of being barred from the afterlife as nothing more than clever propaganda, a fable invented to control society. People would do as they were told because they couldn't afford not to.

Imaly had always thought that Caratacus, who'd allegedly presented Imaly's great-grandmother with Ferrol's horn, was an invented person. He had to be. At best, she imagined him as a fictitious amalgamation of ideas someone had needed to put a name to. Imaly never once considered the fabrication to be true—until now.

Why would she lie about such a thing?

It could be that Makareta was just seeking sympathy. Still in her second century, she was a child in so many ways. Her proclamation was likely a cry for attention. *Or maybe she's trying to manipulate me. But . . .*

Then came the hole Imaly kept falling into, the one that didn't make sense. *What if it's actually true? And if so, what about my other assumptions?*

Imaly had no specific evidence that Caratacus didn't exist. And after so many centuries, it was odd that no one in her family had ever let their confidence slip. Surely Gylindora would have told her children the truth—*wouldn't she?* Unless, of course, her great-grandmother had been duped along with everyone else. Perhaps Caratacus *was* a real person, a master swindler who took a common ram's horn and fooled everyone into believing it was magic. This explanation would have satisfied her if not for the Art. Magic should be impossible, but she had witnessed the fane kill Zephyron, watched him punish Makareta's co-conspirators, and had been the personal victim of an enchanted backslap. *And what is the horn if not magic?*

The very foundation of Fhrey society was based on faith in Ferrol's Law—an idea that was just as absurd as the belief in Caratacus. And yet, so was the concept of dying. No one could fully comprehend being dead, trying to do so entered the realm of the preposterous. The idea of losing one's soul by violating Ferrol's Law was equally ridiculous. But then someone who is alive dies, and death stops being merely an idea. Likewise, when a girl with hollow eyes screams that she's lost her soul, that, too, changes things. And if the punishment was real, didn't that mean the gods were, too? There wasn't any point where a line could be drawn. *Is there really a Tetlin Witch?*

Imaly was one of the last to arrive at the Airenthenon, and she took her seat in front next to Volhoric as they waited for the fane. The Umalyn High Priest looked as if he hadn't slept in a week. Volhoric always looked ancient and drawn, but the old Fhrey appeared particularly drained that afternoon, a condition that plagued most of the Aquila.

Osla, who had recently replaced Cintra as the leader of the Asendwayr tribe, sat with hands folded in her lap, head down as if afraid to meet anyone's eyes. Nanagal, tribal head of the Eilywin, brought his work along, busily adding up lists of numbers with his counting frame and a measuring stick. Hermon, the leader of the Gwydry, appeared the least perturbed. He sat with the stoic blank face of the working tribe—a people unfettered by deep thought. Vidar had a similar stone face, but his was likely a mask, as Imaly was fairly certain he knew what the fane would say.

"Do you know what this is about?" Volhoric asked as they sat beneath the great dome on stone benches arranged in a semicircle around the fane's chair.

"Not a clue," she replied.

"The fane doesn't chat over wine and cheese with the Curator of the Aquila anymore?" the high priest said with a cynical smile. "How sad."

"When was the last time he attended one of your spring sacrifices? Perhaps the fane's absence is why Ferrol has forsaken us."

"Don't think I haven't considered that," Volhoric said seriously, looking at the empty chair with a sad frown. "And it's not just the fane. Each year fewer and fewer attend the temple ceremonies. We are becoming a godless people. And when the laws that keep us safe begin and end with our devotion to Ferrol, I fear we are living in a house of oil-soaked cloth while playing with sparks."

First Makareta—now Volhoric. Imaly looked up at the smiling image of Caratacus painted on the Airenthenon's domed ceiling and frowned.

The fane entered, and everyone stood.

He was dressed in his usual white and gold. The fabric of his asica was as pristine as ever, but the Fhrey himself appeared worn. The winter had been hard on him. Lothian had lost a good deal of weight, and his once-blond hair was turning white. Even so, there was a spring in his step and a smile in his eyes that she hadn't expected. Imaly didn't know for sure why the fane had called the meeting, but she had harbored a couple of guesses.

First, summer had come, and that was the season for warfare. They were well past mid-season, and there had been plenty of time for the Rhunes to advance. Imaly half expected that Lothian was going to announce the fall of Avempartha and the enemy's imminent arrival at Estramnadon's gate.

There was one other possibility, and the positive look on the fane's face made her wonder if something truly amazing had happened. Only a week before, she had suggested sending a bird to the Rhune leader with a proposal of peace.

Is it possible an agreement has been reached? Is it conceivable that the war is over?

"My fellow Fhrey," the fane began, and everyone under the dome fell silent. "I have news regarding the war with the Instarya-led Rhunes. Despite having destroyed their base at Alon Rhist, I only wounded the beast, and over the intervening year, it has healed. This spring, they have gone on the offensive and attacked."

The fane didn't sit. Instead, he began to pace slowly and methodically back and forth, much like a teacher in front of a class rather than a fane addressing his subjects.

"Make no mistake, the Rhune threat is formidable. They have a massive population such that even if we kill ten of them for every one of us they kill, we will still lose. Furthermore, Dherg have given them the secrets to their metals and the Orinfar, which can negate the weaves of the Art. Combined with the training the Rhunes received from the Instarya, they have become extremely dangerous in combat. They have also invented new weapons of war—spear throwers and horse-pulled carts—that have proved deadly on the open fields of the High Spear Valley. Yet more than any of these, the biggest threat has come from a dragon."

Lothian paused to let this settle, and he appeared a bit disappointed there wasn't a great gasp at the comment.

Everyone knew about the beast, which wasn't really a dragon but a conjuration of the Art. Only those who took part in the infamous battle knew the full story of their defeat, but everyone knew that the dragon had tipped the scales in the Rhunes' favor—and had nearly killed the fane.

The Miralyith leader raised his hand. "Where did the dragon come from?" Vidar asked, apparently not as enlightened as Imaly had expected.

"There is some debate on that," Lothian replied. "The creature was obviously conjured; the question then becomes, by whom?"

"Arion is the only one who could have—"

The fane interrupted Vidar. "One might think that, but Arion was dead before the dragon emerged. Jerydd and Mawyndulë had killed her the day before." Lothian pointed toward his son, who stood near the door and nodded in agreement.

This, too, was common knowledge, and Imaly grew impatient. *If the Rhunes are marching on Estramnadon, you might want to speed up the speech a bit and let people at least get drunk and say goodbye to one another.*

"We believe that the dragon was created by a Rhune."

Interesting.

This, at least, was new. Imaly hadn't heard it before, and, looking at the other faces under the dome, she concluded that no one else had, either— not even Vidar, who looked livid as he shook his head and blurted out, "That's not possible. The Rhunes are incapable of wielding the Art, much less creating a creature of such magnitude."

The fane looked to his son and waved him over to the dais. Mawyndulë only took a few steps, then stopped, leaning in as if he were poking his head through a doorway. "It's true," he told the room in a weak voice. "I saw her first in Rhulyn the day First Minister Gryndal was killed. At the time, I thought it was a trick—or a lie spun by Arion. But at Alon Rhist, Jerydd and I fought her. We think the traitor Arion trained her somehow."

The fane nodded at his son, and Mawyndulë shrank back.

"Thanks to the combination of all these factors—the dragon's protection, the Rhunes' overwhelming numbers, spear throwers, and racing carts—they have pushed our forces back to the Harwood."

This sounds so dire. So why are you smiling, Lothian? Is it because of a bird?

"But I come to you this day with good news."

It is a bird!

"As expected, Rhune Art has its limitations, and so do the tricks of Instarya warfare. Within the eaves of the Great Harwood, the winds of war have shifted. The trees, forever our allies, have hindered their carts, and we have managed to replicate and improve on their spear throwers. We have broken up their massive lines, removing the advantage of their numbers. But more than anything, their dragon appears to be neutralized. Reports say the beast never strays far from the Rhune base camp, which hasn't been moved in over a year. We've concluded it can't progress any farther. The reason isn't known, but the fact remains undeniable."

Lothian paused to let the full ramifications of this statement sink in. His smile became a full grin as he spread his arms dramatically. "I come to you today to report that our forces have won a massive victory in the eaves of the forest. Thousands of Rhunes were killed, and Nyphron was forced to retreat to the safety of his dragon to lick his many wounds.

"Fortunes have reversed. The Rhunes can throw their numbers against our bulwark of trees, and we will continue to slaughter them. And once they are weakened and demoralized, we will marshal our forces and eliminate the Rhune threat just as my mother, Fenelyus, delivered us from the Dherg."

A Gwydry entered with a cup and handed it to Lothian. As he did, a dozen other servants moved about the chamber, handing out similar cups of wine. Imaly took one offered to her by a young Fhrey with a happy face.

"Today we celebrate the start of our victory!" Lothian raised his cup to the dome. "Today we toast the rising dawn of a brighter future!"

Everyone drank and applauded, except Imaly, who did neither. Somehow, she didn't think it would be that easy. It never was.

PART III

CHAPTER NINE

Stalemate

The Battle of the Harwood began with a series of Fhrey victories. What followed were years of slow, costly progress that witnessed the deaths of thousands. It ended when our army finally reached the Nidwalden River and the tower of Avempartha. What should have been a three-day journey took five years.

— THE BOOK OF BRIN

"Which one are you?" Nyphron asked, pulling off his helm and slapping it on the table.

The gray-bearded dwarf looked up. Shock filled his face and he took a step backward, staring with wide eyes.

"Did you hear me?" Nyphron asked. "Speak up!"

"Lord Nyphron!"

"No, *I'm* Lord Nyphron. I'm asking for *your* name."

"Oh—ah, Flood, sir." He blinked and began to stroke his gray beard as if it were a magic talisman grown to ward off exactly this kind of confrontation.

"Well, Flood, I'm here to inspect the bridge, or more accurately the lack thereof."

"Ah—okay." The little guy looked terrified. "I'm quite certain *my brother* can give you a tour."

"And where is he?"

"Over there." Flood pointed toward the river.

"And what's his name?"

"Frost, sir."

"That's right, Frost and Flood." Nyphron thought a moment. "Did your parents hate you?"

Flood couldn't find words to reply and so responded with a shrug.

With a shake of his head, Nyphron left the little creature and crossed the bald rock, drawing stares from everyone he passed. He was a golden-haired god trailing a brilliant-blue cape, wading through a sweaty herd of filthy laborers. Reaching the eastern side, he entered into the cloud of mist rising from the falls and faced an unparalleled view. The Nidwalden River plummeted several hundred feet to a forested world far below. There the thin blue line meandered lazily to the shimmering Green Sea on the horizon.

He could also see his bridge. The road that had taken years to build through the Harwood continued out across a series of great stone arches that rose up four stories from the river's surface and extended across the Nidwalden toward the tower. Beautiful in every detail, it was a masterpiece that only Dherg could produce. The span's piers, like the granite slab in the center of the river, were besieged by the water that frothed at their feet.

The bridge was beautiful, but only a little more than halfway to the tower.

Nyphron found Frost near the river's edge. This Dherg had a white beard and was up on a wooden platform, waving a green flag at a host of workmen. The workers in turn operated a wooden arm with a counterweight, swinging a massive stone block into place.

"Frost!" Nyphron shouted over the river's roar as he climbed.

Frost looked up with a perturbed scowl, then mirrored his brother's shocked expression at the sight of the commander. "Your Lordship! What are you doing here?"

"Seeing for myself what is taking so long."

"We are working as hard as we can, I assure you."

"And yet it's still not done—*it's been five years.* I constructed this marvelous road so you could haul slabs from the quarry. I sent you the best masons. I've provided everything you asked for, so why isn't it finished? The reports haven't provided sufficient detail."

"Well, we—for Drome's sake!" Frost dropped the green flag, pulled out a black one, and waved it at the crews below. The stone was swinging wildly. "Haul those ropes!" Frost shouted to no effect. Then he resorted to pointing with savage jabs, but it didn't appear as if anyone below was looking his way. "They aren't putting enough tension on the guidelines!"

The dwarf held out a blue flag in his right hand and waved a white flag in his left, first up and down, then left and right. "No! You idiots!" Frost shouted. "Draw it left! Left! You can't—"

Despite the noise of the river, Nyphron still heard the snap. One of the lines holding the slab broke and whipped back. It hit one man standing on the balustrade. With a sharp cry, he went into the river and was swept over the falls. With only three straps clutching the slab, the stone listed sharply. Its edges sliced against the remaining ropes, fraying them.

Frost dropped his blue and white flags, grabbed up a red one, and waved it frantically over his head.

Men fled the bridge, racing for the bank as the slab's remaining ties snapped and fell. It hit the edge of the previously laid span, chipping it. The scaffolding and crane, which were partially tethered to the plummeting stone, were dragged forward. The crane's long arm, the size of a massive tree trunk, swept the surface of the bridge clear of everything—including a half-dozen workers.

Frost threw the red flag on the platform's floor and jumped on it three times. Then he pulled on the locks of his beard. "That! That's why it takes so long!" The Dherg actually growled like a mad dog. "Rhunes! They don't know what they're doing. Even your *masons*"—he said sarcastically—"are nothing more than stone stackers. Most of these idiots were farmers or sword swingers until they came here. They aren't builders. They have no idea how to properly heave a stone, and Flood and I can't be everywhere!"

He took a long disagreeable breath, frowning as he surveyed the damage. "And this—this is a good day! At least no one was shot. Usually, we lose two or three workers from arrows launched from the undergrowth. Or men just disappear when they go to piss in the woods."

Nyphron was still looking at the carnage below, where the remains of the splintered crane were wrapped in a tangle of ropes. "You're still being attacked on this side? Have you spoken to Tesh? I appointed him to the position of forward commander of the Northern Legion. He's responsible for protecting you."

His fear of Nyphron vanished, and Frost erupted. "Aye, I spoke to the prymus! He's out there right now hunting, but just as Flood and I can't be everywhere, neither can Tesh. He flushes them out, gives chase, but they come back. And then there's the tower, isn't there?" Frost extended both hands, presenting Avempartha to Nyphron as if he might not have noticed the massive structure.

"What about it?"

"Having idiot laborers is only part of the problem. The tower also interferes."

"How? You use Orinfar markings, don't you?"

"Yep, and the stone blocks you just watched fall were marked on all six sides. So were the crane and the scaffolding. But it isn't easy putting the markings on ropes, and engraving chains is tedious work. In order to speed up the progress, shortcuts are sometimes taken."

"You're saying the tower did that?"

"Aye, what do you think made the slab sway?" Frost took a moment to spit into the falls. "They conjure breezes to get them moving. Then if the workers don't get the block under control in time, the Miralyith cut the rope when it can do the most damage. But like I said, today has gone better than most."

"How so?"

"No one is allowed near the water without wearing the Orinfar. But it's hot, and the Rhunes tend to take their shirts off. They paint markings on their skin, but as they sweat, the pattern can smear. You can hear the pops when they explode. It's hard to get a crew back to work after seeing one of their comrades burst like a soap bubble. Sometimes the tower waits, and then unleashes a coordinated attack. It sounds like a crackling fire down there when that happens, and no one works for days after that. Our production today is actually quite good, aided by the lowest water level I've seen in months." He pointed.

Nyphron saw strings of green algae and the tops of normally submerged plants.

"Usually it's up to the third block of the piers," Frost continued. "Being as low as it is, we've been able to lay that forward pier without losing a single life. That's an unheard-of achievement. Do we have you to thank for that?"

Nyphron stared at the Dherg, puzzled. "What are you talking about?"

"The river. You dammed it, right? Somewhere upstream?"

Nyphron shook his head. "It would take an army of giants to do that. And while there are plenty of Grenmorians up that way, they'd rather kill us than help us. We'd have to start another war with them, and tactically, that's not a good idea."

"Oh, I meant—I thought maybe you got Suri to do some magic."

Nyphron frowned at the very thought. The mystic was a sore spot with him, a festering splinter that defied logic. "That child is useless."

"She's a woman now, isn't she?"

"Whatever she is, she's no help. Refuses to do anything useful. This war could have been over years ago if she'd burned down the forest, dammed up the river, made more dragons, or done any of a hundred other things, but she won't lift a finger. I have no idea why she's still around."

Frost hung his head over the railing of the platform and stared down at the river. "I was sure you'd done something. It's so low, and it hasn't been a dry summer or fall." He shook his head. "I'd even go so far as to say it's been wet. Rained much of last week. Come to think of it, that was when the water level began to drop, which doesn't make any sense."

From across the river, Nyphron heard a sound, voices rising above the river's roar. Looking over, he spotted a gathering of Fhrey on a balcony. There looked to be as many as ten, each in a fluttering asica, completely bald, and looking at him. One pointed.

"Tet!" Nyphron cursed, realizing he'd left his helm on the table.

He jumped down and ran back toward the cabins, where he'd met Flood.

"What's going on?" Frost asked, chasing after him.

Nyphron didn't answer, certain a lightning bolt was on its way. Being so focused on getting his helm, it wasn't until he reached the table that he realized several things weren't right. First, the sky remained clear. Usually the Miralyith brought in clouds to facilitate their lightning, but the sky was a brilliant autumn blue. Second, everything had become quiet. The rush of water flowing over the falls had stopped. The river was no longer low—it was dry.

Frost looked back. "That's not good."

His brother Flood shook his head in a rare moment of agreement. "Aye, you're right, not good at all."

Now the singing from the tower was easily heard. An airy chant that chilled Nyphron. *They've been waiting for me!* Realizing there was no way they could have known he was coming, he reconsidered. *Maybe not waiting, but certainly they're taking advantage of seeing me here.*

Thunder rolled in from the north, but it wasn't thunder.

"What's that?" Flood asked Frost.

"If you want to live, follow me!" Nyphron yelled and raced down the slope to where his chariot waited. "Abryll!" he shouted. "Turn around. We're leaving!"

"What's going on?" Flood asked as all three crowded onto the chariot, and Abryll slapped the reins, sending the horse charging back up the forest road.

Workers and support crew watched them race by with confused expressions. Others hardly noticed the chariot as they looked north, trying to determine if a storm was coming. A few, the almost smart ones, ran for the shelter of the cabins.

Those wooden boxes will be their coffins, Nyphron thought as he urged his driver to whip the animal.

The two Dherg hung tightly to the top rail of the chariot as it raced along the road. Neither was tall enough to see over the cart's sides.

"What's that noise?" Flood asked.

"Putting runes on ropes may be difficult," Nyphron said. "But it's impossible to put them on water."

Behind them came a roar so loud it sounded as if the world was ending. Abryll was whipping the horse hard, driving the white stallion to its limit.

I love this road! Nyphron thought as they flew across the smooth gravel. Looking back, he saw trees toppling, boulders thrown, dirt and muck churning.

"The river is back, but my bridge is gone."

No one knew if it had been Nyphron or Persephone who came up with the idea of dividing the camp into four square sections, each according to its purpose: crafting, food preparation, healing, and military strategy. Suri suspected it had been Nyphron. He was the sort to think in straight lines—in squares rather than circles. But he was a male, and men preferred sharp corners. Women were more inclined to curves. As nothing in nature was ever so rigid, one only needed to see a bubble to understand the nature of Elan or her opinion on the subject.

The domed tents resembled roundhouses, and their proximity to the Harwood Forest reminded Suri of Dahl Rhen—minus the ghastly lodge and wall. She thought the lack of a tree-cadaver cage was an improvement. The forest, however, was a different matter.

She had visited it only once and hadn't cared for the place. The Harwood was nothing like the Crescent. Forests, Suri came to understand, were like people. The Crescent was a friendly, welcoming aunt who smelled of fresh-baked bread and greeted you with a hearty hug. The Harwood was a crotchety old uncle who stank of sour milk, grumbled, and spat at his visitors. Still, even an unpleasant uncle was better than no relation at all, and anything was preferable to the desolation of Dureya.

Persephone's tent stood at the center of the massive encampment, where two worn-to-dirt pathways crossed, dividing the quadrants. Roan referred to it as *the hub of the wheel,* a phrase Suri liked but didn't understand. Persephone called it *the lodge,* which Suri understood but didn't like. The keenig's tent was a gathering of tied wooden poles and felted cloth. Different from the others only in its size, it was large enough to hold a dozen people and so tall that no one had to stoop while inside. A canopy extended across the front, making a porch. Thick red carpets with floral designs covered most of the area beneath the awning. Everyone seemed to like this except the grass, but turf was only happy when its tassels blew in a summer wind, and that season was over. Small tables, pillows, clay pots, and wooden boxes lay scattered over the rugs. Wood and metal shields hung along the eaves, and a large fire smoldered and smoked out front.

Such a practice made Suri wonder about the wisdom of people. To them, fire was a tool, but Suri saw flames as living beasts, wild creatures. She had once invited a squirrel into Tura's home and learned the hard way the nature of untamed things. Fire was far less domesticated, and much more destructive, than a squirrel.

Habet, the fire tender, sat before the ashen ring, watching the glowing coals with a distant expression. He looked up at her approach and smiled. He had a way with smiles. Some people were stingy and managed only smirks. Others grinned—a selfish expression full of homemade delight. Habet was different. His were generous gifts of heartfelt happiness, and he appeared to have an inexhaustible supply.

"Your fire is out," she told him as they both watched the glowing embers.

Habet's brows furrowed as he slowly shook his head. He raised a finger to his lips, then whispered, "Sleeping."

Suri took a second look at the coals, nodded, and whispered back, "My mistake."

This made Habet smile all the more. Without a word, he got up, walked around the fire ring, and hugged her. This wasn't the first time. Habet embraced just about everyone. The simple man wasn't much of a talker, but he was a first-rate squeezer. Still silent, Habet returned to where he'd been, sat down, and stared once more at the coals.

Rain was on its way, but she saw no point in telling him. *Bad news can always wait.*

Habet wasn't the only one out front. Two Fhrey warriors stood to either side of the entrance. Dressed in full armor, each held an intimidating double-bladed spear. They weren't huggers. The Fhrey in general, and the Instarya in particular, were not prone to open displays of affection. They did occasionally grab each other in a violent backslapping manner, which Suri deemed a good-natured throttle. The Fhrey were an aloof sort, proud and isolated. Even Arion, who had loved Suri, was strangely reserved, even distant.

Suri arrived a few hours after midday. Overhead, gray clouds had rolled in, the sort that in another month might hold snow but for now were only full of rain. Still, she felt they also held a warning of the winter to come—a prophecy. Some predictions were easy.

The guards didn't stop Suri or ask questions. For the most part, they did their best to ignore her. She was a Rhune who wielded the Art, and that was as odd as a talking badger. They didn't know what to make of her, and Suri's own people had difficulty figuring her out. When she had been a fourteen-year-old mystic, they regarded her as a novelty and smiled while shaking their heads. Occasionally, they laughed. After rumors about her leveling a mountain circulated, that novelty had worn off. She was still just a child, so they tolerated her, but everyone kept a safe distance. Now, at twenty, after she'd held up the walls of Alon Rhist and created a dragon, Suri didn't need the Art to sense the people's terror. Children held their breath at her approach, and men pulled wives back as she passed. How to refer to Suri puzzled the Rhunes. *Witch* was too small by a mile and *Miralyith* too foreign. Despite outgrowing the term, they still used *mystic*, but that title meant something different now.

Suri had been expected, and she passed the Fhrey guards, who reacted with external indifference, even while the Art shouted *fear*. Suri glanced back at Habet. He waved, his smile even wider, and the Art whispered *peace*.

Such is the difference between intelligence and wisdom, she thought, and for a moment Suri could have sworn she felt a brush of fur against her leg. She looked down, but nothing was there.

"Suri." Persephone smiled as she entered the tent.

Inside, Suri expected to find Nyphron, red-faced and demanding once more that she aid his war. After news of the bridge's collapse, she anticipated a particularly contentious encounter with him. She was pleased to discover only Persephone, Brin, Justine, and Nolyn waiting inside.

The keenig's eyes were wreathed in dark circles. Wrinkles and gray hair had changed the person Suri used to know into someone else. More than older, Persephone appeared weathered, a tree that had suffered many storms and lost so many leaves she couldn't catch the light anymore. She held Nolyn on her lap. The little boy was dressed in a rustic shirt and tiny leigh mor, which followed proper Rhune fashion. He had a bit of drool on his face, smeared across reddened cheeks.

"Suri!" The child fought his mother. Nolyn was bigger than the last time she'd seen him, but still a ball of energy with a blazing head of yellow hair, bright-green eyes, and Rhune-round ears.

"Suri's here!" the boy cried. The moment his little feet hit the floor, he ran to her.

The mystic caught him up in a hug. A proper, Habet-style embrace. Crouching down, she held up an index finger where a single tongue of flame danced off the tip. The boy swiped at it. Each time his little hands came close, the flame flickered out, only to reappear.

"Justine, can you please take Nolyn outside?" Persephone asked. "I need to speak to Suri."

The boy's nurse approached, but she made no attempt to take the child.

"Blow," Suri told Nolyn.

His face lit up, and with bulging cheeks, he sucked in a great breath and blew at her burning finger. The flame winked out, and the boy squealed in delight.

Suri smiled at Justine, and the woman snatched the child away as if saving him from the clutches of a rabid bear. She quickly stepped outside, leaving Suri with the keenig and Brin.

Neither of them looked happy. The Art provided little insight at the moment. All she sensed was noise. Artistically, the camp felt like she was wading into a massive crowd of excited people all shouting at once. Voices talked over one another such that only one thing was certain—something major was going on; something great was about to happen. The Art told her that Persephone's tent was the spiritual equivalent of a crossroads, a decision point, not just for her, but perhaps for the entire world.

Slowly standing back up, Suri swallowed twice. *What is going on?* She eyed the keenig and the Keeper of Ways. The last time Suri had felt this much significance was in the smithy when Malcolm had asked her to make another gilarabrywn. He was far more than he appeared; what *that* was, she still hadn't figured out. Suri hadn't seen him in years. As far as she knew, no one had. Thinking that this confluence of monumental portents might herald the strange man's return, she took another look around the tent, but Malcolm wasn't there. Just Persephone, Brin, and her—*upon us three the world will spin?*

"I haven't seen you in a while," Persephone began. "You look good. You've grown so much."

With such momentous apprehension filling the little space, the mundane chitchat was absurd. *Is it possible they can't feel it? I know it's not like what I'm experiencing. Still, I'm sure they sense something. They have to.* Matching Persephone's this-is-just-an-ordinary-visit stance, Suri retorted, "So, we are playing that old game, are we? The one where you state the obvious, and I'm supposed to do the same? Okay. You look old and tired; Nolyn is taller, and Brin has ink stains on her fingers. How's that?"

Suri could see it on their faces. Both had that taut pull of someone on the verge of exploding with news. There was also concern, a serious worry about how the meeting would turn out. They had something important to tell her—*no, they have something to ask me*—but they had no understanding of how truly significant what they were about to say would be.

"Umm..." Persephone clearly searched for words. "How are Gifford's lessons going?"

"Fine. Can we get to the good part now?"

"The good part?" Persephone looked bewildered.

"You're going to ask me something that will likely change the course of the world, which I have to admit sounds far more exciting than talking about what I had for dinner last night, if that is what you were planning on asking next. I see Nyphron isn't here, so I won't be saying no a thousand times before he catches on. But there is something important you're dying to ask. So, what is it?"

The two exchanged smiles, Brin shrugged, and Persephone took a breath. Then the keenig's eyes grew serious. "Suri, I sent a message to the fane during the Battle of Grandford, asking for peace."

"Arion's message?" Suri grinned at the news.

"Yes, exactly."

"And?"

"And we didn't hear a reply for a year. When it finally arrived, the fane said he was interested. That was five years ago, not long after the Battle of the High Plains, which had been a great victory for us. Then it was Nyphron's turn to be indifferent, and I'm sorry to say I didn't push.

Fortunes reversed in the First Battle of the Harwood, a crushing defeat, and since then, we've had five years of warring and death on both sides. Nyphron can't get his army across the Nidwalden, and even though we lose many brave men in the forest raids, our forces remain strong. The Fhrey are powerless against our numbers, and we are powerless against their river, and so the war goes on and on." Persephone paused and took a deep breath. "Any talk of peace has been silent over these many years—until now." She gestured for Brin to speak.

"The method we use to talk to the fane isn't very sophisticated. Birds are used to carry messages, which must be small and light. Also, the Fhrey writing consists of a finite set of symbols that represent individual words. It's meant to report simple events or make requests. Complex conversations would require many pigeons that are trained to fly to Estramnadon, and those are in short supply. With such a system, it's impossible to negotiate a peace." The Keeper revealed a little strip of parchment. "This is what has just arrived from the fane." She unrolled the note and read,

"Want stop fight.
Meet Avempartha.
Send one.
No send traitor Fhrey.
No send Rhune leader.
Send Rhune Miralyith."

"Like I said, we only have a few symbols to work with," Brin apologized. "It might not make much sense."

She appeared frustrated by her inability to explain, but she shouldn't have worried. Suri understood quite well. The process wasn't unlike reading a god's message from chicken bones.

"The way we've interpreted it," Brin went on, "is that they refuse to discuss anything with Nyphron or the other Instarya, whom they most likely see as outlaws. They also don't trust Persephone, probably because they think she incited the war by taking Alon Rhist. Plus, she's human, something they're not exactly comfortable with. But we're guessing they see you as somewhere in between—a Rhune they can relate to."

"They want you to travel to Avempartha," Persephone said, "and you have to go there alone. In some ways, that's good. I suspect a delegation would take a long time to reach a consensus. If it's just one-on-one, we'll have a better chance."

Persephone stepped forward and placed her hands on the mystic's shoulders. "Suri, you've done so much. You saved my life in the Crescent Forest, and our entire party in Neith. Alon Rhist would have been overrun without you. And none of that compares to the horror you've had to endure when making . . . when sacrificing . . ." She paused and swallowed hard. "You've done far more than anyone, and I have no right to ask—"

"I'll do it," Suri declared.

Persephone appeared taken aback at her sudden acceptance. "Suri, this is extremely dangerous. You'll be all alone."

The mystic nodded.

"Suri, there are dozens, perhaps hundreds of Miralyith in and around that tower. They could kill you. This could be a ploy. The fane knows what you are capable of, and this may be a trap to eliminate you. I think you should take some time and think about—"

"I said, I'll do it."

Persephone looked frustrated. "I don't think you understand the full—"

Suri shook her head. "With Nyphron it's all no, no, no, and still he doesn't hear. And now you're deaf to yes, yes, yes."

Persephone ran a hand through her hair as if wiping that notion away. "Suri, I'm only concerned that you might not be thinking this through carefully."

"No, that's not it, but it's okay." Suri reached out and took the keenig's hand. "Trust me. I know *a lot* about guilt. And you needn't feel any. I'm not going for you, or because it's what the fane requested. I'm doing this because it's my path. This is what Arion saw. This is *my* Gifford's Race. And for once, it'll be only my life at risk. That'll be a welcome change." She smiled. "I knew this was coming. I've been waiting for it. Well, not *this* exactly, but Malcolm asked me to stay, and he said I would know why when the time came. This is it."

"Malcolm? What does he have to do with—"

"Let's just say I was waiting on the leaves, and now it's my turn to touch the Black Tree. Arion gave me wings. It's time for me to use them."

CHAPTER TEN

The Trouble With Tressa

Kindness is often as simple as seeing what others choose to ignore.
— THE BOOK OF BRIN

The rain had started to fall during Brin's meeting with Persephone and Suri, but when it came time to leave, Brin was pleased to discover a momentary pause in the downpour. Before she reached her tent, the sound of sobbing caught the Keeper's attention, but after chasing it down, she discovered only Tressa. Brin told herself to keep walking.

Normally she avoided the older woman. Tressa had never been pleasant, but since the death of her husband, she had been worse than horrible. She drank heavily, cursed the gods at every opportunity, and cussed at everyone else with her remaining breath. Rumors claimed that she threw rocks at men and spat on children.

Everyone treated Tressa as a ghost, not merely ignoring her, but going so far as to pretend she didn't exist. As far as the rest of the world was concerned, the woman was dead. Seeing how completely Tressa had been severed from the clan, Brin almost felt sorry for her, but she stopped short of actually caring because she knew—as everyone did—that Tressa deserved her fate. No one could prove she had plotted with her husband to kill Persephone, but general opinion held that she should have been executed or at least exiled. Instead, Persephone showed mercy; the rest of the clan did not. That's how ghosts were made of living people, but it was Tressa's own fault.

That afternoon, Brin found Tressa in the mud just outside the Healing Quarter. She was bent over on her hands and knees, sobbing so hard that her body convulsed. The woman's old breckon mor had long since rotted off her shoulders, and the ghastly oversized man's shirt that replaced it was soaked. Her matted hair hung down into the mud, and bits of grass stuck to her upper arms. Spittle dripped from her mouth, connected to the puddle inches below her face by a liquid string.

It's just Tressa. Probably drunk. Keep walking. But Brin's feet refused to move. She'd never seen anyone so miserable before.

"Why?" Tressa cried out and slapped the puddle with her fist, causing an explosion. She lifted her head toward the heavy gray clouds and screamed, "Was that too much to ask for? Couldn't you let me have . . ." The rest of her words were lost to sobs as she clutched her stomach and doubled over once more, wailing into the sodden earth.

Brin remained rooted to the spot. Seeing Tressa like this was painful to witness, regardless of what she'd done.

"Tressa?" Brin spoke the forbidden word.

The despicable woman raised her head in bewilderment.

"What's wrong?" Brin asked. The question was foolish. The woman was no doubt upset that her husband was dead and she left alone and hated. Still, the question was infinitely better than asking if she was okay. Tressa hadn't been *okay* in years.

Tressa didn't speak, just stared at Brin and whimpered.

On any other day, Brin might have been concerned that Tressa, who was a bit crazy and a lot dangerous, would leap forward and attack. The woman was famous for irrational acts, and at that moment, she looked to have gone insane. But in Tressa's red and puffy eyes, Brin didn't see hate or anger. All she saw was helplessness and exhaustion. In Tressa's dark pupils, Brin saw her own reflection.

"Brin?" Tressa said. "What do *you* want?"

Brin moved closer. "Is there anything I can do?"

Still heaving for breath, Tressa shook her head and managed to spit out, "He's dead."

"Konniger?"

Tressa's eyes went wide and she launched into another wail. For a moment, Brin thought she was crying again, but then she realized she was mistaken. Tressa's voice pealed with wild, hysterical laughter.

She's finally gone completely insane.

"Elan's fat ass, no!" Tressa said. Her laughter sputtered, and she hung in a state of limbo, as when a ball thrown upward hovers for a heartbeat before falling back down. Then she started crying again.

"Who then?" Brin took another step, inching around the puddle that Tressa didn't appear to notice.

With a gasp, Tressa sucked in enough air to reply, "Gelston." She managed a deeper breath. "Bastard survived a culling lightning bolt, lived through the Battle of Grandford, but today . . . today . . ." She hitched, gasped, and sniffled. "He just kicked off. I found him lying in his bed, his eyes on the tent's flap. He seemed like he had been waiting for me. Although most of the time the old bastard didn't know who the Tet I was."

It started raining again, but Brin hardly noticed.

Gelston was her uncle, her father's brother. The day Brin's parents had died, he survived a lightning strike but never recovered. Sickly and suffering from a spotty memory, he hadn't recognized Brin during her infrequent visits. The last time, he called her *a sweet bit of honey* and grabbed her wrist hard enough to leave a mark. After that, she found excuses not to come around. She heard someone was taking care of him, but she never dreamed it was Tressa.

"I should be happy, you know?" Tressa said, wiping her mouth with the back of a muddy hand. "Nearly seven years together and he never once thanked me, even though I cleaned his sheets, cooked for him, fed him, and washed his ass when he soiled his pants." Her mouth was hooked in a deep frown as she looked out at the increasing rain. "But"—Tressa began to shake again—"he did hug me once." Her lower lip trembled, and her arms clutched her body as she began to rock. "It was a few years ago, and I can still remember what it was like to feel . . . to feel . . . that at least one person didn't hate me." The sobs returned.

Now, Brin was crying as well.

"I know your mother taught you better than that," Padera told Brin as the younger woman stood just inside the entrance of their tent, dripping wet and shivering with enough force to churn butter.

Brin looked out at the pouring rain. Gray sheets were coming in at angles across the field, making the tents on the far side of the Healing Quarter appear hazy and washed out. The noise of the storm was loud, a heavy drumming on the canvas.

"Get those clothes off." Padera grabbed a blanket off the bed. "And tell me what happened. Why were you out in such weather?"

Brin began the arduous process of pulling at her wet dress, which stubbornly refused to let go. "Gelston is dead."

"Something kill him?"

"No," Brin said while peeling the dress away from her goosefleshed skin. "Tressa said he just died. Passed away in his bed."

"Tressa?" Padera said with a suspicious and disapproving tone.

"She's been taking care of him. He was my uncle, *my* blood, but it was *Tressa* who did all the work."

"Trading his things for mead and ale, you mean."

"No, it wasn't like that," she said, but then she realized it had been Gelston's shirt that Tressa was wearing.

"Oh? You think so, do you?" Padera asked while wrapping the blanket around Brin and scrubbing her hair with a large rag, flinging the water free. "Why? 'Cause that's what she told you? Did she explain her selflessness over the rim of an ale jug?"

Brin stopped Padera and looked her in the eye. "Tressa was sitting in the mud, sobbing like . . . well, like no one I've ever seen. I think—I think she loved him."

Padera's face grimaced, which was something akin to seeing milk curdle. "Even struck dumb by lightning, Gelston had better taste than to—"

"Not in *that* way." Brin finished, shaking out her hair, since the old woman's hands had moved to her hips to help make her point. "You had to have been there; it's the saddest thing I ever saw. I can't imagine being so hated."

"There are good reasons why people hate Tressa."

"But what I'm saying is that Gelston was all she had. In the entire world, he was the only one, and . . . and he couldn't even manage to remember her from one day to the next. Don't you see how pitiful that is?"

"And how would you have felt if she had succeeded in killing Persephone? And let's not forget she *did* kill Reglan."

"No, she didn't. That was Konniger's doing."

"She was his wife."

"That doesn't make her guilty, just a poor judge of men. And Persephone could have ordered Tressa's death, but she didn't. If the keenig doesn't think she's guilty, who are we to judge?"

Padera took Brin by the shoulders and guided her past the spinning wheel to the bed. The large bag of straw covered in layers of soft woolen blankets whispered as they sat. Overhead, the rain drummed on the cloth roof, and the wind played with the entrance flap.

"Persephone is too kind for her own good."

"That's probably true, but what if she's right? What if Tressa is innocent? Maybe she had no idea what Konniger was up to. That makes us guilty of punishing an innocent person." Padera opened her mouth to protest, but Brin went on. "And even if she helped plan it, well, water doesn't retreat from her lips when she needs to drink, and the sun doesn't refuse to shine on her face. So who are *we* to punish Tressa? It all seems so cruel."

"You didn't feel this way yesterday."

"That was before I saw Tressa sobbing in the mud. I used to think of her as a haughty witch who had no right to sit in Persephone's chair. The one who had fought with my mother and thought Moya should be married to The Stump."

"And now?"

"I don't know." Brin looked back out at the rain. "But I do feel sorry for her." She searched Padera's shriveled face. "You think I'm being ridiculous. That I'm just a young, stupid, naïve girl."

Padera drew Brin's legs up and laid them across her own lap to dry the Keeper's feet. "First, you're not a *girl* anymore. You're a grown woman. Second, I think you're a lot like Persephone." Then she shrugged. "And I wish the world was filled with more young, stupid, naïve women like you two. It'd be a better place if that were so."

"I'm going to look for her first thing tomorrow."

"What for?" the old woman asked.

"To be her friend."

"Tressa doesn't deserve any and certainly not one as good as you."

"I don't care."

"I wouldn't get your hopes up. Tressa is as stubborn as they come; she doesn't make friends easily."

"Maybe that's because she hasn't been given the chance. And she doesn't have to do anything. She already has a friend, just doesn't know it yet. As such, I'm going to help her."

"How you gonna do that? Shove a soul down her throat?"

Brin frowned. "She doesn't have anything to do now that Gelston is gone. She lacks a purpose, a reason to live. Like anyone, she needs to feel useful and that she's making a difference. Having something she's good at will give her pride."

"Only thing Tressa is good at is drinking."

"I'm going to give her something else." Brin smiled. "I'll teach her to read."

Tressa looked at the neatly piled stack of parchments that measured more than a full hand in height. She'd never seen anything like them. Each sheet was covered with small markings, lines running in rows from one side to the other. Tressa lifted a page and then another. All of them were beautiful. "You made these?"

The younger woman nodded proudly, like she'd chugged a huge mug of beer without burping or having any come back up.

She and Brin sat on a blanket near the bank of the little creek that ran just to the west of the encampment. The rain from the day before had swelled the brook so it gurgled noisily over the rocks. The Keeper had gotten Tressa to come by promising to sew her a new dress. Tressa knew there would be strings attached but was willing to hear what Brin had in mind.

"What are they for?" Tressa asked.

"To keep a permanent record so future generations will know what happened."

"Wouldn't that put you out of work?"

Brin shook her head. "It'd give me a new job, and you can have one, too. I want to teach you to read, to understand these markings."

"Wait, you want to make me a Keeper?"

Brin shook her head. "Not exactly, no. I just want to—"

"How long will it take?" She eyed the stack warily. Something wasn't adding up. She wanted the dress, but at what cost?

Brin chuckled. "You have pressing engagements elsewhere, do you?"

"Maybe not," Tressa said, not liking the woman's attitude, "but I want to know what I'm getting into." She touched the stack as if it might bite her. "Are you as good as your mother at weaving and sewing?"

Brin nodded. "Yup, she taught me well. I already have the thread and cloth."

Tressa looked at Brin's garment, made in the traditional Rhen pattern—beautiful, neat, clean. "Will you dye the thread to match?"

"Sure."

Tressa stared longingly at the cloth. Gelston's old nightshirt was filthy and ragged, and the holes at the elbows grew bigger every day. When it finally fell apart, she'd have nothing.

Not that it matters. No one looks my way.

But it did matter.

Tressa had fallen so far and so fast, she was surprised she'd survived the drop. She'd been Second Chair—the chieftain's wife. Now, she fought with the camp's dogs for scraps. After her talk with Malcolm, she thought her life would improve, but that was six years ago. His parting gift hadn't made a bit of difference. *The most valuable thing in the world* had failed to live up to its reputation. Malcolm disappeared, and the cage he mentioned never showed up. *Maybe it's like what he told Raithe—maybe the future got altered by someone kicking a falling stone from its expected path.* For Tressa, nothing had happened, nothing changed.

Yeah, it did, she corrected herself. *It got worse.*

Gelston had died.

Tressa was left with a worthless key, a filthy shirt, and her pride—the last two of which were in the same condition. Her dignity was ragged, stained, and falling apart, but she continued to clutch at the remaining shreds, trying to hold them together.

Realization dawned then. Brin wasn't actually offering to make her a dress. No one gave Tressa anything. "Why you doing this all a sudden? Is this some kind of trick? A way to humiliate me?"

As she said it, the pieces began falling into place. "You got others watching? They're out in the tall grass, aren't they? Got people hiding and sniggering at my stupidity? You're gonna try to get me to think scribbles can talk, just so you can laugh at how pathetic you think I am. You thought

I'd do anything for a dress because all I got is this—" She motioned to her filthy, oversized shirt.

Tressa's throat tightened as if a hand had squeezed it closed. She thought once more of Gelston. Of how he'd handed her the shirt off his back. A man who had been hit by lightning and turned into an idiot had shown her more compassion than this . . . this . . .

Her face tightened in anger. "You're a rotten bitch, just like your mother. That's what you are. Well, you know what you can do with your dress and your"—Tressa looked at the ridiculous parchments so meticulously stacked—"lousy book!"

Before Brin could stop her, Tressa grabbed half the stack and threw it toward the river. The individual pages scattered in midair then settled like fall leaves. Several hit the water and floated away.

She expected Brin to frown in disappointment because Tressa hadn't fallen for whatever sick and twisted hoax this was supposed to be, but she didn't. Tressa had another handful of pages ready to throw when—

Brin screamed in horror.

The young woman ran for the stream and Tressa watched, dumbfounded, as the Keeper nearly killed herself on the jagged rocks at the river's edge while diving in to save as many pages as she could. Out of maybe a hundred, she came away with no more than twenty. The rest were lost, snatched away by the swollen current. Brin pulled herself to shore and collapsed to her knees, half in and half out of the water. She clutched the pages to her heaving chest, crying.

When she looked back at Tressa, who was still holding the remaining parchments, she began to beg. "No, please!" Brin pleaded between sobs. "Please don't, please. I've spent so long . . . I've worked so hard. My parents are in those pages . . . my family . . . my . . ."

Tressa stared at her, confused.

Brin wiped her eyes, and climbed back up the bank. The Keeper didn't say anything else as she pulled the remaining pages from Tressa's hands. Then she gathered them all up in the blanket.

Brin cradled her bundle, and said, "Padera was right. She always is." As new tears fell, she turned and walked back toward her home.

"Not the end of the world," Padera told Brin when the Keeper still hadn't gotten out of bed by afternoon of the next day. This was the eighth time she'd said it. "You of all people know that worse can happen."

What remained of *The Book of Brin*'s diminished stack was still wadded in the blanket, dropped from the day before.

"You don't understand," Brin said, her voice muffled as she spoke into the pillow. "This is the second time. My first book was destroyed in Alon Rhist."

"So, you already know how to fix it. Now get up and do something about it. Quit feeling sorry for yourself. Go to Roan's, get more ink, and start again. Wallowing here isn't helping anything."

"The pages aren't the problem. Don't you see?"

The baffled look on the old woman's face revealed she clearly didn't.

Brin sat up. She was still in the dress that she'd failed to take off the day before when she crawled into bed, hoping never to see the light of another day. She wished Tesh were there, wanted to feel his arms around her, but he was always gone. As prymus of the Northern Legion, he rarely left the forest.

For years, ever since her conversation with Malcolm, Brin had tried to teach others to read. At first, everyone had been too busy. Afterward, they were still too busy. She'd tried to teach Roan, figuring she'd be the best at it. Everything went wonderfully at first. Roan understood the system immediately, but she had so little time. Everyone wanted her for something. Tressa was the only person in the camp who didn't have a job to do because no one wanted to talk to her long enough to assign the miserable woman any tasks.

"The pages mean nothing," Brin told Padera. "Not if no one can read them."

"The Fhrey read."

"Not really. Their system is for lists and commands. One symbol for one word. It's not flexible, and it's *so* limited. My marks represent sounds, so anything you can say I can write. The Fhrey can't read my pages any more than anyone else. Malcolm said my writing could become universal, and in the future, everyone would read my book, but it looks like he was wrong."

The confusion disappeared from Padera's face, and the old woman sat down beside her. "Tressa didn't just destroy a few pages. She crushed your dream."

Tears slipped down Brin's cheeks as Padera hugged her close.

"No, it's worse than that. She destroyed our chance at a complete and accurate history. Centuries from now, no one will know what happened. I won't rewrite the pages. I won't ever write again. I can't."

"Then you really *are* stupid," Tressa said.

They both looked toward the tent flap where Tressa stood, silhouetted by the late-afternoon light.

"And *you* are going to be black and blue once I lay hands on my cudgel!" Padera growled and moved to get up.

"Relax, old hag, I'm not here to cause trouble."

"You've done nothing else since the day you were born," Padera shot back.

"Ain't it the truth, but not today. I just came by because—well, here."

Brin heard something slap the floor. Looking over the edge of the bed, she saw a stack of damp parchments, maybe as many as fifty.

"Don't know if I got them all, but they were all I could find, and I looked pretty hard." Tressa moved back a step, and Brin could see just how filthy she was. Not just dirty, like when they'd last met, but a real sight. The woman was caked in mud. The old shirt of Gelston's was torn in places and Tressa had scratches on her cheeks, forehead, and arms. Some were still bleeding. "Anyway, there they are."

Tressa turned to leave.

"Wait!" Brin bolted from the bed.

"What?" Tressa whirled. "You want an apology or something?"

"That's the least you could do, you vile drunk," Padera hooted at her.

"No," Brin said. "No I—I just, I . . ." Brin rushed to the basket beside the bed and pulled out a bolt of wool cloth woven in the same Rhen pattern as Brin's dress. "I wanted to know if this would be all right. You know, for your dress?"

Tressa stood just outside the tent looking back, that same disbelief in her eyes.

"I mean, assuming you learn to read, of course."

Padera made a *pfft* sound, which made Tressa shake her head. "The old hag is right. I can't learn nothin'. It'd be a waste of time for both of us."

"I'll make it anyway. You can have it if you just *try* to learn."

Tressa narrowed her eyes. "Don't be stupid. That doesn't make any sense."

"The same can be said about you—you blighted curse upon the world," Padera said. "You're walking around in stolen, thin linen with winter coming on, and this woman is offering to make you as fine a garment as—well, better than the likes of you deserve—and you're squawking? If Brin is stupid, you're—you're—there just ain't no word low enough to describe you. But that's fine because she shouldn't be wasting her time doing anything nice for the likes of you. So go back to Gelston's tent and curl up next to his cold corpse, like the raow you are."

Tressa tightened her jaw, folded her arms, and shot a defiant stare in Padera's direction, but she spoke to the Keeper. "Okay, Brin, sure. You've got a deal. If that old witch doesn't want me to do it, then I'd like nothing better. And that dress had best have a folded hem and low neckline. I'm still young enough to get another man."

Brin smiled as she watched Tressa walk away. When the woman was across the quad and out of sight, Padera clapped the Keeper on the shoulder. "No sense in begging when dealing with the likes of Tressa. Say what you will, but she's a fighter. And to get someone like that to do what you want—give them something to battle against." The old woman gave her a wink and a grin. "Now go get those wet pages off my floor."

CHAPTER ELEVEN

Techylors

They fell like leaves in the forest. I had no idea what it was like out there for him, for all of them. I stayed in camp, wrote my book, worked with Tressa, and worried myself sick.

— THE BOOK OF BRIN

The moment the arrows landed, the instant Tesh realized he hadn't been hit, he knew they would survive. He lay on the forest floor, both elbows planted in damp leaves, stomach draped uncomfortably over a tree's root. He peered through the clasped hands of yellowing ferns that quivered with his breath. Overhead, the white-feathered arrow meant for him—now a weather vane showing the direction of his enemies—stood out from the mossy bark of the chestnut tree. Tesh had slithered around the base to the *safe side*—the side without the arrow—where he lay listening, breathing dead leaves and moist dirt.

He couldn't tell how many had been hit by the ambush; his men were trained not to cry out. A few had to be dead. It wasn't possible to take a volley like that and not lose at least some. As it turned out, the elves were natural archers, and Rhune soldiers no longer wore metal in the Harwood. A lucky pause in his step was what had saved Tesh's life. Good things sometimes happened. Mostly they didn't, but on rare occasions, luck worked magic that even the Orinfar couldn't stop.

"Prymus?" Tesh heard a soft, concerned voice calling from the ferns to his right.

"Meeks?" Tesh asked.

"What should I do, sir?" The words were spit out in a rush, a little slurred, a lot shaken.

Meeks was new and far from a full Techylor. Those who fought in Tesh's legion were trained in all of the seven disciplines he'd adapted from the Galantians. The process was considered ridiculous by many—too long, too demanding, and definitely too extreme. Most of his men failed to complete their full apprenticeship. Over the last five years, only Brigham Killian had achieved what Tesh considered competence in all the disciplines, but those that had at least some proficiency in each were admitted to his elite squadron, the Harwood Techylors. Needing to field a fighting force, Tesh was required to send out partially trained soldiers. Meeks was one of those. Just seventeen, the kid was making his first trip into the Harwood.

It's difficult to believe I was his age during my first visit to this wretched forest. But I was old even before that day. Dureya, and what the Galantians did to it, made me grow up faster than anyone should.

First trips to the Harwood were always difficult. Years of training did nothing to prepare the recruits for the reality of the forest and the indescribable terror that accompanied an invisible foe trying to kill you.

"Stay low and on the "—Tesh looked up—"south side of a tree. You *are* behind a tree, right?"

A rustle. "Am now."

Tesh shook his head and marveled that the elves had missed Meeks. The only answer had to be that the boy hadn't been shot at. "Good. Stay there. No peeking."

"We gonna be okay?"

"We aren't dead, Meeks. They always get a free shot. It's the price we pay for finding them. Relax, we're gonna be fine."

Sounding like a sudden downpour of hard rain, another bombardment of arrows ripped through the fall leaves. None landed anywhere near Tesh, and he quickly blew three loud whistles. On the third note, he rolled left and drew both swords while leaping to his feet. He sprinted forward two steps, planted a foot, spun left, then ran again. He aimed for big trees, ran right at them, then veered away at the last minute. Either an arrow or a late-season hornet buzzed past his cheek. A moment later, another chipped bark off an oak as he rushed past. *Definitely not a hornet.*

The elves who'd ambushed them would be up in the trees on the north side of the trail. Fight then flight was the elves' best tactic, and sticking to one side of their target made that easier. The one drawback of hiding in a tree was having to climb down to run away. Elves were fast, but not that quick.

The maple tree.

Tesh focused on the one with the red leaves and a broad set of easy-to-climb limbs. After years of fighting, he didn't have to see his enemy to know what was needed. Because only one arrow had come his way, and none at Meeks, Tesh guessed there were fewer elves than Techylors. He guessed four or five; they wouldn't attack with less. The feathers on the arrow had been white. No white birds existed in the Harwood, and white arrows didn't remain that way long. The archer was a new recruit. With the age of elves sent to the war becoming increasingly younger, Tesh could surmise he was fighting a pack of inexperienced kids, assuming the term *kid* could apply to someone a few centuries old.

Tesh heard a yelp to his right, a high-pitched elven cry. Either one of the Fhrey had fallen in his rush to climb down—unlikely, but he'd seen it happen—or one of Tesh's men had beaten the prymus to first blood. Tesh's disappointment lifted after he spotted two targets in a tiny glade. Pointed ears twitched as their heads snapped around to stare at him, so deerlike. These two wore forest-green cloaks layered and dyed to blend with foliage. Given that elves had stolen the Rhunes' secret of bows, Tesh thought it fair play to adopt their deceptive garb. This made it difficult to tell friend from foe, at least until they moved. Fhrey moved like deer.

In the quiet span that separated two heartbeats, a pair of arrows flew at Tesh. He couldn't see them. All Tesh registered was the twang of bows. His reaction was instinct and reflex. He cross-sliced over his body with both swords and felt the thrilling snap of wooden shafts clipped between his blades. One was close enough to slap his chest.

The two elves in shambling green hoods stared with gaping mouths.

"Your turn," he told them in Rhunic, knowing neither would understand. He didn't care. Tesh only wanted to attract their attention, keep them off balance. That was the important thing when fighting elves— taking away their equilibrium. Without it, they were as helpless as a cat in a pond. Risking a dozen decades of life, these too-recent immigrants to the bloody Harwood were well spooked, and they never saw Edgar or Atkins taking aim at them. The arrows were nearly silent, and the elves made even less noise when they fell.

"That's it," Edgar told Tesh, bending down to search the bodies. At thirty-eight, Edgar had become *the old man*, a title made all the more apt by the growing rash of gray in his beard and a cowardly hairline that retreated under his hood—what the man referred to as his *stress line*.

"Seriously?" Tesh asked, disappointed. He looked to the forest, hoping he was wrong.

"Sorry," Edgar said, handing up the arrows to Atkins. He studied one of the elven bows, then tossed it away. "Kids again. Not even a hundred years old, I'll bet."

They didn't linger. Leaving the bodies where they lay, the three began walking back through the trees toward the trail.

Disgusted, Tesh shook his head. "This is ridiculous. How many were there?"

"Five."

"That's all?" Tesh frowned. "A couple of years ago, Gray Arrows were behind every tree! You couldn't enter the forest without coming away with blood on your sword."

"It's like overhunting back home," Atkins said. "The Harwood was theirs; now it's ours."

"But it's still dangerous," Edgar declared, pointing to where Meeks lay in the ferns, an arrow embedded in his left eye.

"He peeked." Tesh sighed. "Anyone else?"

"Nope," Edgar reported. "Oh, well, Brigham took one through the hand, but he'll be okay."

"Really? What was he doing? Waving at them?"

Edgar shrugged. "Never know with him. He's a lot like you."

Tesh grinned. "He is, isn't he?"

"That's not a compliment."

"We'll have to agree to disagree."

The other new recruit, a Melen by the name of Vargus, joined them.

Tesh looked around. "What about Anwir?"

With a glance and a nod, Edgar referred him to Atkins. The short southerner, who had grown a partial beard Tesh was still getting used to, was stuffing the captured arrows into his overfull satchel. "He's fine."

"Didn't do anything, though," Vargus reported. "I was right beside him. Galantians are supposed to be such great warriors, but that Fhrey just watched."

"They never do anything," Brigham said as he appeared out of the trees, one bloody hand wrapped in a cloth. "Can't defend themselves against their own kind because their god won't let them. If I were Anwir, I'd be looking for a new god."

"Does seem a bit asinine," Edgar admitted.

"That's likely why Anwir, Tekchin, and Nyphron are all that's left of the Galantians."

"How many were there?" Vargus asked.

Brigham paused to count. "Sebek, Vorath, and Grygor lost their lives in the Battle of Grandford, right?"

Tesh nodded.

"And Eres died right here in the Harwood; so, seven."

"Eight," Tesh corrected. "There was another one named Medak— Eres's brother. He died in Rhen before Grandford." He looked around. "Where is Anwir?"

"Tracking the white-feathers that got away," Vargus replied. "Said he wanted to see if he could find out where they were crossing the river."

Before long, the others—minus Meeks, who was dead, and Horace and Pliny, who were on point-and-pommel duty—had gathered around. Anwir was the last to join them. He wasn't a regular member of the Techylor war band; Tesh had asked him along to help find elves.

Anwir had always been the oddly quiet, strangely thoughtful Galantian. His long face, braided hair, and penchant for knots and slings had made him a misfit in that glory-seeking group of Fhrey marauders. He didn't drink, never sang, and often prayed. For what, Tesh had no idea. What could an elf pray for? Certainly not long life. They'd already been blessed with that. Anwir spent his time tying and untying knots and inventing new ones. He had a childlike fascination with the things, which was evident from the knotted loops of rawhide he wore as necklaces and bracelets, and the elaborate braids in his hair. Tesh guessed the reason for the contrast was that Anwir was the only Fhrey Galantian not from the Instarya tribe. Anwir was an Asendwayr—a hunter who was good at tracking.

"Anything?" Tesh asked the Fhrey.

Anwir shook his head and sighed.

"Too bad," Tesh replied with disgust. "Guess we better start digging a place for Meeks."

"Don't we need to get back?" Brigham asked while fiddling with the wrapping on his hand. "We have a rendezvous, remember?"

Tesh didn't.

"The mystic. Isn't she arriving today?"

"Oh, Tetlin's ass, that's right." He looked around and ran a hand through his hair, feeling the sweat. "We're already late, aren't we?"

Brigham nodded.

"Dammit. All right, let's head back."

"What about Meeks?" Atkins asked. His south Warric accent made the name come out as *Makes*. He pointed at the body with the last two arrows he hadn't found room for in his quiver but couldn't bear to drop. "Can't leave him here."

"He's dead and not going anywhere. We're already late. If Suri is killed while in my forest, I won't just get crap from Nyphron, I'll be strung up by Persephone *and* Moya."

"Need to bury him, Prymus. Can't leave men to rot. You want a manes haunting you?"

"Meeks would be the type, too." Edgar stared down at the dead face, which was a frozen portrait of shock. "Spiteful kid. He'll track you down."

"No time. We'll come back after," Tesh told them. "And if we're too late, I'd rather have an undead Meeks on my tail than a live Moya."

Tesh spotted the woman standing before the tents.

The Techylors' base camp was a miserable cluster of torn, stained, listless shelters. The soldiers suffered from inadequate poles and ropes, which left their quarters deflated and sad. Dirty, drying clothes hung on lines. Their stink fought with the campfire smoke for worst smell. Tesh wasn't one for tight discipline when in camp, and as a result, half-naked men were sprawled everywhere: eating, drinking, and sleeping. The mystic didn't seem to notice. She stood amid piles of fly-infested apple cores and discarded animal bones, looking eastward down the road.

Tesh hadn't seen the mystic in years. The last time was at Raithe's funeral, but he mostly remembered her from Tirre. He'd been fourteen and guessed she was about the same age. Back then, she'd dressed in odd clothing, talked to animals, and played in the ocean. Suri had become a woman, but still wore strange clothes. Now in place of her leather vest and belt made of teeth, she wore the asica of a Fhrey Miralyith.

"Suri?" he called. "Sorry I'm late."

Confusion formed on her face. She didn't recognize him.

"I'm Tesh, prymus of the Northern Legion and commander of the Harwood Advance." He pulled off his pack and tossed it onto the ground beside the water barrels. "Welcome to our humble home."

She looked around at the tents as if just noticing them.

"I was told you were coming," he said. "I'll try to make your visit as comfortable as possible, although we lack the comforts you're likely used to at the Dragon Camp."

"How far is it to the tower?" she asked.

"The tower?" Tesh glanced at Edgar and Brigham, who flanked him as they pulled off gear.

"Avempartha," Suri clarified.

"Oh, don't worry." Tesh offered her a casual wave. "It's too far away to harm us."

"How far is it? Can I get there before dark?"

"Hold on." Tesh, who'd been in the process of unbuckling his sword belt, stopped. "You aren't planning on going there, are you?"

"You can't," Brigham said. "Even if you were painted in the Orinfar, it's too dangerous."

"The Miralyith keep a constant vigil," Anwir explained. The Galantian pulled a cup of water from the barrel and drank.

"He's right," Tesh added. "Miralyith are stationed all along the far bank. They watch our side. It's a game with them."

"A game?" she asked.

"Yeah." Tesh dropped the last of his gear, then threw himself down on the dirt, propping his head up with a sack of apples. A wild orchard lay not far to the south, and since it was autumn, the fruit was plentiful. Brinks and Pliny had been trying to make hard cider, so far without luck. "I suppose for them it's like fishing. Since destroying the bridge, they try to hook us. They lure us into just the right spot, and then a tree topples or the river washes away a bank and sends someone over the falls. Persephone wouldn't want you getting anywhere near that tower."

"Yes, she does. She's the one who sent me."

"Why?"

"I'm going to talk to the Fhrey and end this war."

"You can't be serious." Tesh looked incredulously at everyone around and let out a little laugh. "You go near that tower and they'll kill you."

"It's okay." Suri smiled at him, then she looked eastward again. "I was invited."

CHAPTER TWELVE

Avempartha

*Everything is so obvious when you look back. It is the first time
through the garden-of-fear-and-doubt that messes with your head.*
— The Book of Brin

The canopy hid most of the stars, except along the scar of the road. The
chalk-white gravel, illuminated by the sliver of pale light, looked eerie in
the dark, a magic path into the unknown that both reassured and terrified.
Suri saw the gleaming trail as a sign from Wogan that she was heading
in the right direction, but that did nothing to eliminate the fear of where
that road would lead. Suri had few illusions about her future, except that
the path before her was necessary. She'd always known that becoming a
butterfly would come at a cost, but she'd never dreamed there would be so
many payments.

Suri had left Tesh and his men at the cluster of tents. They had wanted
to escort her, or so they'd said. She didn't need the Art to sense their relief
when she explained that she had to go alone.

Suri slowed her pace as the road entered a clearing, and it was there
that she first spotted Avempartha. She'd expected a dark, frightening
silhouette marring a star-filled sky. What Suri saw instead took her breath
with its beauty. In the middle of the pale river rose a shimmering pinnacle

of wonder, like a lady dressed in a gown of silver and blue, swirling on the edge of the world, arms thrust skyward in jubilation as she danced and kicked up a mist. Rising in the center of the Nidwalden on the brink of the falls, Avempartha was no less than the embodiment of joy captured in glimmering stone.

Enraptured, Suri hardly noticed that while she continued to walk, the constant crunch and crackle of her feet on gravel had long since stopped. She was on the bedrock that reached right to the water's edge. And from there she saw balconies, lighted windows, doorways, and stairs dotting the surface of Avempartha. This was nothing like any building she had ever seen. This wasn't brutally set upon the land or hacked from stone, and it certainly wasn't assembled from the carcasses of trees. The tower hadn't been forced into existence; it had been invited, *born* into the world. It belonged to Elan just as much as the rivers, mountains, or forests. She felt joined to the tower as they stood across from each other—Suri gazing at the tower and the tower looking back.

At least, someone was watching her.

Suri sensed eyes. *Are you Mawyndulë? Someone else?*

She couldn't tell. The Art was rarely so specific. Those odd sensations of dread without cause, a general suspicion that one ought to stay in bed on a given day, or the knowledge that choosing *this* was better than choosing *that*—these were the hallmarks of the Art. This ability to hear the voice of Elan wasn't limited to Artists; everyone heard Her, but Artists were trained to *listen*.

Suri stood there, waiting. That was the scary part. Unlike everyone else who came near Avempartha, she didn't wear Orinfar runes. Wearing them would block her ability to use the Art, which would defeat much of her purpose for the trip.

Arion's words to Persephone wafted back to Suri like the scent of lilac on a warm summer's day. *My people think Rhunes are animals, mindless beasts. They feel no guilt about killing your kind. Just like you don't consider it wrong to kill a deer. I know. I thought the same way before I met you. We need to prove to my fane . . . to all the Fhrey . . . that you are worthy of life and deserve respect, dignity, and sovereignty. If they can see we are more similar than they think, they'll understand their mistake.*

Suri was confident about defending herself against the Art, one-on-one, at least. But she wasn't so certain how she'd fare against the power of Avempartha, which was filled with who knew how many Miralyith. She was well within range of any assault they might wish to conjure, but she hadn't even bothered with a shield. She wasn't there to fight. Gripping Tura's staff tightly, she waited to see if the ruler of the tower would attack.

Nothing happened.

This was both good and bad. Suri liked not being exploded or struck by lightning, but . . . *Now what?*

Suri tapped the ground with the staff, slid her lips left then right, took a breath, and sighed it out. "Hello?" she called, but the roar of the falls swallowed her tiny voice. The Miralyith knew she was there, understood she was waiting. Suri felt a giant eye glaring at her from inside the tower. Minutes went by and still there was no reaction.

Suri sat down on the stone, Tura's staff across her lap, and her legs dangling off the edge. She sawed them back and forth. Fishing an apple out of her bag, she ate it, then flung the core at the tower. Suri had a good arm, but the remains of the fruit didn't even reach halfway before disappearing into the mist.

"This is just plain rude." Suri stood again.

She walked away from the river and climbed up a bald-faced escarpment. There she opened her arms and hummed. Suri liked to start weaves that way. She didn't need to anymore, but it did balance her, and a little counterweight helped because the power from the falls—while not as powerful as it would be if she were inside the tower—still delivered quite a kick. She rapped her staff on the stone, and it replied. Drawing from deep underground, she compressed it, thinning the rock much in the way Gifford made pots rise from his spinning wheel by squeezing clay between his fingers. Suri directed the stony cliff to reach out toward the tower.

She began walking even before the stone completed its journey. As she did, she widened her bridge because erratic gusts of wind pummeled her, and the mist made the stone's surface slick. *How stupid would it be to fall right now? The all-powerful Rhune Miralyith is coming and—whoops, there she goes!*

Sensing a weakness in the stone, Suri drew up a support pillar from the bottom of the river. After securing her walkway, she gave a glance to the tower. Nothing had changed. She hoped the Art might grant her a warning if the defenders decided to blast her with a torrent of water or a cyclone of wind. As it was, the night was devoid of both dread and welcome.

Halfway across, Suri looked down at the raging river. Hearing the roar as water flew over the edge, she sensed a reluctance that bordered on terror. Suri hadn't given much thought to how drops felt when plummeting off a cliff. She figured any fear of heights would have been conquered after falling as rain. But perhaps that was like being born. No one remembered their beginnings. Suri sympathized with the droplets' plight. As a youth, she had raced across fallen logs slick with dew and leapt chasms without a moment's hesitation. She and Minna had been fearless. Truth be told, Minna—being the wisest of wolves—was often reluctant to follow but eventually came along. Nowadays, Suri had lost some of her unbridled audacity. Where and when it went wasn't known. Time had sneaked in and stolen her recklessness. This realization was exceedingly apparent as she walked the narrow stone pathway. Suri wasn't scared, merely apprehensive, with a dash of concern added in for good measure. These trepidations gave her pause, and while she didn't drag her feet or crawl, Suri wasn't comfortable with the idea of running. Minna would have approved, which caused Suri to suspect that while age had stolen some of her courage, it had left the gift of wisdom.

Suri aimed for the broad balcony in front of her, the one with a large set of double doors. The sides of it had railings, but the front had been left open as if it were an official dock. Drawing stone from the tower was easier than from the shore. The moment she switched sides, Suri noticed the ease with which the rock extended, as if the stone was experienced at being used for exactly this purpose.

When the two sides of the bridge met, Suri paused, ready to cringe. When she wasn't struck dead, she shrugged and walked the remaining distance. Stepping onto the balcony, she felt an odd sense of relief, especially since she was now squarely in the jaws of her enemy. The roar of the falls was muffled by the building's platform and the wind was blocked by the tower. This left the little space before the big doors oddly quiet.

Taking but three steps forward, she felt an eruption of power so strong it made her dizzy. A loud cracking erupted behind her. The tower's stone returned to whence it came, and the rest of Suri's narrow bridge collapsed and sank.

"Welcome to Avempartha," a voice said in Fhrey.

Whirling around and compounding her vertigo, Suri saw that the big doors had opened. Light poured forth, and the silhouettes of several robe-clad Fhrey approached her. After closing the distance, Suri could see that the party was led by an elderly individual with a long white beard and a wreath of thinning hair. The beard, hair, and wrinkles made him appear far more Rhune-like than Fhrey.

"I'm Jerydd." He looked at her with a quizzical, sidelong stare. "Do you speak Fhrey?"

"I do indeed," she said formally, even adding a bit of an Estramnadon accent. Years ago, Arion had explained how Fhrey from various regions spoke differently. Those from the capital city had a conservative style and a tendency to replace *th* with a *ter* sound, a trait that Suri knew Gifford would hate. Arion also indicated that the Fhrey were acutely aware of *dialect distinctions,* as she had put it. The Estramnadon phrasing, which was far more formal than the way the Instarya spoke, was more respected. She went with that because it was how Arion had talked. "I am Suri."

Jerydd smiled, revealing a host of previously hidden wrinkles that rose beneath his eyes. "We've been expecting you."

She gave a second glance at the lack of bridge behind her.

Jerydd frowned in apology. "Security is a high priority, what with the war and all. I'm sure you understand." As a gust of wind buffeted his hair in a most disrespectful manner, he turned sideways and extended a hand toward the open door. "Please come in, won't you?"

For an instant, Suri sensed a whisper of dread, the same sort that warned of approaching bad weather or the onset of a nasty cold. It could have been anything, but she was pretty sure she wasn't detecting a storm or sniffles.

I'm in the middle of the lake already. The far shore is just as close as swimming back.

Suri pushed away her trepidations and advanced toward the ranks of Fhrey. They all wore similar dark robes, some with raised hoods. The others displayed bald heads. Each stared at her but none spoke. The idea of walking that gauntlet toward that interior space made Suri's stomach crawl into her throat. She hated being indoors, loathed the idea of being trapped inside walls—even those as beautiful as Avempartha's. Tura had always warned against spending too much time inside. *Makes a body crazy, living 'neath a roof that ain't the sky, on a floor that ain't dirt, and 'tween walls made to keep things out but that actually trap what's in. We ain't supposed to live inside a box any more than we's supposed to live 'neath the surface of a pond. Can't breathe, and without air . . . well, you know.*

The dread sidled a few steps closer to doom as Suri neared the great doors.

What if once I go in, I can't get out?

Suri was desperately afraid of being trapped in a small space, or— worst of all—buried alive. She'd learned the phobia from Tura, who was so horrified by the prospect that she made Suri promise to burn her body rather than bury it. Flying skyward with the sparks and ash had to be better than being sealed underground. Gripping Tura's staff with white knuckles, Suri forced herself to walk through the entrance. The moment she did, the sense of dread vanished. The interior of the tower was nothing like she'd expected.

Not a torch or lantern burned, but Suri had no trouble seeing. The walls themselves gave off a soft blue light. Vaulted ceilings a hundred feet high spread out like a forest canopy, with intricately lined designs that suggested ivy and leaves. The glossy floor reminded her of a still lake. Railings looked like the curling tendrils of creeping vines. Nothing was without adornment, every inch imbued with beauty and care. A music filled the place, giving it life. The muted humming of the falls created a low, comforting sound, while wind brushing the tower's curves created soft reassuring tones: wind in leaves. Inside, fountains added to this music with bubbling and trickling. These were the melodies of a forest, the voices of home. Living birds flew up in the high places and sang songs of summer, lazy days, and flowered fields. They ate from feeders, bathed in fountains, and slept in nests of cloth and string.

Jerydd led her up several sets of stairs, through great rooms, and across interior bridges that joined spires. All the while he watched her, and not only with his eyes. She felt the deft touch of the Art probing and investigating. At last they reached a small room where he offered her a seat. This chamber wasn't as elaborate as some of the others. Just two chairs and a little table filled the space, but there was a window that looked out on stars.

After taking a moment to slip off his cloak, he sat. Suri did the same, removing her old traveling cape and draping it on the back of the chair. A few of those who had walked with them began to whisper excitedly until Jerydd asked them to leave with a stern look and a sharp wave.

"Please forgive them," Jerydd said with a dismayed tone. "Most have never seen a Rhune up close, much less one wearing an asica."

"I take no offense at that, but I'm curious. Why didn't you extend a bridge for me? That wasn't very polite."

Jerydd looked surprised by the question. "I was told to expect a well-educated practitioner of the Art, someone who would need no assistance crossing the river."

Suri still found it rude, but because Jerydd bore no resemblance to the horror that was Gryndal, and he seemed more like an old Rhune than a Fhrey, she began to relax.

A porcelain teapot rested on the table, steam escaping its spout. Jerydd filled two small white cups. "Do you have tea in Rhulyn?"

Suri nodded, then realized that a mute response might appear less intelligent, so she added, "Several types—for enjoyment and medicinal purposes." She had taken a chance using the word *medicinal*. Arion had used it a few times, and Suri always thought it sounded smart, but she couldn't be positive she'd used it correctly. Jerydd's face betrayed no hint that she'd made an error, and Suri guessed she'd lucked out. "Arion was never fond of our willow-bark tea."

At the mention of the name, Jerydd perked up. "I was told you were a student of hers. Is that correct?"

Again, Suri nodded, then silently chided herself for it. She needed to talk, to prove that Rhunes were civilized, thinking people. "Arion helped me"—she almost said *become a butterfly* but changed it at the last second— "learn the Art."

"And you believe yourself to be a Miralyith?"

Suri didn't need the Art to know this was a trap. "No. Miralyith is a Fhrey tribe. I am *human*. I can never be a Miralyith."

Suri expected an impressed nod, as she was certain that had sounded smart, but Jerydd appeared unimpressed.

"Then what are you?"

This stumped her. *Butterfly* wasn't going to cut it with this old Fhrey, even though in her own mind that's how she saw herself. She considered all the names others had called her: Rhune Miralyith, witch, sorcerer, magician, spell weaver. None of them fit, and they all had negative connotations. In addition, they were Rhunic words, which would mean nothing to him. She needed something enlightened, something Fhrey, something like—

She smiled. "I'm Cenzlyor."

Jerydd looked puzzled—no, it was more than that: He seemed concerned. "Do you know what *Cenzlyor* means?"

"It'd be ironic if I didn't." Suri ventured a friendly smile. "Swift of mind. It's the title given to Arion by Fane Fenelyus, and a nickname that Arion gave to me."

They both sipped tea, which was different from what Suri was used to, more fragrant, as if brewed from flowers.

Jerydd clutched the cup to his chest with both hands. His left had a slight quiver, which the right helped to steady. She didn't sense that he was frightened. The more probable explanation was that age had weakened him.

And yet, isn't it possible he's putting on a thick mask just like me?

The Fhrey had lost almost every major engagement of the war, the exception being the First Battle of the Harwood. Pushed back to the tower, they were on the brink of destruction. Suri had been a big part of their early defeats. She had made the gilarabrywn that had turned their fortunes at the Battle of Grandford. And while Jerydd may indeed have forced her to extend a bridge to the tower as a means of identification, it was also a test. He didn't know she had refused to build a bridge for Nyphron and his troops, but how could he not be worried about her doing so in the future? Was it so outlandish to believe he could be frightened? He certainly had more at stake than she did. She'd gambled her life, but if peace couldn't be reached, it could mean the destruction of his entire civilization.

She wanted to calm his fears, so she said, "I've been sent to discuss ending this war."

"Nyphron has given you the authority to negotiate?"

"Persephone has. She is the leader of my people."

"Not Nyphron?"

"He is her husband."

Jerydd's eyes widened at that. And while previously the Art had detected only dead air between them, she received a sudden burst of shock, topped with an aftertaste of revulsion. All of it was quickly erased.

Not wanting to appear too passive or submissive, Suri asserted herself. "And are you able to speak for your fane?"

"Actually, no. I was merely instructed to verify that you existed. Now that we've literally crossed that bridge, I'll report my findings and receive additional instructions, but, well . . ." Jerydd set down his cup and stood. "It's late, and I'm certain you had a tiring trip. I've been rude in not offering you food and rest. You are our most distinguished guest, and nothing will be spared to ensure your comfort. I will order a chamber prepared, food brought, and tomorrow we'll know more about how to proceed. Would you care for a bath?"

Suri didn't know how to answer that. She loathed baths. Never understood why Arion had loved them so. The whole idea was preposterous. No one could avoid dirt, and why would anyone care about having some? It wasn't cold like snow or hot like—well, a bath. And how was covering oneself in water better than being covered in dirt? Still, Arion took a bath every chance she got. Concerned that she would be perceived as less cultured by refusing, she said, "Of course. The road was *very* dirty."

Jerydd smiled in understanding. "Absolutely. I'll see it's taken care of. Now if you'll excuse me."

With that, he stepped out, leaving Suri alone with her fragrant tea.

Suri couldn't sleep. She'd always had trouble doing so indoors. Too quiet, and too—there was no other way to describe it—*too dead*. Life was lived under stars and clouds, surrounded by living trees and blades of grass. Nodding off in any room, even one that was no doubt the best in Avempartha, proved to be too difficult, so she was awake to see the tower of Avempartha change colors with the morning light. The glow shifted steadily from blue to a warm, golden hue. As far as rooms went, this was the most beautiful one Suri had ever been in. And yet there was a door—a *closed* door. Thankfully, it wasn't bolted. She had checked that almost as soon as Jerydd left and continued to verify the fact throughout the night. If the door *had* been barred, Suri would have added a large hole in the wall, whether the Fhrey liked it or not. She'd make it a big opening leading to a broad balcony. With the amount of power Avempartha was feeding her, she felt confident she could have built a city.

That was another thing keeping her up. She practically vibrated with raw energy. Suri felt buoyed, almost euphoric. The channeled strength of the falls was a temptation, begging her to try it out, put it to a test. And yet . . . that massive flow wasn't the most power she'd ever felt. Not even close.

They came to her shortly after sunrise. Jerydd, who smiled broadly, and his flock of bald Miralyith, who watched her with suspicious eyes, had entered after a polite knock. One of the group carried a small wooden box.

A gift?

"Slept well, I hope?" Jerydd asked.

Suri only smiled back.

"I've received instructions and have made arrangements for your transportation."

"Trans-per-tey-shun?" Suri didn't know what that meant, and it pained her to show ignorance. *How stupid must I look right now?*

"Ah—yes." Jerydd bit his lip.

He's surprised I don't understand. I was doing so well, and now . . .

"For a person of your importance, I've secured a *carry*."

Suri winced at yet another unfamiliar word.

This time Jerydd appeared to understand and added, "A *carry*, is . . . well, you have them. It's a box on wheels that is pulled by horses."

"Oh, you mean a wagon?"

Jerydd smiled but didn't nod, which made her think he had no idea what the word *wagon* meant. *How do you like feeling ignorant?*

"That's not necessary," she said. "I don't mind walking. I'd actually prefer that."

"This is better. The journey is quite long." He smiled again.

"Where am I going?"

"To Estramnadon. It's our capital, and we want you to be comfortable."

"I thought we were going to be discussing matters here."

Jerydd smiled once more, and there was something in that expression she didn't like. "The fane wishes to conduct negotiations with you personally. A Rhune who can wield the Art is an incredible thing. He feels it's important that our people meet you. Most Fhrey have never encountered a Rhune and their impressions, I'm sorry to say, aren't very enlightened. Seeing you, and hearing how eloquently you speak our language, will make it easier for the fane. The peace process will be accepted as an agreement between equals. Without that, the people would think him weak and wouldn't understand how he could give concessions to a people that are thought to be so inferior."

I'm not likely to meet the fane, am I? Suri's words came to her from the past. She'd been arguing with Arion about the woman's plan to stop the war. At the time, Suri wasn't a real Artist, Arion was considered an outlaw, and she didn't know anyone else who could arrange an audience. Since then, everything had changed.

Jerydd's argument made sense, and Suri knew that meeting the fane face-to-face had always been Arion's wish. "All right," she agreed. "I'll go."

"Wonderful. Ah . . ." Jerydd looked over at the container. "There is one small matter that we need to address for that to happen." The Miralyith holding the box stepped forward and pulled back the lid. Inside was a circular metal band.

Suri recognized the same sort of collar that Malcolm had worn. And just like the ex-slave's, this one had a small but formidable-looking device that would keep it closed.

Before she could say anything—and she had quite a bit to say—Jerydd spoke up. "A personal audience requires this. It has long been the policy of the fane—of any great ruler, I suspect—that no one enters their presence armed with weapons. I hope you can understand that it would be insane to allow you, an enemy combatant and powerful Artist, to have a private audience with our leader. We won't even allow our own people to approach him when armed, and Fhrey don't kill Fhrey. We certainly can't allow you to walk into his chambers with all the power of the Art."

It was then that Suri noticed that the inside of the collar was engraved with markings. She knew them well, having once painted the same symbols on a set of bandages for Arion.

"The Orinfar," she said.

This time Jerydd nodded. "You must surrender your weapon before I can allow you to proceed."

Suri stared at the collar. Persephone hadn't said anything about this. *Did she know?* Suri didn't think so.

"I realize this is unpleasant," Jerydd said. "I certainly wouldn't want to don one of these. But look at it from our point of view. There's no way for us to be sure that you're not going to assassinate our leader. As powerful as you are, it would be beyond foolish for us to let you cross the river, much less get near our fane."

Suri didn't take her eyes off the circlet. She remembered the difficulty Roan had in getting Malcolm's off. She also recalled how much Arion had complained when cut off from the Art.

"Let me ask you this," Jerydd said. "Would you allow our best warrior to bring his extremely sharp sword when visiting your leader? Would you take that chance with . . . what did you say her name was?"

"Persephone."

Suri tried to imagine if the situations were reversed, making it difficult to ignore Jerydd's point. *And yet* . . . "Can't I just speak to you? And then have you talk to the fane? It will take longer, but—"

"That wouldn't solve the issue of having others in Estramnadon meet you. There are members of his council, leaders of each tribe who may not understand his giving in to what they see as a barbaric race." He shook his head. "No, I'm afraid that the only chance for this to work is for you to go to Estramnadon, and to do that we must ensure that you can't obliterate it."

Suri thought about the destruction of Neith, and wondered if he had heard about it. Regardless, he made a valid point.

Her trepidation must have shown because he reached out and closed the lid. "Never mind. I can see you're uncomfortable." He waved to the one holding the box. "Take it away, and extend a bridge for her to the west bank of the river." He then turned his attention back to Suri. "I'm sorry we couldn't work this out. But I do thank you for coming, Suri, and trying to end this awful war."

Arion's words emerged from the past. *One day, when both sides have drunk their fill of blood, the truth about you could provide the honorable excuse to end it. It's just so horrible to think people—so many people—need to die to reveal wisdom that ought to be common sense.*

"Wait," Suri said, stopping the flock of Fhrey and the box from leaving.

If they wanted me dead, they could have killed me before I even crossed the river.

"If I put this on, I'll be given safe passage to the fane and back again?"

"Absolutely," Jerydd replied. "But I don't want you doing anything that you aren't sure about."

Suri probed as best she could, but the Art offered no hint, no suggestion about his intent.

What value is there in Minna's, Raithe's, and Arion's deaths if I walk away now? And how can I deny that this is the path Malcolm wanted me to follow? What good is a butterfly that's too afraid to flutter?

Suri nodded. "If it can bring peace, I accept."

When the lock clicked into place, Jerydd felt a wave of relief pass over him.

It's over. She's ours!

A moment before, he'd felt the power radiating off her like the heat of a massive bonfire. The Rhune's strength had been stunning, and it was little wonder she'd nearly killed Mawyndulë and was capable of conjuring dragons. But with the collar on, the fire had gone out. The woman who had called herself Cenzlyor was now just a Rhune, and Jerydd knew how to deal with their kind.

"Look at it," he said to the others with a sneer. "The traitor dressed it up, taught it to speak, and how to use the Art, but it's no better than any other Rhune now. The fane was right to neutralize this threat. And his plans will certainly end this war. Not through a negotiated peace, but by the annihilation of the entire barbaric horde who dared to wage war against us."

The Rhune backed up and brandished the stick she'd brought. The moment Oscile tried to grab her, she struck him across the side of his head. "You lied!" she shouted.

Jerydd waved a hand, and the staff was ripped from her fingers and thrown across the room. But that was all he could do. The collar prevented the Rhune from using the Art, but it also prevented Jerydd and the other Miralyith from silencing or controlling her. She'd have to be subdued by physical force. She was quick, but outnumbered, and they pushed her back into a corner of the room. Kicking and clawing, she was restrained with thick leather straps. Then four of them lifted and carried her out.

Jerydd ordered, "Lock her up."

CHAPTER THIRTEEN

My Prince

I have always thought children are universally loved, but I find it hard to believe that even a mother could love the likes of Gronbach and Mawyndulë.

—— THE BOOK OF BRIN

Mawyndulë watched with indignation as Treya assembled the tower of twigs. With amused bewilderment, he saw her gather brown pine needles, dead leaves, and a massive wad of withered blond grass. From her pack, she pulled out a bark-stripped stick as thick as his thumb and a little bow that she bent against the ground so that the string could be pulled taut. Then she retrieved a knife and a foot-long board and began cutting a depression in it. Amazingly, there were three other cavities, all scorched.

She's done this before! The thought was mind boggling.

Mawyndulë stretched his legs across the dirt and stole one of Treya's three traveling bags, the soft one with bedding. He propped it behind his head to watch. Frogs peeped in the darkness of the forest. Crickets added to the general noise of the woodland. No fireflies, Mawyndulë noted. Too late in the year, he guessed with a vague disappointment. Chilled, he pulled his cloak and elbows tighter but did nothing to interfere with Treya. A night on the road was devoid of good entertainment.

Placing one end of the stripped stick into the little divot she'd just dug out in the face of the board, Treya wrapped the bow's string around the spindle and began sawing back and forth, spinning the vertical stick. She applied pressure on the butt-end of the spindle with a block of stone and continued to drill the little depression wider. Smoke emerged after only a few seconds. Treya stopped her drilling, which confused Mawyndulë since she had just started making some real progress.

Maybe her arm is tired?

She didn't look fatigued or frustrated. Treya moved methodically and confidently as she began using her ever-present knife to cut a notch from the side of the board to the hole she'd just drilled. Each of the little scorched divots had similar notches. With it cut, Treya abandoned the board to search through her previously gathered pile of odds and ends, picking out a leaf with curled sides. She set it on a large piece of bark, then positioned the hearth board above it so that the leaf was beneath the notch. With a knife, she roughed up the spindle's end and then got back to sawing. When smoke appeared for the second time, she really laid into it such that he could hear the string sing and the wood cry.

Mawyndulë watched closely, but still no flame or fire. Once more, Treya stopped.

Something's wrong. Wood too wet, maybe?

Treya didn't appear disheartened in the slightest, nor did she look surprised. She pulled the board away. A bit of smoking wood dust, which had been ground out of the hole, remained on the leaf. This she gingerly lifted and deposited on her wadded nest of dead grass. Then, lifting it close to her face, she began to blow. As she did, the nest smoked. Only a bit at first, but after several puffs the grass was hidden in a thick cloud. She set the whole thing down near her tower of twigs and continued to wheeze on it until finally a tiny flame appeared.

Treya looked up, saw him watching, and offered a self-satisfied grin.

"Do you seriously go through all that for every meal or cup of tea?" Mawyndulë asked.

"Of course, my lord." Treya carefully placed her twigs over the infant flame, feeding it like a baby bird while repeatedly looking over at him with that stupid grin.

Mawyndulë couldn't take it anymore. Pushing to his feet, he walked over and stomped the fire out, kicking the whole mess aside.

Treya scrambled away, staring up at him in shock.

"You're pathetic," he told her. "You know that, don't you?"

He clapped his hands, and three massive logs rolled out of the nearby trees. They huddled together where once the carefully built tower of twigs had stood. Mawyndulë rubbed his palms together, hummed a tune, then squeezed a fist. The logs burst into a bonfire that illuminated the woodland clearing where the two had settled.

"*That,* Treya"—he pointed—"is a fire."

"Ah, yes, my lord. Of course. My apologies." Treya had drawn away from both him and the fire that blackened the ground around it.

"I'm genuinely horrified to think what else you do on a day-to-day basis. Do you fetch water from the river in buckets? Use needle and thread to sew my clothes?" He lifted the edge of his cloak to peer at his asica as if it had offended him. "It's like I'm living with a Rhune, for Ferrol's sake. Do you howl at the moon and worship the sun like they do?"

"Of course not!" Treya rocked up to her knees.

Insulting her faith had started another, very different, fire. She glared at him, at her prince, with defiance unbecoming a servant. Her jaw was set, her little hands made into fists. "Ferrol is the only god I recognize. She is the only true—"

"She?" Mawyndulë stopped her.

Thrown off balance by the one-word question, Treya looked puzzled. "Ah, yes, my lord—*She.*"

"You think Ferrol is female?"

She nodded.

Mawyndulë wasn't an expert on religion. He went to the ceremonies in midwinter and midsummer like everyone else but rarely listened to Volhoric's sermons. The sound of the priest's voice always made Mawyndulë drowsy. The best religious education Mawyndulë had received had come from Gryndal, who'd preached that the Miralyith were gods—a belief that was undergoing a crisis of faith as of late. But Gryndal had always spoken of Ferrol as male. And Volhoric himself had referred to *His law* and *His blessings.*

"But the Umalyn say—" Mawyndulë began, but he stopped when Treya frowned and turned away. "You don't accept the word of the priests?"

"Not my place to speak ill about such esteemed Fhrey." Treya began gathering up her fire-making tools and stuffing them back into her bag.

"So, what makes you think Ferrol is female? Is it just wishful thinking based on your own gender?"

Again, he got a nasty look, the same one he'd seen his entire life. Usually it was accompanied by the words *my prince!* Normally, she referred to him as *my lord,* or simply *sir.* But if he tracked mud through the palace, was late getting up for one of his father's meetings, or killed his goldfish out of neglect, she addressed him *that way,* and gave him *the look.* Those two words, said in her condemning, accusatory tone, had sent chills down his back like nothing else—a leftover irritation from his childhood.

Treya had been Mawyndulë's servant for as long as he could remember. It was possible she might even have been his wet nurse, although he tried not to think about that. Such thoughts made him nauseous, but it wasn't because he hated her. Mawyndulë hardly thought of her at all, but he'd recently realized she was perhaps the only person in the world he could tolerate for any length of time. She was always around and had always been that way. Treya was as comfortable as a well-worn shoe, and she might be the only one who truly loved him.

"A look is not an answer," he reprimanded. "I'm asking a legitimate question."

"My grandmother told me." Treya had surrendered her glare and finished putting her notched board and spindle away, along with the stone she'd cupped in her palm while drilling.

He was amused that she packed it—as if the forest weren't filled with thousands of ones just like it. "I thought your family was Gwydry?"

She jerked the bag's strings, closing it, and gave him only a smirk this time. "A Gwydry can't know something about Ferrol that the Umalyn do not?"

"Ah . . . yeah. Isn't that why we have that tribe? Next, you'll be saying you can build houses better than the Eilywin, or—" He shook his head. "No, I think it's obvious you can't make a fire better than a Miralyith."

"You shouldn't be so certain of everything, *my prince.*"

Mawyndulë cringed. *Why doesn't she just scrape her teeth across a fork? It'd produce the same result.*

"Pride is—" She stopped, the smirk replaced by a look of pity. She bit her lip, turned away, and went to retrieve a different bag, the one that rattled.

Mawyndulë had heard that bag's contents clattering against Treya's back the whole day. He didn't know what was in it, but he knew it annoyed him.

Opening the sack, she pulled out pots and pans. "Before I offend you further, my lord, I'll need water. With your permission, I'll—"

Mawyndulë frowned and held up a hand, stopping her.

The trail they'd been walking followed a pleasant stream that made a faint rushing sound. Even if Mawyndulë couldn't see or hear it, he'd have known the stream was there the same way a person would realize a lit candle was in a dark room. The power of that stream was what he'd used to create the fire, which he found humorous in a way only a Miralyith would.

Mawyndulë lifted three balls of water from the river just as he'd done when going to the Airenthenon as a junior councilor for the first time. On that occasion, Vidar had chastised him. This time, Treya merely watched in awe as the gelatinous globes wobbled over and collapsed into the pots.

"If you heat the water," Treya said, "we won't even need the fire, except perhaps to keep bears away. Although I suppose you can do that, too, can't you?" She pulled assorted vegetables from the bag and began cutting them with a knife. "I suppose you could build us a whole house if needed. Isn't that right?" Her tone was far less than admiring, but far short of sarcastic.

"What were you going to say?" Mawyndulë asked.

Treya gave him an ignorant, innocent look.

"You started to say something about *pride*."

"Oh? Did I? I don't remember."

That's the worst lie I've ever heard. She's not even trying, Mawyndulë thought, then reconsidered. *No, she doesn't know how to lie. When has she ever had a need?*

Treya changed the subject. "Do you think you'll have any trouble bringing the Rhune back to Estramnadon?"

Up until that moment, he hadn't thought she knew where they were going, let alone why. She hadn't asked, but apparently, Treya knew more than she'd let on. Servants were like that. The practice came from listening in the shadows, and it made him wonder who her grandmother had been eavesdropping on when she heard Ferrol was female. *And where was it she'd learned about pride?* Treya wouldn't tell him about either, not now. Servants were like mice: If you caught them off guard, you had a chance; but once spooked, they ran, and there was no catching them.

"No," Mawyndulë answered and lay down again, hooking his hands behind his head. "The hardest part will be dealing with the horse pulling the cage. I don't like horses."

"She's in a cage?"

"That's what you do with dangerous animals."

Treya looked west through the trees. "How can a Rhune be dangerous?"

He knew what she was thinking. If he could protect them from bears, what problem could a Rhune be? But Mawyndulë could still remember running for his life while descending the rocky bluff across from Alon Rhist. As he ran, Jerydd had said, *Talent is one thing. A knack is another. But a moment ago, we were nearly hit by enough raw power to make me think Avempartha has a twin!*

Mawyndulë still didn't know how it was possible; neither did Jerydd. If Mawyndulë had been an instant slower, he would have died.

Died.

Mawyndulë had only been twenty-six at the time. *How insane is it that I almost perished so soon after being born? Crowds of awful, dusty relics have been staggering around the face of Elan for thousands of years, and I was nearly snuffed out at a quarter century?*

The thought still rattled him. Even if the Rhune wore the collar and was caged, Mawyndulë wasn't at all eager to meet her again. But Jerydd couldn't afford to spare even one Miralyith from his defense of the river, and Mawyndulë was available. Furthermore, he was familiar with this Rhune—they had a history—and Mawyndulë wasn't likely to underestimate her again.

Mawyndulë forced a smile. "Any wild animal can be dangerous. But there's no need to worry as long as I'm with you. I'm a Miralyith, and it . . . well, it's just a Rhune."

CHAPTER FOURTEEN

Down by the Riverbank

They say seeing is believing, but people often see what they want rather than what is, which makes me wonder about the virtues of blindness.

— THE BOOK OF BRIN

Suri shivered in the cold of the little room. They'd taken her asica and cloak, leaving her in only her thin linen shift. Hugging her legs to her chest, she balled herself up in a corner of the vacant cell. But the cold wasn't the biggest problem. Suri couldn't breathe. The cell had no window, and whenever she tried to hammer on the sealed door, the answer was always the same. "Back!" an angry voice would shout.

I have to get out! I have to get out!

The five words screamed in her head—sometimes in Rhunic, other times in Fhrey, and oftentimes in both—as she exchanged various words without thinking. Her heart fluttered as fast as a hummingbird's wings, and every muscle in her body was clenched so tightly it hurt. And that wasn't all.

I have to get out! I have to get out!

She had lots of pains. Her arms and hands hurt the worst because of beating on the door. She'd also thrown her body against it, even against the stone walls, screaming all the while. She'd seriously injured her shoulder and banged her head so hard she saw stars. The pain had actually helped. The physical agony superseded the panic, at least for a while.

Suri had never felt panic before, but she'd known dread and fear. They were old pals in comparison, but the exposed-nerve horror she'd experienced since the door closed was new and excruciating. For several hours, she stopped being herself. Who she had turned into, she had no idea. The one thing that saved her was that most of that time was thankfully obliterated from her memory by a sensation that she was outside, looking back at herself.

That can't be me, she thought. *If it is, I've gone mad.*

She remembered hearing laughter—lots of laughter.

"Vicious little thing!"

"Look how ugly it is."

"It's throwing itself against the door again!"

"Should we do something? It's going to kill itself."

"Look, it's bleeding."

"That's strange . . . its blood is red. Would have thought it would be green or maybe black."

Eventually, the voices stopped, and in the silence, Suri's body ran out of strength. Battered, bruised, and bloodied, she collapsed. Curled into a tight ball, all she could do was whimper and moan. The room was lined with straw, and even though she'd gathered what she could, it was little defense against the ever-present chill. The once inviting tower had become a terror.

I have to get out! I have to get out!

She squeezed her fists and eyes shut and clenched her teeth. She tried to hum, tried to summon the support of the world through the Art, but that had been stripped away. She was alone, isolated, abandoned, and utterly lost.

Whether days or hours passed, Suri couldn't tell. There was nothing but the cold and the five words repeating over and over in a loop. And then the cycle was broken when someone asked, "Can you hear me?"

She didn't answer—couldn't if she wanted to.

"Mawyndulë is coming to get you. He's on his way. Do you know who that is? Do you know what that means?"

She heard a tapping on the door and heavy raspy breathing.

"Have you been enjoying your stay, Rhune? Too bad there haven't been any more baths." This was followed by laughter; then even that sound faded.

As it did, Suri realized she'd stopped hearing *I have to get out!* A new, more terrible phrase began to repeat in her head: *Mawyndulë is coming to get you.*

Avempartha. The tower had become more popular than the Tetlin Witch when cursing. Like everyone born of a human mother, Tesh hated it but couldn't help marveling at the sight. Rising out of the mist, the tower looked to have been created when a giant piece of sky fell with great force and the resulting splash turned solid at its apex. Everyone knew it was made of stone, but at that distance and shining in the morning sun, Tesh could have sworn the glinting blue tower was made of ice—jagged and sharp. He'd seen the tower many times. The ghostly apparition, always partially hidden behind pale mist thrown by the falls, was the most notable landmark along the bank and utterly impossible to mistake for anything else. The tower was the final goal, the treasure forever out of reach. Being the elves' only remaining frontier defense, Avempartha was the last obstacle, and it had been that way for three years.

"Well?" Tesh asked, as Anwir stood on the rocky shore. The Galantian was looking across the river with an expression that might have been considered sad if Tesh had been more sympathetic to him or his kind. On that far shore lay the elven realm—Anwir's homeland. He was barred from setting foot on that bank just as much as any Rhune.

The Fhrey looked down near his feet, then up the bank. He sighed while shaking his head. "It just stops."

"That's not possible. Are you saying the elves swam across?"

"I'm telling you the trail ends here."

Tesh looked at the fast flowing water. He tossed a twig in the river and watched as it was swept over the falls. *They couldn't swim it.*

"Tesh?" Brigham interrupted. "Shouldn't we see about burying Meeks?"

Tesh shook his head and gestured at the tower. "I want to escort her back out through the forest."

"It's been three days."

"So she ought to be coming out soon, right? Let's give it another few more days. Besides, this may be our best chance to discover how the elves have been crossing."

The night Suri had approached the tower, all of Tesh's men had feared the mystic was committing suicide. Watching from a safe distance in Orinfar armor, they had watched her create a bridge, cross over, and enter. To their great surprise, there was no lightning, fire, or explosions.

Looks like she was right about being invited, Tesh had thought.

If peace talks were actually under way, and it certainly seemed like that was the case, this gave Tesh an exceptional opportunity to search the riverbank. He theorized that the elves wouldn't do anything to jeopardize the negotiations, so he and his companions had spent the next three days searching for the secret to how their enemies had been getting back across the Nidwalden. They'd found some fresh tracks near the site of Nyphron's destroyed bridge, but the mystery remained unsolved.

Even when not turned into a weapon used to destroy the Dherg's bridge, the current of the river made crossing impossible, and yet somehow the elves were doing it with amazing regularity. At first, Tesh suspected the Miralyith were extending bridges at night, as they had at Alon Rhist. But sentries had proven that theory wrong.

Anwir continued to search, but as the Fhrey fidgeted with a knotted bit of rawhide, Tesh wondered if his heart was in the work. Nyphron was fixated on crossing, frantic to obliterate the tower and crush the fane, but Anwir wasn't like him.

Tesh had hoped to uncover the secret that had vexed them for years, but it was becoming clear that wasn't going to happen. On the other hand, apparently he was right about the truce because the Miralyith had been ignoring them.

"Hey, look at that," Edgar said, pointing across the water.

A span had extended to the eastern bank, but that wasn't unusual. The elves made bridges on that side all the time. Wagons of supplies were always being delivered. The Miralyith made the bridges in minutes, but the Great and Glorious Nyphron couldn't build one on their side despite five full years of trying.

"What of it?" Atkins asked.

"There's a wagon setting out, but it's odd; ain't got no sides—well, I guess it does, sort of."

Anwir peered across the river. "Bars," he told them. "It's an animal cage, but that one is on wheels."

Tesh squinted but couldn't make out much. "A cage on wheels?"

Anwir nodded, then went back to his knotting, this time using his hair. How he managed it, Tesh never learned. Knots in his own hair usually fell out, but the Fhrey somehow got his to stay.

"Big cage." Tesh stood up to get a better look.

"Probably for sheep," Brigham said. "Back in Rhen we had pens to separate out the rams from the ewes."

"I thought you Killians raised wheat or barley, something like that," Atkins said.

"Did," Brigham replied. "I didn't mean *we* as in my family. I meant the dahl in general. Me and my brothers helped out Gelston and Delwin."

"What for?" Edgar asked. "What'd they give you for helping?"

"Wasn't like that." Brigham shook his head, then shrugged. "Everyone pitched in where needed in the dahl. That's just how things were back then."

Tesh sat down and took off his boot to look again for the pebble that had been bothering him since setting out. He'd shaken and slapped the boot, but nothing ever came out. Finally, he resorted to stuffing his hand down inside and groping the leather seams, searching with his fingertips. He found a knobby bump of worn hide that might be the culprit and was about to reach for his belt knife when he heard the screams.

Even the roar of the falls wasn't sufficient to drown out the shrieks that cut across the river. Tesh's first thought was that the elves were burning a goat alive, a sacrifice or something.

Anwir dropped his braid, his sight focused on the tower.

Across the river, the animal cage had been opened. A group of elves came out of the tower carrying something, or trying to. Their captive bucked, kicked, and screamed; the shrieks were terrifying. One elf fell. The remaining ones dumped what they were carrying into the cage and slammed the gate closed. Not until they had did Tesh get a clear view of what was trapped inside.

"Sorry, Brigham," Tesh said. "I think Meeks is going to have to wait."

CHAPTER FIFTEEN

The Animal in the Cage

I often wonder how that first meeting would have gone without the collar.

— THE BOOK OF BRIN

Mawyndulë saw the horse and wagon as he approached the tower. The thing made him uneasy. Even the name was grating. The Fhrey had no word for a cart hauled by a horse. The word *carry* was sometimes used, but a *carry*, or *lift*, was a device traditionally used to move the powerful, the sick, or the old, and doing so never involved animals. Horses were noble creatures who allowed themselves to be ridden by worthy Fhrey. It was so like the Rhunes to dishonor and humiliate a majestic beast.

The wheels of the wagon were different, too. They weren't solid disks but rather a thin rim of curved metal with pole-like supports radiating out from the center. The contraption appeared inadequate to the task of holding up the cage. That, too, was a *Rhune thing*. Chariots, arrows, dragons, and the Orinfar were the four scourges that had plagued the Fhrey. None of them really originated with the Rhunes. The savages were incapable of invention in the same way that sheep failed to grasp metalwork. The Dherg had taught them all these insidious tricks—the vile moles, who continued to harbor hatred for losing a war that they themselves had started out of greed.

We really should kill them all as well. Fenelyus was wrong for not wiping out the Dherg, and now her mistake has come back to plague us.

The cowardly Dherg had joined forces with the disgruntled Instarya, and together they yoked the Rhunes to fight for them. In a way, Mawyndulë nearly felt sorry for the Rhunes—nearly. How could anyone truly feel that way for a dumb animal?

Mawyndulë saw a dark lump to one side of the cage, as he and Treya passed by on their way to the tower. He made out skin, straw, and hair. The figure was curled up like a dog.

"Is that the Rhune?" Treya asked, hanging back.

"It's *a* Rhune, and as I doubt Jerydd has an assortment on hand, we can assume that is indeed *the* Rhune as well."

Jerydd came out of the tower just as Mawyndulë and Treya paused to stare at the occupant of the cage. The kel of Avempartha had been in contact with Mawyndulë off and on all morning. Jerydd was impatient and stressing the urgency of the mission, but Mawyndulë believed the old kel just wanted to get rid of the disgusting Rhune on his doorstep. The smell alone was enough to make him want to put as much distance between it and him as possible. He and Treya were downwind, and the odor was unmistakable, like a breeze blowing over the mouth of a piss-pot.

I'll be traveling with that for three days? he thought with a grimace.

"You took your sweet time!" Jerydd barked as he shambled his way down the road. Jerydd and Mawyndulë met halfway between the cage and the tower.

The kel looked older. *How is that even possible? That's like water being wetter or snow being colder.* The Fhrey was no longer dusty, he was practically powder. The way he walked had a lot to do with that impression. The last time Mawyndulë had seen him, Jerydd wasn't exactly doing backflips, but he'd walked normally enough. The Fhrey coming at him now shuffled with one hand out for balance as if he were navigating a tightrope. Each step appeared labored, and a sheen of sweat shone on his face.

Perhaps there was another reason for the urgency.

Mawyndulë remembered visiting Fenelyus in the weeks before she had died. The old fane couldn't walk. She was bedridden and appeared withered and thin. Now, Jerydd had that same look. *Transparent,* he thought, as if one of the kel's feet were already in Phyre. Along with Jerydd came Indus and Krem, both young Miralyith presumably on hand to catch the kel should he fall. All three stood with asicas flapping in the wind.

"We set out as soon as you instructed," Mawyndulë replied. "You know that."

Jerydd scowled. "Then you strolled your way here. Haven't I made it clear that the survival of Erivan hangs like a droplet?"

This wasn't the first time Mawyndulë had heard this. Jerydd had been venting his frustration for days using the Art. On the way there, Mawyndulë had been forced to listen to diatribes on how the prince was lazy and ultimately unworthy of the gift that Ferrol—and Jerydd, mostly Jerydd—was handing him. But all those conversations had been waged in the privacy of his head. Mawyndulë thought Jerydd might be so old he forgot he'd already said this very thing just a few hours before, then realized the kel remembered just fine. Jerydd wanted witnesses. What good were private insults? Ridicule was best delivered before an audience.

"Now take the Rhune directly to your father. Let him know we are in desperate need of a dragon to hold the tower."

This is new. "Why? What's the problem?"

"Your little mind isn't equipped to hold more than one thought at a time, so just remember to have the fane send us a dragon as soon as he can."

Mawyndulë glanced at Indus and Krem. "Hold on, do you mean you want us to turn around right now? We just hiked all day. We're tired. I was planning to spend the night in Avempartha, have a decent meal, sleep in a bed, and set out tomorrow."

"Do you see?" Jerydd said to Indus, then turned to Krem. "This is what I'm dealing with."

Wisely, neither Indus nor Krem offered so much as an expression in reply.

"You *will* take this Rhune to Estramnadon," Jerydd ordered. "And you will travel with all due haste. Kill the horse if you have to, but get this Rhune to the fane. Impress upon him with your tired, bloodshot eyes how imperative it is that he get the secret and send help."

Another Fhrey, who looked like he might be a Gwydry, walked past them and on down to where the cage was. He checked over the straps holding the horse to the wagon, then gathered up the animal's lead and waited for Mawyndulë.

"And don't take that collar off," Jerydd said. "And stay away from Imaly. That Fhrey is poison."

The kel shook his head. He was breathing hard and looking desperate. For a moment, Mawyndulë thought he might cry. "If only I were younger. You need to do this, boy. You need to do this properly. Now go. Go and save Erivan. Save our people."

The Gwydry held out the horse's lead toward Mawyndulë, which he promptly ordered Treya to take. He sighed, shook his head, and with one longing look at the tower, said, "Let's go."

When Suri became conscious again, the wagon was moving. She didn't think of it as waking because she hadn't fallen asleep. Sleep was a pleasant thing, a wonderful satisfying end to a well-lived day. She had passed out. At some point, her mind and body had mercifully overpowered the panic on her behalf. As the wagon bumped, bounced, and jostled side-to-side while banging over rocks and sticks, she opened her eyes to see that the nightmare had worsened.

She tried to think of something else, something nice, something pretty. Instead, all that came to mind was the lack of air. The two wide sides of the wagon were open, with large windows of narrow-set metal bars allowing a cool breeze to blow through the cage. Despite this, Suri had trouble breathing. She focused on pulling in each breath, then pushing it back out, her eyes fixed on the bars that trapped her.

Her heart was thumping at a rapid pace. She could feel the beat in her throat as it throbbed against the metal collar. Her hands hurt. She didn't know why. Her fingertips were bloody, and she spotted a red smear on the floor of the cage where a tiny bit of the wood had been stripped. A few of Suri's nails had white creases where they had bent back. Two of them still had splinters lodged underneath.

Once more, Suri began to rock and moan. She tried not to. *It's just a box. It's better than the cell. I can feel the air. I won't be in here forever. They'll let me out soon. It's not like the last time, when I couldn't even tell how long I'd been there.* The voice in her head sounded reasonable, but the things it said didn't matter inside a small cage. Nor would they to any sensible person chained to the bottom of a lake and told, "You will *eventually* be allowed to breathe." No matter how reassuringly or rationally the voice in her head presented the facts, she wasn't interested. Suri didn't want facts. She wanted out. It took all her concentration to resist throwing herself against the bars again or clawing at the floor.

For hours, she rolled along through a forest of beautiful trees, ancient behemoths. They ought to have soothed her, but the bars and the collar made them a separate reality, an image on a rolling wall. She was alone in a box she couldn't escape, so where the box was didn't matter at all.

"She doesn't look good." Suri heard a voice say in Fhrey.

"Of course not, it's a Rhune."

"Well . . . yes, but what I mean is she looks sick or something. Not well, at least."

Suri lifted her head. Walking alongside the wagon was a small female Fhrey. Her hair was surprisingly dark, most of it tucked up under a yellow wrap that exposed a long neck and oblong ears. She wasn't wearing an asica, just a simple smock tunic and a cloak left open in the front so it hung like a cape. Not nearly as beautiful as Arion, this Fhrey lacked her grace and elegance, but her face—her face, at least, looked kind.

"You're an expert on animals now?" The other voice came from somewhere ahead and out of Suri's view because the front, roof, and rear of the box was solid wood.

"How much of an authority does one have to be to tell when someone is miserable?" She said this while staring at Suri with an intense pity that made the Fhrey's face wrinkle.

"It's locked in a cage. All animals are miserable when trapped."

"I don't know. I think she might be ill. Do you think they fed her?"

"Jerydd didn't even feed us—so I doubt he gave *it* any food." The Fhrey she couldn't see made an exasperated noise. "I can't believe he just turned us around like that. Couldn't he even spare me a bowl of soup?"

"I think he was in a hurry because he's afraid she might die."

"I think he was afraid *he* might die. Did you see him? My only hope is that Jerydd lives long enough for me to make his life a waking nightmare for mistreating me so."

The lady Fhrey came closer. She placed a hand on the bars, looking in. She looked about to cry. Suri wondered why, then realized the Fhrey was a mirror, reflecting what she saw. Sympathetic and sad, the Fhrey searched Suri's eyes, then reached out.

Suri opened her mouth to speak—

"Hey!" The wagon lurched to a stop, jolting Suri forward. "Watch out. Don't get so close. This thing is wild. It's likely to bite. Then you'll get some awful disease."

Suri was an inch away from another panic attack. She dug the remains of her fingernails into the skin of her forearms. The pain kept her rooted, but it was a tenuous grip.

The Fhrey who had cautioned the other one came into view. He had a stick and clapped it against the bars, making them ring.

Suri flinched.

"Hah! See?" he said and added a triumphant laugh. "Just a dumb Rhune."

"Mawyndulë, please *don't*. You're scaring her."

Mawyndulë. The single word cut through the haze of her prison like a shining beacon. Suri forgot about the bars, the cage, and about being trapped. Her eyes came up and focused on him once more, and she remembered the prince who had come to Dahl Rhen.

"You're Mawyndulë," she whispered to herself, but the words were loud enough for them to hear.

He drew back at the sound. Even without the Art, Suri sensed his fear.

"She talks!" the female said, blinking in amazement. "You never said they could talk."

"You killed Arion." Suri glared at Mawyndulë.

The prince recovered, gathered himself, and took a step closer. "Yes, I did." He glanced at the lady Fhrey, and in a lowered voice, he added, "She was a traitor."

"I loved her," Suri told him.

Both Fhrey looked at her in surprise.

The female Fhrey continued to stare at her, astounded. "She speaks so well."

"That's good. I hope Arion trained it sufficiently so it can tell my father about the secret of dragons."

Suri heard laughter. For a moment, she thought it was one of the Fhrey, but she was looking at them and neither made a sound.

"Why is she laughing?" the female Fhrey asked Mawyndulë.

Realizing she was the one chuckling, Suri laughed all the harder. It felt good. The sound, the feeling, the look on their faces all combined to push back the walls. She could breathe.

CHAPTER SIXTEEN

Six Dead, One Captured

It has been said that nothing ever goes according to plan, but I guess that depends on whose plan you are talking about.

— THE BOOK OF BRIN

"*Captured?* Are you sure?" Persephone asked.

Tesh nodded. "Suri walked into the tower fine enough, but something musta happened. A couple of days later, she was brought out, and it definitely wasn't by her choice."

"Why do you say that?"

Tesh glanced at Edgar, and both of them frowned. "She was screaming her head off as they dumped her inside a wagon."

"More like a cage," Edgar clarified.

"Yeah, what he said. She tried to fight them off but couldn't. Not long after that, an escort party came and the wagon was pulled east into the forest."

Persephone reached out for the chair behind her but missed. She staggered backward, nearly falling. She felt like Tesh had stabbed her.

Why didn't Suri stop them? She'd crushed Neith beneath a mountain, collapsed a bridge at Alon Rhist, and held up the fortress walls in the Battle of Grandford, but she did nothing as they carted her away? That doesn't make sense. Then it came to her. *The Orinfar.*

Tesh and Edgar stood before Persephone in the Keenig's Lodge. Nyphron had escorted the pair, announcing they had arrived with "important news." Her husband had thought he and the keenig should hear it together and in private. He was right. As big as the tent was, it still felt crowded. Wind buffeted the canvas and rattled the support poles. Cold weather was coming.

Tesh may have said more, but she didn't hear. Her mind returned to the conversation when he paused and said, "Also . . ."

"There's more?" Nyphron asked. He had taken the news with less outward shock, but his voice, and those words, betrayed him.

"We lost six this trip: Meeks, Brinks, Ethan, Seth, Prichard, as well as Anwir."

"Anwir?" Nyphron asked, his eyes darkening. "How?"

"Ambushed just before we left the forest on our way here."

Nyphron stared hard at Tesh, but the Techylor continued to stand at attention. "Anything else?"

"No, sir."

Having found the chair, Persephone sat down. She stared at the ground while running a hand over her face.

"Dismissed," she heard Nyphron tell his troops.

Tesh retreated from the tent, followed by Edgar, who seemed equally relieved to get out. The Techylors were back in the Dragon Camp after months in the wilderness. Having completed his report, Tesh looked forward to better food, drink, and seeing Brin—although not in that order. Edgar's priority must have been beer because he headed toward the tent where the barrels were stored.

Tesh knew where to find Brin, but he wanted to clean up first. He and his men had returned *wearing the forest*—a phrase that needed no explanation. Covered in dirt and blood, he probably looked hideous and smelled worse. This wasn't how he wanted to greet her after being away for so long. He veered toward the river, but word of their return must have spread because he'd barely reached the Healing Quarter when Brin found him.

She ran his way, one fist full of her pages. Somehow, she managed to hold on to them as she tackled him.

"I missed you *so* much!" she squealed between kisses and smoothing back his hair. They lay on the grass between a barrack tent and a stack of shields. She was wearing her breckon mor, the same one she always wore, he guessed. But he couldn't be sure, since all Rhen folk used the same pattern and color of cloth. He liked the way she twisted the wrap tight around her waist, the shortness of the skirt, and how the folds gathered across her breasts. The old style had its charm, and Rhen's plaid complemented Brin's brown eyes.

"It's been ages since you left. I've worried about you every single day."

Those joy-filled eyes, the hair spilling down in cascades to her shoulders, and that smile . . . She was so perfect. If only . . .

"I heard you were in a meeting with Persephone." Brin's smile faded. "How many this time?"

"Just five."

"Five? After so long, well, that's good. That's really good, isn't it?"

He shrugged. "The elves are running out of fighters. Most of the ones we encounter now are little more than kids."

"The men you lost . . . was it anyone . . . ah . . ." She hesitated, her face strained. "It wasn't Edgar or Atkins or . . ."

"No, all of them were new recruits. Meeks, Brinks, and that lot. Barely knew them, really."

"I liked Meeks," Brin said sadly. "He always called me ma'am."

Tesh didn't want to talk about death, and he didn't like seeing Brin unhappy. He'd preferred to separate his two worlds. The Harwood was the ugly one, this was the beautiful. Seeing Brin silhouetted above him was a pristine moment, his reward for his time in the wood. "How's the book coming?" he said, changing the subject. Brin loved sharing her progress with him. Asking about it was the easiest way out of any awkward conversation. "Did you finish the part with the Battle of Grandford?"

An eager smile grew on her face. "Oh, yes, months ago. Came out real good, too . . . I think." She gave a little shrug. There was always a qualifier, for fear of displaying pride.

Brin was brilliant. Keepers had to be—even those who didn't learn how to transcribe language onto parchments. He loved Brin, but he hated her humility. *Why can't she see how wonderful she is?* The mindset didn't stop with just her. So many of the people Tesh fought for were still *Rhunes,* miserable creatures who bowed without thought before those they no longer saw as gods but still feared as if they were.

They see pride as a deficiency instead of a birthright.

"Tell me some of it," he said, trying to look eager.

Brin seemed stunned. "Really? Right here? Now?"

"Absolutely."

A smile filled her face. "Okay." She let him up and they sat together, shoulder to shoulder.

She sifted through the parchments, then stared at a page. Running a finger across the marks, she mumbled, then shuffled again.

"You're the Keeper of Ways, and you can't remember the story?" he asked.

"I remember all of them, but not the exact words—"

"You don't have to be so precise, do you?"

She shot him a look as if he'd insulted her mother. "Well, yeah. That's kinda the whole point." Once more, she searched through the pages and found the part she had been looking for.

"They came with hardly a warning,
thousands beautiful and terrible;
They came across bridges of stone,
wearing shining gold and shimmering blue;
They came with powerful whirlwinds,
and giants, fire, and death;
They came and nothing could stop them,
Save honorable men."

"That's great," Tesh said and meant it. He didn't remember her other stuff sounding so good.

Her smile widened. "You think so?"

"Absolutely! It's *really* wonderful, Brin. Seriously. Is all of it like that?"

She shrugged. "I hope so."

Tesh looked at all the sheets on her lap. "Then you shouldn't be so careless."

"What do you mean?"

"Get a bag or something." He started gathering the pages she had leafed through, straightening them.

With a gentle touch, Brin stopped his efforts to move the pages around. He'd seen mothers less protective of newborns.

"Oh, well, Roan has an idea to sew them together in sections then put them between boards of wood wrapped in leather, but she can't until I'm done."

"You could have her work on what you've finished so far. It'd be better than losing pages."

Brin smiled awkwardly. "I suppose. Hey, you know what? I could still show you how to read. I'm already teaching Tressa of all people, and she's—"

"I don't have the time." Tesh had to close that door fast. He didn't want to get her hopes up.

"But it's really not that hard. We could—"

"Maybe after we're married."

"When will that be, by the way?" Brin asked, a sharpness edging into her voice.

"I don't know. Soon."

"Why not now? Roan and Gifford are married; even Moya and Tekchin live together. Meanwhile, I'm still tenting with Padera. Don't you want us to be together? Wouldn't it be wonderful to fall asleep in each other's arms? To have children?"

"Of course I want that, all of it. But I can't, not yet."

"Why not?" Brin asked, entwining his arm with hers and laying her chin on his shoulder.

"I can't be a good husband *and* an effective soldier. I have to win this war first. You understand, don't you?" He took a breath and one of her hands. "I watched the elves butcher my mother and father. Saw them kill children—toddlers who sat in the mud with tears streaking their dirty cheeks. They—"

"I know," she cut in.

"Well, I don't want that happening to us. I can't have our kids going through that. Until this is over, I have to be out there." He pointed east toward the ghostly haze of trees. "Part of why I'm so good is my willingness to take chances. I can't do that knowing I might end up abandoning you with a child. It'd make me hesitate, and that wouldn't put just my life at risk, but the lives of my men as well. You have to let me win this war. Then, if I survive"—he saw fear fill her eyes, then added—"and I will survive. That's when we can find a pretty place where I can hang up my swords and learn how to raise sheep and rye."

"But . . ." She brushed away a tear that was threatening to fall, then sighed.

"What?"

Brin shook her head. "Nothing." Arguments drew lines on her face. She didn't agree, but didn't want to fight. "Oh!" Her eyes brightened. "What about Suri? You might be a farmer earlier than you think. Did she get into Avempartha? Did you see her?"

He didn't want to answer. Brin and Suri were friends.

"What?" she pressed. "What's wrong?"

Holding back the tent flap, Nyphron stared at the sky that was clouding up again. Like anyone—except maybe farmers—Nyphron preferred sunny days to rain. Not because he enjoyed the light or warmth, or held a warrior's instinctual disdain for mud, although all those things were true.

He didn't like storms because they reminded him of Miralyith. This day's gray overcast, however, wasn't the result of magic. What rolled in that afternoon was a general dullness, a mirror casting back his own dreary disposition. By his most conservative calculations, he should've seen Estramnadon burn two years ago.

"You sent Suri? To Avempartha of all places?" Nyphron said while still looking out at the sky. "You didn't even discuss it with me."

"You wouldn't have agreed."

"Of course not, and you should have known better." Nyphron regretted the statement even as the words left his lips. Not usually one for remorse, he was upset because he'd been trying so hard to keep his composure. He poured himself wine, aware he was drinking two jugs a day. *Five years, and I'm still sitting in a tent while Lothian kicks his feet up on the Forest Throne.* The whole situation was beyond absurd; it was unacceptable. *Another winter is on its way, and I'm no closer than the last time snow fell. It wasn't supposed to be this way.*

Nyphron turned and let the flap fall, darkening the interior of the tent. "What were you expecting her to do?"

"She went as an ambassador, to discuss the possibility of peace."

"If that's what you wanted, you could have sent anyone. Why her, of all people?"

Persephone shook her head. "No, not anyone. Arion had always been convinced a meeting between Suri and the fane could end the war. Besides, she was the only one the fane was willing to talk to."

He sadly shook his head. "Arion was a fool; you're not. So I'm baffled. How could you agree?" Nyphron was angry, a boiling pot with a rattling lid, and yet he wasn't oblivious to Persephone's pain. She was already paying a high price for her mistake, and ranting wouldn't help. Instead, he forced his voice lower and spoke as gently as he could. "If the fane truly wanted peace, he would have insisted on speaking to me."

"In his eyes, you're a traitor, and he specifically ruled you out." She paused a moment, then added, "And me as well. He made it quite clear that Suri was the only one he would speak to."

"The fane considers all Rhunes to be little more than dumb animals. He'd never surrender to one."

"We weren't talking about surrendering. We've had six years of killing, hardships on both sides. But we can't get past the Nidwalden, and Lothian can't put a dent in our numbers. He sees the same thing I do; we've reached an impasse, and ending the war on mutually agreeable terms is the best solution."

Nyphron sighed. "What the fane sees is that he is a god. He had no intention of discussing a mutual peace. Doing so would be humiliating beyond imagination."

Persephone looked confused. "Then why—"

"You still don't see it?"

She stared at him, her eyes shifting back and forth.

"He wants the secret to making dragons," Nyphron said.

Persephone shook her head. "It won't work. Suri won't be able to cast the weave. She was telling the truth about how the spell works. She would need to sacrifice someone dear. Few on this side of the river meet that requirement, and there's no one she loves east of the Nidwalden."

"She won't have to be the one who casts the spell," Nyphron said. "She only has to tell Lothian how to do it. Then he'll have his Miralyith sacrifice their loved ones. In a week, maybe two, the skies will darken with fleets of dragons." Nyphron felt himself losing his struggle to keep his temper, so he moved to the exit. Pausing at the flap he added, "By seeking peace, you've provided the fane the victory that should have been ours. The war will end, but only after Lothian has swept us from the face of Elan."

CHAPTER SEVENTEEN

Malcolm Told Me

It would be easy for me to skip this part, especially since I am now in a hurry to get everything recorded. I could pretend that I believed her from the start, but that would be a lie, and I know, now more than ever, that lying is more than deceitful. It is dangerous.

— THE BOOK OF BRIN

"Sorry I'm late," Brin called out as she ran, dodging around the tent ropes like a ten-year-old who was late for dinner.

It's like she never grew up, Tressa thought with a mixture of amazement and irritation. Life wasn't fair, but somehow Brin had escaped the poison that came with the pain. The little cruelties that shredded innocence and left behind hateful adults hadn't found a foothold in the girl. And yet, Tressa knew the life Brin had lived, and that left her puzzled. *How does she do it?*

Tressa could never remember being . . . she struggled for a word that summed up Brin. She couldn't. *Naïve* was the closest, but that wasn't quite right. *Young* was another option, but Brin wasn't a child anymore. She was twenty-two years old. There had been a celebration that spring, one of the few festivities held in the camp. Padera had made a cake, and people danced and sang around a bonfire. Tressa hadn't been invited. She watched from the darkness, wondering what the cake tasted like.

By Brin's age, Tressa had already buried one husband, married a second, and lost two children, neither of whom made it past eight—not eight years—eight days. If she'd died along with the infants, maybe someone would have mourned her like they'd done when Aria died giving birth to Gifford. Giving birth to children too weak to survive was the hallmark of a bad mother. By twenty-two, all of Tressa's dreams had been ground up like grain and blown away like chaff. She forgot how to smile, at least the happy version. But here was Brin, grinning and clutching that stupid book of hers like she didn't have a care.

Brin fell to her knees next to the water barrel that was stationed between the big spit and the laundry tubs. This was where they met every day so the Keeper could teach Tressa to read. The spot wasn't very nice, but it was out of the way. Tressa had suffered through only a few lessons, and little of it was making sense. She understood the concept: An image stood for a sound. Problem was that Tressa couldn't fathom how anyone could memorize all the pairings. The more she learned, the more Tressa realized the project was hopeless. There was just too much. Brin could likely do it because of her Keeper's mind, which had been trained for her role from a young age. Tressa had a hard time remembering when to spit and when to swallow. But she enjoyed her time with Brin.

"I got distracted," Brin said, puffing for air. "Tesh is back."

"I'm surprised you came at all then."

Brin frowned as she set the pages on the ground. "He's not why I'm late. And I can't stay. I just brought some pages that I thought you might practice with on your own. I really do have to get back."

"Back where?"

"To the Keenig's Lodge." Brin neatened the stack and put a rock on top to hold it against the breeze. "Things have happened that I need to record."

"What sort of *things*?"

Brin was already back on her feet, looking frustrated by the questions. Tressa could see the debate in the Keeper's eyes. She wanted to leave, but hesitated. Then Tressa realized that Brin didn't want to be rude . . . to *her*. For Tressa, that was like seeing a double rainbow. She'd heard about them but had never actually seen one.

What is it with her? It's like she doesn't live in the same reality.

"We just found out Suri's been captured by the Fhrey," Brin said quickly. "The whole thing is a mess! Suri was invited to the tower to talk about a possible peace, but it was a trick. We're trying to figure out what to do. Nyphron thinks they're taking Suri to Estramnadon, the elven capital city, which is even farther away. He believes they're going to force her to teach them how to make dragons. If they do, well, it's not hard to figure out what that means. Persephone sent Justine for Moya, so I came here to drop off these pages. It won't take long, so I really do need to get back." Brin took a breath, shaking her head and putting a hand over her mouth as if she might vomit, then said, "Tesh said they put Suri in a cage."

"Cage?" Tressa said.

"Yeah, so I'm—Tressa, are you all right?"

"There has to be something we can do," Moya was saying from inside the tent as Tressa approached. Tressa had never visited the keenig's tent before. She hadn't spoken to Persephone since handing over Reglan's ring. Even then, all Tressa remembered having said was, "Here." This meant the last time they had talked was when Persephone lied about Konniger's death. She'd done it to be kind, which was pretty insane, considering Konniger had died trying to kill Persephone. Everyone knew about it and believed Tressa had been aware of the plot, a sentiment that didn't exactly endear her to the residents of Dahl Rhen. But it wasn't like she had ever been popular.

Habet was crouched on the ground, fussing with the fire and staring up at her.

"What are you looking at?" she growled.

He shrugged and smiled.

The simpleton was another of Dahl Rhen's misery dodgers. Like Brin, the Moron of the Eternal Flame was immune to life's savageries. *Idiocy has its advantages.*

Tressa briefly considered announcing herself and asking permission to enter, but that would give Moya the opportunity to say no. She couldn't let that happen. This was the first step and the easiest. If she couldn't handle it, how could she ever manage the rest?

Tressa pulled back the flap and entered. Inside, Persephone sat on a chair that Tressa guessed had been brought from Alon Rhist, Moya at her side. Brin, who had returned to the keenig while Tressa was still working up the courage to come over, was on the floor where a half-completed page indicated she'd already been taking notes. Nyphron stood at the center of it all. Everyone looked at her.

"Hello," she said stupidly. Tressa had nightmares like this, where she walked into the middle of the camp naked and everyone gawked.

"What are—" Moya said as her eyes first widened and then narrowed. She took a step toward the entrance.

I've got two seconds before she throws me out. So here goes . . . "I know how to save Suri," she announced.

Persephone caught Moya by the wrist and pulled her back. "What did you say?"

"You need to get across the river, right? I know how."

"*You* do?" Moya said in disbelief. "How is it you even know something happened to Suri?"

"I told her," Brin said. She had a guilty look on her face, as if she'd sinned against the gods.

Moya didn't berate the Keeper. She didn't take out a switch and whip the woman for her crime. Instead, the Shield to the keenig glared at Tressa as if she had corrupted the pure one. "You don't know Tet! Get out of here, Tressa!"

"No, wait," Persephone said. "I want to hear this."

"Well," Tressa started, knowing how crazy she was about to sound, "there's a door that goes to Es-tra-ma-something, the Fhrey's capital city. That's where they're taking her, right?"

Persephone looked at Brin, who looked at Moya, who said, "You're culling drunk, aren't you, Tressa? Whose bottle did you steal this time?"

Tressa ignored Moya. She had no chance with her. Instead, she kept her sights on Persephone; she was listening. "That door is connected to an underground passageway, and its entrance is near a swamp not far from here. So if we go there, we can pop out of the Fhrey door and save Suri."

Nyphron rolled his eyes. The women all stared, but not even Moya looked angry now. What Tressa saw was far worse than anger or hate. Their faces were painted in pity.

In a sad, pathetic voice that made even Tressa question herself, she added, "I know it sounds crazy, but I'm not making it up. Malcolm told me about it."

Persephone slowly nodded, and said "Thank you, Tressa. I appreciate you coming and telling us."

The gentle tone made Tressa want to cry. She couldn't bear the thought of standing there, bawling in front of them. She turned and ran out.

CHAPTER EIGHTEEN

The Mystery in the Garden

The world of the Fhrey is still such a puzzle to me, but now I know
that much of it is a mystery to them, too.

— THE BOOK OF BRIN

Imaly was filled with an odd combination of dread and elation when she spotted him in the Garden, sitting on the same bench—the one directly across from the Door. She had come in search of the odd stranger who'd called himself Trilos, but part of her had hoped he wouldn't be there, in the same way someone suffering a toothache hoped the healer might be busy elsewhere.

Over the years, Imaly had seen her share of oddities. She'd witnessed whirlwinds tearing trees up by their roots, the moon blocking out the sun, foxfire in the forest, a winter without snow, and the Shinara River frozen solid. But all those things paled in comparison to what had happened when she was three hundred years and fourteen days old. That was when the war with the Dherg had started. Five years later, Fenelyus of the tribe Eilywin began performing magic.

The war had been raging ever since Fane Ghika of the Asendwayr was murdered. Alon Rhist of the Instarya had become the new fane and fought as best he could against the iron weapons. Then he, too, was killed, and the Dherg marched unopposed with their massive army toward the Nidwalden and the Fhrey homeland. No one wanted the *honor* of being the last fane, and Fenelyus Mira was chosen without a challenger. Seven days after accepting the mantle of leadership, she stopped the army on the Plains of Mador. She managed this all by herself, single-handedly killing tens of thousands and creating a mountain in the process. No one questioned her methods. No one was even concerned. Fenelyus was the fane, and she had stopped the invasion. What was there to worry about?

The Umalyn leaders declared that she had been endowed by Ferrol with the gift of the Art in their time of need—just as Gylindora Fane had been given the horn. In Fenelyus's case, she was able to teach others her gift, and her students became known as *Miralyith*, literally "Mira-followers."

After that, Imaly saw daily miracles. The sick and injured were magically healed; trees were *asked* to grow in particular directions to accommodate buildings; rivers temporarily flowed backward to aid the transport of supplies; rain was scheduled and seasons tempered. Festivals were wondrous occasions adorned with magical decorations and lights. For a time, in the early centuries of Fane Fenelyus's reign, it truly seemed as if Ferrol had blessed them. It took a while before certain people started espousing that some Fhrey were more blessed than others.

Fenelyus had saved the Fhrey from obliteration at the hands of King Mideon, rescuing them at the last moment. For this, she was revered as a hero, but she had also released a poison into their society that slowly ate away at its foundation. Fenelyus had saved the leaves but infected the roots.

Two major mysteries surrounded her. The first was how she had obtained the gift of magic, and the second was why she had failed to fully obliterate the Dherg. Both centered on the Garden and the Door. The official versions, as recounted by the Umalyn High Priest, said that Fenelyus was rewarded with the Art while kneeling before the Door and praying to Ferrol for guidance. Later, when she had crushed King Mideon and driven her enemy back to their last stronghold of Drumindor, she once more visited the Garden. There Ferrol asked her to show mercy toward the Dherg, which she did.

As a lifelong councilor in the Aquila, Imaly knew a lie when she heard one. These weren't even good fabrications. They didn't have to be. When people needed to believe in something, they made allowances.

Imaly's problem was that she couldn't bend so far or delude herself with fantasies. She was the great-granddaughter of Gylindora Fane, the Curator of the Aquila, the sentinel and watchdog for a fragile system that had preserved their way of life for millennia. Fenelyus had broken Fhrey society, and it was Imaly's responsibility to fix it.

She viewed the Door as the epicenter where everything had started. Set in a rock wall that enclosed an area a bit larger than the Airenthenon, the Door appeared to be made of simple wood and ordinary hinges. The Umalyn priests said it was the gateway to the afterlife. Imaly didn't believe that. She saw it as just a symbol. The Door most likely wasn't even a real opening; it probably hung like a picture on a wall with nothing behind it. The *idea of it* was all that mattered. The Door represented the difference between the living and the dead and embodied how a person could be barred from paradise if they failed to follow the Law of Ferrol. This parable, for which the Door was a physical reminder, taught that defying society would result in exclusion and banishment. Chaos was kept at bay by logic, but for those unswayed by reason, there was fear.

All that was fine, perfect even, except that while the Door was a wonderful symbol, it overachieved its goal. Not only couldn't the Door be opened, which made perfect sense both metaphorically and physically, it also couldn't be harmed. No ax could cut it, no fire could burn it, and even the Art was useless against it. As a symbol, the Door was enduring, but as a door, it was disturbing.

So was the fellow who made a habit of sitting across from it.

It had been almost seven years, and yet he hadn't changed. Trilos remained in the same shoddy clothes—or at least ones that were similarly shoddy. Imaly hadn't paid that much attention to his attire the first time. In any case, he looked as unkempt as ever.

"May I?" she asked, indicating the open space next to him.

"Of course." Trilos slid a tad to the side to grant her more room.

Imaly took a moment to gather her robe before sitting. "Thank you."

Winter was coming, and the trees were shedding. Falling leaves blew by, swirling and dancing in the corners.

"Are you always here?" Imaly asked. She didn't bother introducing herself or taking the time to mention they'd previously met. Their singular conversation had lasted for only a few minutes, but he'd known her then, so she expected he knew her now. Trilos the Door Watcher had known a great many things without being told. This was why she had sought him out.

"It's what I do," he said. Trilos didn't bother to look at her. He kept his eyes on the Door, as if afraid he might miss something.

"But why?"

"Same reason you do what you do." He sat forward, his elbows on his knees in a most undignified slouch. His hands were together, fingers absently folding and unfolding, interacting like a pair of mating crabs.

Mating crabs? Imaly found her analogy bizarre. She'd never seen crabs copulate. She'd rarely even seen them at all, but perhaps that was the reason she'd conjured that thought. The way they moved was strange, exotic, unnatural.

Still fascinated by his hands, she said, "I administer the Aquila and advise the fane on how best to rule his people in order to ensure our society remains safe. So why—"

"And is that why you're here? To help your fane?" he asked, as if he didn't believe her, as if he knew better.

Imaly gestured toward the Door before them. "I'm here as a worshipper of Ferrol, paying my respects to the Door, same as you."

Trilos chuckled. Like his hands, the laughter was odd, off somehow. Once more, she had the impression that it was unnatural.

"Did I say something humorous?"

"Comedy exists when truths and lies masquerade as each other." He leaned over, tilting his head slightly toward her as if they were old pals. The act made her want to recoil, but she held steady. Every muscle in her body tensed, but no one could see that. At least she didn't think so. "Everything you said was a lie, even the part you thought was true—*that's* what made it funny."

She wished to ask more, to question him about his meditations on the mysteries of the Door. But more than anything she wanted to know about the disappearance of Mawyndulë—*that* was the real reason she'd sought him. She couldn't, though, not now. He'd just accused her of both ignorance and lying. Ignoring the comment would suggest agreement. Denying it would be indefensible, as he had been completely correct. Admitting the falsehood would place her in a weakened position. Declaring piety before the Door should have been a perfect and unassailable shield, and yet here she was beaten by her own defense. They had barely entered into the conversation, and already he had the upper hand. Imaly had always considered herself a master of discourse and debate. At that moment, she felt as if she were a child at the adult table.

"She went in, you know," Trilos said, inexplicably.

Freed by the unintelligible statement that blew the whole discussion off course, or at least from the direction *she'd* wanted it to take, Imaly asked, "I'm sorry, what?"

"Fenelyus went in that door."

This time was Imaly's turn to laugh. "No, she didn't. I don't even think that's a real door."

"Oh, I assure you, it is."

"Then why can't anyone open it?" she asked.

"It's locked."

Imaly chuckled at the simple but absurd statement. "No, it's not. There's no keyhole, no latch, no bar."

"Not that kind of a lock." He grinned at the door as if he and it shared a secret. "Because it's not that kind of door."

"So it's a magic door then, is it?" Imaly's tone was condescending as she tried to regain her footing in the conversation.

"Of course, but that's nothing unusual. The sun rising each morning is magical, too."

"That's not magic. The rising of the sun is a natural occurrence."

"What's *natural* about a ball of light rising up out of nowhere to illuminate and heat the world then crossing the sky before falling back into nothing? And even more bizarrely, it'll do it again the next day. The only reason you don't see it as magical is because you're used to it. If you hadn't seen it happen, and do so every day since you were born, you'd think I was making the whole thing up. And when you saw it for the first time, you'd certainly believe it to be magic. The same could be said about snow or rain." He took his eyes off the Door and looked up. "Everything that comes from the sky is magical, mysterious, and eternal." Reaching down, he scraped up a bit of dirt, lifted it, and let it fall. The specks scattered in the wind. "That which comes from Elan is fleeting, doomed from birth. The problem lies in those things that have common ancestry in both. Those made of dirt and sky, the unwanted children of warring parents."

"You're not from around here, are you?"

"Not originally, no. I'm from the east, but then everyone is. They just don't know it. Everything started out there. Sadly, there isn't much left anymore—neglectful tenants were left in charge and ruined the place."

"Where were you before here?"

"For a long time, I was in prison."

That's not a surprise. "Really?"

"Oh, yes."

"Why were you locked up?"

Imaly saw Trilos stumble. He paused, his eyes looking around in thought. Finally, he replied. "I honestly don't know." Then he looked at the door. "But I know who imprisoned me, and I intend to find him and repay the kindness."

He's insane or at the very least a fool. Imaly wondered why it had taken so long to figure that out. Staring at a piece of wood all day should have been a huge clue. Even Volhoric, for all his piety, didn't do that. This understanding arrived with equal parts relief and disappointment. She needn't be afraid or concerned about him *watching her*, something he had ominously mentioned at their other meeting. She also wouldn't be able to learn anything useful from him.

She sighed and started to stand.

"You're leaving? I thought you wanted to know where Mawyndulë is," Trilos said. "That's why you came, isn't it?"

Imaly sat back down as a dozen questions and hundreds of warnings popped into her head, but she focused on the opportunity presented. "Do you know?"

"He went to Avempartha. Just him and Treya." Trilos laughed again. "That's another farce. Another truth pretending to be a lie. Although that one is a very bitter joke. Cruelty is also a great source of humor. Everyone laughs when someone falls, don't they? Poor Treya. It's one of the many reasons I have so little sympathy for Lothian. He believes making Treya a servant to Mawyndulë was a virtuous act. He feels he was being kind." Trilos shook his head. "He was being compassionate in the same way that a thief leaves behind a loaf of bread after stealing all else."

Imaly had no idea what he was talking about. She thought she should, sensed there was a nugget of importance connected to that random comment, but this wasn't why she'd come. "Why did Mawyndulë go to Avempartha?"

"To fetch a Rhune. He's bringing her back to Daddy. Showing off his princely chops."

While Trilos might not be entirely sane, he did appear to have access to a surprising amount of information. "Why would he do that?"

"The fane ordered him." Trilos smiled at her. "There's another joke, in that *you* have no idea what's happening despite playing such a large role in it."

"I don't understand. What do you mean?"

"Frustrating, isn't it?" he said, still focused on the Door, his crab hands once more folding over each other. "Being the confused one, I mean."

He was right, and pointing it out didn't help. "Tell me what I did."

"You told the fane about the message from the Rhunes, the offer of peace."

Feeling a dash of fear that Trilos might know a bit too much, Imaly made a quick mental search of everyone who knew about her receiving the message from the Rhune leader. She recalled speaking of it openly when Lothian first returned from the Battle of Grandford. *Anyone could have heard me.*

Trilos continued, "This gave the fane the idea to use a pigeon to set a trap. He invited a Rhune to come as a representative to talk about peace, but Lothian doesn't want that. He wants the secret."

"Which is?"

"The Rhune that Mawyndulë has been sent to fetch knows how to make dragons, or what Lothian thinks are dragons. The fane intends to learn that from her."

Imaly nodded. "I see."

"I doubt that," he said. He finally turned to look at her. "Or rather I suspect you're seeing the wrong thing."

"Which is?"

He smiled, but she didn't know why. "You're recognizing the obvious but failing to put the pieces together. You remind me a bit of my sister—the older one, not the younger." He said this as if Imaly invited his family over for parties on a regular basis. "She was too smart for her own good and yet often fails to put together the simplest connections. But you're both cunning and vicious, and that has served you two well."

Imaly noted that he spoke of his sister—the older not the younger—in the past and present tenses, but given the whole of his statement, that was the least of her concerns.

"So, what is it I'm missing?" she asked.

"You don't have enough pieces on the board to achieve your goal. You're working with just enough to succeed, but plans never go as intended. You should anticipate setbacks. Complications always arise. You feel you're doing the best you can, given your limited resources. But your best won't be good enough. You're going to need a second Miralyith, Imaly, or it isn't going to work."

He knows about Makareta! And what I plan to do with her. But that's impossible! I haven't told anyone!

"What you are ignorant of," he said, "what you're failing to realize, is that the other Miralyith doesn't have to be a Fhrey."

"Did you find Mawyndulë?" Makareta asked the moment Imaly returned home. "Is he okay?"

"You shouldn't be so close to the door. What if I was someone else?" Imaly snapped, shutting the door quickly and loudly.

"I knew it was you; the Art told me."

"You can't use the Art!" she shouted.

Makareta was lounging on the settee, her mouse slippers abandoned on the floor. Three dirty teacups and a beach of crumbs littered the little table in front of her. "I didn't *use* the Art!" The Miralyith child grew angry, placing a hand on the back of the settee and straightening up.

"You just said so."

"No, you just don't understand how the Art works."

Imaly took the time to properly hang up her cloak, as it gave her something sensible to do besides screaming. "Enlighten me."

"Using the Art is like talking, and yeah, if I did that, someone might hear. But another part is listening. You can't notice someone listening. And why are you so mad right now?"

"I'm not!"

"The Art is telling me—"

"Oh, just stop it, will you!" Imaly, frustrated with the hook, threw her cloak across the room, shocking Makareta, who stared openmouthed. A moment of silence reigned as they both stared at the sprawled garment on the floor. "Okay, I'm a little worked up."

"Why? Is Mawyndulë all right?" The degree of concern that spewed from Makareta surprised Imaly.

The girl had used Mawyndulë for her schemes. She'd unabashedly manipulated the prince, seduced him into betraying his own father, and yet . . . *Is she trying to confuse me? Does Makareta think she can control me like she did him?*

"He's fine, I suppose."

"What do you mean, *you suppose?*"

There it was again, that odd note of sincerity in her worried pretense.

"I mean that I have no reason to think anything unpleasant has happened, but I haven't personally verified that."

"Why? Where is he?"

Imaly sighed and walked across the little room to pick up her cloak. "His father sent him to escort a Rhune prisoner back here to Estramnadon."

"Oh." Makareta, previously puffed up by fear and anger, deflated, collapsing down on the settee into her usual slump. Then she looked at Imaly with a perplexed expression. "Wait . . . what's wrong then?"

Imaly placed the cloak on the hook. Turning back, she said nothing.

I have no idea.

CHAPTER NINETEEN

In the Land of Nog

I have always had a hard time throwing things away: old clothes
that are little more than rags, sandals with holes and broken straps,
a wad of hopelessly tangled string, even people who have hurt me.
I cannot bring myself to throw them away because, as it turns out,
sometimes I need them.

— THE BOOK OF BRIN

Tressa tripped on a sledgehammer left outside for so long that it had been
hidden by tall grass. If she had fallen, she would have smashed her face on
the corner of the stone furnace. *Typical.* She was annoyed that her reward
for trying to do something good was nearly having her teeth bashed in.
Maybe I'm just not good at this kind of thing.

Roan and Gifford's tent was at the center of the Crafting Quarter.
Anvils circled it, as did piles of charcoal, scraps of metal, crates of ore,
and furnaces—some hot and cooking, others cold and waiting. People had
taken to calling it the Land of Nog, the place where crimbals lived and
all things miraculous could happen. A small, single stall housed Naraspur,
whom Gifford had adopted and doted on. The horse acted as a stand-
in for the child the couple lacked. Tressa didn't think their childlessness
was because of any judgment from the gods, but more likely the result of

Roan's intimacy issues. Things had gotten better between the potter and the inventor, and yet their relationship was far from perfect. Roan didn't recoil at Gifford's touch, but anyone could tell some things were still off-limits.

Everyone has troubles. Gifford's and Roan's are just more obvious than most.

The tent glowed as if it were a monstrous firefly. Standing outside in the dark, Tressa went through the process of working up her nerve—again.

After the disaster at the Keenig's Lodge, she'd nearly given up on the idea of persuading others to come. She might have quit entirely if not for the memory of the silver ring. Malcolm had told those gathered in the smithy that everyone present that night had to do their part. Tressa was certain Malcolm didn't mean that she would be involved in saving the world, but he had, and she was. In her entire life, contributing that ring to the making of the sword was—pathetic as it seemed—her proudest moment. No one had asked her to hand it over. She'd given it out of love and respect for a man she'd hardly known. And while even Tressa didn't know why she had done so, Malcolm had known she would. He knew everything.

In the autumn, several years from now, when everything has gone poorly, Tesh will bring news about the cage, and no one will know what to do. That's when you'll need to step forward.

He hadn't actually said *who* she was supposed to tell. Tressa assumed he meant Persephone, but that hadn't worked out so well. Having tried, Tressa nearly chalked the effort up as good enough, except she remembered something else Malcolm had said: *And you'll have to take others with you, seven to be exact.*

Just as she had once done with the ring, Tressa played with the idea that Malcolm was mistaken. She lacked faith, not in him but in herself. *Who will go anywhere with me?* With no clear option, Tressa nearly set off alone, except, *I had doubted him before, too.* Crazy was only crazy . . . until it happened.

Roan and Gifford's tent felt a lot like the smithy, wonderfully nostalgic in an inexpressibly good way. Here was the best place for a last try. More than that, aside from Brin's inexplicable interest in her, Roan and Gifford were the closest things she had to friends.

"I'll try one more time," she told the starry sky. "'Cause I can't think of nothing else to do. But if this ain't good enough, then I guess you shouldn't have picked me."

With a deep breath, she strode across the remaining debris field and patted the canvas. "Hey in there. You aren't doing nothing perverted at the moment, are you?"

"Twessa?" Gifford called.

"Yeah, I wanna talk to you two. Can we do that? Or do you need to put clothes on or hide a sheep or something?"

The tent flap pulled back and a fully clothed Gifford greeted her with a surprised, lopsided smile, but that was the way he always looked so she couldn't tell anything by it. He waved her inside, and Tressa ducked under the flap.

The interior of the tent was lit by three surprisingly large lanterns that hung from the ceiling ribs. They were yellow balls made of thin cloth, with a clay vessel at the bottom. They resembled a trio of golden mushrooms and illuminated the place brilliantly. Roan lay on the floor with her legs up on a toppled basket, a lock of hair in her mouth. She held a piece of slate on her chest that she marked on with chalk. Not looking up from her tablet, the woman didn't appear to notice Tressa had entered.

"See, we not doing nothing," Gifford said.

"Sorry to hear that, Giff," Tressa offered in condolence, then studied the lights again. "Nice lanterns." She meant it, although the words came out with a sarcastic tone. This was part of her normal inflection, a nasty accent that was all hers. Her mother used to tell Tressa that if she rolled her eyes too much they might get stuck up in her head and never come down. Mothers were always saying stuff like that, screwing with their kids, scaring them into doing what they wanted. Tressa's eyes never got stuck, but the theory wasn't as stupid as it seemed. After years of acting like a bitch, Tressa didn't know how to act otherwise.

Gifford wasn't the sort to take offense, not with anyone. And when it came to Tressa, he was well acquainted with her disagreeable demeanor. She'd been a regular visitor to Hopeless House, where Gifford and Gelston had roomed together.

"Moss soaked in animal fat is what fuels them," he told her. "I made the clay vessels with little chimneys the way Woan wanted. The big ball evens out the light, softens it. A couple months ago we had diffewent ones. Woan caught a bunch of lightning bugs and put them inside. Wasn't as bwight, but no smoky smell."

Tressa nodded.

"What did you want to talk about?"

"I was wondering if you two would come with me to save Suri." Tressa tossed the words out with all the hope of the village idiot asking the belle of the autumn harvest to dance. She saw it as mere formality. In her head, Tressa had already heard the rejection and was mentally packing her sack for the next morning's journey.

"How we gonna do that?" Gifford asked with his normal deadpan acceptance of the impossible. Tressa could excuse it, given that the man was a cripple but had won a race to save humanity.

"Well . . ." Tressa took a deep breath so she could get through it as fast as possible. "Malcolm told me to go north to a swamp where—"

"Malcolm told you?" Roan was now looking up.

"He's back?" Gifford asked.

"No, he told me this a long time ago."

"When?"

"As we were leaving Alon Rhist. That's when he said—"

"Malcolm told you how to save Su-wee . . . back then?" Gifford asked.

"Yeah, I know." Tressa nodded with an insecure smile. "It was *before* she was captured, and that doesn't make any sense, but he said I had to take others, and—"

"Did he mention us?" Roan asked. She was on her feet now, still clutching the slate to her chest and inching toward her. The intensity of her expression was drawing concerned looks from Gifford.

"Well, not exactly—not by name, but he said I needed to bring seven people with me."

"Did you tell Pe'sephone about this?" Gifford asked.

"I did, but she and *Moya*, well . . . I suspect they had a good laugh after I left. Persephone likes to pretend she's all proper, but she and Moya probably went on and on about *that drunken idiot Tressa*. Thing is, I haven't touched a jug since Gelston died. I tried to stop when Malcolm dropped this news in my lap. I felt that he'd picked me special, and that I ought to live up to that expectation—be a good person, you know? Only I . . ." She laughed self-consciously, miserably. "I discovered I ain't special, and I ain't a good person. I'm a weak, bitter old woman, and I drink when I can get it. I'd like to say I've been dry because I made a vow, but the truth is . . . no one will give me any." She looked Gifford square in the eye. "I'd be drunk right now if I could."

"He said seven?" Roan asked, as if she hadn't heard anything else but the number.

"Huh? Oh." Tressa nodded. "That's why I came here." She made a sad face. "As sick as it sounds, you two, and now maybe Brin, are the only people who don't hate me. At least, I don't *think* you do. I hope not."

"We don't hate you, Twessa."

"And that makes you the only people who might listen. If it wasn't for that, I wouldn't even try. I only asked you two 'cause Malcolm said I needed others. I don't know what made him think I could muster up seven soulmates. But then I don't know what good he thinks I can do anyway. I'm just glad he seems to have faith in me."

"And Persephone won't go with you?" Roan asked.

Tressa shook her head. "Can't blame her. If I wasn't in the smithy that night, if I hadn't witnessed what Malcolm did, what he said, if I hadn't felt it, I wouldn't believe me, either. She probably thinks I'm nutty."

"I was there," Roan said. "You're . . . not nutty." She looked down at the slate in her hands. She rubbed her fingers over the surface, slowly erasing what had been there. Then she let the tablet fall, and the chalk quickly following. Her sight shifted to Gifford. She offered him a sad, apologetic expression. "I'm going to go with Tressa."

Gifford's eyes widened. "Go? You don't even know . . ." He made a motion rolling his hands over each other.

"Where?" Roan finished for him.

"Yes!" Gifford said. "How can you agwee if you don't know that?"

Roan looked down at the slate. "Because it's to save Suri. And because Malcolm said so. Nothing else matters."

Coming out of Roan's mouth, the words didn't sound so stupid. As messed up as she was, the woman was famous for being a genius. The ex-slave of a sadistic monster had once tied a string to a stick and changed warfare. She had declared that a pottery wheel could help carry an entire dahl's supplies, and she was right. Tressa suffered from a reputation for dishonesty, but Roan had one for plausibility. She could say rain would fall upward and make it sound likely. Hearing Roan say Tressa wasn't insane was more than a shock; to Tressa, it felt like an undeserved kindness. It felt like the time Gelston had hugged her.

Funny how a crumb can seem like a banquet to the starving. Only it wasn't humorous. Tressa knew that much. It was sad.

With Gifford and Roan willing to go, Tressa found the courage to try once more to convince others to come. She explained that Brin was an unlikely candidate because she hadn't been swayed in the Keening's Lodge when she had talked to Persephone, but Roan had insisted that they invite the Keeper just the same.

In Roan's unfathomable mind, a place Tressa envisioned as even more cluttered than her lawn, there were two reasons for this. The first was that Tressa had named her as another potential friend, and the second was that Brin hadn't been in the smithy that night. She couldn't possibly understand what was going on but might if she heard the whole story. Only Tressa, Roan, Suri, Raithe, Malcolm, and the three dwarfs had been there. Roan invited the little men over as well. The digger was amiable enough, but the bearded twins grumbled their way in. All three were probably more drawn by the offer of beer and cheese than by any interest in listening to Tressa.

Roan was back at her slate, wiping it clear with her forearm and making new marks, when Gifford returned with not only Brin but Tesh as well. The two came in smiling, but Brin pulled up short when she spotted Tressa. This suggested Gifford hadn't explained everything—maybe not anything. The man had a tendency to keep his remarks short.

"What's going on, Roan?" Brin asked, standing just inside the entrance before the seated circle of dwarfs, who were helping themselves to the wheel of cheese.

Roan didn't say anything. Instead, she looked at Tressa. "You tell her."

"I already did."

"Is this about Suri?" Brin asked.

Tressa should have known Gifford hadn't told her the subject of the meeting—he couldn't say the mystic's name.

Roan nodded.

"She's right. I was there when Tressa told Persephone. There's no reason to—"

"But you don't know about Malcolm," Roan said.

At the sound of his name the three dwarfs stopped fussing over the cheese and looked up. "Malcolm? What about him?" Frost asked.

"*He* told Twessa to save Su-wee," Gifford said. "And that was long ago, be-foe she was taken."

This touched off a round of serious, knowing looks among the dwarfs.

"But that's impossible," Brin muttered, puzzled.

"Woan and I am going with Twessa."

"What?" Brin asked, stunned. "Why?"

"Suri saved us, more than once," Roan said. "She killed Minna and Raithe. I owe her."

"We all do," Brin replied, exasperated. "But we can't do anything."

Tressa suspected Roan would see Brin's reaction as an indication that the Keeper didn't care by flatly refusing to help. That was the sort of behavior that made a person look bad. For Tressa, reputation-guarding was a mere memory. Years ago, it had been important to be seen as kind or generous, but Tressa didn't exist to most people anymore. Brin still had a reputation to protect; Tressa didn't. In many ways, she was happy to be rid of it. There was a lot less crap to deal with when no one cared.

"Look, I would give up my life if I thought it could help Suri," Brin said. "But there's nothing we can do."

"There is," Tressa said. "Malcolm told me how."

Brin did that eye-rolling thing that Tressa's mother had so adamantly warned against, then shook her head as her face took on a greater level of frustration. "Yes, you keep mentioning him, but I don't see how he has anything to do with this."

Roan and the dwarfs exchanged more looks while Tesh, Brin, and Gifford watched with curiosity.

"Is it a secret?" Tesh asked while reaching out for the cheese that the dwarfs appeared to think was meant for them alone.

Everyone looked to Tressa, who sighed. "It won't sound believable coming from me."

"But you're the one Malcolm talked to," Roan said.

Tressa glared at Roan. She was right. *Roan didn't go from slave to sage by being wrong all the time, now, did she? Tet.*

Tressa wiped her mouth and nodded. "Okay, it's like this. Malcolm isn't who you think he is. If you thought about it, you'd realize that. He's always in just the right place at just the right time. He's the one who hit Arion with the rock. If he hadn't, she would have taken Nyphron back to Estramnadon. Can you just imagine how things would have been different if that had happened? He told Suri to destroy the bridge at Alon Rhist. And we'd all be dead if he hadn't convinced Suri to kill Raithe and make him a dragon."

"That doesn't prove anything. Those could just be coincidences. Everyone did something important."

Tressa nodded. "But he also knows things. Things he couldn't possibly know. Like the fact that the Fhrey would build seven bridges. Not two or five or eight, but seven."

She pointed at Gifford. "He even said Giff would succeed in his night ride to Perdif and that the Gula would come, but they'd be too late. And all of it happened."

The dwarfs' heads were bobbing up and down with the look of deep sincerity that only dwarfs were capable of. Roan stared at Tressa, wide-eyed, captivated, as if it was all new to her.

"Malcolm knew things about all of us—stuff he shouldn't know. Personal things that a body only shares with the gods on nights when no one else can hear. He knew the future and the past, and every word he said proved true. He was able to convince Raithe that he needed to give up his life, and he was able to persuade Suri to take it. That right there should prove something. He was able to do that because . . ."

Tressa paused, and everyone waited. She struggled to find the right words. She wasn't like Persephone, who could persuade others to follow. But this was important. She had to persuade the people in that tent. "It wasn't just what Malcolm said and did, it was how he made us feel. In that smithy, for the first time since Reglan died—" She shook her head. "No, for the first time since I was a child, I felt *good*. I felt brave, courageous, and . . . and clean."

"What are you saying?" Brin asked.

The words caught in her throat. She'd never said them out loud before. And only thought them once in her head. Things that were obvious in the confines of the heart often failed to translate well when expressed through the inadequate filter of language. Still, she didn't have any choice. "Everyone always said that the Fhrey were gods, but we know they aren't. I don't think the same can be said about Malcolm."

Brin stared at her. The expression wasn't of disbelief but of bewilderment.

Tressa was surprised. Moya would be laughing, Persephone shaking her head sadly. But then Brin didn't have their wisdom, their years, their cynicism. For Brin, the world was still a place with empty spaces, blank voids where anything might dwell. Nothing was really impossible. Not yet. Age and experience proved suspicions, hardened rules, deadened imagination. Brin, Tressa felt, was still just young enough to believe the unbelievable.

Brin looked at Roan, and then the dwarfs. She took time to read each face carefully. "Roan? Do *you* believe this?"

"I was there. I know what happened. I can't explain it, but yes, I think Tressa is right about Malcolm."

"And based on that you're willing to . . ." Brin looked at Tressa. "What are you planning to do again?"

"We are going to go north." Tressa pointed in what she hoped was that direction. "About a day's walk to a swamp."

"That's the Swamp of Ith," Tesh said. "Not a nice place. Even the war went around it."

Tressa nodded. "There's a little island where the swamp and the Green Sea meet. We're supposed to go there."

"How does that help Suri?"

"From there we're going to travel underground so we won't have any problem crossing the river."

"Underground?" Rain asked. "How deep?"

"Pretty deep, I'm guessing, because we have to go under the sea. We'll come out in the city. Then all we have to do is find Suri and go back the way we came."

Tesh laughed, and quite loudly. "Ah—sorry." He caught himself. "It's just, well, that doesn't sound like much of a plan. I kinda do that now, making battle plans, that is. So, assuming there *is* a route under the river to the city, um . . . how do you find her once you're there? I mean, you pop up out of some tunnel and you're in the middle of this unfamiliar place filled with the enemy, right? Suri is bound to be under guard somewhere, but you don't know where. What are you going to do? Wander around? Ask for directions? Walk up to the first elf you meet and say, 'Excuse me, but do you know where they are keeping the Rhune who looks a lot like me?' That's if you could speak Fhrey, which I don't think you can. What happens when you run into resistance? Something I think is pretty likely, by the way. And how do you plan to get away? Even if you aren't killed in the first few seconds, are you just going to run for it? I'm pretty sure they will follow you."

"I don't know," Tressa said. "Malcolm didn't explain those details."

"Details!" Tesh laughed again.

"He just seemed to suggest it would all work out." She looked at her hands. "But then he also said I would have seven people go with me, and I don't think that's going to happen."

"There are seven people in this tent not including Tressa," Roan said.

"Oh, no. Hold on there, lass. I never said I was going anywhere," Frost declared.

"Me neither," Flood said.

"And Brin and I aren't going," Tesh declared for the pair.

"Roan?" Brin asked.

"I'm still going," she replied.

"Which means me, too," Gifford said, taking Roan's hand and smiling that lopsided grin.

"What do you say, Brin?" Roan asked.

"You really think that Malcolm is—"

"Malcolm isn't a god," Tesh insisted. "Trust me on this. I lived with the man. And as for that swamp? It isn't the sort of place to take a hike in. It's dangerous. The Swamp of Ith is right on the border with the forest. Do you know what my men call the Harwood? *Horrorwood*, and for good reason. There's likely to be elven scouts in there, or goblins, or worse. It's no place for—"

"But if there's even a chance we could save Suri . . ."

"You're not going to save Suri with this group," Tesh said. "You'd need an army."

Brin nodded and smiled as if Tesh had unwittingly solved everything. "If it's true, it certainly would take more than us to save her, but the keenig won't take it seriously unless—don't you see? If there is a secret passage under the river, all we need to do is find it. It's just a day's walk, right?" She looked at Tesh but didn't wait for the answer. "So, we go there, find it, come back, and then tell Persephone and Nyphron. Then they can send in the troops. We wouldn't just save Suri, we'd win the war. Isn't that worth a day's hike through a swamp?"

"I—I suppose," Tesh said. Then he looked back at Tressa. "How big is this passage? How many men could we walk abreast? Is it well hidden?"

"How the Tet should I know? Malcolm didn't exactly draw me a map and paint pictures. Although . . ." Tressa snorted. "That brings up something else I suppose I ought to mention." There were actually a number of things that needed saying, but she was making progress, and if she told the whole story, no one, not even Roan, would go. "I didn't bring it up before because I thought you wouldn't believe me."

"Seriously? Oh, this ought to be good," Flood said, chewing a mouthful of cheese. "Maybe you ought to wait until I've swallowed, then."

"Like I care if you choke," Tressa snapped. "So, yeah, I guess maybe the entrance is pretty well hidden, 'cause Malcolm said we'd need help finding it."

"What kind of help?" Gifford asked.

"There's a person living on the island to show us the way."

"Someone lives in the Swamp of Ith?" Tesh asked skeptically.

"Yeah." Tressa dragged the word out, the same way she might drag her heels toward a place she didn't want to go.

"Who?"

"The Tetlin Witch."

෨

Everyone agreed they had to tell Persephone before leaving. Not surprisingly, Tressa refused to be the one. Brin was the obvious choice, and after arriving back at the Keenig's Lodge, she received the usual friendly wave from Habet.

The tent had been a hive of activity all day. Most of it caused by Nyphron, who met there with his legion commanders to discuss a new strategy. They referred to it as the Long Shot and the Last Resort because with Suri's abduction, it had come to that. The idea was to send a party of Fhrey north toward the headwaters of the Nidwalden, in Grenmorian territory. Elysan was slated to lead the troops. His mission would be to speak to Furgenrok, the ruler of the giants, and try to persuade him to switch sides in the conflict, or at least let the Rhune legion pass through his lands. By the sound of it, Brin didn't think any of them held out much hope of the plan succeeding.

When Brin returned, she was pleased to find the Fhrey commanders were gone, and so was Nyphron. The only ones inside were Persephone, Justine, and Nolyn. The little boy was asleep with Persephone curled around him, and Justine was straightening up the mess left behind by the day's turmoil.

"Why aren't you with Tesh?" Persephone whispered. "I kept you here all day. I thought you'd—"

"This is important."

"Oh?" Persephone carefully pushed herself up until she was sitting. "What is it?"

"Roan, Gifford, Tressa, and I are going to the Swamp of Ith."

"What? Why? Does this have to do with what Tressa told us earlier?"

Brin nodded. "After talking with her more, we think there's a chance that she actually might know a way to cross under the river."

"Through a passageway that leads to a door in the center of the Fhrey capital?" Persephone asked skeptically.

Brin shrugged. "We don't know what it is. Tressa doesn't, either, but it's only a day's walk to the swamp. And if she happens to be right, then we'll come back with the news and you can send a legion over. If we're wrong . . . well, who cares if the four of us spend a day tramping through a swamp?"

"I do," Persephone said. "It's dangerous up that way."

"I could get Tesh to come. He wasn't initially interested, but I'm certain I can persuade him."

"I know he is formidable, but even with him I can't let you go wandering up near the Harwood." Persephone looked down at Nolyn breathing softly in the bundle of blankets. "I've already lost Suri. I can't risk you and Roan as well."

"Seph," Brin said softly, "they're going to want Suri to tell them how to make dragons."

"I know."

"Suri won't want to do that."

Persephone lowered her head.

"They're going to torture her, Seph."

Persephone put a hand on Nolyn's back and gently rubbed. "This is my fourth child. Did you know that? All except Mahn died before you were born. Mothers shouldn't outlive their children. I didn't bring Suri into this world, but she's still my daughter."

"When we didn't have swords, you took us across the sea to Neith. Just a few of us, not a huge army. But look what we did."

Persephone nodded. "Yes, but there wasn't a war raging in Neith, and we had a Miralyith and an Artist-in-training. They were an army unto themselves. But you, Tesh, Tressa, Roan, and Gifford? Are you serious?"

"We're just going to look. It'll probably be nothing, and we'll come back, and that will be the end of it. But how can we live with ourselves if we don't at least give it a try? Suri's done so much for us. We love her, too."

"Brin"—Persephone shook her head—"I can't let you. I'm sorry. I just can't. It's too dangerous."

Brin frowned. "Fine," she said, her fingers clenching into fists. "Forget I said anything."

The Keeper turned and walked out.

CHAPTER TWENTY

Beyond the Light of Day

Tressa was known for many things; singing wasn't one of them, but maybe it should have been.

— THE BOOK OF BRIN

The next morning, the gilarabrywn that lay with its head between its front claws looked asleep. No, less than asleep; it appeared carved of stone. The only movement came from the wind flapping the leathery edges of its two great wings, folded up against the beast's sides. Bigger than a horse, bigger than a moose, bigger than a two-story house with a peaked roof, it was the largest thing that moved under its own power that Brin had ever seen, and she stood less than ten feet from it. She had never been that close before. Few had.

Everyone in the camp avoided Dragon Hill, and not surprisingly, Brin was alone. She was the first to wade through the tall wet grass, the first to reach the meeting place.

She had a strapped bag slung over her shoulders, the very same one that Roan had given her to carry *The Book of Brin*. Her finished pages remained in a stack in her tent. She didn't think she'd have the chance to write, and she needed the space for food and a blanket. Brin had packed a meal made by Padera. The old woman was suffering from a nagging cold, but she'd insisted on making it. The swamp wasn't much more than a day's walk, and while she'd brought very little, the pack still felt unpleasantly heavy for a hike.

Roan and Gifford, who led Naraspur, appeared. They moved through the tents, then scaled the hill together, hand in hand. The sun hadn't quite cleared the horizon, but Roan would have been awake for hours. The three trudged up the long slope from the camp, which in the misty morning light looked like a checkerboard of white and dark squares.

"Good day," Gifford called out with a smile, just as if they were meeting once again at the old well in Dahl Rhen.

Gods, that seems so long ago! Brin thought.

"Morning," she said.

A breeze that didn't exist down in the valley blew in from the north, and Brin shivered. She flipped the hood of her woolen cloak over her head. Impossibly, the garment still smelled of her mother, who'd woven it only days before she died. Or maybe it was that her mother had just smelled of wool. As the three got closer, Brin could hear Gifford's brace squeak. He sounded like the door to the old lodge. Brin remembered that the left one always made an odd noise, but the right door never made a sound. *Funny the things you recall.*

Gifford and Roan were a lot like those doors. The world of Brin's youth was forever gone, but coming up the hillside was its spirit. The two wore heavy cloaks of the Rhen pattern. On the horse, the same clever shoulder packs were strapped, as well as little metal water carriers.

"Where's your armor?" Brin asked Gifford.

He looked up with a sheen of sweat on his face. "I think we all know I am slow enough without it. And it's too heavy fo' hiking. You might be supwised to know, but I'm not good on long walks."

"Aren't you going to ride Naraspur?"

Gifford nodded. "I'm gonna use the old gal to get to the swamp, but I suspect I'll have to leave Naw-as-pa behind to get to the island. She can wait till we come back."

Roan pulled their intertwined hands to her lips and kissed Gifford's fingers, then gave him an admiring look that, autumn wind be damned, warmed Brin from the inside. She envied the two and hoped she and Tesh would one day be like them.

The three dwarfs came next. Given Frost's and Flood's denials during yesterday's meeting, Brin was surprised to see them. Then she noticed they didn't carry packs, so they were only there to see the party off. All three spoke in their native language of sharp chopped tones, which sounded a bit angry, but their language always sounded that way.

Tressa came up the hill behind them, walking alone. She had a full pack strapped to her shoulders as if she planned on being gone a year. Watching her, Brin wondered if the dahl had misjudged the woman or whether the events of the last few years had made her a better person. She felt it was a bit of both. The idea bothered Brin on a professional level and reminded her of what Malcolm had said about truth. Life was never as simple as told in tales. So what did that say about them? Were they truth or fabrications?

"Brin!" Tesh called as he easily jogged up the slope despite his armor and dual swords.

"Morning, dear!" She waved brightly.

He scowled in return. "We talked about this last night. We *aren't* going, *remember?*"

"You are right. We did talk, and *I am* going, *remember?*"

After leaving Persephone's tent, Brin had told Tesh she was joining them and asked him to come. He had ranted about how she, Tressa, Gifford, and Roan had no idea what it was like up north. They had argued for hours, but it hadn't changed her decision any more than Persephone's edict had. Apparently, Tesh hadn't gotten the message.

Tesh clenched his teeth and rolled his eyes. "This is"—he searched for a word, probably *stupid* or *pointless*, as he'd used those several times the night before, but what came out was— *"dangerous."*

"We're just going on a little hike," she said.

"No, you're not. I forbid it."

"Excuse me?" Brin was stunned. "You're what now? My husband? Even if you were, it wouldn't matter."

Tesh didn't answer, but he was fuming. "But you have no reason to go."

"Suri is *my friend*. What part of that do you still not understand?"

"I don't mean that. I meant—"

"What do we have here?"

Brin was so busy fighting with Tesh that she hadn't noticed Moya and Tekchin approaching. They, too, climbed the hill. "Going somewhere, Brin?"

Brin turned her back on Moya, which left her facing the dragon. "Cinnamon sticks!"

"What?" Tesh whispered, inching closer.

"Persephone sent her," Brin whispered back.

"I got that, but what's the thing about . . . *cinnamon sticks*? Is that a curse?"

"My mother used to say it when our dog, Darby, got in the wool."

"Wow, your mother was a real firebrand, wasn't she?"

From behind, Brin could hear Moya getting closer. "Persephone said you couldn't go. Do you remember that conversation, Brin?"

"There's way too much forbidding going on," Brin whispered to herself.

"I know you can hear me," Moya said.

"Mo-ning, Moya," Gifford called to her.

"Morning, Gifford," she replied.

"Morning, Moya," Tressa offered.

"Shut up, Tressa," Moya shot back.

Brin folded her arms and clenched her teeth.

"Brin?" Moya was close now. "Did you forget to tell everyone that Persephone said no one is allowed to go?"

"She told us," Gifford said. "That's why we meeting up on this hill and away fwom the camp."

Oh thanks, Gifford, Brin thought.

"So this was supposed to be a secret meeting?" Tekchin asked. "A clandestine rendezvous?"

"Ain't my boyfriend fancy sounding?" Moya said. Her footsteps had stopped.

Brin still refused to turn.

"Did you really think Persephone was that stupid?" Moya said. "You—"

Brin whirled around. Her cheeks glistened with tears. "It's Suri, Moya! It's Suri! And we're not going to sit here and do nothing. Besides, we're only gonna look! I just can't . . . I can't . . ."

Moya reached out and hugged her. "I know. It's okay."

"I just wanted to do something," Brin cried into her shoulder. "I need to help her. I have to at least try. After all she did for us . . ."

"I understand. I do. It's okay."

Brin put her arms around Moya, and she felt something. Pulling away she asked, "Why are you wearing a pack?"

"'Cause I heard this trip was going to take all day, maybe two. Sorta an overnight camping thing, right?"

"What are you saying?"

"Seph said it was too dangerous with just a single Techylor for protection." She looked at the prymus. "No offense, Tesh." Turning her attention back to Brin, she said, "So, guess what? The keenig ordered me to play babysitter." Moya displayed a sarcastic smile. "Thanks for this by the way. I *sooooo* wanted to spend the day wading through a disgusting swamp with Tressa."

"I love you, too, Moya," Tressa said.

"Shut the Tet up, Tressa."

"Tekchin coming, too?" Brin asked.

"Uh-huh. I'll need someone to rub my feet after the walk." Moya grinned at him.

"Yeah," Tekchin replied. "That's exactly why she'll be moaning from the tall grass at night—it's 'cause I'm rubbing her feet."

Brin wiped away her tears, and said, "Thank you."

"Don't thank me, darling. I wouldn't be doing this if Seph hadn't ordered me to."

"I don't believe that for a second."

"Well, maybe she didn't have to twist my arm *too* much."

Tesh said to Moya, "I had no intention of going, but if Persephone is sending you and Tekchin, I'll go with you." He looked at Brin. "Give me your pack."

"I can carry it just fine," Brin said.

The scowl returned. "You're not going, Brin."

"Tesh, I know what danger is. I went to Neith. I almost died there— more than once."

"And that's why I won't let you go. I don't *want* you to die. I *can't* lose you."

"If you're coming, you can protect me."

"I can't!" he snapped. "It doesn't work that way. People die in the blink of an eye out there." He pointed toward Mount Mador as if the mountain were some sort of monster. "I'd bring my whole troop if I thought it would help, but it wouldn't. The elves ambush. They always get the first shot. You're not going, and that's it!"

"I *am* going, Tesh. This isn't up to you. I'm not one of your soldiers. You can't stop me."

"What if I told you . . ." He hesitated again, his lips a tight, unhappy line. "What if I said that if you go, it's over between us."

"What?" Brin felt as if he'd struck her, hard. The blow hit her chest, and she didn't have the air to speak. She stared at him in disbelief. "Tesh— don't" was all she got out. She took a step back, a step away, one hand covering her mouth. "Don't."

He stared hard at her, and for the first time, she saw what he normally left in the forest. Tesh never spoke of his days in the Harwood, and all she'd ever known from him was warmth and tenderness, but beneath it lay a jagged rock. She'd figured it was there, a hard, cold edge. How else could he do the job he did? But she never thought she'd see it turned on her.

All of this must have shown on her face because the brutality quickly faded from his eyes and he reluctantly nodded. "Fine," he said, and then he reached out and took her by the shoulders. "But you have to promise me one thing—one lousy thing."

"What?"

He reached up and took her face in his hands. "That if things go bad, you'll run—you'll run as fast and as far as you can to save yourself. Run right back here. I couldn't bear it if you died. You can't wait. If we get into trouble, and I tell you to—you run. Will you promise me that much? Please, Brin, promise me that."

"Okay," she said.

He shook his head. "Not good enough. Say the words. Make the vow."

She nodded. "I promise. I'll run."

Tesh threw his arms around Brin and hugged her tight. "Okay then."

"Assuming this has any chance of actually working"—Moya squinted into the brilliant first rays of the sun's face as it inched above the tree line—"we need to get going. No telling how much time Suri's got."

"Wait," Roan said. "We can't go."

"Now what?" Moya asked.

"That's only six," Roan said.

"Huh?" Moya replied.

Roan used her finger to point and count. "Me, Gifford, Brin, Tesh, Moya, and Tekchin—that's only six."

"Yes, it is, Roan, and we're all quite impressed that you can count," Moya said.

"But Malcolm said there would be seven."

"Who cares what Malcolm—"

"I'm going," Rain said.

Frost glared at the dwarf. "No."

"You're not gonna find her where they're going," Flood blurted out. Together he and Frost converged like protective parents on the smaller and younger looking dwarf. Frost had a finger out and pointed. "You're being ridiculous."

"Okay, now what the Tet are you three talking about?" Moya asked.

"You don't know that," Rain said to Frost. "I might find her."

"You looking for someone?" Moya asked. "In a swamp? Who?"

Rain looked sheepish. "I dunno."

Frost made a sound in his throat signifying disbelief. "O' course not. Knowing who it is would make too much sense, wouldn't it? But it's not 'cause of the swamp he's going. It's 'cause the trip is underground."

"There is a person, a Belgriclungreian, who is trapped at the bottom of the world," Rain explained, and Brin realized this was the most words in a row she'd ever heard the youngest dwarf speak. "She has been calling to me for years."

"She has not," Flood barked at him, bouncing on his toes, his eyes flaring.

"Wait, how do you—" Moya paused. "If she's trapped, and you don't know where, how do you even know about her?"

"She comes ta me. In me dreams," Rain said.

"Oh," Moya replied. "Oh-*kay*."

"They need one more," Rain said. "It's a sign."

"O' course it's not a sign, you damn fool."

"Malcolm told her seven." Rain pointed at Tressa. "It's a sign. It's why I went into Neith—both times."

"And remember how well that worked out," Flood said.

"I'm going, and that's the end of it."

"Are we all set then?" Moya asked. "You need to get a blanket or something, Rain? How about you, Tesh?"

"Aye. For a day and a night, I'm good a'right," Rain answered.

Tesh put his hands on the pommels of his swords. "I got all I need for a short trip."

"Okay then, let's go," Moya commanded.

Frost and Flood looked at Rain, and they both sighed. Rain put down his big pickax and gave each an embrace, clapping backs. Then both Frost and Flood tugged once on Rain's little beard. Why, Brin hadn't a clue.

With a final deep breath, Moya and Tekchin led the group down the slope to the north, eight walking into an unknown world and an uncertain fate.

After many days of rain, the morning stood out brilliantly. Not just cloudless, the hazy face of summer had been replaced by a fierce glare born out of a deep-blue sky. Heat vanquished by a chill, the air was crisp and smelled of dying leaves instead of baking grass. Sharp blades of sunlight cut through trees and burned away mists that had pooled during the night in deep hollows.

Brin had always loved fall. Food was plentiful; the work was light; the forest became a painting of bright reds and yellows, and there was the promise of the coming cold, when the dahl's residents would gather around fires and tell stories to pass the many dark hours. She missed those days cuddled between her mother and father, wrapped in layers of soft wool. Safe and warm, she heard neither the crackling fire nor the howling wind, which was drowned out by the booming voices of storytellers recounting adventures with expressive hands that cast shadows of monsters on the lodge's walls. Those same winter winds were now on their way, and she was wearing her mother's wool once more, but the story being told was hers, and the monsters would not be mere shadows.

Tekchin and Moya walked in the lead of their little group of eight. Brin had begun the pleasant downhill trip beside Tesh. She'd taken his hand at the start, but he'd let go. For miles, they hadn't exchanged a word. She thought he was still angry, but she knew that sometimes Tesh was just quiet. That morning he'd seemed as chilly as the weather. By midday, he had moved up alongside Rain while Brin had fallen in beside Gifford and

Roan, who both rode on Naraspur's back. Roan had protested, not wanting to burden the animal with two, but it was clear Gifford loved riding with Roan's arms around his waist.

Walking alongside, Brin had a perfect view of Gifford's leg, strapped into the brace Roan had made for him. "Does it hurt?" she asked. "Having your leg tied up like that, I mean."

"No," he replied. "Well, not much."

Roan glanced down to the brace with a concerned look. "I can loosen the straps if you—"

"It's fine," he assured her. "I want them tight."

"Okay," Roan said, but she didn't look better. She seemed just as pained as Gifford, maybe more.

Brin picked a different subject. "I hear you can do magic like Suri, Gifford. That's amazing."

Gifford smiled his lopsided grin. "Well, not exactly, but she has taught me a few things. I managed a location weave. It's simple, and I just follow the steps. It's a beginning, I guess."

"He's scared," Roan said as she rocked with the movement of the horse.

"Really?" Brin asked.

Gifford nodded. "I suppose so."

Brin waited, but Gifford didn't add anything. "Scared of what?"

Roan and Gifford exchanged uncomfortable looks.

"It's okay," Brin said. "I was just making conversation."

Brin fondly remembered the discussions they'd had on the ship to Neith that had passed the hours, but this trip was different. Tesh seemed upset with her for coming. Moya didn't want to be there at all, Tressa was abrasive, and Rain and Roan were always quiet. Now even Gifford, whom she saw as her last refuge, had become awkward.

This is going to be a long walk, Brin thought.

"It's just," Gifford began unexpectedly at the same time that he wiped the sweat from his nose, "I don't want to upset anyone."

"Huh?" Brin asked.

"He means he doesn't want to *terrify* people," Roan explained. "He just can't pronounce the word."

"Oh," Brin said.

"Su-wee says a bad life with obstacles and pain amplifies the magic," Gifford explained. "If you have big, ah . . . pwoblems, then you can have a lot of intensity, a lot of pow-ah."

"Power?" Brin asked.

Gifford nodded, embarrassed, and Brin thought that was strange. Funny the things that bothered people. She felt that if she couldn't talk clearly, it wouldn't concern her. At least she wanted to believe that, but if she were Gifford, maybe she would feel differently.

"Magic is made by pulling pow-ah fwom the outside, fwom living things, like dipping a bucket in a well. But people have wells inside them, too. I guess I have an unusually deep well because I've had lots of pwoblems."

"Oh," Brin said, again.

He made a face at her that looked to be part smirk, part grin, part pout, and totally indecipherable.

Brin smiled back, but it wasn't a happy face she made. She knew parents who pointed at Gifford when warning their children about angering the gods. Such accusations made no sense, as Gifford had never done anything to deserve any punishment, nor had his parents, but there was no doubt the gods hated all three of them. His mother died giving birth to their only child, and his father had to live with her sacrifice in exchange for Gifford. And Gifford—well, he had to be Gifford.

"So when I do stuff," he went on, "I'm anxious that I might . . . you know . . ."

"Kill everyone," Roan said. "When he tried to light the signal fire at Perdif, he incinerated the whole village. Singed some of his own hair."

"I see," Brin said.

Gifford pointed to his eyebrows. "Came back." Again, he showed that inscrutable expression that Brin suspected would have been a self-deprecating half smile if it had been worn by anyone else.

That afternoon, as Brin walked through hip-deep grass and waved away gnats while struggling with a heavy pack, the odds of actually finding a way to save Suri felt remote. Reality was back, and the tangible world held contempt for dreams. "Do you think it's possible? Can the Tetlin Witch really be alive, and will she be willing to show us a way to get into the Fhrey city? I mean, last night it all seemed like it was possible, but now . . ." She looked up at the bright-blue sky. "I don't know."

"Why not?" Gifford said. "Amazing things happen all the time. Look at me. *I'm* still alive."

Brin smiled, thinking it a joke, and then she wasn't so sure.

They continued all that day hiking downhill across open ground of late-season flowers and brown tasseled grass. Everyone kept glancing to the right as they passed Mount Mador—just too big, too magnificent to ignore. The snowcapped peak appeared a living thing, a white-haired god holding up the sky. To the north, just beyond a river, lay a huge forest. Hill upon hill, its dark trees blanketed everything as far as the eye could see. The wood didn't look like the Crescent Forest. The Harwood was denser, less inviting, and Brin was happy to hear they weren't going in. Their path turned due east, following the river—actually more like a wetland.

Down by the water's edge, the view grew hazy, as a stubborn mist lingered. They rested on a grassy bank and ate alongside the rushes, listening to water gurgling a pretty tune. Cloaks and capes were cast aside, spread on the grass like picnic blankets as the sun grew warmer. Brin was once again beside Tesh, eating one of her apples and watching the tall grass blow in the breeze. Tesh still hadn't said much, but she no longer thought he was angry. He wasn't *not* talking to her, just not talking at all. The man was moody. Most likely, he was worried about her. Instead, Brin tried to enjoy the moment by leaning back and feeling the sun on her face. *Beautiful days shouldn't be ignored.*

"It gets more difficult from this point," Tekchin declared. "You said we were looking for an island where the swamp meets the sea, right?" he asked Tressa, who nodded. "Okay, so be sure to fill up on water, and drink deep while you can. That's the bog below us." Tekchin pointed downstream toward where the pretty rushes grew dense. Brambles rose, and stunted trees crowded together. "Plenty of freshwater creeks like this feed into it, but the water turns briny and black as we head east toward the sea."

"So we're almost there?" Brin asked.

"You *are* there. You're looking at the Swamp of Ith—the start of it, anyway."

This admission turned everyone's head toward the mist downstream, where Brin noticed dark birds circling. She found it hard to imagine they were already there. Somehow, she'd thought it would take longer. The alleged home of the Tetlin Witch turned out to be only a few hours away. The sheer convenience felt contrived to the point that Brin was all the more certain that Tressa was lying—well, perhaps not lying, but certainly wrong.

"Doesn't look *too* bad," Moya said as if she didn't believe her own admission. "I mean, it *is* just a swamp."

"It gets worse." Tekchin reclined on his side near Moya, an arm propping his head, the sun shining off his bronze armor. "Years ago, the Galantians came down this way, and we ducked our heads inside. Miserable place, really." He looked at Gifford. "Be best if you left Naraspur up here where there's plenty of water and grass. Down there, the ground gets soft and muddy. You don't want her to get mired. You can tether her to a line between a couple of trees. She should be okay for a day or even two."

Roan pulled a bit of rope out of a pack, tied it to Naraspur, and set to work.

"What exactly are we trying to find out there?" Moya aimed her question at Brin, but everyone looked at Tressa.

"Malcolm said it was an island," the woman explained. "A sort of a secret island, I guess."

"Secret?" Moya said doubtfully. "How is an island secret?"

"I'm not sure, he just said it wasn't easy to find. That she makes it that way."

"She?"

"The Tetlin Witch."

Moya stared at Tressa. "You aren't serious." She turned to look at Brin. "She's not, is she?"

Brin nodded. "Malcolm told her the Tetlin Witch lived on the island, and the witch will show us the underground passage, which I guess is also hidden, right?"

Tressa nodded.

"Tressa," Moya said, "are you making all this up? Is this some kind of joke? It is, isn't it?"

Tressa continued to sit on her blanket, eating an apple of her own.

"The Tetlin Witch is just a legend. If you make me go down there, and I find out this is all a lie, I will—"

Tressa spit out what she'd been chewing and began to sing:

"Far beyond the woodland hills, beyond the mountains vile,
Hidden in a mist-soaked swamp upon an awful isle.
She haunts the lapping blackened pools and creeping ivy ways,
And there awaits with hair of brown and eyes of greenish-gray."

"What the Tet is that?" Moya asked.

Tressa had a surprisingly nice voice. Not beautiful—she had no real talent for singing—but Brin never would have expected anything remotely pleasant to come out of Tressa, who, like most full-time drunks, spoke as if a family of frogs had made a home in her throat.

"It's a song Malcolm taught me."

Brin was shocked. "Never heard that one before."

"Malcolm mentioned it's really old," Tressa said.

Moya stood up. "Let me get this straight." She held up a finger. "We're going through that swamp to find the hidden home of the legendary Tetlin Witch." She held up a second. "And she's going to show us a secret passage." She added a third. "And it's going to take us to the Fhrey capital city. Is that right? Do I have that straight?"

"Look at that, everyone." Tressa grinned at her. "It's so easy even Moya can follow it."

Moya closed her pack and hoisted it on a shoulder. "I really hope you're not messing with us, Tressa. I really do—for the sake of your face and my knuckles. Let's do this!" Moya grabbed up Audrey, which she'd been using like a walking stick. "Let's go knock on a witch's door."

CHAPTER TWENTY-ONE

The Swamp of Ith

We all have many secrets. Some we tell, and others we bury. The worst ones are those that come back to haunt us.

— THE BOOK OF BRIN

The swamp wasn't the Harwood, but even so, Tesh was worried.

I should never have let her come.

He'd started cursing himself only hours after setting out. There was no protecting people in the wild. Tesh remembered the arrow in Meeks's left eye and realized he should have stood his ground and demanded that Brin stay behind. She was the one good thing in his life. Perhaps the only good thing in all the world. She wasn't like anyone else. The woman was kind, and good, and beautiful. The rest of the world could burn to ash, and it wouldn't matter so long as she was safe.

I should have gone to Nyphron. He felt certain the commander didn't know about this trip. If he had, he would have put a stop to it. Being keenig, Persephone could have overridden his order, but she rarely intervened in military decisions. *Brin would have hated me, and I would have lost her forever, but she'd be alive. This whole thing is stupid.*

He tried to remind himself that it wasn't the Harwood. They were a day or two away from the action, from the war. This would only be a long, unpleasant, and fruitless hike. But they were in a place he didn't know, and his Dureyan "optimism" was kicking in. In the Harwood, he'd developed a special sense, an ability to smell danger, to know when things weren't right. He'd learned to rely on that instinct. Doing so had saved his life and the lives of his men, but in this swamp, in this unfamiliar place, he was blind, and he wasn't in charge. And it wasn't just his special sense that was diminished; everything was difficult to see. Visibility dropped the moment they entered the bog, and it grew worse with each step. The mist thickened, the grass grew taller, and the trees—if he could even call them that, as they were wretchedly warped things—rose all around, growing out of the murky water on arched roots, as if revolted by where they stood. Mounds of moss-wrapped stones created a patchwork of foothold islets in an endless black pond. The wet surface was covered by a thin skin of green scum, under which who knew what might be lurking.

Weighed down by armor, Tesh was caught in a world saturated by alien sounds and the pungent stench of decay. The woman he loved waded somewhere ahead of him through the same leech-infested mud. She was only steps away but too far for him to see her clearly, and—with his feet shackled by muck and water—too far to reach if something awful happened. Tesh continued to wade forward through hip-deep water and neck-high fear. Nothing had happened. Not a sound that couldn't have been a bird, frog, or insect disturbed their trek, and he'd seen nothing but shadows and mist. But that only made it worse. Tesh rarely feared the adversary he could see, the one he knew. It was the enemy he couldn't find, who he didn't even know was there, that was the greatest threat.

That and his own mind.

In his head, he saw Brin shot with an arrow, stabbed with a spear, beheaded, or cleaved in two by some ax or sword. Each image was wrought in fine detail, drawn from his vast collection of memories. Tesh had always known he was haunted—first by his parents, who cried out for revenge, and then Sebek, who still whispered in his ear at night, *Time for another lesson.* Then as he entered the war, he was hounded by all those he had slain. He remembered each one. He forced himself to stare, to ponder, to reflect on each death, to savor it. He'd tasted their blood, washed in it. And once, he had spent a night beside a decapitated elf, using his head as a pillow. Even Edgar thought him strange for that. The blood never sated him, even when he literally drank it. Mere blood wasn't enough to drown the one memory he still carried—the night everyone he'd ever known had been killed.

Sloshing through the Swamp of Ith, his fear consumed him. Having seen, and been, the face of death, his mind was quick to supply the nightmares to justify his concern. He wished he had Edgar, Atkins, and Brigham—people he could count on, people who could—

Not the Harwood, he reassured himself. *No elves here.* Then he looked over at Tekchin. *Well, not many elves, that is.*

Tesh took a deep breath of decomposing air and tried to focus. He waded forward, feeling his feet being sucked into soft, root-meshed muck and noticing that where his legs cut the surface there was dark water below. They weren't following any path he could tell. Brin had moved forward to speak to Moya, leaving Tesh to trudge behind Tressa. In the tall, dense grass, he could only reliably see Tressa's back.

They were called *blades of grass* for good reason. Tesh had cut his hand more than once when his palms slid along a stiff razor-like edge. After the first cut, he began using his dagger to pry his way through, but when he heard Tressa curse, he'd given the blade to her. He hoped Brin wasn't in similar straits and wished she would wait for him. He considered passing Tressa but guessed Brin was still mad. She hadn't said much that whole day, and when they had set off, she purposefully dropped back to talk with Roan and Gifford rather than stay with him. He couldn't blame her. She just hadn't seen what he had. She didn't know how horrible the world could get and couldn't possibly understand. In so many ways, she was still a child. His job was to protect her, even if she hated him for it.

Best to leave her be. Let the anger run its course.

Tesh grimaced and pressed on in Tressa's wake. Dressed in a man's shirt many sizes too large and belted at the waist with a strap whose excess tongue hung down and slapped her thighs, Tressa looked as if she'd already been through her own war. But she hadn't given up. Tesh appreciated that—that and her thorny temperament. She'd accused him of lying when he offered her his dagger. When he handed it over, she'd hesitated and asked what he wanted in return. This, and knowing everyone else hated the woman, convinced him she had to have Dureyan blood. He couldn't help liking her.

"Snake!" He heard Moya call.

"Snake!" shouted Brin.

Tesh drew his left sword and pushed forward.

"Snake!" Tressa yelled.

Tesh didn't take another step, as out of the grass, skimming across the surface of the water, came a massive serpent as thick as his own thigh and too long to judge, black-and-green scales curling through the slime. Without a passing glance, it slithered by.

"Snake!" he called back to Roan and Gifford, who were bringing up the rear.

With a pounding heart he watched it go, disappearing into the grass. Maybe that would be the worst of it.

A moment later, he realized it was getting dark.

"We can't sleep up here," Tekchin said.

"Sleep?" Moya blurted. "Who do you think is going to be doing that tonight? I'd hoped we would have been there by now, but we're not making very good time."

They were all mostly huddled out of the water, some on a small mossy mound that might have been rocks or a trio of rotting tree stumps. In the growing dark, it was difficult to tell. Moya had called the halt to their aquatic trek, and Tekchin wasn't pleased. No one was, but they did appreciate the opportunity to climb out of the water that had been thigh-high for most of them and waist-high for Rain.

Tesh took the chance to reunite with Brin. Her anger appeared to have burned out, since she buried her head in his chest. Her hands were wrapped in strips of soaked cloth. She was breathing hard and looked exhausted. Squeezing her, he was reminded how small she was and how angry he was with himself.

"Anyone else have leeches?" Tressa asked.

"I'm afraid to look," Brin said.

"We need to find solid ground before we run out of light," Tekchin insisted.

"What are you talking about? It's already dark," Brin said.

"Fhrey eyes see better than ours in low light," Moya explained. "Look, we aren't Galantians. We can't go all night without stopping."

Tesh understood this to be the problem of going into the wilds with novices. They didn't understand the hardships required to survive. "You're both right. We can't stay here, but we can't continue to wade around aimlessly. Tekchin and I will scout ahead. We can make a sweep. The two of us have a much better chance to find—"

"No," Moya said. "We aren't splitting up."

"But together, Tekchin and I could—"

"I said no, Tesh." Her tone was firm and final. "We only need to rest a bit."

They stood there, listening to the creaks and caws of the swamp as it settled into the night. Finally, Moya ordered them forward once more.

Night in the swamp was a surreal thing. Crawling vines hanging from splintered logs that protruded from the water became fractured bones wrapped in shredded clothes. Swelling trees shrouded in leaves masqueraded as a host of shambling ghouls. But these were illusions. Years spent in the Harwood had taught Tesh never to rely on sight alone nor to allow fear to conquer reason.

It's only a swamp. Just murky water, rotting wood, grass, mud, vines, bugs and . . .

Tesh spotted a nest tucked in a low tree only inches above the waterline. A precarious place for a bird's home even if the local snakes weren't the size of battering rams. Tesh would have thought it abandoned, fallen from somewhere above, except it wasn't empty.

Eggs in autumn? Tesh wondered.

He veered toward it.

Amid the woven twigs, grass, and black feathers, lay three glistening eyeballs. One looked up, another pointed to the left, and the third was so mangled and torn that the pupil was missing altogether.

"What in the blessed name of Elan is that?" Tesh whispered to himself.

Tekchin's Fhrey ears heard him, and the Galantian waded over and peered in. He stared for a moment then asked, "Why *three*, do you think?"

"Seriously? The number is what surprises you?"

"Just that most things have two eyes."

Tesh only looked at him.

Tekchin shrugged. "Just makes you wonder if there are things in here with three eyes."

"Or three things with one eye," Tesh muttered as he turned and struggled to penetrate the shadows that surrounded them. Listening was useless. The swamp rattled with the noise of a million peeping frogs, whining insects, and lapping water. Everything was louder with the darkness, and the night seemed deeper after finding the nest of eyes.

"What is it?" Moya asked. She'd stopped the line while they studied the nest.

"Nothing," Tesh and Tekchin said together and headed back to the group.

"You're like a thousand years old, right?" Tesh whispered to Tekchin. "Ever seen anything like that before?"

"Saw a vulture messing with an arm once," Tekchin replied softly. "Was pecking at the elbow end, pulling on tendons, making the fingers move like the hand was beckoning—but no, nothing like that."

"Not a *good* omen then, I'm guessing."

"Wouldn't think so."

"Can you determine what color they were?" In the dim light, Tesh hadn't been able to tell, but he thought the elf might have seen.

"Why do you care?" Tekchin asked.

"Brown eyes, human. Blue eyes, Fhrey."

"Oh," Tekchin said. "Couldn't tell, but if you want to go back and carry them around until morning—"

"That's okay. Not that curious."

Splunk!

Something splashed. Something big.

Tesh pulled both swords and peered hard into the dark, but he failed to catch any movement.

"What are you seeing, Tek?" Moya called.

"Nothing," he said, his own sword out and catching what little of the moonlight pierced the swamp thatch.

"I thought Moya said Fhrey can see in the dark," Tressa said.

"We see better than Rhunes, but nothing can see in the dark," Tekchin replied. "Not even owls or goblins. How about dwarfs?" he called back.

"Aye, yer right," Rain replied. "Can't see a thing in total darkness."

"And you don't see anything out there?" Moya asked again.

"Nope."

They waited. Nothing happened.

"C'mon," Moya said, sloshing forward, "but keep your swords out."

Wading through cold, putrid water as the last memories of sunlight faded, Moya wanted to kill Tressa. And it wasn't just because it was her fault that Moya likely had a dozen or more leeches sucking on her ankles and calves. The woman had been a misery ever since she spread Heath Coswall's story that Moya had slept with him down by the White Oak Bridge. Moya had, but Tressa insinuated that Coswall was just one of many. Everyone believed her because part of the story was true, and the rest was exactly what they'd expected from Moya. Even her own mother had believed it.

Tressa was four years older than Moya, which didn't make any difference now that the two women were in their thirties, but when Moya was thirteen and Tressa seventeen, it meant the world. Tressa wasn't just older, she'd had four sisters, three brothers, and a pair of respected parents. Moya was the only child of Audrey, the dahl's washerwoman, who couldn't recall the name of Moya's father. Moya's mother had a bad reputation, and when Moya turned fourteen and exhibited the same wild tendencies, assumptions were made. Tressa could have wielded her seventeen-year-old clout to defend Moya but chose to attack her instead. Easy targets were comfortable stepping-stones for the likes of Tressa.

Age had only ripened the poison inside the woman. She went from childhood brat to a full-grown bitch without ever losing her love for bullying. No one could convince Moya that Tressa hadn't known about Konniger's plans to kill Reglan and Persephone.

Tressa likely masterminded the whole thing. Konniger was always a few seeds short of a harvest, and ambitious plotting is Tressa's kind of thing. This is likely another scheme. The problem stumping Moya: *What is the point? What's to gain? I could understand it if she wasn't here, too, but the woman is in the soup along with us. She is just as miserable as everyone else.*

"We not alone," Gifford said ominously.

Moya stopped. She looked around, saw nothing, and then tried to see down the line, but it was too dark. "What do you mean?" she asked, straining to hear beyond the racket of nightly chirps and chatters. The continual creaking, croaking, and hooting was beyond aggravating.

"Something is close," Gifford said.

"Something? Or do you mean someone?"

"Some*thing*," Gifford confirmed.

"Tekchin, you see anything?"

"No," the Galantian replied. "Nothing but water and trees."

Moya struggled to bend Audrey and loop the string without letting her touch the water, which was impossible, and she was forced to dip the bow in order to press the end against the poor excuse for ground. *If something is coming, why haven't the crickets and frogs shut up? They do when something is around.*

"I don't see anything," she said, testing the strength of her line and finding it reassuringly stiff. She didn't let it twang. Moya didn't want to give anything away.

"Me neither," Brin said. She was two people back from Moya, with Tesh quickly moving to her side.

"By Mari," Tressa burst out, "what in Rel are you seeing, Gifford?"

"I don't *see* it," Gifford admitted. "I *feel* it. This whole place is . . . ee-we."

"Eerie," Roan said, feeling the need to clarify.

"You *feel it?*" Moya asked. "Is this some kind of magic thing?"

"Yeah, I guess so. And I'm not usually good at it. Most times it's just a fleeting sensation like a chill o' something. That's what Su-wee taught me, but I had a tough time telling what was what. Only now . . ."

"Yes?"

"I'm kinda not having that pwoblem. I'm getting lots of feelings."

"But it's *just* a feeling, right?" Moya stopped short of nocking an arrow. "'Cause, I mean, I've got plenty of those myself."

"No, it's not the same."

Moya could only reliably see a few feet. Beyond that, something would have to step into one of the few pools of moonlight for her to have a chance of hitting it. "Okay, so what does it *feel* like? What's out there?"

Gifford was quiet, and all the heads Moya could see turned in his direction.

"I'm not—I—I don't know."

"C'mon, Giff, give me something, for Tet's sake. Raow, snake, giant, human, dwarf, Fhrey, animal, vegetable, mineral. What?"

"None of those."

"None of—ah—oooh-kay." Moya didn't like the sound of that, and she hesitated to ask her next question. "If you had to make a guess, would you say it felt good or bad?"

"Bad," Gifford answered far too quickly.

Moya didn't care for the way he said the word, either; it came out with an apprehensive weight.

"Most unquestionably bad," he felt compelled to add. "Actually, I feel lots of *bad* moving about. This place is . . ."

"Is what, Gifford?"

"Honestly? Only way I can say it is—*haunted*."

"Haunted," Moya repeated. She wasn't questioning him; she believed it with every fiber of her being. Gifford had merely put a name to what she'd been feeling since they entered. *Haunted*. Saying it out loud made it real.

"Is it the witch?"

"I don't know. Maybe."

"Coming or going?"

Another pause. The silent vacuum filled with the nerve-ripping concert of the swamp.

"Coming or going, Gifford?" Moya's voice rose higher than she'd intended.

"Coming," he finally replied, his voice growing softer. "And . . . I think they listening to us."

"They?"

"Over there!" Tekchin pointed into the trees off to their left.

"What is it?" Moya asked, but before Tekchin could answer, she saw for herself.

A man walked through a patch of moonlight. Dressed in forest armor, the sort Tesh and his Techylors wore in the Harwood, he was walking toward them.

"Shoot him!" Tesh shouted.

Moya hesitated. She wasn't about to release an arrow at an unknown man, and the guy she was looking at was clearly that, a human wearing familiar gear.

We're not far from the front lines of the war, she thought. *This guy might have been separated from his squad in the forest, run south, and got lost in the swamp.*

"Shoot him, Moya!" Tesh shouted again.

"Why?"

Part of her answer came from noticing that the lost soldier wasn't coming at her, but making straight for Tesh, who drew both of his blades and stepped in front of Brin.

"Shoot him, Moya!" This time it was Brin who yelled.

As he grew closer, the lost soldier burst into a run. That was when Moya noticed the odd lack of splashing. The soldier left no wake in the water. She also noticed a faint but undeniable glow around him. But neither of these caused her to shoot. Instead, it was the broken end of an arrow sticking out of his left eye socket. Moya drew back and let her own arrow fly.

A perfect shot, but it failed to hit the target. The arrow zipped through the man's chest and continued until it hit black water with a resounding *ʒoop!* An instant later, the lost soldier was gone.

Moya searched the darkness. "What just happened?" Everyone Moya could see was staring wide-eyed and breathing hard, but no one answered. "What was that?"

"I—I recognized him," Tesh said. "And I'm guessing Brin did as well. That was Meeks."

"One of Tesh's new recruits, who was killed," Brin said. "The one who always called me *ma'am.*"

Moya saw Brin's hands trembling, and realized her own were doing the same. She was cold, but not that cold. Her heart was trotting, and if anything, she felt numb. *Haunted,* she thought.

"Giff? Is it gone?"

"Nope."

Moya searched the gloom, pivoting as best she could in the muck, but saw nothing. Tekchin was beside her, his sword out. He, too, peered into the night.

"This is all your fault, Tesh!" A voice, oddly muffled, fluttered in and out as if something were trying to block the words. Meeks was calling from the dark, howling and fading like a rush of winter wind; the unnatural sound of the words sent a chill up Moya's back. *"You really should have taken the time to bury me, Prymus."*

"It's a manes," Tesh said with miserable certainty.

"Anyone know where it is?" Moya asked.

"You should have buried me, Tessshhh," the voice hissed. *"How could you leave me like that? I was just a kid. I trusted you, believed in you. You got me killed, then left me—left me to be eaten by animals. I have no stone!"* The voice grew to an inhuman volume, shaking the trees around them. *"No STONE!"*

"Sorry about that," Tesh replied. "We were in a hurry."

"A hurry! I have no way to enter Phyre! For eternity, I will walk the face of Elan. I am but a wraith trapped between two worlds because you were too busy!"

"What's a manes, Brin?" Moya asked.

"A ghost," she replied. "The spirit of the dead unable or unwilling to pass into the afterlife. They roam the world, often tormenting those who wronged them."

"Can it hurt us?" Moya asked.

"I don't know. We shouldn't be able to interact at all. A manes is a spirit, and we're flesh. Different worlds entirely, but . . ."

"But what?"

"We shouldn't be able to see him."

"Oh! I can hurt you, Tesshhh!" The ghostly glowing figure of Meeks appeared once more, this time far more translucent and hazy. He had a sinister grin on his face as he glared at his old commander. *"Only two left. Isn't that right, Tesh? Or do you include Moya? She's a Galantian, too, isn't she?"*

Hearing it speak her name, Moya shivered. *It knows who I am?*

Tesh advanced on the shade, pushing through the water with swords high.

"Tesh, don't!" Brin called.

He swung, but his blades passed through the manes as if it were smoke, and Meeks laughed. *"What's wrong, Prymus? Don't want me to tell them your secret?"*

Tesh swung again.

The shimmering image of Meeks laughed. *"Tesh killed Sebek in his sickbed the night of the final attack on Alon Rhist. He killed Eres in the Harwood. The prymus made it look like just another casualty of war. He did the same thing with Anwir. Invited him out away from the camp as the others were setting up to leave. He took his time. After he had severed the Galantian's hands, and while he slowly cut off each one of Anwir's precious knots, Tesh told his story, believing Anwir would never have the chance to breathe it to another living soul. He didn't, but he told me. You didn't give Anwir a stone, either, Tesh. That was your mistake. Anwir isn't the vengeful sort like I am. Still, that didn't stop him from telling me what you did. I'm betting Tesh is saving Nyphron for last, which means, Tekchin, you're next."*

"It's not true," Brin said.

"It is! He's hunted and murdered all the Galantians. Only two left . . . only two, but maybe now you won't get a chance to finish, Tesh. So close. So very close. How disappointing to die unfulfilled. How does it feel, Tesh? To come so near and yet be unable to take that final step? Don't worry, Tesh. I won't leave you alone. I'll be with you always. Look for me in your dreams; watch for me in the dark."

The image faded, and once more they were alone with the concert of the swamp. No one moved or said anything for a long moment.

"Is it true?" Moya asked Tesh.

She and Tekchin stared at him.

"Anwir was killed in an ambush as we were getting ready to leave the Harwood," Tesh said.

It sounded like a denial, but it wasn't, and Moya took a step closer.

"Meeks is lying," Tekchin said. Both Tesh and Moya looked at the Fhrey, surprised. "No offense to Tesh, but a Rhune couldn't have killed

Sebek even when he was wounded, much less a healthy Fhrey like Eres. And there is no way he could have gotten the better of Anwir—certainly not in a forest—not to his face. Their deaths were their fates. It was Ferrol's will. Anwir's days were done, and he was given an honorable death in battle."

Moya pointed at Tesh. "He was with each one of them when they died."

Tekchin made a dismissive sound. "Everyone knows Sebek was killed by the Shahdi. Tesh was just a boy then, and it would have taken five or six Fhrey to kill Sebek, even wounded as he was. Eres . . ." Tekchin hesitated. "Eres was never the same after Medak died. Even Galantians have their limits, and he blamed himself for his brother's death. Tesh didn't kill them. He couldn't have."

"Of course he didn't kill them!" Brin declared. "Moya, what's wrong with you?"

Moya continued to stare at Tesh.

You hate them, don't you? she had asked Tesh years ago when he was only a boy. She couldn't remember his reply, but she couldn't forget the murderous look in his eye. She didn't know what it was then, but she thought she did now. *I caught a glimpse of his soul.*

CHAPTER TWENTY-TWO

Treya's Gifts

I was cold, hungry, exhausted, and oh-so scared. I felt sorry for myself, believing that I—that we—were sacrificing so much more than everyone else. Then I thought of Suri, and I felt ashamed.

— THE BOOK OF BRIN

Mawyndulë didn't like the way it kept staring. The Rhune glared out through the bars at him, legs up in a tight ball and back against the rear of the cage. In the darkness, the campfire flickered in its eyes, giving the Rhune a sinister, demonic look. He wondered what it was thinking, then caught himself and realized it wasn't—it was a Rhune.

But even animals have thoughts, don't they?

He got up and moved closer to the campfire. The Rhune's eyes never left him. If it did think, if it was capable of thought, Mawyndulë didn't suppose it was wishing for him to have a long and prosperous life.

It hates me. It wants to kill me because of what I did to Arion.

The sensation was disturbing. To feel the thing's gaze while only a few feet away was like standing on the edge of a cliff, looking down and wondering how it would feel to take that step—what it would be like to fall. Mawyndulë had been to war; he'd faced the enemy across the Grandford, but it hadn't felt like this. The enemy at Alon Rhist was a faceless thing on the far side of the river that existed more as a vague idea, and the hate was distributed across an army. This—this glaring Rhune in a box—this was personal.

It's not going to give up the secret. Not now.

Mawyndulë frowned. His father and Jerydd, in their combined dusty stupidity, had ruined everything. None of it was Mawyndulë's fault, but they would blame him somehow. People always wanted to hold others accountable when catastrophes occurred.

They should have placated the Rhune longer, humored it more.

No, Mawyndulë realized. *Wouldn't have mattered.* The old kel was too arrogant. He couldn't have managed to pretend, even for a moment, that the deal was legitimate. Mawyndulë tried to imagine Jerydd politely chatting with the Rhune, having tea and smiling. He found it easier to imagine rain falling up. On that at least, Mawyndulë sympathized. The idea of placating a Rhune was unimaginable.

I would never have agreed to escort it to Estramnadon if the thing wasn't locked in a box.

The very thought of its being free sent a chill through him, and he shivered. On the other side of their camp, the Rhune noticed, and for a second, he thought it smiled.

Doesn't matter. We'll get the secret somehow. Vasek will cut it out if he has to.

For a moment, Mawyndulë considered how he could extract the information himself. He could put bugs in its head—or make the Rhune think he had. He could burn it, boil its blood, melt its hands, freeze its fingers and shatter them with a stick. The Art was far superior to any traditional torture.

Mawyndulë sat down near the fire, poking at it with a stick and realizing that if he got the secret from the Rhune, he wouldn't have to cart it back. He could kill it right there and be done. Then he could return with the problem solved. Mawyndulë would be the hero of Erivan, savior of his people.

I could even make the first dragon and send it to Jerydd myself, maybe this very night.

He began thinking of the best method for extracting the secret, something that would produce the most anguish but not impair the creature's ability to speak.

It would be best if I didn't need to extort the information. Better if I could think of some way to pull it out directly.

He stared at the Rhune as he contemplated a way to use the Art to either search its thoughts or compel it to answer his questions. He smiled as various possibilities trickled through his head. Then his sight fell on the collar.

Ferrol be damned! He frowned in frustration, recalling the Rhune fighters who had defied the attacks of the Spider Corps.

He could still torture the Rhune, but he'd have to do it conventionally. The Orinfar collar protected as much as it hindered. Mawyndulë didn't relish the idea of getting into that cage with a stick, a brand, or a knife. Besides, it was too easy to make a mistake. The last thing he could afford to do was accidentally kill it. Both his father and Jerydd would hate him if he returned with a dead Rhune.

"Your bed is ready, my lord." Treya came over. "Are you done eating?"

Mawyndulë looked down at the bowl. "That was terrible, you know?"

"There's not much I can do on the road, my lord. I'll make you a nice pigeon pie when we get back." She smiled at him.

"Whatever." He scowled and resumed poking the burning logs. The end of the stick caught fire. He waved it out and watched as the smoking tip glowed orange. *I wonder how the Rhune would squeal if I jabbed it with this? Bet it would stop staring at me.*

"Going to be cold tonight." Treya was looking up at the dark canopy of trees and pulled her cloak tight to her neck, then glanced at the cage. "Poor thing will freeze. That shift is so thin."

"So?" He caught the stick on fire again, let it burn a bit, then once more waved the flames out.

Treya hadn't replied, and when he turned, he saw she, too, was staring at him. She wore that *my prince* expression.

"What?" he asked, throwing up his hands.

"You should give her your extra blanket."

"Absolutely not!"

"Why?"

"Are you insane? That's disgusting. I'd have to burn it afterward."

"You would not." Treya frowned at him as if she had the right to do so. "Look over there." She pointed at the cage. "See how the poor thing is shivering."

"Let it. I don't care."

Treya folded her arms. "What if she dies of exposure tonight, and we return to Estramnadon with a frozen corpse?"

"It won't get *that* cold."

"Doesn't have to be freezing for someone who's weak to die." She pursed her lips and raised her eyebrows. "Do we even know if they fed her while waiting for us to arrive? It may have been days since she ate. And what about water? Thirst is an even more pressing danger than the cold." She said all this with that familiar and annoying look that said: *I may only be your servant, but I'm smarter than you—and you know it.*

Mawyndulë rolled his eyes. "Okay, go ahead and give it the stupid blanket."

"And the leftover food?"

"What? Are you serious?"

Treya pointed to the pot where she had boiled the vegetables and millet. "If you don't want it, why can't she have it?"

Mawyndulë didn't want to give the Rhune anything, but he couldn't think of a reason to say no. Treya took his silence as permission and gathered up what was left in the pot, scooping it into a bowl.

"Remember which one that is," he told her sternly, "and don't ever serve me food from it."

"I'll be certain to burn it and bury the ashes while saying a prayer to Ferrol that He unmake the dust that it becomes." She said this with enough seriousness that Mawyndulë couldn't be certain if she was insulting him or not. Treya was good at that. He imagined most servants were.

"Watch yourself," he told her. "Be careful it doesn't grab your arm. Probably can't tell the difference between it and food."

Treya frowned back at him. "Of course she can. Why are you being this way? You're taking her to your father so she can tell him the secret to making dragons. If she's as primitive as you say, how can she instruct the fane in the Art?"

"It isn't going to instruct my father in the Art!" he burst out, loud enough to make Treya jump. "That's ridiculous! A Rhune can't teach a Miralyith anything! It may *have* a secret, the same way that rattling bag of yours *has* pots in it, but the bag can't teach you to cook! I can't believe you just said that. But I guess that's the sort of thing a lousy Gwydry would think, isn't it?" Mawyndulë threw the smoking stick into the fire, both he and it fuming.

How dare she say such a thing? I should punish her for that! Suggesting that the fane—the fane—could be schooled by a Rhune. And in the Art of all things! What an idiot!

"I'm sorry, my lord." Treya stood holding the bowl with both hands, a worried look on her face.

I scared her.

Mawyndulë felt awful. He almost never yelled at Treya. She was the only person who remembered his birthday, and she gave him a gift every year. The items were cheap and silly, but she never failed to give him a present, something made by hand. She was the only one who had cared when he failed his entrance exam to the Academy, telling him moronic jokes and putting fresh flowers in his room to cheer him up. And when he was sick, she brought him tea and sat at his bedside day and night. She'd even sung him lullabies when he was a child.

I'd forgotten that.

Looking at the hurt in her face, Mawyndulë felt uncomfortable. He wanted to say he was sorry, but he was the prince. It wouldn't be proper to apologize to a Gwydry servant. Such things would only lead to future problems.

He stood up. "I'm going for a walk. Have things taken care of by the time I get back."

Treya nodded and watched as he walked off into the trees.

Mawyndulë didn't go a long way, just down the slope along the bank of the river, far enough to be out of sight. He plopped himself down in the ferns, looked up at the forest canopy, and begged, "Why is it so hard being me?"

"Here you go," Treya said, passing the food between the bars. Despite her earlier bravado, she placed the bowl at the end of the cage farthest from Suri.

The mystic frowned in disappointment. *You don't believe your own words.*

Suri's indignation was short-lived when she noticed the servant wiping away tears. Once more, Suri wished she could tap the Art and explore Treya's feelings. Something wasn't right. The Fhrey appeared strong and intelligent, and yet she could be brought to tears by a rude outburst from a spoiled brat. Suri was missing something, but then again, she was missing a great many things: food and something warm to wear were tops on that list. As she crawled across the cage to the bowl, she hoped Treya hadn't forgotten about giving her a blanket. She *was* freezing. The intermittent bouts of shaking had left her physically exhausted, but they did provide an unexpected benefit. When her physical needs became more desperate, her mental state calmed. The primal demands for food and drink combined with the pain brought by the cold night's wind had beaten back the fear of imprisonment. Conscious thought returned, and that was a relief, even if it was mostly about food and the promise of something warm.

"Thank you," Suri told her as she clutched the bowl just below her chin and shoveled food into her mouth, an oatmeal-like grain with some kind of vegetable. Suri didn't know exactly what it was, and she didn't care. It was food, and she swallowed every morsel, licking her fingers, hands, and the bowl.

"Do you have a name?" Treya asked.

Of course I have a name! Didn't you just get done explaining to the bloodsucking leech of a prince how I'm not an animal? Suri thought. But with the hopes of a blanket still on her mind, she replied, "Yes, my name is Suri."

She held out the spotless bowl. "And this was extremely good. You're an excellent cook." This might have been a lie; Suri didn't know. She had no recollection of the taste of what she'd just consumed. That bowl full of *whatever* was the first thing she'd eaten in days. It could have been rat innards, and she would have been happy.

"May I have some water, as well?"

Treya stared at her, dumbfounded.

This is the difference between saying something you believe to be true and facing the truth of your words.

"I—ah—yes. Yes, of course." Treya left without taking the bowl.

Suri took pity on the Fhrey and moved away, putting as much distance as possible between the bowl and herself.

Treya returned with a waterskin. Without pause, she poured from it into the bowl.

I suppose letting me drink directly from the container would be too much to hope for. I should be happy she didn't pour it on the ground and expect me to lap it up.

"Thank you again," Suri told her. She went to the bowl and struggled to drink without spilling. She got most of it in her mouth. Treya gave her more, and Suri did better with the second helping. "I'm so cold that it's hard to hold the bowl steady." This at least was half true.

"Oh!" Treya said and rushed off. She returned with a bundle of cloth. "Here." She stuffed the wad through the bars. While not directly in front of Suri, it was nevertheless closer than she had set the bowl.

In the bundle was a knee-length smock as well as a blanket.

"That's my spare dress," Treya said, biting her lip as Suri lifted it.

The garment was clean and showed creases from where it had been folded. "Are you sure you want to give me this?" Suri asked even as she pulled the dress over her head. The thing was too big and the wide neck hung off one shoulder, but it was warm. "He didn't say you could give me clothes."

Treya looked in the direction Mawyndulë had walked. Suri expected to see fear, but what she saw instead was sadness. *She wasn't frightened about being yelled at or even angry about his lack of respect. She was hurt. Maybe they're lovers?* Suri was no expert on people or relationships, so she wasn't sure, but there was something going on between them.

"He's not awful, you know," Treya said. "He's a prince—he has to be strong and self-confident because one day he will rule."

It seemed like Treya was trying to convince herself as well as Suri about that.

Suri wrapped the blanket around her shoulders and pulled it tight to her neck. "You've been very kind to me. Why?"

Treya looked surprised, then thoughtful, and then she shrugged. "I've never met a Rhune. I've heard all sorts of stories about big hairy brutes with sharp fangs that want to kill all of us, but you aren't any of those things. You're actually kind of pretty. I even like the markings." She traced a finger on her own face. "Do they mean anything?"

Suri nodded. "They mean *me*."

Treya looked puzzled for a moment then nodded as if she understood. "I wouldn't want to see a dog treated the way you've been—and you're not a dog."

"But I'm not Fhrey, either."

"No . . ." Treya said. "But not all Fhrey are treated the same. I'm not a Miralyith. I'm a Gwydry."

"I heard."

Treya nodded and again looked to the forest. "Sometimes I think they forget we're Fhrey, too. That's not good for a future fane."

"I don't suppose you'd consider letting me out of this cage?" Suri asked.

Treya's eyes grew wide at the thought.

"I promise not to run away or bite your arm off or anything—honest. I—I just have a problem with being sealed up. It—it scares me. The walls, they—I need to be able to get out. It's not a normal Rhune thing. It's just me. I feel sort of sick. I don't even like houses."

"I'm sorry. I can't do that." Treya was shaking her head. "I don't—" Her lips betrayed a smile as she realized. "I don't even have the key. I *can't* let you out."

Suri didn't know what a key was, although Arion had used the word often, and usually when referring to Suri. "Well, thank you for the food and clothes. It's possible—no, likely—that you saved my life." Suri looked at the forest. "He wouldn't have given me anything."

Treya took the bowl back, nodding as she did. "Don't hate him."

Oh, that milk was spilled when he killed Arion. If this collar weren't around my neck, I'd turn that two-legged tick into a bloated pus-filled pimple and then pop him. Suri didn't say any of that, either, but she also couldn't lie, not to someone whom she suspected really might have saved her life. Instead, she simply nodded.

"We'll be in Estramnadon soon," Treya said. "I'm certain they'll let you out there."

Again, Suri nodded, but she wasn't certain of anything anymore except that she did like Treya.

Not all Fhrey are bad, she remembered. Then she looked to where Mawyndulë had gone. *But, like humans, a lot of them are.*

With food in her stomach and the blanket and smock warming her, Suri's attention was drawn to the bars that trapped her. Once more, she began to tremble. Again, she found it hard to breathe.

CHAPTER TWENTY-THREE

Whispers in the Mist

Sometimes our need to believe blinds us to reality, and sometimes seeing reality blinds us to what we need to believe.

— THE BOOK OF BRIN

A parade of people came into view, moving between trees, marching through the swamp. Moya felt as if she were late to a cookout that had just ended and she was heading upstream through homeward-bound revelers. This strange host came at them in various-sized groups, but most often as individuals. Silent travelers on a watery road, they journeyed without splash or ripple. Disordered and staggered, the procession included all sorts. Moya spotted men, women, and children. Seeing little ones who were no more than five or six, whimpering as they plodded through the dark, made her want to cry. There were humans, dwarfs, and even a few Fhrey. Many of the men were dressed like soldiers, but others looked to be farmers fresh from their fields. Almost all the women were weeping; some wailed. As diverse as they were, the procession of souls shared a common miserable appearance, as if every step was an agony.

A tearful woman holding a pile of bloody rags paused and looked at Moya. "Why?" she asked.

266 · *Michael J. Sullivan*

Moya didn't have an answer. She didn't understand the question. The woman shook her head in disgust and walked on.

Perhaps a hundred or more lost souls had passed them that night as they continued to wade. When the last of that most recent ghostly troop faded, swallowed by the dark, Moya looked at Gifford. "Definitely haunted."

Gifford didn't reply, didn't even look at her. His head was turned skyward, his eyes searching overhead.

"Gifford?" Roan said. "What's wrong?"

"Listen," Gifford told everyone.

Crickets, frogs, mosquitoes, wind in the leaves—they all made noise, but the loudest thing Moya heard was her own breathing.

"Listen to what?" Rain asked.

"The voices."

"The ghosts?" Moya asked.

Noticing her look, Gifford shook his head. "Not them. Something else is—is whispewing."

"I don't hear anything," Moya said. "Anyone else hear it? Tekchin, you have the best ears."

The Fhrey shook his head.

"Giff?" Tressa asked ominously. "Are any of these voices telling you to kill the rest of us?"

Gifford shook his head. "No. The voices not even talking to me—talking among themselves."

"More ghosts, then?" Moya asked. "Invisible ones?"

"I don't think so."

"What then?" Tekchin asked.

"I think"—Gifford swished his lips side-to-side—"I think it's the twees."

"The trees?" Moya said. "Are you serious?"

"Suri talks to trees," Roan said as she moved closer to Gifford and wrapped his arm in hers.

"I kinda thought she made that up," Moya said, "just like she pretended to have conversations with her wolf."

"I think maybe she could do both." Roan looked up. "What are they saying?"

"Talking about us," Gifford said. "Wonde'ing what we doing."

"I've been asking myself the same thing." Moya said. She was openly shivering now that the night had turned steadily colder. "Are these voices—do you think they're a problem? A threat to us?"

Gifford shook his head. "No, just twees talking among themselves."

"What do we do, Moya?" Brin asked. The Keeper looked exhausted. Her eyes struggled to stay open, and she, too, shivered, her teeth chattering as she spoke.

Persephone had sent Moya to safeguard and lead the party, but there was a problem with that. Other than the time she had commanded the archers in the Battle of Grandford, Moya had never really taken charge of anything. On that one occasion with the archers, it'd been easy. She was part of a bigger whole and tasked with something she was good at. All it took was courage, stupid mindless bravery. This required something else.

They expected her to have answers, which she didn't. They wanted her to be smart, which she wasn't. Moya had plenty of bravery but no brains. She'd led them to the center of a horrid swamp filled with ghosts, snakes, and who knew what else, and she didn't know where to go next. Worse than that, she didn't know how to get out. For some time, she'd been concerned that all the water would mean no clear path to follow for the return trip. There was an excellent chance they could all die out here.

She held Audrey wrapped in her arms and horizontal to keep the bow from touching the water. She glanced up, hoping to see stars, but all Moya found was darkness. Seven tired, scared, wet people looked to her for answers or at least a direction to travel. She had neither.

"It's late; we have to rest. I guess we'll take turns on the log over there."

"It's not big enough to sleep on," Tressa said.

"If you're tired enough," Tesh said, "you'd be surprised where you can drop off."

"Even if we doze a bit, the bigger question is, what then?" The woman had a face that invited a punch. She wore a perpetual frown, the sort that said she was always judging and finding fault. Even her rare smiles appeared sinister.

"We came because of you," Moya told her. "You and your Cult of Malcolm. Well, we're here. Do you have any ideas?"

Tressa thought a moment, and Moya figured she was thinking up a good insult, but when she finally replied, it was unexpected. Tressa looked down the log at Gifford. "Why not ask the trees?"

"Oh, sure, great idea," Moya said. "Why not ask the snakes while we're at it?"

"Persephone asked Magda questions," Brin said, "and Suri heard the answers. Remember her telling us that in Roan's roundhouse?"

Moya stared at Brin for a moment. She couldn't actually recall the conversation, but she did think there had been one. *Which is why Brin is the Keeper and I'm not.* "Can you do that, Gifford?"

"Maybe. I can give it a twy."

Gifford tilted his head back as if addressing Eton. He took a moment to clear his throat and then said, "Ah—hello, I'm Gif-fud. If it isn't too much twouble, we would be most happy if you could suggest someplace we might sleep."

"Dry land," Roan added.

"Yes"—Gifford nodded—"someplace that isn't wet."

Brin, Rain, and Roan all nodded their agreement to that last part in particular. Then everyone stood still and silent, waiting. Some looked up at the darkness; others studied Gifford for a sign. Moya struggled to hear.

If their situation weren't so dire, Moya might have laughed. They were two men, four women, a Fhrey, and a dwarf, all standing knee-deep in filthy, cold water, desperately hoping the trees would tell them where to go to take a nap. In any other circumstance, Moya would pray the trees *didn't* talk to her.

Several minutes passed, and then a faint breeze blew. Moya couldn't feel it, but she could hear the rustle overhead. Then even Moya thought she heard something. She looked at Gifford and saw him nodding.

"Can you help us, please?" Gifford asked.

There was a pause.

"We seek to find the witch—the Tetlin Witch."

Another pause.

"Can you help us?"

Moya couldn't tell if Gifford was holding a conversation or just shouting out at the night and hoping for a reply.

A handful of leaves began to fall. No one noticed anything strange about that at first. Then Roan, who always had a bizarre fascination with the trivial world, said, "Leaves are falling."

"Yes, Roan," Moya said. "That happens in autumn."

"Not in a straight line it doesn't."

Moya looked. They all did. Just as Roan said, floating on the surface of the still water lay a row of leaves. "Will this take us to dry land or the witch?"

Gifford was less than helpful as he looked back and shrugged.

"Ask."

"I can't."

"Why not?"

Gifford's face flushed, and he lowered his head, embarrassed.

Roan spoke for him. "He can't say *dry* and he certainly can't say *or.*"

Gifford looked to Roan. "You help me—help me speak."

She nodded but looked scared. Roan had difficulty talking to the likes of Padera, and Gifford wanted her to have a chat with creepy swamp trees?

Gifford looked up. "Excuse me again, but do these leaves lead to the witch . . ." He pointed to Roan.

"Or to dry . . ." Roan added.

"Land," Gifford finished.

They waited, and as they did, Gifford smiled proudly at Roan as if she'd just done a backflip. His wife covered a modest smile.

It's as if neither of you realizes where you are, Moya thought, amazed.

More leaves fell, filling in the gaps and creating a distinct and very long single line across the water.

"Well?" Moya asked.

Gifford shrugged once more.

"Thank the Grand Mother we got that settled." Moya sighed. "All roads lead forward, right?" She didn't wait for anyone to answer and began following the trail.

The walk was surprisingly short, and to Moya's shock it ended at a beach. The sand was black, and there were plenty of jagged rocks, but it was undoubtedly a shore. She heard waves but didn't see them. In the dark, all Moya saw was a flat emptiness, but the crash and roll she recognized from the trip to Neith. The water's edge was nothing more than a wide sandbar where sea met swamp, grass met sand, and neither held sway. But it was dry, clear, and generally flat—exactly what an exhausted person could hope for.

"The rest of you sleep," Moya said. "Audrey and I will take the first watch."

Moya wanted to turn in just as much as anyone. She even made a case in her own head that because of the stress related to leadership, she was more deserving than the others, but . . . *Persephone would stay up.* Moya figured that since she wasn't as smart as the keenig, she should at least try to emulate her.

No one protested. They didn't even speak. Most hardly bothered to lay out a blanket before laying their heads down, and in moments they were asleep.

Tekchin was the last to turn in. "You wake me the moment your eyes begin to droop," he told her.

She didn't bother mentioning that had been two hours ago. They kissed, and he curled up beside her.

Moya had picked a spot near a big, black, water-smoothed rock, and once Tekchin was asleep, she peeled off both boots and sat with her legs stretched out on the sand, giving her feet to the air.

Grand Mother, it feels good to get out of the water!

A damp chill blew in. She shivered. Reaching into her pack, Moya dug out a blanket. Miraculously, the wool was dry. She wrapped it around her shoulders, leaned back against the rock, and relaxed.

Bad idea. I'm too comfortable. I should stand up. I should at least take off the . . .

Her eyes closed, and her head drooped. Her chin bobbed against her chest, and she jerked awake.

Tetlin's ass!

Hating herself and that damn swamp, Moya stood up and walked around, making a small ring of footprints that soon became a little trench. She left her boots off. Not even a raow could force her to put those back on. Feeling a little dizzy, she stopped her spiraling trek. Still standing, Moya dug her toes into the sand and looked out at the endless night. Behind her were vague irregular shapes of varying shades of black-on-black—trees, bushes, and tall grass, but peering into the wind the other way, she saw nothing.

Just a void out there. This could be it—the edge of the world. Five more steps that way, and off I'd go.

Moya had no idea where she was with regard to the wider world. Growing up in Dahl Rhen, she'd assumed that Elan was made up of just the Crescent Forest and a few outer villages. When she got older, she realized Rhulyn was bigger than that after hearing stories of the land of the Gula to the north. She knew Alon Rhist was out there, too—which she had always believed was the land of the Fhrey—and that the Dherg lived south across something called the Blue Sea. She had lived with this mental map that was bounded by distinct edges for decades; now the edges had grown fuzzy.

She'd crossed the Blue Sea and found that the world went on, and she'd traveled to Alon Rhist and discovered no end or edge. Rhulyn, it seemed, was small—the world of her youth insignificant. How much farther did the land go? Maybe no one knew, but perhaps she had finally found an edge.

What would happen if I stepped off? Would I die? Or would I just keep falling?

Moya looked across the little dune isle at the others. Tekchin slept on his back the way he always did. He'd start snoring in a little while. Gifford and Roan fit together so perfectly that they made a single person. Rain had dug a little nest in the sand to keep the wind at bay. Brin curled up with Tesh, drawing him around her like a blanket.

Tesh did it. The idea that had fluttered around her head finally landed. Regardless of Tesh's denial and Tekchin's assertions, she knew Tesh had murdered the Galantians.

Anwir, Eres, and Sebek—he was with each one, or close enough to have killed him. No one knew where he was in the last Battle of Grandford. He showed up late to Persephone's room, covered in blood. Eres was his commander in the First Battle of the Harwood, and Tesh had personally requested Anwir to be his tracker.

That leaves only Nyphron and Tekchin. Is that why he came? And when he suggested that he and Tekchin should go off together to search for a place to sleep, was that a ploy? Is he along just to get Tekchin?

All of it made so much sense that Moya was left wondering what she would do if Tesh attacked. She focused on Brin, who looked happy and content in his arms.

Will she ever forgive me if I kill him?

She sighed and looked out over the dark water once more.

This whole trip is stupid.

Moya had told herself that from the start. She knew it was impossible when Tressa first spoke to Persephone, and since then it'd spiraled out of control. The Tetlin Witch didn't exist. She was like the rumor of Fhrey being gods. Everything was made up. They were risking their lives merely to save themselves the guilt of doing nothing to save Suri. They were trying to convince themselves that they could prevent the fane from getting the secret of dragons. But wanting something didn't make it real. *Hope and faith don't put no food on the table,* Moya's mother used to say.

Does Roan know this? Does Gifford? Smart as the two of them are, they have blind spots. It's all Tressa's fault! What's with her pretending to be a hero all of a sudden? Dear Mari, how I hate that woman!

Moya looked over to where Tressa slept, curled up and at a noticeable distance from everyone else. That woman knew she was unwanted and disliked and had the presence of mind to keep her distance. Tressa shivered alone in the cold.

Stupid bitch!

Why in the name of the Grand Mother of All would Tressa send us out here? This whole trip has to be nonsense, doesn't it? Moya needed to sandbag against that wave because she didn't want to accept that not only was the Tetlin Witch real, but she could be very close.

The witch was the source of all evil in the world. She created the demons and the raow. She was the source of all sickness and disease. She ate children, cooking them in a pot with carrots and basil leaves. If she did exist, Moya discovered a terrible flaw in Tressa's plan. Thing was, no one really believed they would find the Tetlin Witch. It would be like finding Mari, or . . . *like chatting with a ghost?*

She saw Meeks. He was in the darkness, coming closer.

"Moya?"

Moya opened her eyes and was surprised to see Tressa's face peering at her in the darkness. Moya lurched, terrified. "What? What?"

"It's okay. You just fell asleep."

"Huh?" Moya's heart was racing, her breath coming in rapid, short gasps. Audrey was across her lap, and her feet were still bare. She shivered with the chill. "Oh."

"Go lie down," Tressa said. "I'll take over for a while."

Moya's head was groggy.

"It's okay," Tressa said and followed it with a yawn. "I won't say anything. You still have a reputation to uphold."

Moya nodded, too tired to argue. She crawled over and curled up next to a snoring Tekchin. Moya pulled the blanket around both of them. It was warm there, warm and safe. She laid her head down.

Tressa. Moya rocked her head. *Oh how I hate that woman.*

Moya woke with a stiff neck, sand in her mouth, and the discovery she was lost in a cloud. They all were. The thick dark of night had been replaced with the opaque white of a dense fog. Roan, Gifford, and Rain tended a small campfire while Tekchin, Tressa, and Tesh gathered driftwood. Brin sat huddled, wrapped tightly in her blanket and just staring at the little flames and the stream of smoke that billowed and blew away when the breeze slapped it.

"Mornings are getting cold," Tesh said, dropping his tiny gathering of wood and rubbing his own arms for warmth.

Roan snatched two of the newly delivered logs and placed them strategically on the fire.

"Is this *okay?*" Moya asked, looking at Gifford and then at the fog-shrouded trees. "With, you know . . ."

Gifford looked over his shoulder, puzzled for a moment, then nodded. "Oh, yeah—no complaints yet."

"We haven't used any live wood," Rain explained. "Figured that would be . . ." He shrugged.

"Rude?" Brin asked.

"Sick and twisted," Gifford added.

The new sticks caught easily and the flames kicked out a pleasant heat that toasted Moya's face and hands, forcing her to sit up and lean away. In the distance, the sound of waves continued. Moya didn't know why she thought the noise might have stopped, but she found it odd just the same.

"Has everyone eaten?"

Tekchin nodded. Sitting beside her, he brushed hair away from Moya's face and dusted the sand from her cheek. "Nothing formal, just bites."

Moya rummaged blindly in her own bag and found a wedge of cheese she hadn't touched yet. As she ate, the others gathered around the fire, and once again their eyes focused on her. That's when it hit: *They've been waiting for me to wake up and tell them what to do next.*

"Tesh, Rain, and I did a little exploring this morning," Tekchin said. "We're on the edge of the Green Sea. The Ithil river pours out of the swamp into the bay, and this is the mouth of the estuary. So we're through the swamp, but"—he looked at Moya—"no island."

"It has to be out there." Tressa pointed at the sound of the waves.

"Maybe," Tekchin said.

"That's a big *maybe*," Tesh said, "but it could just as well be back in there." He pointed at the trees. "Or it might not exist at all. And if it is out across the water, there's no way to get there."

"We could swim," Moya said.

All three shook their heads.

"Tried that after the sun came up," Tekchin said.

"And?"

"Well, the water is real cold for one thing," Tesh said.

"And the second?" Moya asked.

Tesh turned and pointed to his side at a rip in his tunic. "Something tried to take a bite out of me. More than one something, I think. So, if the island is out there, we're not getting to it without a boat."

"Well," Moya said, "I guess that's it then. If there's no island, and no way to get to one, I don't see—"

"Oh please." Tressa rolled her eyes. "He wouldn't have sent us if we couldn't make it."

"Who?" Moya asked. "Malcolm?"

"Of course Malcolm." The woman took it upon herself to place new wood on the fire.

"What is it with you two?" Moya asked. "Have you slept together?"

"No!" Tressa exploded, aghast. She shoved back away from all of them with a hateful look in her eyes.

"What?" Moya was genuinely shocked at her outrage. The question was possibly the most cordial thing she'd said to the woman in recent memory. "Konniger has been dead for years, and Malcolm is pleasant enough. You certainly could do a lot worse."

"It's not like that—not like that *at all!* You people are so blind. Malcolm knows everything," Tressa said.

"He doesn't know *everything.*"

"No, really—he does. He knows the moment you were born. What your favorite food is. The thing you're most ashamed of that you've never shared with another living soul. He knows we are sitting here right now and what we're saying. He probably even knows what you're thinking and what you'll say next."

Moya pressed her lips together to avoid laughing. She didn't know why. Two days ago, she'd have laughed in Tressa's face and thought nothing of it. She'd often gone out of her way to do just that. *How I hate this woman!*

"It's true!" Tressa shouted at her. "You'll see." She pointed toward the waves. "We're going to find the island. It's going to be right out there and we won't need a boat—or we'll find one or something. Malcolm has already seen us succeed. He knows we're going to do it."

"He doesn't *know,*" Roan said softly. She was staring into the flames.

This caught Tressa's attention. "How can you say that?" Unlike with Moya, Tressa didn't shout at Roan. Her tone was soft, hurt, as if Roan had betrayed her somehow.

"He said himself that he doesn't know everything," Roan explained. "About the past maybe, but not the future. Someone's foot can get in the way, remember? So while he's seen the future, he also knows it can be changed."

"Not you, too," Moya said. "Roan, of all people—"

"You can add me to the list," Rain said. "I was there that night in the smithy when Suri . . . well, when she did what she did."

"What the Tet happened to make you all think Malcolm is so special?"

"You might want to avoid that particular curse, going forward," Tressa said, returning to the little pile of wood Tekchin had dropped. She resumed feeding the campfire, which spit and hissed in the foggy morning air.

"What? *Tet?*"

Tressa nodded. "Given who we are hoping to meet, yes. It might be considered insulting."

"Oh please." Moya shook her head. "But seriously, why are you all so dead set on raising Malcolm onto a pedestal?"

"Haven't you heard? He's a god," Tesh said skeptically.

"God?" Moya laughed. When no one laughed with her, she stopped. "Oh—come—on."

Moya turned to Brin, who shrugged with a concerned look. "I wasn't there. But," Brin said slowly, thinking, "he does seem to know a lot, and when I told him about the Ancient One, he ran off like he was going to hunt him down. And he told Tressa about Suri being taken years before she was."

"That's only if you can believe Tressa, which I don't." Moya glared down at the older woman, who smiled back. "Okay, whatever. Malcolm's a know-it-all, fine. It doesn't matter anyway because we can't find this island . . ." She looked out at the impenetrable mist.

"Even if it is out there," Tesh said, "we don't know how far or in what direction." He stood up and took a few steps toward the water as if he was going swimming again.

Moya saw the rip in his clothes, and there was a small stain of blood, too.

"So we wait for the fog to burn off," Tressa said.

"And if it doesn't?" Moya asked.

"Can't be like this all the time," Tressa said.

Moya gave her an amazed look. "A ghost talked to us last night. We all watched a parade of dead people march by, and Tekchin told me he and Tesh found a nest with eyeballs in place of eggs. Oh, and the trees here whisper to each other. No, Tressa, I think the fog could very easily *always* be here."

"Look, if anyone wants to pack up for home, go ahead," Tressa said. "I can find the isle without you."

"Because Malcolm said you'd succeed." Moya finished the unstated thought.

Tressa nodded. "Yeah."

"Fine," Moya said. "You want to stay, that's okay by me. The rest of us—"

"What *do* the trees say?" Brin asked Gifford. "Do they know how to get to the island?"

Gifford shook his head. "I asked about it. I even went over to them." He pointed at a clump of trees. "I spoke to those. Didn't say anything to me."

"Maybe they only talk at night," Brin suggested.

"Maybe."

"We have to wait." It was Roan again, her little voice barely audible above the crackle of the fire.

"Wait?" Moya asked. "For what, Roan? This was supposed to be an overnight trip. We don't have much food and water left. We'll be lucky to get back without getting lost. Every minute we stick around, we run the risk of getting ourselves in real trouble."

"It's just like in Tirre," Roan said.

Moya put the cheese back into her pack and inched forward. "What is, Roan?"

"The water—it goes down."

"Goes down?"

"In Tirre, sometimes it was high and other times it was low. If you look at the base of the trees, you'll see a discoloration. It's a water mark. It shows where the waterline sometimes is."

Moya looked at the trees Gifford said he'd tried speaking to and saw no discoloration. "There's nothing there."

"No," Roan said, "because the water is high right now, but it will go down. In a few hours, it will go much lower."

"Then what?" Moya asked.

"Obvious, isn't it?" Tressa said with a faraway look and a dreamy smile. "We'll just walk to the island. I told you. Malcolm is always right."

"How long do we have to wait?"

Roan shrugged. "I don't know."

Moya sighed.

The whole trip had seemed like such a waste of time, except . . . Roan thought it was possible, and hadn't she created miracles? After all, there really was a haunted swamp.

But can the Tetlin Witch really be out there? Moya faced the fog and wondered. *And what will I do if we find her, and it all turns out to be true? And more important . . . what will she do to us?*

CHAPTER TWENTY-FOUR

Unpleasant Paths

Distilling barley makes liquor. Doing it again loses a little of the flavor but makes the intoxicant much stronger.

— THE BOOK OF BRIN

Rolling through the outer villages, the wagon gathered a following. Most Fhrey had never seen a Rhune before, and the Gwydry in particular left their daily toil to walk alongside and peer through the bars at the caged beast. Mawyndulë found them a nuisance. They got in the way and startled the horse, which was hard enough to keep under control. Not that this was his problem. Mawyndulë had Treya lead the animal most of the time.

"Did you capture this yourself?"

"Is it dangerous?"

"What will you do with it? Put it on display in the capital?"

The questions came by the dozens, but Mawyndulë didn't answer any. He was too miserable to be friendly. He had a blister on his left foot, stubble on his head, and he was tired of Treya's traveling meals. The bread was gone, and the thin soup didn't fill his stomach after an all-day walk. What galled him the most was that the Rhune got to ride the whole way.

Word began to spread, and the number of people waiting at each village grew larger. By the time they reached Alluriville, the crowd that assailed them was a mob. Mawyndulë had planned to stop there. He'd promised his sore feet and empty stomach they would be rewarded by a way-station visit, but the masses had been too excited, and he pushed on instead.

Through all their travels, the Rhune watched him.

She wore one of Treya's tunics. His servant shouldn't have sacrificed a spare outfit like that, but seeing the Rhune dressed up in "people clothes" was funny. At the spring fair, they often put a hat on a goat or a cloak on a cow, making people laugh. The Rhune in Treya's outfit had the same effect.

"Does it have fangs?"

"What does it eat?"

"Does it make sounds if you poke it?"

A few people threw stones at the Rhune. Treya yelled at them to stop, begging Mawyndulë to do something. He didn't. The people just wanted to make the Rhune get up, see it move. Given that he had walked all the way to Avempartha and back while the monster rode comfortably in the wagon, Mawyndulë didn't see a problem with prodding it to do something for a change. He considered getting a stick and poking the thing himself.

They didn't make it to Estramnadon before the sun set, which only served to put Mawyndulë on edge. He wanted to be home. He wanted to be done with this awful trip, but there was no way he would travel at night. He'd already tripped on two roots. He was tired. His feet were sore, and the nights were getting cold. Mawyndulë was slow in reaching the realization that they'd have to stop, thinking that Estramnadon would be right around the next bend. It wasn't, and by the time he gave up and ordered a halt, Treya was left unprepared and hustling in the dark to set up camp and make the meal. He took pity on her and made the fire himself.

"Here you go," Treya said, taking the Rhune a bowl of food. "Careful, it's hot."

"Why do you do that?" Mawyndulë asked while watching Treya pass a steaming bowl through the bars.

"Do what? Feed her? You feed the horse. Why shouldn't we feed her?"

"No, not the food. I meant why do you talk to it like it's a person?"

Treya looked puzzled. "She *is* a person."

Mawyndulë laughed. "It's an animal."

"Animals don't talk. She does."

"Some birds have been trained to mimic. That doesn't make them people. This one was trained—that's all."

Treya looked back at the Rhune, whose face was mostly hidden as it slurped from the rim of the bowl. "I don't think that—"

"For Ferrol's sake, don't try and think. You're a Gwydry; you aren't built for it. Look, we've been traveling with it for days. If it could talk—I mean really talk intelligently and not just babble words drilled into it by Arion—it would have. If you were in a cage, you'd be demanding to be let out, wouldn't you? But it hasn't because it doesn't really understand any more than a goat would. It isn't a person."

Treya shook her head. "She talked to me a little. Said thank you when I gave her food, complimented me on it, and—"

"Yes, yes, I just told you the thing was trained to do simple tasks. The Instarya stable master has a horse that can count with its hoof, but that doesn't mean it's capable of serving on the Aquila, does it? The Instarya are clever. They trained the creature to make it appear intelligent, but look at it. It just sits there cowering. It babbles. It drools. It wails. And you've seen how it keeps throwing itself against the bars like it's insane. There's no intelligence behind those eyes."

"She's scared. That's why she shakes. It has to do with being sealed up in a small space. That's what she told me."

Mawyndulë frowned and shook his head. "What *she* told you? Do you hear yourself?"

"I'm not saying she's intelligent like a Fhrey, but I don't think she's like a cow or goat, either. She has feelings, and she can express them."

"So can a cow and a goat."

"You know what I mean."

"I know what you *think* you mean, and I am telling you, you're wrong." Mawyndulë set down his own bowl of awful vegetable gruel and walked away. "Tomorrow we'll take it to my father, and he can extract whatever Arion taught her."

"What will he do to her?"

Treya was going there again, but he would have none of it. "I have no idea."

"So you don't believe she has the Art?"

He hesitated as Jerydd's words echoed once more out of the past. *Talent is one thing, a knack is another, but a moment ago the entire might of Avempartha was slapped aside.* At the time, even Mawyndulë had believed it was true, but after seeing her, after hauling the creature for two days and watching the thing drool, he realized his mistake. In his shock, brought on by nearly dying, he had jumped to conclusions. *There are likely a dozen explanations for what happened at Alon Rhist, none of which require the existence of a true Rhune Artist. Besides* . . . "What Artist would let themselves be caged?"

He saw the confusion appear on Treya's face. If his servant knew anything about the Orinfar, she might have argued that the collar made any Artist, Rhune or Fhrey, helpless. Or if she were more intelligent than a goldfish, she might have surmised that the young woman had been tricked into being caged. But Treya merely accepted Mawyndulë's premise and nodded. "What will happen to her after your father is done?"

Mawyndulë shrugged. "Who cares?"

The trip had been a nightmarish blur of pain, nausea, dizziness, and mind-numbing fear. This toxic cloud was penetrated at different points by the Fhrey servant who gave her food and spoke kindly, and by crowds of hideous faces who laughed, jabbed, and threw things at her. A stone had struck her head, and she had seen stars.

Suri tried to imagine herself someplace else. She closed her eyes and concentrated on her home in the Hawthorn Glen, on its open glade. That helped a little. She felt as if she were fighting against an oozing blanket of tar that enveloped and threatened to smother her. Her focus on the Hawthorn was her way out, pushing against the tar blanket with splayed hands, but the tar would seep between her fingers, work its way in, and before long she would lose her grip on the vision of the open forest of her youth. The effort was exhausting. Her sweat-covered body was chilled even with the blanket. Her stomach fluttered uneasily with that queer sensation she used to get when jumping off the falls back in the Crescent Forest. Most of the time, Suri suffered from debilitating headaches, and there were incidents when the walls seemed to close in and she fainted. She would wake confused and lost, only to remember she was trapped. Then the fear would hit her again. Try as she might at such moments, Suri couldn't keep from throwing herself against the bars. The bruises only added to her agony.

Death would be better than this.

For a fleeting moment, she saw something in her mind, a flash of fluttering color.

Butterfly.

With eyes firmly shut, Suri searched her mind for it, and it wasn't hard to find.

Butterflies aren't the sort to hide.

She saw it clearly, orange outlined in black with little white dots around the edges. Beautiful.

Before that.

The glory of wings vanished and instead she saw what almost looked like a thick green bean dangling from a tiny branch.

Chrysalis.

Caterpillars sealed themselves up in dangling prisons.

How horrible.

Even for a caterpillar the idea of imprisonment had to be terrible, and yet . . . *What if that's the point? Wings are not given, they're grown, developed from within. Cut off from the outside world, caterpillars must draw strength from inside themselves. Without help, without support, without resources of any kind, they must find the ability to survive. In doing so, they change—they have to.*

But Suri had already become a butterfly. Arion had said so. She had her wings. She'd earned them.

So, what emerges after a butterfly is sealed inside a chrysalis?

CHAPTER TWENTY-FIVE

The Hidden Isle

Seeing is often a matter of knowing what you are looking for. Knowing what you are looking for comes with wisdom. Wisdom is sometimes abandoned with the tide—especially when it has teeth.
— THE BOOK OF BRIN

Hurry.

Gifford barely heard the word.

Like many of them, he was dozing. The day had turned wonderfully warm despite the prevailing fog, and with little to do but sit and wait, few could resist a nap. Those who did defy sleep consisted of Roan, who believed sleep was a waste of time, and Tressa, both of whom Brin was teaching to read.

"Try again," Brin told the older woman.

Tressa scowled at the marks Brin had made in the sand as if they were insulting her, and maybe they were; Gifford had no idea. What he was certain of was that Brin had invented a new magic. *What wondrous people I know.*

Hurry!

Gifford lifted his head and glanced around, looking for Tesh. The voice almost sounded like him, if he were whispering. But he spotted Tesh sleeping on the bit of grass just before where the sand started. Rain was sleeping there, too.

Hurry! Hurry! Hurry! More than one voice this time. The word was spoken by a trio or more.

Gifford sat up so fast he drew looks from everyone.

"Bad dream?" Tressa asked, with a sympathetic expression that said, *Been there*.

"I had one," Brin said. "More than one, really."

"Let me guess," Tressa said. "Meeks?"

Brin frowned and nodded. "Is that what *you* dreamed about, Gifford?"

He shook his head and spotted Moya with Tekchin, and as it turned out they weren't napping with the rest. They were walking the perimeter of their tiny encampment, following a worn path that nearly everyone had trod.

"What's wrong?" Brin asked.

"I think we have a pwoblem," he said, waving to Moya, who trotted over—nothing on their little sandbar being more than fifty yards away from anything else.

"What?" Moya asked. "What's going on?"

"The twees talking again," he told her.

This caught everyone's attention. Even Tesh and Rain sat up.

Moya knelt down in front of Gifford. "What are they saying?"

"Saying—ah—" He struggled to find words that didn't have the *rrr* sound. "We need to be—ah—fast."

"Fast? Fast at what?"

Gifford shrugged. "Don't know." Then he thought a moment and added, "Maybe getting to the island."

The trees didn't say this, but ever since waking from his late-afternoon nap, Gifford had felt it: a nervousness, a growing tension. Working with Suri had taught him not to ignore the peripheral feelings that lingered at the edges of his mind. These fleeting thoughts that he usually ignored only broke through the noise in times of crisis, like when the giants attacked

Dahl Rhen and he knew to take shelter in the storage pit. At the time, he hadn't known it was the Art, but hindsight let him see the patterns of his life and the straight paths that, at the time, had seemed like circles. Normally, Gifford struggled to hear, to feel the subtle messages that the Art sent, but not in this place. In the Swamp of Ith, the normal whisperings had become shouts in his ear.

Get moving!

"Roan?" Moya called, and the woman's head came up. "Check your stick."

Everyone got to their feet as Roan ran down to the water's edge to the five-foot pole she had scored with hash marks and planted at the waterline. She bent down, putting her face near the lapping waves. She counted.

"How many?" Moya called.

"Eight."

"Eight? Wasn't it nine before?"

Roan nodded.

"Refresh my memory, Roan. Eight is fewer than nine, right? So that means . . . ?"

"The water level has gone down as far as it's going to and is rising again." Roan said this as if she were admitting to a murder.

"But you said we just had to wait. And you"—Moya turned to Tressa—"said we were *just going to walk* to the island." Moya pointed out at the sea that continued to bleed into the stubborn fog. The tide had gone out. They had more beach than a few hours before, but the sea remained, and no island had shown itself.

For once, Tressa didn't say anything in her defense. Like Roan, she was baffled.

In their silence, Moya turned to Gifford. "Are the trees saying anything else? Anything helpful, like what we should do?"

Gifford shook his head.

Moya ran a hand through her hair, pulling it back so forcefully it must have hurt. "Look, I'm not Persephone. I need help. One of you has to give

me something. Roan? You're my resident genius. Do you have anything?"
Moya paced, flexing her hands as if the returning tide were an hourglass.

She's feeling the same thing, Gifford realized. *Probably doesn't know it any more than I did, but the world is talking to her. It's this place.*

As he thought of this, an image formed in Gifford's mind of a swirling cone—a funnel, a drain. *The walls are thinner here,* he thought. *The walls between the worlds.*

Roan's face took on a serious, focused expression as she pulled on her hair and then began to chew on the ends. After nearly a minute, she still hadn't said anything.

"The song . . ." Tressa said, and began to sing the tune again.

"For Tet's sake, Tressa," Moya said, "please don't sing. You'll scare the trees."

Tressa frowned, her eyes shifting side-to-side in thought. Then she began to mutter the words. *"Hidden in a mist-soaked swamp, upon an awful isle."*

"Tressa," Tesh said, "we're in the swamp. There just hasn't been an island. The song is wrong."

Gifford turned to Roan; she had that look on her face. Her eyes were open and clear, but not seeing, or seeing well beyond what normal people could.

"Hidden," Roan muttered. Then as if she heard something, she spun around and looked out at the water.

"What is it, Woan?"

"Hidden," she repeated. "It's there, out in the mist, but it's hidden."

"We know that," Moya said. "Well, we don't *know,* but I'm guessing that's the general hope at least."

"How do you find something you can't see?" Roan asked.

Brin closed her eyes, and a moment later, she said, "You feel for it?"

This drew an incredulous look from Moya. "Kinda hard to feel an island that might be miles away."

"You're right," Roan said. "So that's not it. Can't touch it, can't smell it, can't taste it . . ."

"Hear it?" Moya asked, and Roan nodded.

"How do you *hear* an island?" Tesh asked.

Roan went back to chewing on her hair. A moment later, she jumped up. "Audrey!"

"Huh?" Moya said.

"Shoot an arrow into the mist."

"Which way?"

"Out there!" She pointed toward the waves.

Moya stared at her dumbfounded for a moment, then shrugged. Grabbing up her bow, she took an arrow from the quiver.

Everyone was silent as Moya drew back, so that Gifford could hear Audrey's wood creak with the rise of tension in the string. Moya tilted her aim up and let go.

Thew.

The arrow sped into the mist and was gone in an instant.

Plip.

"Water," Roan said, her eyes closed. "Try again. Aim to the left a little."

Moya let another go.

Plip.

"Try the other way."

"Roan," Moya said. "You understand I only have so many arrows, right?"

"You want to save arrows or find the island?" Tressa asked.

"Might not be one," Moya pointed out.

"There *is* one," Tressa insisted.

"Doesn't matter if we find the island," Tesh said. "We still can't get there."

"The other way," Roan insisted.

Moya sighed, turned, and let another arrow fly.

Plip.

Moya's shoulders slumped.

Hurry! Must hurry! No time left! The trio had become a chorus in Gifford's mind. "The twees say we need to be quick. Time is almost gone, they say."

"See!" Tressa said. "Even the trees are on my side."

Roan had bent down and was drawing lines in the sand. "More to the right."

"Roan," Moya said in an exasperated tone, "are you sure that—"

"Do it!" Tressa shouted.

Moya sighed and pulled another arrow from her dwindling supply. She looked to Tekchin and shook her head. Tilting her aim a tad farther to the right of the last shot, she sent another arrow into the mist.

Tink!

Everyone's eyes widened.

"That wasn't water," Moya was the first to declare.

"No, it wasn't," Tressa said.

Roan dug a definitive gouge through the sand. "Do it again. Same direction only not as far."

Moya nodded and sent another arrow out.

Tink!

Roan stood up. "That's it."

Go now! Go now, or it is too late!

"The twees say we have to go now," Gifford announced.

"Go where?" Tesh asked. "Let me remind you, swimming is *not* an option."

"Roan?" Moya asked.

Roan was walking toward the water.

"Woan?" Gifford called nervously. When Roan was focused, she saw little else. Gifford worried she had forgotten there was a dangerous sea between her and whatever was out there.

Roan didn't stop. She kept walking, a strong confident stride.

"Everyone, gather your stuff and follow Roan," Moya ordered. "Move!"

In a mad dash, they all rushed back to the fire. A lazy day had prompted many of them to lay out wet clothes. Gifford was no exception, and his things were scattered. Without a care or thought, he grabbed everything, including a good deal of accompanying sand, and stuffed the whole mess into his pack. He picked up Roan's bag, too. Hooking one pack on each shoulder, Gifford turned, then stopped in shock.

Roan was gone.

"Woan?" he shouted. "Woan?"

This caught the attention of them all. Moya, who was hopping on one foot as she struggled to pull on a boot, shouted, "Roan?"

"This way!" Roan called back.

Gifford didn't wait for the others. He staggered down the sandy slope to the water's edge. "Woan?"

"Here!" she called.

Gifford tracked toward the sound of her voice and finally spotted her, a vague hazy outline of a person in the mist. Then his mouth dropped open.

"Where is—" Moya appeared at his side. Following the line of his sight. She gasped.

Roan's faint silhouette looked like a ghost gliding across the surface of the sea.

Tressa exclaimed, "I told you. I told you so!"

"Grand Mother of All, she's walking on water!" Tesh said.

Roan waved at them to follow. "Hurry! We don't have much time! Start where I planted the stick and follow me."

Gifford searched the beach until he spotted the stick she'd been using to check the height of the water—now jammed in a new place.

"How is she doing that?" Brin asked, looking at the surface of the sea with its placid but intimidating endlessness.

"I'm not a very good swimmer," Rain admitted.

"Usually, I'm pwetty good, but . . ." Gifford pointed at the metal anchor on his leg.

It's Roan, Gifford thought. *What else matters?*

He was the first to follow her. Icy cold, like dead hands, the water clasped his ankles. He pushed on, splashing forward, and to his surprise the water never deepened. Beneath him was a hidden walkway, a barely submerged bridge. "It's a shelf, a sandbar or something just beneath the su'face."

"A land bridge!" Tekchin said.

Swinging his dead leg over the water was a challenge, and Gifford sprayed his way out into the fog. His normally slow speed was cut to a crawl, and he waved the others past. Each went by, creating a froth in the seawater. Roan waited, smiling at his approach. She took her pack, which helped, but he still struggled. His dead leg, the one he couldn't bend, kept dragging through the water. Gifford was forced to push his thigh ahead with his hands, plant the leg, then vault with it. The process was tedious, slow, and after only a short while he understood why the trees had told him to hurry.

The water was rising.

The icy dead hands of the sea had gone from grabbing his ankles to slapping his calves. This did nothing to speed his progress, making it all the harder to force his leg forward. Gifford looked up from his efforts and peered ahead, hoping to see the elusive island, but all was mist.

"How fa' is it, do you think?"

"I don't know," Roan replied.

No time left! Gifford remembered the trees' chorus. "You should go ahead. Catch up to the west."

Roan stared at him, puzzled, then down at the water, at his leg, and finally she, too, peered ahead at the mist. "Put your arm over my shoulder."

"Woan, you should go. I'm too slow."

"Lean on me and hop. We'll be okay."

"But Woan—you can't swim."

"I can."

"Not well."

"Won't have to if you hop. Now do it!"

They pushed forward through the rising sea, moving as one awkward creature, a crab with two arms and four legs. Behind them, the swamp and the bit of sand where they had spent the night were gone. So, too, were the others—everything swallowed by the white haze. In every direction, the view was the same: the opaque white of drifting, surface-bound clouds, out of which came the cries of unseen gulls.

The water inched up above their knees.

Underneath, Gifford could feel rocks. They weren't walking on sand anymore—maybe they never had been. Instead, he felt smooth stones, seashells, and other things—stringy, slithering tendrils that wrapped around his ankles. The sea didn't just have hands; it had fingers. At first, he thought it might be fish or even snakes, but when a swell rushed past, he spotted a clump of tuberous seaweed floating by. That's what his feet were feeling. This set him at ease, but along with the wayward aquatic plant, he also became aware that the water had risen to his hips, and that hopping wasn't helping. His dead leg was no longer the problem. Just plowing through the water—even if both legs worked like champions—would have been tough. Roan's face was glistening with sweat, and as the water crept higher, he saw fear.

Roan had never liked water. Her two encounters had both been painful and terrifying. The first was when her absentmindedness caused her to fall into the Crescent Creek, breaking her ankle. The second was with Persephone in Neith when she'd fallen along with the others into an underground flume and nearly drowned. Number three didn't look to be very promising, either.

Gifford stopped asking her to leave him behind and started trying to think of how he might swim and drag *her* along at the same time. He'd have to abandon the packs. Maybe if he lay on his back, she could climb up on him like a raft and he could—

Something brushed his good leg, and it wasn't seaweed.

"Did you feel that?" Roan asked.

"Keep moving," Gifford said, and he began paddling with his free hand. As he did, he brushed something solid that slithered past his fingertips, something scaly, something big.

Moving fast wasn't easy. In the water, nothing was quick—except the thing that had brushed by.

"Hang on to me, Woan," he told her and employed both of his arms in the effort.

His legs were useless, but Gifford's arms were strong. Roan clung to his neck as Gifford stroked. His arms were like a pair of powerful oars. Looking up, Gifford could finally see the outline of trees appearing out of the gloom. The island was only a little way off. This brought a smile to his lips.

We're going to make it! We are going to—

Massive jaws bit his leg.

Gifford cried out as teeth clamped down, but the outburst was more from terror than pain. Whatever was under the water, the creature that had bitten him had powerful jaws but poor judgment. It had chosen his bad leg—the one with the brace.

He felt it thrash and jerk, trying to rip his flesh, but the steel brace worked as well as armor. Gifford beat at the thing with his fist, landing several hits before it let go. Then with renewed energy, Gifford swam forward with all his might.

He submerged his head to get bigger pulls, coming up every other stroke for air. He gave up looking ahead. Doing so took time, and he couldn't afford to slow down. All Gifford could think of was that creature, and whether there was more than one. His mind kept conjuring images of it sinking its teeth into Roan's arm or leg and ripping her flesh. He could feel her clutching him with one arm, the other paddling as best she could, her legs kicking. Kicking was good, kicking was great, if nothing else it might keep the monster off them.

With each stroke, every dive, and each mouthful of air, he anticipated the pain of the thing's toothy bite, or the greater pain of Roan's shriek.

Then he felt something grab him again, but this time by the arm. Just as before, there was no pain. He raised his free arm to swing—

"Gifford! Gifford!" Tesh was yelling. "You made it." Tesh had a hold on him with one hand. His other held a naked sword at the ready.

"Just put your feet down," Moya said. She was there, too, reaching out for Roan.

Gifford felt for the ground and discovered the water was hip-deep again, the land rising sharply.

All of them scrambled uphill and collapsed on a new beach where they lay panting, dripping, and smiling.

We made it. But where exactly have we made it to?

CHAPTER TWENTY-SIX

Dragon Hill

No one knew she went up there at night. If they did, they certainly could not have guessed why. I did not know any of it. If I had, it would have broken my heart. By the time I learned, my heart was already broken.

— THE BOOK OF BRIN

The wet grass soaked the hem of Persephone's dress as she once more climbed the northeast hill. It was still dark, the morning—*hours away?* She couldn't sleep, and that wasn't good, not for her, not for Nolyn, not for her people. She climbed the hill in the dark, in the silent predawn hours, best that no one saw, best if Nyphron had no idea. He was sound asleep in his own tent. Nyphron never had any trouble sleeping.

Persephone shivered and pulled her cloak tight to her neck, holding the front closed with her hands. This made her think of how excited Roan had been when she saw her first button on a Fhrey garment. This made her stop. She was only halfway up the hill, but the thought hit her like a blow, and she couldn't help looking east.

I should have gone. But how could I? I have Nolyn now, and I'm keenig, and maybe if I repeat these things enough times, I'll start believing. Doubtful, but there's a slim hope.

The wind on the hill was bitterly cold, with the sort of damp teeth that bit through skin and went for bone. On the open expanse of the hill at an hour before even the earliest of risers opened their eyes, Persephone was alone. She'd felt that way for years, but this was the first time she truly was. Even the ghost of a dead husband no longer haunted her. Everyone had left, but even if they hadn't gone off to the swamp, she couldn't have spoken to Moya, Roan, or Brin. She loved them all, but they couldn't understand.

No. There's only one who could have done that.

The dragon lay on the crest of the hill as it had for years. Persephone had climbed the slope dozens of times to speak to the beast. The unmoving creature had become her silent confidant, an imaginary friend whom she pretended could hear her. Persephone never went too close, but this time was different. She had something important to say, even if it was only to hear herself say it.

She planned to walk right up to the beast, maybe even touch it, but halted when one of its eyes opened. A pupil dilated in the dark, its vertical slit spreading left and right, opening like a door, focusing on her. Nothing else moved, not so much as a wrinkle on its scaly skin. She might have lost her nerve if it had. The sheer size of the thing was heart-stopping. A single tooth was the length of her arm, and had those eyes really been doors, she'd barely have to duck to pass through. She was a mouse in the field, inching toward a lion-sized cat. That Suri could have created it was unimaginable. *And yet she destroyed a city.* Persephone was there, she'd seen it. Suri had brought the whole mountain down. No one was in the city— Suri had always been odd, not evil, but the dragon looked malevolent. The scales, the deep-set eyes with oblong pupils, and those fangs—this wasn't a puppy Suri had birthed, and if it had moved more than its eyes, Persephone thought she would have screamed.

Halted by the opening of that eye, she didn't have the courage to go closer, not with it watching. "They're gone," she said, having no idea if it understood. "Moya, Roan, Gifford, Brin, Tesh, Tekchin, Rain and"—she laughed—"even Tressa." She shook her head. "Tressa, of all people."

Persephone adjusted her hands on her cloak as another gust of wind struck her. The wind coursed through the grass, making it sway and Persephone stagger. It did nothing to the dragon. Not even the eye blinked.

"They went to save Suri. She's in Estramnadon by now. The Fhrey will probably kill her. In all likelihood, they're torturing her right now. She's like a daughter to me, did you know that?" Persephone looked down at her feet, wet in the dewy grass. "I never told her, either. I should have. Maybe she knows. I hope she does. Thing is, you always think of the things you want to say to someone after it's too late."

Tears welled in her eyes. She didn't wipe them, and they brimmed on her lids, clinging to the edges as she stared at the beast.

"I don't even know if you can hear me. Maybe you're just—I don't know—just a thing like a rake or a snowball, but I need to tell you something—something I had hoped to tell you six years ago." Persephone sniffled. "I should have, and I did try. The night of the attack, I sent Padera to fetch you. I would have come myself, would have run to you, except I was trapped on that stupid bed, my stomach was . . . And I thought—I thought there would be time. There would be a tomorrow because there had always been one before. Can you really blame me for not knowing?"

She looked at the beast's eye, that massive door. It glared back at her unwavering, unblinking. She had her answer. "Of course you can, and you're right to do so."

"Anyway"—Persephone sniffled again, finding it hard to breathe—"I wanted—that night—I wanted to tell you that I didn't mean what I said, and that—that . . ."

She started to cry. Letting go of her cloak, she covered her face with both hands and wept. She stood wavering on the hill. More than half a decade had passed, but in one sense, not a minute had slipped. She could still see his face, that look, that terrible expression of pain. He was the God Killer, the great warrior, but she had dealt the mortal blow from a sickbed, wielding nothing but words.

Had he gone right then? Had he chased down Suri and asked her? Or had she come to him and, having nothing to live for, he'd agreed?

He volunteered, given his life so that everyone else could live.

"And to think I called "—she sucked in a ragged breath—"that I called *you* selfish. That I said you didn't care about us."

She fell to her knees, sobbing too hard to stand.

Suri can't make another dragon because there aren't any more Raithes.

"I love you, Raithe. And I'm so, so sorry."

The eye blinked, with a sound like the unfolding of a sheet.

Persephone looked up, surprised. She waited but the gilarabrywn did nothing more.

She could feel the wetness from the grass soaking into her dress. The wind picked up again, tossing her hair and pulling at her cloak.

Of all the decisions to get wrong. And yet, what if I had gotten it right? What if Padera had somehow managed to reach him? Or what if I hadn't been injured and could have gone to him myself? If I had told him the truth, if I'd told him how I really felt, would he still have done it? And if he hadn't, wouldn't everyone have died? There would be no Nolyn. Gifford would have returned to find Roan's dead body. Brin and Tesh would never have had any time together, and that would have been true for oh-so-many others. Was his life too much to ask?

Raithe didn't think so.

She just wished . . .

Persephone climbed back to her feet. The dawn would break soon. She could feel it. The world still plodding on its inevitable march toward who knew what, and who really cared anymore. Still, the keenig couldn't be caught weeping on the Dragon Hill. Folks might ask why, and if they did, she might just tell them the truth.

"Raithe," she said to the beast, "what I said at your funeral . . . I didn't mean that, either. I was hurt. I was angry. And I missed you so much."

She wiped her face. "I don't know if you can hear me, but if you can, please, I beg you, please don't hate me. I didn't say it then. I couldn't, not when you asked. But I did love you—I still do, and I always will. Please, please don't hate me."

Persephone waited until she could breathe again, until she could walk once more without fear of falling. Then she turned and started back down the slope. She had only taken a few steps when she heard a rustle from behind. Turning, she saw that the great head of the gilarabrywn had risen. Leaves and bits of grass fell from it.

Persephone gasped and froze in fear. She was close enough that if it wanted, the beast could kill her in a dozen different ways, and when it opened its mouth, her heart stopped. She imagined it snatching her up in its jaws, swallowing her whole. But it didn't attack, and for a long moment, they looked at each other. Then as the first rays of morning light filled the eastern sky, the dragon spoke. It said only two words, but they were enough to drive Persephone back to her knees.

"Even now."

CHAPTER TWENTY-SEVEN

The Tetlin Witch

As far as I know, the island does not have a name, and I am certainly not about to give it one. Some places should remain anonymous, some words unspoken, some people undisturbed.

— THE BOOK OF BRIN

Rocks on the island looked like faces. Old men mostly but a few shriveled hags were sprinkled in as well. There was even the occasional child with an upturned nose and wide eyes. One even looked remarkably like the profile of a snarling wolf, complete with fur represented by fuzzy moss and the pale tooth of a bleached, dead tree root. They were probably just tricks of light playing on Brin's very gullible mind. Each was unpleasant and definitely unwelcoming.

The group clustered close, clinging to the tiny beach where they gathered to recover from the crossing. No one was hurt—merely wet, exhausted, and shocked they'd done it. There actually was a *hidden isle*, and they were on it.

Brin looked through the clefts between the many giant stone faces that lined the beach, huge boulders that broke away from the cliffs ages ago.

Is she up there?

Brin spotted cracks and crevices that would grant passage up the escarpment to the interior of the island where . . .

Does the Tetlin Witch really live here?

As Keeper of Ways, Brin knew every story about her, except apparently Malcolm's song. She struggled to recollect every bit of information on the witch, who was known to be the mother of all things horrible. The witch was said to be so hideous that a person would turn to stone just by looking at her, and so wicked that Nifrel—that part of the underworld where evil went—refused to have her. There were many tales of her cruelty, like when she gave the gift of song to a lover of music and then struck him deaf. She was responsible for winter. Sickness was all her doing. Illnesses, fevers, and disease—even the sniffles—were of her making. Some particularly bad afflictions were known as the Witch's Gift or Tetlin's Curse.

Famous the world over, she was feared and detested by Rhunes, Fhrey, and Dherg alike. She was kin to all the spirits of evil, the mother of demons and raow. There were myriad tales in which she lured travelers into her cottage, where she would cook them in a huge blackened pot and then eat the poor victims for dinner, drinking their blood like wine. In all the tales Brin could recall, she noted some commonalities: The witch was usually waiting for time to end; she sat on a stool, and nearly every story had her living near a pond. Brin had remembered quite a bit, but nothing that mattered to their current situation. All the tales about the Tetlin Witch were awful, terrifying things.

And this is her home.

Brin looked up once more at the horrible cliff.

It suits her.

The dark misshapen rocks, the creeping vines dangling from twisted branches, and the impenetrable mist made this as perfect a place as Brin could imagine for the Tetlin Witch to dwell. *Did the witch come here because it suited her, or was this once a paradise that she ruined?*

"You okay?" Tesh asked. He spoke in a whisper. Everyone did, when they talked at all.

She nodded rather than risk making too much noise.

Most simply stared at the rocks surrounding them with anticipation in their eyes. Rain stood entranced. Moya held Audrey, which was strung with an arrow lying across the wood. Only Roan appeared indifferent to their surroundings as she focused on Gifford's leg brace and its strange pair of dents.

"How we gonna do this?" Tesh asked Moya. He double-checked his gear and the hang of his swords.

Moya didn't look happy. "What do you mean?"

"Do you have a strategy?" Tesh asked.

"Strategy?" Tressa said. "What are you talking about? Do you normally make a *battle plan* when visiting someone? We are not hunting her. We aren't here to kill. We're here to ask a favor. Besides, I didn't think any of you believed in the witch. She's just a fairy tale, isn't that right?"

Moya looked at Tressa, then back at Tesh. "Honestly? I don't know. But then I haven't known much about anything since we started, and we're doing pretty good so far." She managed a smile. "I mean, we're here, aren't we? We're on . . . *her* island. Assuming, of course, she does exist." Moya added this last part while nodding at Tressa.

A day ago, almost all of them had been happy to spit the name of Tetlin like the shells of sunflower seeds. Since crossing the land bridge, no one had used her name. Not even Moya had slipped, and she had once won the dubious, though unofficial, award for Dahl Rhen's foulest mouth.

"Oh great, it's raining." Moya shook her head while looking up at the sky with a palm turned up to shield against the droplets. "What is it with this place and wanting to keep us soaked?"

"Whatever we're doing, we ought to do it soon," Tekchin said. "Days are shorter than they used to be. Best not to be 'not hunting her' in the dark."

"All right." Moya straightened up. "Okay, let's do this. Everyone stay close. No spreading out. I don't want anyone getting lost." She faced Tressa. "I can't believe I'm asking, but what do *you* think? How should we proceed if we aren't supposed to . . . you know?" She glanced at Tesh.

Tressa licked her lips, then shook her head. "I suspect we need to find her and ask politely if she can show us the way to the secret underground passage."

"Something tells me it's not going to be that easy," Moya said.

Everyone hoisted their packs, drew up hoods, and formed behind Moya, who led the way through the forest of giant faces and up the rocky cliff.

The trip from the beach was strenuous. Steep ledges required hands, feet, roots, rocks, and vines to climb. On two occasions Moya, Gifford, Tressa, and Roan needed a boost, and Rain needed a pair of hoists. Being agile and thin, Brin was proud that she didn't need any assistance, and she'd never understood how anyone could be afraid of heights.

Once at the top, they found an overgrown but deeply dug path and followed it into a forest. The trees were stunted, with huge knobby trunks, black, wrinkled bark, and low branches. Some had lost their leaves, exposing delicate bony fingers that groped for something too far to touch. For all her previous urgency, Moya now moved hesitantly, peering through the mist. She jumped when a raven took flight, but then so did Tekchin, who walked just behind her. Brin was surprised Moya hadn't dropped the bird in mid-flight with an arrow, or at least shouted out "Tet!"

"Path splits," Moya told everyone, coming to a stop. Their neat little parade broke pattern to look forward.

They had arrived at a mysterious and spooky standing stone that towered a good seven feet in height but only four feet wide. The dark rock was speckled in a pale blue-green lichen, but offered no marking, no indication why it was there or where each path went.

Moya looked to Brin and Tressa. "Any ideas?"

Brin had none; neither did Tressa; and both of them shrugged.

Moya agreed with this conversation of ignorance and shrugged, too, then continued up the right-hand path. That wasn't the direction Brin would have taken because it was the darker way, deeper into the forest. Yet the choice made sense. They weren't looking for a place to picnic.

As they walked, grass diminished and trees grew dense. Naked branches, painted black by the rain, managed to join hands overhead, creating a stick-roofed tunnel. Beneath their feet, rocks and sprawling roots conspired to trip them. Everything else remained a mystery shrouded in mist. Not long after the split, the rain that had pattered lightly for hours stopped quibbling and came down in earnest, drumming thunderously on what few leaves remained. The trail turned into a trickling stream. While she couldn't be certain given the mist and clouds, Brin thought it might be getting dark.

Again, Moya stopped, and the line halted behind her.

They waited, but Moya didn't move or speak. Brin stepped out of line to look ahead, and in the growing dark, she saw a yellow light through the haze. Moya began moving again, slower, more cautiously. They passed a bucket sitting on a tree stump that Moya took a hard look at. The pail, which was close enough so that it wasn't lost in the fog but far enough away to appear unreal, sat upright and was filled with little stones. *Plink*s and *plunk*s played by the rain on its rim made a mournful, haunting sound.

The trail ended at a clearing where a small hut sat next to a little pond. Built of intertwined branches pale with age and piles of moss-covered stone, the little place was round, with a roof of heavy thatch and vines shaped into a lopsided peak like a traditional witch's hat. A steady stream of smoke issued through a chimney made of loosely stacked stones, and a light flickered through a small window beside a wooden door.

"There it is," Tressa said and began to softly sing:

> *"She waits they say for time to end and for her life to be through,*
> *Until that time, she waits for me and also waits for you.*
> *Within a hut of tilted peak, the Tetlin Witch does dwell."*

"There's more to that song?" Moya asked, her voice a harsh whisper.

Tressa frowned. "Yeah."

"Why didn't you tell us before?"

306 · Michael J. Sullivan

"Didn't think it mattered. If we never found the island, it wouldn't have. And after I sang that first verse, you were all looking at me like I was nuts. Extending the serenade wasn't gonna help my cause."

They had gathered to either side of Moya, who stood between the pond and a chopping block adorned with a wedged hatchet. Dark, ruddy patches stained the top of the block as well as the blade. The rain continued to fall, flowing off the roof and striking the ax's handle. The fat droplets made the pond dance and pinged off the sides of another stone-filled bucket, which was near the door of the house.

"Since we aren't here to raid the place, shall I go knock?" Tesh asked. After getting no response, he took a step forward.

"Wait." Moya dragged wet hair out of her eyes. "I'll do it." She held Audrey out to Tekchin. "I don't think I'll need her for this." Then she took off her pack and set it on the grass. Turning around, she looked at the rest of them. "I guess this is it."

Moya sucked in a deep conscious breath, fisted her hands, and faced the hut.

"I'll go with you," Tekchin said.

"No." Moya shook her head. "There's a difference between a woman knocking on an old person's door and a man in battle gear doing it."

"I'll go with you, then," Brin said, quickly pulling off her pack.

"Brin," Tesh protested. "You—"

She dropped her gear and held up a hand. "I'm going."

"That's not an old woman in there," Tesh said. "This isn't a neighborly visit."

"I actually have to agree with Tesh here." Tekchin folded his arms over Audrey. "Treating the ah—her—like Padera might not be the best strategy."

"And approaching her like she's a murderous bear in a den would be?" Moya said. "Wanna make spears? Maybe build a fire to flush her out? If this is you-know-who, she's been around a long time, and I'm sure she's dealt with worse than the likes of us."

Tekchin scowled.

"Malcolm wouldn't send us here if she was going to eat us," Tressa said.

"See?" Moya grinned.

"You're listening to *Tressa* now?" Tekchin asked.

"He's right," Tesh said. "Malcolm doesn't know anything. I lived with him. He has trouble putting boots on."

"You saved that for now, did you?" Moya asked. "Listen, I want the rest of you to stay here. If Brin and I are eaten, then you can do what you feel is best."

"I didn't come along to let Brin get *eaten*," Tesh said.

Brin looked up at him. "I thought you came because you loved me."

"I did."

"Then wait here."

He started to speak, but Brin put fingers to his lips. "You risk your life going to the Harwood. I let you go because I love you, and that's what you want to do. I know that doing so is part of who you are."

"But I'm a warrior. That's my job. You know that."

Brin nodded. "And you know I'm the Keeper of Ways, right? This is *my job*."

"It's not supposed to be dangerous," Tesh insisted.

"Can we argue about this later?" Moya asked.

"There might not be a later," Tesh snapped. "I don't want her to die."

"It's my job to witness. It's who I am. Aside from helping to save Suri, that's why I came. That's what I do—what *I want* to do."

"Maybe that's why Malcolm picked you," Tressa said, more to herself than to Brin.

"Except he didn't. He never said a word about it," Brin said.

"Then why are you here?"

"To help Suri."

"No." Tressa shook her head. "That's too simple." The woman was speaking more to herself than anyone else. She looked around at all of them.

"It's just like in the smithy. I had to bring seven others because each of us has to do our part. Rain has his own quest. Roan knows about tides. Gifford can talk to trees. Tekchin and Tesh can fight. Moya has her bow. Malcolm picked me because he considers me a mason, but why is *Brin* here?"

"I told you, to save Suri."

"You've been teaching me to read. How come?"

"Because Malcolm said—" Brin stopped then continued with a slight quiver in her voice. "He said I had to teach others to read."

"Just a touch," Tressa said, "a hint, a light nudge. That's how he does it. Because he told you that, you were nice to me. And since you were nice to me, Roan and Gifford included you in the meeting about this trip." Tressa nodded. "Malcolm wanted you here."

Brin was terrified but more determined than ever. She turned to Moya. "Let's go."

Rain looked at Tressa. "I didn't know you were a mason."

"Neither did I."

Moya and Brin strode forward. They were only a few dozen yards from the door, but the distance seemed like miles. Flat paving stones made a walkway, and when at last they stood at the end, Moya reached up and knocked. Then they both stood still in the rain and held their breath. In Brin's head she reran the little song Tressa had most recently sung:

> *She waits they say for time to end and for her life to be through,*
> *Until that time, she waits for me and also waits for you.*
> *Within a hut of tilted peak, the Tetlin Witch does dwell . . .*

They heard a latch lift.

Brin's body rocked with the beat of her heart. The sound of the rain came and went with the same rhythm as blood pulsing in her ears. At the last minute, she reached out and took hold of Moya's hand. Moya accepted it and squeezed.

The door drew back, letting light escape. They saw a woman. Done up in brown braids, her hair revealed a long neck and high forehead. The dangling earrings made of tiny threaded stones rattled when she moved. She wasn't old nor was she young. Her cheeks were high, neck smooth, hair dark. Some creases flirted with the corners of her mouth and around her eyes. Brin had expected her pupils to glow or to find the whole of her eyes to be opaque black—or maybe white. Instead, they were normal, albeit an odd color. Unlike the brown eyes of the Rhunes, the pale gray of the Dherg, or the blue eyes of the Fhrey, hers were a greenish-gray. Brin thought only Nolyn had green eyes, but while the child's were bright with youth, this woman's were deep and disturbing. Peering into them gave Brin the same sensation as looking at a starry night—as if she were seeing eternity and beyond.

"Hello?" The woman greeted them pleasantly enough.

"Ah . . . hi," Moya replied, her face devastated with crushing confusion.

Brin knew exactly how she felt. *Is* this *the witch? She doesn't look the part.*

The greenish-eyed woman waited a bit longer, holding the door. When Moya still didn't say anything, she peered up at the sky. "Something of a wet night to be out wandering. Can I assume you're lost?"

"Are you the Tetlin Witch?" Moya burst out, and Brin felt her heart stop.

The woman's brows rose, and Moya grimaced, cringing in expectation of disaster.

"Are you *looking* for the Tetlin Witch?" the woman asked.

"Yes . . . yes, we are. It's very important."

"Important, is it?" The woman narrowed her eyes. Somewhere behind her came the crackle of a fire. "Maybe you should come inside then. Would you like that?"

Moya glanced at Brin. In that look Brin saw a million questions, and she didn't have a single answer.

"You don't have to," the woman said quite kindly. "It's just"—she looked up at the water running off the roof—"raining pretty hard."

The woman backed up, leaving the door open. Inside was a warm, dry room with a wooden floor and rugs. A stone fireplace burned three logs and illuminated a rocking chair with a basket beside it. The woman returned to the chair, where she picked up knitting needles connected to a work in progress, then sat down.

"Please don't leave the door open. The water splashes in, and there's a chill."

Moya, still holding Brin's hand, stepped inside and let the door close. Nothing was frightening. This could have been Brin's old roundhouse, for all its hominess.

The smell of baking bread and the warmth of the hearth greeted them with a friendly embrace, which was beyond wonderful in contrast with the previous night in the swamp. To be honest, it was better than any place she'd been since the fall of Alon Rhist—possibly since Dahl Rhen. That's what it felt like: her own home.

Looking around, Brin saw herbs, spatulas, mallets, and pots hanging from the rafters, but what she noticed most were the stones. They were everywhere. Many had a hole in the center, allowing them to be threaded like beads. The rocks filled ceramic bowls, cups, jars, and baskets. A pile of small stones littered the little wooden table, only the corner of which was revealed by the firelight. A butter churn was tucked to one side, and a series of wet clothes were hung up near the fire. The inside of the little hut appeared far larger than the outside promised, but most was lost to darkness as the fire burned low.

"So what brings you to the island?" the woman asked. She was wearing a pleasant but simple brown dress with a tan shawl. Her face was round, and her ears had a slight angle, but they weren't pointed like a Fhrey. She looked human, except for the odd-colored eyes. She rocked slowly while knitting. In many ways, she reminded Brin of her own mother.

This is so odd. Maybe it's an enchantment? Is the witch making everything so pleasant to lure us in, catch us off guard? That's what happened in the stories.

Moya took two steps and stood before the woman in her rocker. "Are you the witch?"

The woman frowned as water drizzled down Moya's clothes onto the rug.

"My name is Muriel. This is my home, and would you mind standing off the rug until you stop dripping?"

Moya shuffled back to the wood floor. Again, Moya glanced at Brin, this time with far less panic but just as much desperation and confusion. "So you're not a witch?"

Muriel smiled. "No, not a witch. Does that disappoint you?"

"Ah . . . actually, yes . . . yes, it does. We've come a long way—well, not really all that far, but it's been a harrowing trip, and we were hoping . . ." Moya focused on the fire and bit her lip.

"Yes?"

Moya laughed self-consciously. "We were hoping the witch could show us a passage to the Fhrey homeland."

"Across the Green Sea?" Muriel raised her brows again.

There was a knock on the door.

"Busy night," Muriel said with a smile. She gave them a helpless look as she held up the knitting in her hands that might one day be a scarf. "Can you get that?"

Before Brin could reach it, the door opened and Tekchin and Tesh burst in with swords drawn.

"It's okay," Moya said, stopping them. "We're fine. It's all right. She's not . . ." Moya sighed. "She's not the witch."

The two warriors gave a quick look around to confirm this, then adopted awkward, apologetic frowns. Tressa, Roan, Gifford, and Rain crept up behind them, each slowly entering, peering around nervously.

"Oh, yes, please, everyone just walk right in," Muriel said sarcastically. "Don't mind the rugs. Just puddle where you like."

"Listen," Moya said to the woman, sighing and shaking her head, "I'm sorry about all this. I think we were misinformed." She took a moment to glare at Tressa.

"Oh? Someone told you to come here?" Muriel made a soft clicking with her knitting needles.

"A friend of ours named Malcolm told Tressa"—Moya pointed at her—"that the Tetlin Witch lived on this island and that she could show us a secret way to Estramnadon. There was supposed to be a tunnel." Moya shrugged self-consciously. "You see, we're desperate to save a friend of ours who is trapped over there, and we thought this might be a way of doing that. But I guess not."

Muriel shook her head and smacked her lips in regret. "I'm sorry. There's no tunnel here."

"It's not a tunnel," Tressa said.

Moya put hands to hips. "You said it was."

"No, I said it was a *passageway*."

"There's no passage across the sea from here, either," Muriel said.

"It's at a pool," Tressa declared. "That's where the entrance is."

The moment Tressa said this, Muriel's face lost its kindly smile. She turned her head to better study Tressa, eyes narrowing, brow wrinkling. "There *is* a pool, but it doesn't lead to the Fhrey lands."

"It goes to a garden door," Tressa went on. "A special door right in the middle of the Fhrey city. Right in the heart of it. A door that can't normally be opened."

Tekchin's eyes widened. In the six years Moya had known him, she had never seen such an expression, a surreal mix of surprise and—fear.

"You're not talking about a door," he said. "You're speaking of *the Door*."

"Who cares which door it is?" Moya said. "The only thing that matters is how do we get to it?"

Tekchin took hold of Moya. "You don't understand. She's talking about the Door in the Garden."

Moya relaxed. "The way you're acting, I would have expected something more ominous. A garden door sounds nice."

He struggled to find the words. "It's hard to explain to someone who isn't Fhrey. It's believed to be the gateway between this world and the next. Between Elan and Phyre."

"And this is an *actual* door?" Moya asked. "You have a real door in your hometown that leads to the afterlife?"

Tekchin nodded. "It might just be symbolic. But the Umalyn—the priests of our people—believe it's real. It's a simple wooden thing right in the center of the city of Estramnadon, but no one has ever been able to open it. A lot of people think that's a good thing because beyond the Door is the world of the dead."

This left all of them looking to one another with raised brows.

"So okay, wait." Moya tilted her head at Tressa. "What are you saying? How would we, ah . . ." She hesitated, thinking it through as illustrated by the way she rotated her hands around each other as if she were winding up thread. "Are you saying that to go through this *passageway* of yours we need to—to die?"

Tressa looked down at her feet. "I told you the path goes underground—far, far underground."

"How far, Tressa?"

"Through the underworld," Tressa said softly. Then looking up hastily, she added, "I know it sounds kind of crazy, but—"

Moya's eyes widened. "Oh, there's nothing *kind of* about it. That's full-out eat-rocks-and-spit-pebbles insane."

"Malcolm told me this is the only way to save Suri. The entrance is at a pool near here, and that is where we need to go in. That's where we start."

"You mean that's where we die," Moya corrected.

Tressa frowned. "The underworld is smaller than the real one. Because it's inside Elan, the trip will be shorter. We'll be able to catch up to Suri—"

"This was all—oh, Tressa, this was one huge mistake. I can just see going back to Persephone and telling her, *All we need to do is kill the whole legion and send them over.*"

"The legion isn't supposed to go," Tressa said. "Just us."

"Us?" Roan asked, peeking out from behind Gifford.

Tressa nodded. "Seven are supposed to go with me into Rel."

"Into—wait—you knew?" Moya started to laugh. "Oh, Tressa. You didn't bring us here thinking we'd join you in a group suicide, did you?"

"I brought you here because this is the only way to save Suri before she is tortured by the fane into giving up the secret of dragons. If that happens, we're all going to die anyway, so what difference does it make?"

Moya nodded, looking disgusted. "When I think of all those leeches I pulled off me . . ." She used a fingernail to hook the wet hair from her face. "Look, I'm sorry we bothered you—Muriel, is it?"

The woman nodded.

Moya shook her head. "This has been just a terrible—"

Tressa began singing again, taking it from the top this time:

> *"Far beyond the woodland hills, beyond the mountains vile,*
> *Hidden in a mist-soaked swamp upon an awful isle.*
> *She haunts the lapping blackened pools and creeping ivy ways,*
> *And there awaits with hair of brown and eyes of greenish-gray."*

As she finished the stanza, Tressa pointed at Muriel as evidence, then went on:

> *"She waits they say for time to end and for her life to be through,*
> *Until that time, she waits for me and also waits for you.*
> *Within a hut of tilted peak, the Tetlin Witch does dwell,*
> *And watches at the fetid pond, the door that leads to Rel."*

Moya glared at her. "You lied to us! Giving us just part of your little puzzle a piece at a time because you knew we—is there more to that stupid song?"

Tressa nodded and continued:

> *"And there she sits upon her stool beside the very brink,*
> *And watches as the fated fools down into darkness sink.*
> *Beware the Tetlin Witch, my friend, and never go astray,*
> *Beyond the woodland hills, beyond the light of day.*
>
> *Or you, too, may find yourself caught up in the mire,*
> *Sinking, screaming uselessly, helpless till you tire.*
> *Then under the muck, under the water, thrashing to and fro,*
> *All of you lost, forever gone, the witch cackling as you go."*

"I can see why you kept the rest to yourself," Moya said.

Tressa took a breath. "She *is* the Tetlin Witch. There *is* a pool, and there *is* a passageway that connects to the door in Estramnadon."

Brin took a step forward, a step closer to Muriel. "Your hair is brown, and your eyes are a greenish-gray. No one has greenish-gray eyes."

The woman didn't reply.

"Odd place to live all by yourself," Tressa observed.

"It's quiet—usually." Muriel smiled. "I like quiet."

"Who are you?" Brin asked.

"I'm an old woman who lives on an island past a swamp that most visitors avoid. Which raises the question . . . Who are *you?*"

Brin didn't answer. Something wasn't right in that little hut, and she was glad to have Tesh with her. But this wasn't like when they faced a raow. Brin found nothing frightening about the woman, and yet she couldn't help feeling uneasy.

"This is Brin, who has apparently forgotten her manners," Moya volunteered. "You've already met Tressa. And I'm Moya. We are all originally from Dahl Rhen. I'm the Shield to Keenig Persephone. We're all—"

Muriel tilted her head slightly as a smile grew. "So *you're* Moya."

Narrowing her eyes, Moya looked closer at the woman in the rocker. "You know me?"

"I know *of* you. Met your mother once."

"My *mother?*" Moya shook her head. "You couldn't have met my mother. She never left the dahl."

"Her name was Audrey, yes?"

Moya nodded, stunned.

"She said you weren't a very good daughter." Muriel looked down at her knitting. "Supposedly, she had trouble with you her whole life because you never listened to her. No matter how many times she told you to do something, you just didn't. She was convinced you acted that way out of spite."

"Sounds like her," Moya said. "And she was right—at least about the spite thing."

Muriel nodded. "Is that why you didn't give her a stone?"

"Pardon?"

Muriel stopped knitting to look up. "A burial stone. A person usually puts one in the hands of loved ones before burying them. It's the responsibility of the next of kin."

"I—ah—ah . . . I left the funeral early. I wasn't even there when she went into the ground. Are you saying . . ." Concern spread across her face.

Muriel sighed and went back to clicking her needles. "Even if you two didn't get along, that's really no excuse. She was quite upset about it."

"Wait—" Moya glared at the woman with the green-gray eyes. "Are you saying—do you expect me to believe you met my mother *after* she died?"

Muriel nodded. "She came here. She was angry that you didn't have the decency to put her to rest properly. You can thank me for not being visited by her."

"*Visited* by her?"

"Some do that," Muriel said, pulling on a difficult line of yarn that protested before leaving the basket. "The angry ones. When they can't get into Phyre and have nowhere else to go, they walk home. Their presence can be quite disconcerting to those they left behind. When far away from the entrance to Phyre, you can't generally see or hear them, but they may move things around, blow doors or windows open, or just make you feel a deep chill. The really angry ones, well, they can do more. They channel that anger into a force that can drive a living person insane, even make them harm themselves.

"Truth be told, she probably wouldn't have sought you out. She wasn't *that* mad. Like I said, we had a nice chat, and she eventually calmed down. I took care of her."

"How?"

"A stone. I gave her one. As you can see, I keep a good many on hand."

"*You* gave my mother a stone?"

"Can't get into Phyre without one."

Brin looked around at the little stones stacked on tables, piled near the door, and filling the baskets.

Muriel caught her looking and nodded. "Many come here. Must be the light in the window. That's who I thought *you* were, to be honest." She looked at Tesh and Tekchin. "Figured there had been a battle or something. It's unusual for so many to show up at the same time. I thought maybe a small village had been attacked by the sort of men that don't mind killing women, or maybe a flood took all of you. That's usually how it happens, you know, something sudden, something where the bodies can't be found. Otherwise, your kin would give you a proper burial, complete with a stone. Imagine my surprise when you turned out to be alive." She chuckled.

"Then the entrance to Phyre—to Rel—really is here?" Brin asked.

"You can get into Phyre from anywhere . . . Brin, is it? You merely need to die."

Hearing her say it, hearing her name, Brin felt a chill that had nothing to do with being wet on a cold night.

"But the song says there's a pool and a door that leads to Rel," Brin protested.

"Creative discretion, I suppose. This island is a weak place, a point where this world and the afterworld come very close to touching." She set down her knitting in order to illustrate the point by bringing her two index fingers together. "Where the walls separating the two are very thin. When you die, you travel to one of the three realms of Phyre on a river. That river acts like all rivers, emptying into a larger one, in the same manner the nearby swamp marks the mouth of the Ithil River. This world and the other mimic each other. The pool you speak of is the very intersection between the worlds, the point where they touch."

"How do you know all this?"

"They tell me."

"They?"

Muriel displayed that cozy, good-natured smile of hers, but Brin wasn't taken in. Still, she was happy, considering what the other alternatives might be.

"You see, spirits who have stones ride the River of Death to this point—to the mouth—and then they sink right down to Phyre. But the ones who weren't given one, well, they pop up and begin to wander. Oftentimes they make their way here and bob about in this shallow place at the end of the ride."

Muriel stepped away from them and waved at the interior of her firelit hut, with its beautiful rustic baskets and tables with pretty designs carved into them. "Because the worlds are so close here, spirits can be seen and heard, and they come up here all the time. Lost and confused, most of them have no idea where to go or what to do. They come and sit by the fire." She indicated the pair of seats. "We chat. They tell me about their lives, their loves, and their regrets. They talk a lot, but eventually they just settle into staring at the fire. That's when I offer a stone. With some I can see the realization, but others surprisingly have no clue. *Need it to cross into Phyre,* I tell them. Some nod with understanding. They try to take the stone, but of course they can't. It takes some explaining then—how the stone is a symbol of weight—that's why it doesn't need to be a big stone. It's just an idea. When it's buried with them, the whole thing is intuitive. Gets a little trickier when I have to explain it to them in front of a fire. Of course, some don't want to hear. The angry ones . . ." Muriel shook her head, her expression changing to frustration. "Some are so furious at their family that they refuse the stone and head home, seeking to punish them."

"Manes," Tesh said.

Muriel nodded. "Others—well, others just don't want to be dead, refuse to accept the truth. So they stay. Angry and frustrated, they head out to haunt the world, but usually they just go back to what was familiar: the place they used to live, a place they were once happy, or sometimes the place where they died."

"And you don't find it odd that all these ghosts visit you all the time?" Moya asked.

Muriel shook her head. "Not anymore. I've been here a long time. What's odd is getting a visit from live people, let alone eight of them at once. And that song, 'Beyond the Woodland Hills,' I'm surprised it hasn't been forgotten by now. Who taught it to you?"

"His name is Malcolm," Tressa said proudly.

"And how does he know about me?"

"Malcolm knows everything," Tressa said.

"I doubt that. If he sent you to travel through Phyre as a means of getting to Estramnadon, it doesn't sound like he knows much." The woman had resumed her knitting with the same sort of suppressed amusement a mother might express to a five-year-old child who was explaining how they were going to run away from home and join a band of thieves. "Only the dead can enter Phyre. And once in, you can't get back out. That's sort of the thing about death. It tends to be permanent. The spirit separates from the body, then the body rots to dust—pretty quickly, too. So, even if you could get out of the underworld, which you can't because the doors lock behind you, there wouldn't be a functioning body to re-inhabit."

At the word *lock,* Tressa smiled and placed a hand on her chest.

"Yeah, see, we didn't know that was the plan," Moya said. "That part about Rel was sort of left out of the story when I heard it." She moved from the warmth of the fire to peer out the windows of the hut. "Look, this was a mistake, and you have my sincere apologies, but it's still raining pretty hard out there. Would you mind if we stayed until it lets up? We won't cause any trouble. It's cold outside, and we are kinda tired of being wet. Do you mind?"

Muriel was still looking at Tressa, her sight shifting from her face to the hand on her chest. "Stay as long as you like."

CHAPTER TWENTY-EIGHT

The Key

*Now that I know where the legend came from and the truth behind
the tales, I can see why we were taught what we were. But we had it
wrong. So very wrong. Truth, I learned, is so much more terrifying
than myth.*

— THE BOOK OF BRIN

"I wasn't expecting visitors," Muriel said as they gathered on the floor
before the hearth, where she stirred a blackened pot. "I generally don't eat
much, which means I don't have much on hand."

The woman had made soup. That's what she said at least; Brin wasn't
so sure. Muriel had cooked it up in a big black cauldron that hung from
a soot-covered metal arm that swiveled over and off the fire. There were
a lot of black chains and hooks dangling from the bottom of the mantel:
fishhooks, pot hooks, bread toasters, and milk warmers. And then there
were the tools: peelers, scrapers, shovels, tongs, brooms, knives—lots
of knives—and one massive saw. Also, to either side were ceramic pots,
pitchers, and pans, all different sizes and shapes, each with some form of
liquid inside.

A cauldron. Brin stared at the huge fire-scorched pot as Muriel stirred
it with a great wooden spoon. If Brin had been asked to create a picture
of the Tetlin Witch, this would be the scene she would draw. All of it was

right there, perfect in its homey horror. Muriel herself didn't quite fit. She wasn't the old crone with the hooked nose and warts that she was reputed to be. As Brin watched her cut carrots and potatoes, Muriel only built on Brin's earlier impression of a spinster aunt—one whom Brin would have enjoyed visiting.

The woman dipped a wooden bowl into the pot, scraped the drip off the side, then handed it to Moya. "Careful, it's hot."

"Moya?" Brin said as casually as she could. "Could I talk to you?" She said this while jerking her head toward the door.

"What, now?"

Brin nodded.

Moya looked miffed. She was cold, wet, and hungry, and a steaming bowl of wonderful-smelling soup had just been handed to her. Brin was getting in the way.

"What is it, Brin?" Moya asked.

"Could you come over here, maybe?"

"She wants to warn you not to eat the soup," Muriel said. "I'm guessing she doesn't like the look of my cooking pot. A little too witchy for her comfort. And food is dangerous. The aroma is so enticing when you're hungry. And hot food when you're cold and wet, well, that's hard to pass up, isn't it?"

Moya looked at the bowl, now with some suspicion.

Outside, the rain continued to pour, drumming on the roof and slapping the windows.

"Food is always a danger in old stories, isn't it, Brin?" Muriel said. "That's how *they* get you, right? How the *witch* gets you. I bet you've never been able to understand how people in the stories are so easily duped into eating food offered to them in caves and witches' kitchens. The legends speak about how irresistible the food is, but you could never see how it could be *that* seductive that people would cast caution to the wind." Muriel gestured toward Moya's bowl. "It's not poison or bewitched. It's chicken soup. I ate the last of the bird yesterday and have been boiling down the carcass all morning. Her name was Mildred, and she made the fatal mistake of no longer laying eggs. So, I chopped her head off and roasted her over this fire. I'm quite certain that at least Mildred would agree with you that I'm not to be trusted."

"Is that what you wanted to tell me, Brin?"

Brin nodded.

"You don't have to eat it, and . . ." Muriel lifted the bowl to her own lips and slurped. "Yep, it is definitely not very good. Not my best at all."

Moya looked at the bowl.

"Careful," Muriel warned her. "I was serious before. It's hot."

Moya dipped her bread in, soaked up the broth, and ate. "I wonder what your best is, 'cause this is great," she said while chewing.

"It's because you're hungry."

They all gave Moya a second to swallow and then a moment more. Tekchin sat beside her with a concerned face.

"She's right," Moya finally said, exasperated with the stares. "It's chicken soup."

She held out the bowl to Tekchin. "Try it."

The Fhrey carefully slurped and smiled. "Very good."

Muriel only had one wooden bowl so they passed it around the circle, refilling it as needed. Everyone but Brin had some, which left her feeling stupid and wondering what she would do if all of them suddenly turned into toads or fell asleep and couldn't be woken up.

Muriel then made tea that she poured into three ceramic cups and these, too, were passed around. Tressa helped hand them out as Muriel returned the pot to the hearth. "I have to admit it's nice to have living, breathing visitors. I get lonely out here sometimes."

"Lonely?" Moya chuckled. "Of course you do. Look where you live. Why don't you move to a town, a nice village with people?"

Muriel sat on the floor with the rest of them, putting her back to the hearthstone. "I used to live in a perfectly nice village. A beautiful place in a green valley between two mountains, which had a lovely stream running through it." She smiled, looking beyond all of them. "Beautiful place. The hills were such a striking color—well, you just don't see that shade anymore. If you did, you'd think it strange. Too green, you'd say. But it wasn't; it was perfect. Today, people don't understand perfection. Everything has to have a flaw or it isn't real. Those hills were real. I can still see them, and that stream, and that sky."

"The sky was different?" Tesh asked.

"Everything was—the same way your sandals are different the first time you wear them compared to the last. And the smells, and the tastes . . ." She continued to stare as if she might say more, but she didn't.

"Why'd you leave?" Brin asked.

"Because it's depressing to watch people you love die. Seems like you just get to know them, start to really care about someone, and then"—she threw up her hands—"they're gone. Every. Single. One. No exceptions. They all leave, and you're still there. Each time, a little bit of you goes with them, until you start feeling empty, like one of those old hollowed-out trees—the ones you wonder how they're still standing. So you start to avoid making friends because you know you'll just get hurt. But people don't like recluses. They think they're up to no good and have something to hide. When everyone else ages and you do not, and when everyone else gets sick, but you never do, it bothers some people—*most* people, as it turns out. When you're held underwater for an hour or are tied to a huge pile of wood that's set on fire, and you still don't die, well, folks don't like that even more."

"Tetlin," Roan said. "The village between the mountains was named Tetlin."

"You *are* the Tetlin Witch, aren't you?" Brin blurted out.

"I'm not a *witch*," Muriel said pointedly, even a bit irritated.

"Sorry," Brin said. "But when people use that name, it's you who they are referring to, right?"

Muriel shrugged. "Folks talk behind people's backs all the time. I'm sure people have called you names, too. Some you know; others you don't."

"Everyone . . ." Brin hesitated. "Everyone says you're evil."

"*Everyone,* really? Odd. You eight are the first living souls I've seen in generations. I'm guessing there are a lot of rumors floating round. And one"—she looked at Tressa—"seems to suggest I guard a gateway to the Door in Estramnadon's Garden."

"Do you?" Tressa asked.

"No. And I told you: Once you enter Phyre, there is no way out."

"What if there was?" Tressa asked. "Would it be possible to pass through and come out in this Fhrey city?"

"No. It isn't possible."

Tressa looked shocked, then angry. "You don't know anything."

Muriel watched her, brows wrinkling again. "You believe you can get out. Why?"

"None of your business," Tressa snapped.

Muriel leaned forward toward her. "You made it my business when you entered my home. Why won't you tell me? Is it because"—she flashed a look at Brin—"you think I'm evil? Are you afraid I plan on stuffing you into my cooking pot?"

Brin felt herself flush, but Tressa just shook her head. "He told me to keep it safe."

"This Malcolm fellow did?"

Tressa nodded.

"The same person who knew where I lived and sent you to ask for my help?"

Tressa nodded again, but more slowly and with less confidence.

"And did he specifically say *not* to tell me?"

It took a moment, but Tressa finally shook her head with a frown.

"But you're still not going to, are you?" When Tressa didn't answer, Muriel sighed. "Fine. So who is this person? This one called Malcolm," she said, looking around at all of them. "How does he know me? How does he know I live on this island? It's not like I make announcements."

"Malcolm knows everything," Tressa said.

"Oh, right, I forgot. Is he an oracle, then?"

Tressa looked insulted. "If you must know, he's a god."

"Oh," Muriel said. "I'm not familiar with a god named Malcolm. Is he new? What is he the god of?"

Tressa folded her arms, scowling.

"You don't know? You're certain he's a god but don't know what of?"

"I'm pretty certain you're a witch, and I don't know much about you, either," Tressa said.

"Adds a whole new dimension to the phrase *Takes one to know one,* doesn't it?" Moya said.

"Are you Fhrey? Is that why you live so long?" Roan asked Muriel as if she hadn't heard anything since she made the connection about Muriel being from the village of Tetlin. "You don't look Fhrey."

"I'm not. But I remember when the Followers of Ferrol moved to Erivan. That was right about the time I moved here, I think."

"That's not possible," Tekchin said. "That would have been over nine thousand years ago."

She nodded. "Something like that. I don't keep track of years anymore. It just depresses me." Muriel looked back at Tressa. "How do you know he's a god? I mean, apparently everyone knows I'm a witch because I live in a hut in a remote island and can remember the dawn of time, right? So how do you know this Malcolm is a god—other than he seems to know a lot about other people's business. And come to think of it, why don't you think *he's* a witch? How does he get god status while I get the title of witch? How does that work? Seems a bit unfair."

Tressa opened her mouth, then shut it.

"Did he *say* he was a god?"

"No."

"Then how—"

"Because he can tell the future," Tressa said. "He knows the destiny and the past of every single person. He knows we're here right now. He knows we're sitting and talking to you."

"Oh, well, that does sound awfully godlike," Muriel said, and Brin couldn't tell if she was being sarcastic or not.

"Malcolm isn't a god," Moya said. "He's a tall, lanky guy with a sharp nose, who I hear has trouble putting his boots on, and he uses a spear he named Narsirabad, which by the way means 'pointy' in Fhrey and illustrates how ungodlike he is."

Muriel went to set her cup down and nearly spilled it. She stared at Moya, shocked.

"What?" Moya asked.

"This *Malcolm,*" she began, still struggling to set down her tea. "*He* sent you *here?*"

"Supposedly . . ." Moya hesitated then jerked a thumb at Tressa. "All we have is her word. She's the one he talked to, and she doesn't really have a stellar reputation for being truthful. Since Malcolm hasn't been around for years, it's not like we could ask him any questions."

Brin expected a response from Tressa, but she stayed silent, her eyes on the witch.

"Why did he send you?" Muriel asked, her tone having turned sharply suspicious. Her demeanor shifted from friendly to defensive as she leaned forward to see them all better.

"I told you," Tressa said. "You're going to show us the way in."

"To Phyre?"

Tressa nodded.

"That doesn't make any sense," Muriel said. "All you—all anyone needs to do to get into Phyre is die. You didn't have to come here to do that."

"We have to go through the entrance near the pool."

"Why?"

"So we can come back out."

Muriel appeared confused and shook her head. "But that's not possible. How are you supposed to do that?"

Tressa once more refused to answer. She even declined to return Muriel's stare, which was odd for Tressa; the woman never shied away from a fight.

"What's around your neck, Tressa?" Muriel asked.

Once more Tressa didn't answer, but a protective hand rose to press between her breasts.

Muriel's brow furrowed once more as her eyes narrowed, and she slowly shook her head. "He couldn't have given *that* to you. And if he had . . . he certainly would never have sent you to *me*."

"What?" Moya asked. "What's going on?"

"This Malcolm," Muriel said, "the tall lanky person who knows the future; has he ever mentioned he might have gone by any other name?"

"He told us his first name," Roan replied.

"He told *Raithe*," Tressa said sharply.

"And what did he say his first name was?" Muriel asked.

Roan looked at Brin, then Moya, and finally Tressa. No one offered any advice. Finally, she said, "Turin."

Muriel got up so quickly that it caused everyone to recoil. After standing, she didn't say a word, didn't move, merely stood stiff, her teeth clenched, hands in fists, breathing hard through flaring nostrils. "I can't believe he would . . ." She lost whatever words she was tracking and ground her teeth.

Muriel walked to the far side of the hut, where she slapped a supporting post hard enough to make herself wince. She shook her injured hand, face bunching up in pain.

"I take it you know him?" Moya asked. She, too, had gotten to her feet. Almost everyone had, except Gifford who had trouble making the transition and Roan who stayed with him.

"Oh, yes. I *know* him." The words seethed through clenched teeth.

"And apparently you don't like him much."

"I *hate* him." Muriel sneered as she spoke. "Yes, that sums it up quite well. I hate him with every particle of my being."

"But he's—" Tressa started, but faltered before the fuming face of the Tetlin Witch. "Why? How could you—how could anyone—*hate* him? He named his spear Pointy."

"That sonofabitch cursed me," Muriel said. "He cursed me with eternal life."

֍

No one said anything for a while. Brin imagined everyone wanted to, but Muriel looked like a red-hot coal, and no one wanted to get burned. Up to this point, Muriel hadn't done anything scary; she hadn't shoved them in an oven, or fed them to wolves, or turned them into toads. She hadn't acted at all like the Tetlin Witch was supposed to. And no one wanted to risk changing that.

After a while and without a word, Muriel began moving around the hut, straightening up the clutter and washing the bowl and cups in a tub of water.

They all watched her, but no one said a word.

The customary motions of cleaning, and the way Muriel appeared hurt, as if she might cry—from either sadness or rage—felt so familiar to Brin. She'd seen her mother clean that way after a fight with her father on hundreds of occasions. The ritual was so similar that Brin lost her fear. She found a cloth and tried to help by wiping down the table, the same way she used to for her mother. Muriel finished the dishes, and as she dried the cups, asked, "Anyone want more tea? I think I could use another cup."

"I'll put a pot on," Brin said and grabbed the kettle.

Muriel watched her. "Are your parents alive, Brin?"

"No," Brin replied.

Muriel nodded. "You're a good daughter."

"Why do you say that?"

"I never met your parents. You must have given them a stone."

"I did." Brin took two steps toward the fire and stopped. "What's it like? In Rel, I mean."

"I can't say for certain. I've never been, and it's unlikely I ever will." Muriel said this with the same biting tone she had displayed earlier. "Like I said, only the dead can enter Phyre. And I can't die."

"I would think that's a good thing," Tekchin proposed.

Muriel looked at the Fhrey with a hint of amusement. "What are you? Twelve, fifteen hundred?"

"Eleven," he said.

She nodded and smiled. "For you, life is still a novelty, isn't it? Still an adventure?"

"How old *are* you?" Tekchin asked, drawing a scowl from Moya.

Muriel showed no offense and simply shrugged as she wrapped the handle of the kettle with a cloth and lifted it off the bracket. "Don't know. There weren't such things as years back then."

Everyone smiled at the unexpected levity. Gifford even laughed. It reminded Brin of a joke Padera would have made.

Muriel stared at them, surprised.

Her open bewilderment cut Gifford's laughter short. He coughed and said, "Nice cups."

"What?" Muriel asked.

"The cups—the teacups—they nice."

"Gifford is a potter," Roan explained. "A really good one, so that's a fine compliment."

"Well, thank you, Gifford. I didn't make them, but thanks." Muriel stood in the shadows, leaning on the table as the crackle of the fire dominated the room.

"I'm sorry," Muriel said eventually, her voice sad and thoughtful. "I'm not used to visitors—living ones, at least. If I had known . . ." She shook her head. "Thin soup isn't a fitting last meal for anyone."

"*Last* meal?" Brin asked, concerned.

"Isn't that why you came?"

"No," Moya said with immediate and absolute conviction. "It isn't."

"It's why I came," Tressa said.

"Get over it, Tressa. There's no way you're going to kill yourself for Malcolm. Why would you? You heard her. Dying won't help Suri because once you're dead, you're dead. When you enter Phyre, you can't get back out."

"Unless you have the key," Muriel said, staring at Tressa.

"What's a key?" Moya asked.

Muriel looked at her, confused. "You don't know what a key is?"

"Should I?"

Muriel opened her mouth to reply, then just stopped, too bewildered to speak.

"A key is something that can open a locked door, one that can't otherwise be opened." Rain's voice came from the back corner, where Brin had lost track of him. The dwarf had a habit of practically disappearing in groups. He was as quiet as Roan and, being smaller, was harder to see. At that moment, he sat between two big baskets of stones, rebuckling his boot. "Usually a key is a bit o' metal shaped in a special way for a particular lock. There's a whole industry in Belgreig around making them. It's how people keep important things safe."

"But we aren't really talking about an *actual* door here, are we?" Moya asked. "I mean, how would that even work?"

"No," Muriel said. "The underworld is not a place of substance. It's not physical. It's spiritual."

"So even if Tressa had a key, it wouldn't matter, right? It's not like she can take it with her when she dies, and there's no real lock to use it on. So I don't understand." Moya looked back and forth between Rain and Muriel.

"If it's the key I think it is, she can," Muriel replied. "*That key*—that's a very special one, and it is able to open any door, any lock, anywhere. Such a device would be incredibly powerful and exactly why Turin would have told her to keep it safe."

Tressa looked nervous under Muriel's watchful eyes.

"So it's a skeleton key, is it?" Rain asked.

"No," Muriel said, "it's Eton's Key."

"Eton?" Brin asked, rerunning the name through her head. *Did she really just say Eton?* Then she pointed up and asked, "You mean, that Eton? The sky Eton?"

Muriel nodded with an apologetic smile that said, *Sorry, but you did ask.* "That's how it can be carried into Phyre. You see, all living things come from the union of Eton, God of the Heavens, and Elan, Grand Mother of

All. He is the sky, the eternal, the unending. She—Elan—is the world that brings forth life and reclaims it. All life born of Eton and Elan has two parts: eternal spirit and temporary body. When the body dies, Elan takes it back. That which is of Eton is eternal and by his edict must be sealed inside Phyre forever. But while they are joined, they are a part of both worlds and can interact with each. The key works the same way. It, too, is made from both Eton and Elan, so it can be touched by both the living and the dead. So, yes, she can take such a key with her."

They were all children around a lodge fire, and Muriel was the storyteller—the sort who relayed a personal tale of events that had occurred long ago on a similar wind-ripped night. People could laugh at such a story in the light of day, but on a mist-soaked, hidden island . . .

"Eton made the key when he created Phyre. It's the only way to open the gates."

Moya gave a slow, off-balance nod. "Ohhhh-kay, but you also said that even if you could get back out of Phyre, you still couldn't get to that garden door from here."

Muriel bent over and leaned on the table, resting her elbows, the drying towel still in her hands. "That's because there are three realms in Phyre: Rel, Nifrel, and Alysin. And then there is the Sacred Grove. All of them must be traversed to reach the Door. Each has its own locked gate, and to get from here to the Door, you'd have to traverse each one."

"But you said Eton's Key opens all locks anywhere, including in Phyre," Tressa said.

"It does."

"So it *is* possible, then?"

"With Eton's Key? Yes," Muriel said. "If you die with Eton's Key, you will take it with you into Phyre, and it will unlock any door, granting you the ability to cross the whole of the underworld and eventually open the Door in Estramnadon."

No one said anything, while outside the wind and what remained of the rain muttered to each other.

"You want me to fetch the legion now, Moya?" Tekchin grinned at her.

"I don't . . ." Moya stumbled. "I don't know what to do with this. This is . . . it's just crazy. That's what it is. It's stupid."

"Go back home, Moya," Tressa said softly. "Everyone go."

"Seven," Roan said. "Seven have to go with you."

"Quit with the numbers, Roan," Moya snapped at her, then glared at Tressa. "And what are you going to do?"

"What I came here for."

"Is that even possible? Do you really have this key? Or is this just some stupid gag of yours?"

Brin thought Moya meant it as an accusation, but it sounded like a plea, more like she hoped it was all a joke.

Tressa hesitated, looking at all of them, then shrugged. "I guess it wouldn't hurt to show you. And she's right; he didn't say I shouldn't." Tressa took hold of the little chain around her neck and drew out the key.

Not gold, not silver, not copper, nor bronze—but the key was some metal. Looking at it, Brin didn't think it all that amazing. It was unusual and pretty in a way—a tiny metallic stem with branches that changed color as it tilted in the light, but nothing about it seemed so grand as what she imagined the key to the afterlife ought to be.

Muriel was shaking her head, and Brin thought for certain she was about to declare that this wasn't the famed key, when she said, "I just can't believe he would send you here with that."

"So, is this Eton's Key?" Moya asked.

Muriel nodded. "Yes, that little bit of metal can throw wide the gates of Phyre."

"When will we do it?" Roan asked, her little voice leaking out of the communal silence that had invaded the hut.

Tressa looked very serious. "I suppose the sooner the better. If we don't save Suri before she gives the secret to the fane, I'm not sure anything else will matter."

"And you're sure you *want* to do this?" Muriel asked. Her words were soft, concerned, sympathetic. She could have been someone's mother.

"Why?" Gifford asked. "Is this a bad idea? I mean, do you think the key won't function? Aw you saying that we can't twust Malcolm?"

"I'm not saying that at all. If Turin gave you that key, and I don't know how else you could have gotten it, and he said it's possible to save this friend with it, then I'm sure that's so—even likely. You see, Turin usually gets his way."

"What do you mean?"

She gestured with her hands, fanning out her fingers and presenting them palms-up. "He's likely hoping you'll beguile me, and you *are* all quite charming. It takes a special kind of person to die for the sake of others. He's betting I'll be moved by that." She shook her head. "But he hasn't really changed. It's just—it's not in his nature."

"Are you saying," Brin started, then stumbled. "I'm sorry. I don't mean to be rude, but are you saying Malcolm is trying to make you fall in love with him?"

"*Me?*" Muriel was so shocked, she began to laugh, then stopped herself and got that faraway look in her eyes again. "You know, I suppose so. In a way, maybe he is. I guess I'm the world in miniature for him."

"So he *can* be twusted?" Gifford asked.

"As far as you're concerned, yes," Muriel said. "It seems he wants you to succeed, and as I said, if Turin wants something, he usually gets it. That's the problem—that's always been the problem."

"Living all the way out here, how well could you possibly know him?" Moya asked.

"Oh, trust me," Muriel said. "I know him very well. He's my father."

CHAPTER TWENTY-NINE

Father and Son

I wonder what sort of relationship Mawyndulë had with his parents. I'm guessing it was not the same as I had with mine. That whole thing with his father just had to be awkward.

— THE BOOK OF BRIN

The wagon came to another stop.

That was good. Movement made it impossible for Suri to ignore where she was, but if the box remained still, and if she kept her eyes closed, she could try to picture herself in a field. Suri struggled to think of nicer places.

Sometimes, the visions helped, and she could relax a little; most times, they didn't, and she went rigid, grinding her teeth and digging half-moon indentations into her palms. When that wasn't enough, she bit herself hard enough to elicit a whimper. She had to because the alternative was to lose control and throw herself against the bars or try to rip up the wood floor. She did her best to think of the box as a cave, one with a big sun-filled entrance, but that was difficult because she could hear people—lots of them. She tried to block them out, but they were close and spoke in excited tones.

"That's a Rhune?"

"How ugly!"

"Why is it wearing clothes?"

"Look at the markings. I'll bet they're war symbols. They do that, you know, paint their faces. They think it gives them power in battle."

"They drink blood, too! Did you know that? Animal blood and the blood of their enemies. And they eat their hearts raw."

Suri tried imagining a bunch of talking rabbits outside her cave, but that didn't help. Rabbits made more sense than those around her. After several minutes, she risked opening her eyes.

The cage was surrounded by Fhrey faces. Young and old, they leered at her. Each expression showed a revolted grimace. Over their heads, she saw a circle of massive trees—the largest trunks Suri had ever seen, including Magda. One was missing, a huge stump marking its absence. To one side, stone steps rose up a hill to a pillared building capped with a dome. To the other stood another hill on which stood a building of similar style, but with more parts: windows, balconies, and wings. Between them was a green area, a neatly tended garden with paths, bushes, trickling streams, and dormant flower beds. A tall curving wall of solid stone was at the center, and in that wall was a door.

Neither Mawyndulë nor Treya was in sight. Several soldiers in gold armor with helms that resembled lion's heads stood around the wagon. They had their backs to her as they faced the crowd. Suri heard clanking, and the box shifted forward then back slightly. A moment later, she saw the horse, which was free of its tack and being led away.

I'm here.

The thought managed to stick in her mind like a pin holding her consciousness steady for the time being. The panic was still there, still needling beneath her skin. Yet the idea she had reached the end of her journey, that she was in Estramnadon, was enough distraction to hold her attention momentarily, diverting it away from the walls.

"Prince Mawyndulë captured it," one of the Fhrey said. "Brought it back from the frontier."

"Why?"

"I don't know."

"Do they all look like this?" one of the Fhrey asked. "How is it taking so long to win the war if they're all so pathetic?"

"Where is the prince?"

"Went into the palace."

"It stinks."

"Looks like it sleeps in its own filth."

"It's nothing but an ugly, skinny pig wearing a dress."

This wasn't how Suri had imagined arriving. She'd seen herself walking proudly into Estramnadon in her lavish asica, chin held high, a friendly smile on her lips. She planned to convince the Fhrey that Rhunes were an enlightened people, explaining as much with her looks, poise, and command of the Art, as with her words—spoken in perfect Estramnadon dialect. Instead, she sneered and said, "And you're a *brideeth eyn mer*."

Suri still didn't know exactly what that meant. Arion had refused to explain the phrase. But it had the effect she was hoping for.

Every eye went wide. Mouths dropped open, and the crowds retreated in fear.

One of the soldiers rapped the bars with a spear. The clang reminded Suri of the cage, of the bars. She began to shudder and shake. Grabbing hold of her legs, she buried her face, closed her eyes, and tried to crawl into the cave again—the cave with the big open mouth that looked out at a shining sun.

ᴘ

Mawyndulë had never cared much for the immense spectacle of the throne room, which he'd always felt was just a little too—Fhrey. The seer Caratacus, who had given Gylindora Fane the Horn of Ferrol, had created the Forest Throne by braiding together six species of living trees—one for each of the original tribes. Thousands of years later, the Forest Throne had grown massive, and the room had been built around it. The throne expanded in all directions, with limbs and leaves pressing along the walls like the splayed hands of someone trying to get out of a box. And while the trees that made up the throne grew out of the ground, there was no visible hole in the floor; the many twisted roots actually created the floor. Likewise, the opening in the great dome was equally hidden by the leafy canopy. While it certainly evoked the innate concert with nature that the Umalyn priests and Eilywin builders insisted on, everything was just too woody for Mawyndulë's taste. He'd always felt that Caratacus had been trying too hard.

"Welcome back," the fane said from his knobby seat.

They weren't alone. As always, Sile and Synne stood on either side of the ridiculous chair. Vasek was there, too, as was First Minister Metis and Commander Taraneh.

"I've brought you the secret of the dragons, my fane." He didn't know why he used the title. Perhaps it simply felt more grown-up than *Father*.

The fane eyed Mawyndulë with a terrible intensity that worried the prince. Mawyndulë had half expected his return to be seen as a moment of triumph—the doubt only existing because his father had never revealed much affection or pride in his son. But seeing Lothian's current expression, Mawyndulë wondered if the rumors about his father becoming dangerously volatile and driven insane by the war might be true.

"All of you, out," the fane ordered. "Leave me with my son."

There was no place in the chamber to sit except for the throne itself, which caused Mawyndulë to stand awkwardly, watching his father. Lothian sat hunched over, elbows on knees, waiting for his subjects to leave. Vasek was the last one through the arch, and he closed the doors behind him, leaving father and son alone in the ancient hall.

"I always thought you were a poor excuse for a son," Lothian said, glaring down at him. "An unbefitting replacement for Pyridian, who was quite near perfect. Did you know that? I don't suppose you did. Because you are the prince, everyone worked to make your life devoid of any problems. They insulated you, even from me—too much, really. But it's true. I thought Ferrol hated me. Gave me a mother who wonderfully became fane, but miserably refused to die, and you for a son: a sniveling, lazy, spoiled, unexceptional, self-absorbed child. Is it true you were afraid of the dark, and until you were ten, you had to have a light in your room before you could fall asleep?"

"Yes," Mawyndulë replied, seeing no point in lying, but overjoyed that his father was unaware he *still* required a light. At ten he'd merely learned to light his own lamp.

"See." The fane gave a miserable laugh, then shook his head.

His father was one of those people whose looks had dramatically withered over the last five years, but he suffered from more than wrinkles. As fane, his father bore the full weight of every bit of bad news. This burden must have been colossal, as Lothian appeared crushed. He sat hunched, his shoulders slouching, his head hanging. Worse than anything, his father had let his hair grow. It came in white with the brittle texture of dead grass. He never cut, washed, or brushed a strand, leaving the whole thing a frightening, oily snarl. He didn't look to have slept much, either. His eyes were red and swollen. Fane Lothian was the closest Mawyndulë thought he would get to seeing the dead walk, or in this case, sit and complain.

"And then the war came. What a miserable gift Ferrol gave to mark my long-delayed climb to this lousy seat." His father leaned back against the polished bark that looked anything but comfortable. He clapped the arms of the throne with a smirk. "Ferrol loved my mother and gave her beauty, wisdom, the Art, and unparalleled success. Next to Gylindora Fane, your grandmother is the most revered ruler of all time, a living legend for most of her life. As if she didn't already have enough, she managed to have *me* as a son." He laughed again, louder and longer. Perhaps he meant it as self-deprecating, but the laugh sounded maniacal.

Mawyndulë shifted his weight. He wasn't used to standing this long in one place, and he was sore from his long hike. The blister on his foot was flaring up, making him curl his toes to avoid standing on it.

"I mostly blame your mother. She never liked me much. Most of them don't. I can see it in their eyes, you know? They stand in front of me like you are now, nodding politely. What else can they do? I'm fane. I can have whatever I want. They don't even complain. Can't. Who would they protest to? Ferrol? He won't listen. He's the one who made me fane, right?"

Mawyndulë realized then that his father was drunk—had to be. The idea had been hovering in his mind for a while, but he'd dismissed it as preposterous. He'd never known his father to overindulge. That was what Gwydry did, what Rhunes did, not Miralyith, and certainly not the fane. Did Ferrol also let Himself become intoxicated? Such a thing might explain a great deal, but Mawyndulë preferred to believe that the god of all Fhrey remained forever sober, always wise. The fane, Mawyndulë finally admitted, was neither. Maybe that was what made the two so different.

He's not insane at all, merely drunk all the time.

"But I don't keep them long. A night—a few days at the most," Lothian went on.

Mawyndulë wondered if he had missed something, as he had no idea what his father was talking about. *Kept who long?* Dusty minds were one thing, but sodden ramblings were impossible to track.

"They never hold my interest for more than that. Must have had hundreds, but your mother was the only one to bear a child, and a son at that. Victory!" Lothian chuckled, showing his teeth and staring at Mawyndulë, his eyes a little unfocused. Lothian licked his lips and wiped his nose. "You see, I had no idea how you'd turn out. In my folly, I believed you'd be another me. Fathers always think that. Think we can mold our protégés like clay. Teach you, build you to be a perfect person. Never happens. People are born who they are. The influence of a parent is minor at best. You don't believe me, do you? Just consider the awful parents who have wonderful children and the great people who have awful brats. Ferrol puts His stamp on everyone. As parents, our effect is minimal. So you see it's stupid, but . . . I thought you'd at least be like Pyridian." He threw up his hands in resignation and began staring at the leaves high above.

In the silence that followed, Mawyndulë wondered if his father had forgotten he was there. He considered saying something, but all he really wanted at that point was to escape. He couldn't just walk away. He considered coughing. That was neatly neutral, no real chance of igniting anger in a drunken all-powerful father, but Mawyndulë wasn't without feelings. What his father said hurt, and that pain came out. "Sorry to disappoint you."

This had the effect he'd hoped for. His father's gaze left the canopy and snapped back to his son. The haze of the fane's sight shifted to a surprisingly lucid focus. Then the fane—his father—truly shocked him. Lothian shook his head and said, "You haven't disappointed me. Is that what you think? I've held you here for what? To berate you for being a louse?" Again, his father laughed.

This time the fane repeatedly slapped the knotted arm of the throne with a flat palm. Mawyndulë thought of how every fane from Gylindora Fane on down had sat in that spot and laid hands on that wood. Caratacus the wizard had formed the thing with some sort of magic before the time of the Art. As Mawyndulë watched his father pound the ancient armrest in his drunken vulgarity, he felt outrage at the heresy. All those past souls were somewhere, looking at Lothian with disgust, and possibly rage.

"I asked you to stay because I wanted to say how proud I am of you. I wanted to let you know that I'm . . . that I was wrong about my son . . . about the coward who was afraid of the dark. Granted, I had my doubts when you were caught up in that Gray Cloak revolt. I mean, what were my options there? My son was either a conspirator or an idiot. Turned out there was a third possibility. You were just innocent. That's another way of saying 'pure' or 'clean.' And you might be the only one. All these others"—he waved and pointed around the empty room—"did nothing. Our world was over. The Rhunes were eating us up like locusts. *Nothing we can do*, they told me. *Nothing at all.* But you, my son, *did* something. You discovered the Rhune Miralyith, and now you've brought it to me."

Lothian leaned forward again, sliding to the edge of the throne's seat, and pointing a wavering finger at him. "You see, it is in times of terrible danger and distress that, well, you know, cream rises to the top of a bucket of milk, doesn't it?"

Mawyndulë nodded out of reflex.

"Exactly." His father slapped the arm once more, this time with such force that the impact echoed across the room and back. "We need to stick together, you and I. We're all we have. We're all anyone has. We are the divine in this world—Ferrol's voice, Ferrol's eyes and ears, Ferrol's hands." Mawyndulë was wondering if his father was going to name every body part the god might possess, when Lothian concluded with, "We can't count on *them*, can we?"

Mawyndulë shook his head.

His father wasn't angry with him. Lothian was proud—at least the wine said so, and maybe it was true—but he had also thought Mawyndulë useless and a coward. The combined news canceled out, and he was left with a father who was drunk and violently striking a sacred throne.

Mawyndulë had never been a strict traditionalist. He'd often made light of religion and ceremony, of all the absurd rules that made no sense. But at that moment, he felt offended. Mawyndulë resented that his father belittled the very seat he had the privilege to sit in.

What good is praise from a drunk? And how dare he sit there? How could Ferrol allow it? No wonder the Rhunes are winning.

Strangely, Mawyndulë, who had long sought his father's approval, discovered that when he got it, Lothian lost his mystique. Mawyndulë had pretended to hold the fane in disdain, but deep down he had respected him, and he believed his father was smarter and wiser than he appeared. Learning that the Rhunes had an Artist and then leading a horse and cart from Avempartha weren't worthy of praise. That his father thought so proved Lothian was less than Mawyndulë had imagined. His father, it turned out, was a fool.

"I just wanted you to know that," Lothian said.

Once more, Mawyndulë nodded, and then he took the opening to escape. "Thank you," he said with a short bow. He took a step backward toward the doors.

Lothian stopped him by speaking again, "With the secret of dragons, we will create a fleet of the vile beasts and take back what is ours, just like my mother did when the Dherg stood on the banks of the Nidwalden and she first discovered the Art." Mawyndulë's father offered his son a friendly sneer. "But unlike her, we'll completely destroy them. Every. Last. One."

Mawyndulë had no problem with that, but he seriously wondered if his father was the right fane for the job.

CHAPTER THIRTY

The Fetid Pool

I have heard that you never forget your first kiss, but I honestly think it is your last that sticks with you most.

— THE BOOK OF BRIN

Gifford and Roan sat near the fire, holding each other. They looked sick. Rain and Tressa didn't look so good, either. All of them crouched in balls, looking out the window or at the fire, not actually seeing anything.

Moya wasn't surprised. This whole thing had seemed so ludicrous and unreal—but there really was an island beyond the swamp and a Tetlin Witch, although Muriel was nothing like in the stories. At that moment, the "witch" was cleaning the last stubborn remains from the pot she'd used to make them dinner, humming pleasantly to herself as she did.

Moya stood, causing Tekchin to look up. "Stay here, will you? I want to talk to her . . . girl talk," she said with a wistful smile.

"Uh-huh." He didn't sound convinced, but he didn't follow her, either. So far, Tekchin had been oddly quiet. The Fhrey was normally loud and talkative, making off-color jokes and insulting anyone within hearing, but since they'd left on this trip, he'd been uncharacteristically subdued. Maybe it was the whole Tesh thing—which, if true, wasn't going to end well. But that was a problem for another day. Right now, Moya had bigger issues.

The tiny hut didn't offer much privacy, but the crackle of the fire and the moaning of the wind made it safe to speak if they did so in whispers. She sidled up next to Muriel as the woman scrubbed the bottom of the pot.

"I need to know something," Moya asked softly, standing close. "Who is Malcolm?"

"I have no idea."

"A little while ago you said he was your father."

"Turin is my father. I can't say that Malcolm is Turin, though my father does make a habit of changing his name."

"Fine, whatever. So, who is Turin?"

"My father."

Moya sighed. She didn't want to play games. This was crucial, and she needed serious answers. "But who is your father?"

It was Muriel's turn to look frustrated. "My father is Turin. Turin is my father. He's the terrible, horrible bastard who ruined my life, then made that misery eternal. That's who he is. What else do you want to know?"

"Look, I'm sorry, but my friends, some really wonderful people, are sitting over there, and I think they're seriously planning on killing themselves because of what Malcolm said. They actually believe they can die, travel to Estramnadon, save our friend Suri, and then come back to life. So, what I'm asking is—"

"Yes, it's possible," Muriel said. "I wasn't lying, if that's what you think. The key . . ." She looked across the room at Tressa. "I can't believe he gave her that and let you come here." She shook her head and rolled her eyes, her lips pulled tight as if trying to hold in a scream. Then she took a breath. "Yes, to answer your question, that key makes it possible. That's Eton's Key. Eton created Phyre, and that thing will open any lock. With it, a person can travel across the realms and come back out. That's not a lie. That's real."

Grand Mother of All! Moya felt her stomach twist. "It can't be."

"Why not?"

"Because it can't—it just can't. Okay?"

Muriel showed her a sad smile. "You came over here so I could admit this was all a lie, a hoax of some kind. That way you could convince them not to do it."

"Yeah, I'm funny that way. I don't like seeing my friends kill themselves." Moya pointed at the others still gathered by the fire. "If Tressa wants to die, fine; but Roan and Gifford are another matter. Roan is special in a lot of ways, not all of them healthy. If she gets it in her head that she can die, go to Rel, and then come back, she'll do it just to see what it's like. And Gifford—well, trust me, if she goes, he goes. And I can't have that."

"I'm sorry. As much as I hate Turin, I don't tell lies, not even white ones. That's more his thing."

Moya stared at her, angry enough to spit teeth. She wasn't ready to believe in Malcolm, and certainly didn't trust Tressa, but Moya was having a tough time making an argument that Muriel had made this up for cheap thrills. The way she spoke of her father was what did it. Moya understood the language of parent-hating and felt she could spot a fake. Muriel was genuine. *No way to fake that to a mirror like me.*

The truth of everything was present in the vehement disgust, the pure anger that only came from an underlying love. A love that, no matter how hard you tried to eradicate it, ended up lingering like a bloodstain.

"Are all of them going?" Muriel asked.

"Just Tressa and Roan, but like I said, Gifford will follow her lead, and I'm not sure about Rain—that's the dwarf over there with the pick."

Muriel frowned.

"What?" Moya asked.

"Look, like I said, I'm not an expert on the hereafter—never been there, obviously, but in this place, the walls between this world and the next are thin. You can hear things. On really quiet nights, you can even hold conversations. What your friends are planning isn't—I don't think it will be easy. Phyre isn't a never-ending celebration like the warriors think. It's a real place, a different place with different rules, but not unlike this one. What I mean is, there'll be dangers."

"Dangers? How can there be dangers? It's not like you can die. I mean, you're already dead, right?"

"There are worse things than death, and of course you *can* still die. If you fail to get back out, or fail to get out before your bodies decompose, you'll stay in Phyre. You'll be dead . . . forever. And . . ."

"And what?"

"That key."

"What about it?"

"It opens all the doors in Phyre."

"You've said that already."

"That's because you need to understand that there are those who would like to get out, those who would very much like to take that key and use it to escape and return to Elan. To be honest, I think most would. And believe me, there are some who are there that we really don't want to get out. Taking the key into Phyre is dangerous in ways you can't begin to imagine—even I can't fully comprehend what your friends will face." Muriel huffed in exasperation as she scrubbed all the harder, then backed up and threw her rag at the pot.

"I can't believe he gave that key to her! It's . . . it's so irresponsible! But that's him all over, isn't it?" She swiped her hair back with her arm. "Are you certain they're capable of such a thing?" Muriel took a moment to look at Moya. "You are brave. I can tell that from just the short time I've known you. Your fortitude is the sort of thing that will be important in Phyre. That's what's needed in there. But what about them?" She nodded in the direction where everyone was huddled. "I doubt it was an accident that you were the first through my door."

"You think I should go?"

Muriel shook her head. "No, I don't think any of you should—not with that key."

Moya picked up the rag and handed it back to Muriel.

"What are you thinking?" Muriel asked.

"I don't know." Moya sighed. "We were supposed to just find out if there was a route to Estramnadon, then report back. Now I feel like I was set up—that we all were."

"That's my father for you. He drops an acorn, and three hundred years later, the oak that grew from it falls over and conveniently kills someone he needs dead."

Moya sadly shook her head.

"What's wrong?"

"I'm in a hut in the middle of nowhere talking to a legend that I thought was invented to scare little kids. And supposedly this person regularly chats with the dead and claims to be immortal. And she is telling me that a guy I've known for the past seven years is her father. Then there's Tressa, the biggest liar I've ever known, telling me this same guy wants her and seven others to die, which, by the way, will somehow save our friend Suri. What am I supposed to do about all that?"

Muriel didn't answer. She rinsed the pot, wiped it dry, and hung it from a hook in the rafters.

Moya looked at Tekchin, who was watching her intently. *He can probably hear everything we're saying.*

"He said eight had to go?" Muriel asked. "These eight?"

"That's what Tressa said."

"And you don't trust her?"

"Not for a minute. She's lied about everything, led us along, withheld information. When we set out, it was to discover a passageway we could send an army through. She knew from the start that wasn't possible. She never told us about having to die or about the key. What else hasn't she mentioned?"

Muriel forced a weak smile. "Maybe I should make some more tea?"

Moya thought it would take more than tea.

Moya came back to the small circle of people clustered around the fire, all of them watching the dancing flames. Tekchin looked up at her approach.

The fire was bright on the side of his face with the scar. She'd always thought it made him seem more real, more human than the other Galantians. Now, she only thought how painful the injury must have been. She didn't know the whole story. It had something to do with mountain goblins, but he'd never told her all the details. For all his boasting, he didn't talk much about his adventures—not to her, at least. Tekchin was often loud, almost as if he considered silence an enemy, but he'd been uncharacteristically quiet on this trip—quiet and watchful. His eyes followed her everywhere, but his look wasn't the usual, lust-filled gawk, or even the wicked grin that made him so appealing. He appeared to be studying her, memorizing what she looked like, as if that would soon be important. Moya got the impression he knew something she didn't.

She offered him a brief smile to let him know she hadn't forgotten him, then sat herself down next to Roan and Gifford, who sat shoulder to shoulder cross-legged in front of the hearth. They stared into the flames with melancholy expressions made more so by the flickering light.

"Don't do this, Roan," Moya said softly, sitting close but being careful not to touch her. "Muriel says it could be dangerous."

"I trust Malcolm," Roan replied, speaking quietly to the fire.

"Okay, let's assume that Malcolm is all you and Muriel are claiming him to be. I can understand being devout. But it's not like he came to you personally, asked you to go. You have no idea if what Tressa has been saying came from him, or if she just lied about everything. This is Tressa, and you don't know her like I do. She lies. She tried to kill Persephone."

Roan turned to face her. "She has Eton's Key, Moya. How does one lie about that?"

"She has a bit of metal around her neck. That may be all it is."

"The Tetlin Witch says that's Eton's Key," Gifford said. "You saying Twessa *and* the witch have a plot to kill us? Because we didn't have to come all this way fo' that."

Moya sighed. "I'm saying I don't want you two to die. If this is real, if people can really walk through the afterlife and reach the Fhrey city, then we should stick to the plan and go back and explain it all to Persephone. She can give that key to a legion and send them in."

Roan shook her head. "Tressa and *seven* others."

Moya wanted to scream but held it in and took a slow breath.

"Not too long ago, Pe'sephone went to Neith to get weapons. She didn't take a legion; didn't need one. Maybe this is like that."

"I'm sorry if this sounds cruel, but there is no way you two and Tressa are going to make this work. I honestly have my doubts the three of you could make it back to the Dragon Camp all by yourselves. Muriel says it will be dangerous."

Roan and Gifford were back to staring at the fire, but they were listening. They had no choice.

"Think about what you're planning on doing. You're going to die, travel through Rel, Nifrel, and Alysin, and come out in the Fhrey capital as what? Ghosts? Then what? How will you be able to do anything?"

"We'll find that out when we get there," Roan replied. "Malcolm wouldn't send us otherwise. So I'm going."

"Me, too," Gifford said.

"I'm going, too," Rain said.

They all looked over, and Gifford smiled at the dwarf.

"Sorry." Rain, hung his head low, looking sheepish. "You're not that far away. Kinda hard not to hear ya."

"Why would you do that?" Moya asked. "Is it all this talk about Malcolm being a god? Because you were in the smithy when Suri made the gilarabrywn?"

"Sort of, but mostly it's me dreams. They've gotten worse since we entered the swamp. She keeps calling to me. Says I've got to come down. I always thought that meant I had to dig, but I think now—I think no one can dig that deep. I think she's dead, and this is the only way I can reach her."

"Who is *she?*" Gifford asked.

Rain shook his head. "I've no idea, but I've had these visions of her all me life. It's why I became a digger in the first place. Since a wee lad, I've been trying to reach her."

"That makes four," Roan said.

"Stop it!" Moya burst out, standing up. "Just stop it, Roan, will you? Just stop." Moya felt angry, frustrated, but mostly terrified. She felt that this wagon of absurdity was rolling downhill, and she couldn't so much as slow it. "I promised Persephone I would keep you safe." She thought to say more, but looking at their blank faces, she knew it wouldn't help.

Moya returned to Tekchin, who remained seated on the far side of the room. She threw herself down beside him.

"What are you thinking?" he asked.

She waved Tesh and Brin over, then proceeded to speak in a whisper. "Roan, Gifford, and Rain are planning on killing themselves with Tressa. This isn't why we came. I can't allow it. I'm thinking we might need to use force to make them come back with us."

"Moya . . ." Brin looked shocked. "What are you going to do? Tie them up?"

"If I have to, yes." Moya was hot, angry, and aggravated—not her best mindset for decision-making, she knew, and yet she didn't see a choice. They weren't giving her one. "Look, Tesh can watch Gifford, and Tekchin can keep a hand on Rain, and I'll handle Tressa."

"And Roan?" Brin asked. "You want me to what? Wrestle her to the ground? Pin her down so you can bind her? I think before we do this, I'd better ask Muriel for some wax to put in my ears so I don't go deaf from all the screaming. Sure, Gifford can touch her, but can anyone else? You remember what she was like. Maybe she's still that way. And if she does start, you think Gifford is just going to stand there? Tesh will have to use force, and Gifford is stronger than he looks. If you hurt Roan, he'll lose his mind. Have you forgotten the beating he took when he returned the javelin Roan took?" Brin paused and took a breath. "Moya, do you really want us to fight one another?"

Moya hadn't forgotten anything. She remembered all too well how she had let Eres nearly kill Gifford, how she had silently watched, and how she vowed never to do that again. And still . . . "What do you want, Brin? I can't let them kill themselves!" she said loudly, much too loudly, and heads turned.

Tressa, who as usual was off by herself near the windows, stood up. "I'm pretty sure you can."

"Tressa! You bitch!" Moya rose to her feet and faced her across the width of the room.

"Eight need to go," Roan reminded them with her incessant fixation on numbers, driving Moya past her boiling point.

"Give it a rest, Roan!"

Tressa crossed the room to where Muriel stood watching. "I think we've waited long enough. We should do this now. Malcolm told me the entrance to Rel was at a pool that—"

"I know the one," Muriel said. "It's just up the path. I'll show you."

She took a heavy cloak off a peg, put it on, and tugged the hood up. It came to a point, and for once Muriel really did look a tad like a witch. From a stack of baskets near the door, she selected a fine, sturdy one with a hooped handle and a lid. Then she picked up a lantern. "Follow me."

Muriel walked to a fenced-in pen behind the hut and picked up a little white duck with a yellow bill. She fought it into her basket and closed the lid.

Then Muriel led them back down the path to the standing stone, where she paused to let the others catch up. The world was dark, cold, and damp. The rain had long since stopped, but the trees continued to drip, and while they waited, Moya drew up the hood of her cloak and pulled the woolen shoulders close around her. Even so, she shivered.

The witch held the lantern high as they waited for Roan and Gifford. The basket dangling from her other hand jerked and shuddered.

"What's with the duck?" Tesh asked.

"Something you'll need" was all Muriel said. Then as Gifford joined them, she turned and followed the path they had passed by on the way to find her.

"We'll need a duck?" Rain asked.

Muriel just smiled.

The trail curved in a wide downhill circle as they descended to a deep bog. There was no avoiding the puddles, and soon Moya's feet were soaked. The air grew wetter—something Moya hadn't thought possible. The trees became short, wretched things marred by bulbous growths, bent trunks, and twisted branches. Black brambles with inch-long, razor-like thorns grew up in abundance, and the tall grass had the brittle look of long, dead hair.

"This is where the two worlds come closest together," Muriel said as she walked, swinging the lantern in far too casual a manner. "There is but a thin skin that separates Elan from the underworld. Phyre bubbles up and bleeds through like a poisoned wellspring, and that corruption, that thin separation, warps the surrounding area. Just as a pond is an oasis for life, this island is a consequence of the gateway. Nothing is as it should be here. Nothing is *natural*."

"Just say it's creepy," Moya said. "Is that why you're here? I mean, because no sane person would ever visit?"

"That's part of it, yes," Muriel said. "But that's really more of a side benefit. As I told you, if I shout, I can talk to my neighbors through the wall. I came a long time ago, hoping to speak to someone."

"Didn't happen?"

She shook her head. "But I discovered I'm needed. Here, the Tetlin Witch has a purpose."

"Giving out stones to the recently deceased?"

"Offering assistance." Muriel nodded and hopped a fallen branch. "The stones are just an idea. Something you can take along to the other side. After death, people continue to think in Elan terms because that's all they know. The lost souls don't take the stones, they take the understanding of them, the concept of weight that helps them sink into Phyre."

Moya marveled at how normal she seemed, how informal and friendly. The infamous Tetlin Witch could have been a friend of hers, and she would have blended in effortlessly with Seph and the others.

"This might not seem significant or important to you. Most people don't give much thought to death. But imagine you're happily living your life, and you go out to pick flowers or fetch a bucket of water and—bam! You die. Maybe a wild animal takes you. Perhaps you fall through ice. It could be a thousand things, some truly ridiculous, like slipping on a stone and cracking your head. The problem is, no one knew you left. No one knows where you went. They don't find your body. You aren't buried, and never get your stone. Next thing you know, you're here." She gestured at the trees with the lantern, which clanked as the handle slapped its cap. "In the case of slipping on a wet rock, you have no idea what happened. It's possible, likely even, that you don't realize you died. You're lost and alone. Maybe for the first time."

"Can't a person just"—Tekchin looked around the ground as they walked—"I dunno, pick up a rock, any rock?"

"No. The dead, their spirits, can't touch any part of Elan."

"Then I don't understand," Moya said. "How can they have the stone they were buried with?"

"The spirit that you encountered in the swamp, he wore clothes, yes?"

Moya and Tekchin nodded.

"But they weren't real, were they?"

Moya remembered how the arrow had passed through Meeks, clothes and all, and she shook her head.

"Those were the clothes he died in, and as I said, you take ideas and memories with you. It doesn't take long for the spirits to reach Phyre. That's why it's so important to bury loved ones with a stone as soon as possible. When they reach the river's end and feel a stone, they know they've died. It's like practicing something repeatedly until, even in an emergency, you know how to react. Funerals are that way."

Moya imagined what it might be like to find herself holding a stone in her hand. If all else had changed, if she were cut off from the rest of the world, that stone—imaginary or not—would provide an explanation of what had happened and what to do. More than that, the stone would be a loving goodbye that could provide needed comfort at the worst possible moment. Alone, completely alone, and scared, Moya thought she'd squeeze tears out of that little imaginary rock.

I didn't give my mother a stone, and no one else did, either. After leaving the funeral, she just assumed someone else would take care of it. Maybe they thought it wasn't their place, and she would come back and do it herself. After all, it was her responsibility. *My mother had nothing to hold on to. How terrible was that! And she thought I'd done it on purpose, out of spite. But that wasn't it. My mother was almost barred from an afterlife because of my oversight.*

"The ones who arrive without stones are usually those who died suddenly," Muriel said. "They don't have time to process the event. So they stand here, confused. I make a point of coming down this way frequently to check. A lot of times I hear crying. Men, women, children, they all do that because they don't understand anything anymore. Others, the more adventurous ones, the ones destined for Nifrel, come right up to my house. We sit and talk. Some take only a minute to figure it out. Others sit for days until they finally pick a stone. I don't know why, but different stones speak to different people; that's why I have so many on hand—to make it easier. The stone remains where it is, but one that looks just like it appears in their hand and off they go down this trail. So sure, the swamp and this island aren't pretty, but if I weren't here, if I didn't do this, what would happen to all of them? Being around as long as I've been, it's hard to find something you can do that still matters."

Down they went in a long spiral that enveloped them in a deep canyon of dripping willows, thorny brush, and wispy grass. The air began to warm a bit as they descended, but with the warmth came a smell, an unpleasant stench that spoke of putrid waters, burnt hair, and rotting things. Moya couldn't see it, but she could hear a flushing-pour splattering somewhere in the dark, a rain-induced waterfall. Then without warning, they reached the bottom.

The trail came to an end in a dismal boggy pool surrounded by sedge, swamp grass, and lethargic cattails. The pool was little more than a puddle, just five or six feet around, and it was filled with a murky, muddy slop that stained the grass surrounding it.

Muriel put her basket and lantern down beside the pool and waited. The rest of them displayed puzzled looks.

Tressa was the first to ask. "Where's the entrance?"

"Right here," the witch said, pointing at the muddy puddle.

This did no more to answer the question for any of them than had she danced a jig. Muriel didn't appear perturbed, or even surprised. Instead, she calmly opened the basket and pulled feathers from the fowl. The bird struggled and squawked violently, but Muriel held it firmly. Then she tied a bit of string around its neck from which dangled one of the little stones with a hole through the center. Without further delay, the witch yanked the duck out of the basket and dropped it into the mucky sludge.

Even in the dark with only the lantern for light, it was easy to see the brilliant white duck as it struggled to use its webbed feet to paddle to the shore, yet it made little progress. The fowl flashed its wings and beat them in a great, fluttering effort to clear itself of the viscous slime. Instead, the duck slipped deeper and deeper into the muck.

"Oh, Grand Mother!" Moya whispered as they all watched the duck squawking and struggling for its life. Despite its best efforts, it slowly descended deeper and deeper until only its long neck and head were above the surface. Then, tilting up in an effort to catch a last breath of air, the bird was gone, swallowed whole by the puddle.

After it disappeared, everyone continued to stare at the pool until the witch turned around and said, "That is the entrance to Phyre."

"No culling way!" Moya said, her eyes wide. She began shaking her head and went so far as to take a step back. Remembering Tressa's stupid song, she thought, *Wasn't all that crap about sinking and cackling made up to scare kids or something? This is . . . this is . . .*

Muriel placed the feathers inside her basket, adding them to the stones already there. Then she set the container on a stool. "Those going should take a stone and a feather. The stone will help you reach Phyre, help you sink. If it is possible to return, you'll come back out this way. This mud is cold, and it'll keep your bodies preserved beneath the surface, at least for a few days, I think. I don't actually know. It's not like this has ever been attempted before. When you return, hopefully they'll be similar to how you left them."

"What are the feathers for?" Tressa asked.

Muriel took one out and held it up, twirling the little white tuft. "Just as a stone is a symbol of weight, of descending, the feather is a symbol of lightness, of rising up, of restoration and redemption. You won't have the real feathers with you, just the idea, but that's the point. In Phyre, my neighbors tell me, ideas can be real. Mind you, I've never been there, and they could be lying to me, but I don't see why."

Muriel replaced the feather in the basket and stood up, waiting.

No one came near her.

Moya was shaking her head. "There's no way." She looked at Roan and Gifford. "No way."

"What were you expecting?" Muriel asked, her casual, friendly attitude seemed decidedly less appealing in light of the duck's disappearing act.

"A cave or maybe a hole, but that's—that's—"

"Disgusting," Gifford provided.

"Yes, exactly!"

"It's a gateway," Muriel said, "an entrance; and all roads to Phyre are the same."

"I'm sorry, but that's just—no. You want people to drown themselves in muck? That's nuts," Moya said.

"I don't want anyone to do anything. You're the ones who came to me. Only the dead can enter. What difference does it matter how you die?" Muriel said this so calmly that it made Moya furious. What she heard instead was, *What's the problem, honey? Can't make a cake without cracking a few eggs, right?*

They were all staring at the pool, and as they watched, slime bubbled up and popped, splattering sludge, burping after its meal.

"No—see—no." Moya was shaking her head again, but more likely she hadn't stopped shaking it since the duck went down. She wore an all-encompassing frown, as if every square inch of her face was thrown into the effort. "Sorry about wasting your duck and all, but there's no way. There's just no way!"

"It does look quite unpleasant," Gifford said, displaying a grimace all his own.

"I didn't think any of you would actually go through with this," Tesh said in a remarkably happy tone. "Though I'll admit you had me worried for a while."

"Yeah . . . well . . ." Moya was still backing away. She bumped into Brin, who was standing behind her, and jumped at the contact. "Tressa, you couldn't have been thinking it'd be like this, could you?"

Tressa didn't answer. She just stared at the pool.

"So, what are we going to do, then?" Tesh asked. "There's no sense standing here if—"

"We just going to go back?" Gifford asked Roan. The question sounded more hopeful than disappointed.

"I—ah," Roan muttered. "I suppose we—"

"Malcolm wouldn't send us here if it wasn't necessary," Tressa said, a tenacious resolve anchoring her voice with a curious weight.

Moya said, "Malcolm can fill a pig for all I care."

"To be fair," Rain said, "how could you tell anyone about *this?*"

"He's right," Tekchin added. "You really have to see it."

"That's why I brought the duck," Muriel explained. "Well, that and the feathers."

"We have to trust him," Tressa said doggedly, and she took a step forward.

"Tressa?" Moya called nervously.

"It's the same as it was with Raithe," Tressa said, "only worse." Moya realized with growing concern that she wasn't talking to any of them. This was her own personal debate. "He knew."

"Tressa, what are you doing?"

To everyone's relief, the woman turned around, but the respite was short-lived when they saw the look in her eyes. She bent down and took items from the basket. When she stood, determination took hold of Tressa just as tightly as she gripped the feather in one hand and a stone in the other. "He did this for me. Don't you see? To everyone else, I no longer existed. But not to Malcolm. He gave me this chance. Now it's up to me to take it. He said it wouldn't be easy. Said it would be harder than even what Raithe had suffered. Don't you see? This is my chance. My one way out. If I don't take it, what am I? What good is living the way I do? I might . . . I might as well *be* dead." She took a backward step closer to the pool.

"Tressa, don't you dare," Moya said.

"I'm sorry I lied to you, Moya, to all of you, but that's why he picked me. When you want to build a wall, it's best to ask a mason. And when you need to deceive good people, you ask me. I'll—I'll wait a little while, in case any of you change your mind," Tressa said, mostly to Gifford and Roan. "Then, if you don't come, I'll go for Suri by myself. I'll understand if you don't. You all have lives. It's just me that doesn't."

"Tressa!" Moya lunged forward, but she was too far away, and Tressa was at the edge of the puddle.

Brin screamed as Tressa threw herself into the pool. She landed with a terrible *plop!* Given the force of her fall, and because she weighed more than the duck, she was immediately swallowed up to her waist.

"Tressa!" Moya shouted, then turned to the onlookers, her eyes frantic. "Give me rope! Give me rope!"

There was none to give.

Moya searched the trees. Jumping up, she tore at vines, ripping them free. Tesh and Tekchin helped her, and together they threw one end to Tressa. By then the woman had sunk down to her shoulders.

"Grab the vine!" Moya ordered.

Tressa shook her head in fluttering jerks. She held her mouth stiff, eyes staring straight out, puffing rapidly through her nose. She was terrified.

Brin fell to her knees, covering her mouth with both hands. "Tressa . . . oh, Blessed Grand Mother . . . Tressa."

As the dark surface of the pool inched up her neck, a smile shattered the stone hardness of her face. "Malcolm *is* a god."

She gasped one last time for air. Then as they all watched, just as with the duck, Tressa was swallowed up.

"Tressa, you stupid bitch!" Moya was on her hands and knees, sobbing at the edge of the pool, vines still gripped in her fingers. "Why did you do that? Why?"

She wasn't the only one crying. Brin, Roan, and Gifford were in tears as well. Maybe they all were. Moya couldn't tell. She couldn't see anything clearly. But she was the loudest, no disputing that. Moya was facedown, pounding the grass with both fists, holding the sod responsible for everything. When that didn't help, she began ripping it up by the handfuls. "Tressa, why did you do that?"

No one said anything for a long moment, as their inharmonious mournful hitch of tears replaced the natural sounds of the pond. *But maybe,* Moya thought, having not remembered hearing a cricket or frog since arriving on the island, *in this place perhaps sorrow is the indigenous song of night.*

Just as the sobs fell to whimpers, Moya wiped her face with the edge of her cloak. That's when she heard Gifford.

"Woan?"

Roan took a step toward the pool.

"Roan?" Moya echoed Gifford. "What are you doing?"

"I can't let Tressa go alone." She said it apologetically, with tears running down her cheeks.

Everyone's heads snapped up.

Gifford took two stones and two feathers from Muriel's basket and moved to Roan's side. "I'll go with you."

Roan shook her head. "No. You don't believe in Malcolm. I can see it in your face. You're worried, scared, terrified—you just can't say any of those words."

"I don't need to believe in him. I believe in you, Woan. And Twessa is my fwiend."

"Roan, Gifford," Tesh said, "Tressa is dead. You can't do anything more for her."

"She used to call you *the freak*," Moya said. "Remember that?"

Gifford nodded. "I know, but it was diffewent when she said it. Twessa knew she was a fweak, too."

He turned to face Roan, who looked up at him with glassy eyes, her lips trembling. "I'd die without you," he told her. "I wasn't alive until we touched, when you twusted me. Woan, I can't live without it now. I won't. I can't." He sucked in a halting breath. "If you leave me, I'll die . . . might as well go to-ge-thah."

"Roan, Gifford, no." Moya was shaking her head again, but this time with a slow helpless rhythm.

"Maybe what Twessa said about Malcolm is twue," Gifford said. "If not"—he looked at Roan with tears slipping down his cheeks—"I've got no we-gwets. Well, just one. I haven't kissed you."

With trembling lips and tear-filled eyes, Roan pushed up on her toes. She put a hand to either side of his face and pulled Gifford to her, kissing him for the first time.

When she let him go, Gifford smiled. "Okay, then," he said. "No we-gwets at all now."

"I love you, Gifford."

"I love you, too, Woan. I always have. And I always will."

They looked at the pool.

"Okay," Gifford said with a firm nod and held out the stones and feathers. "To-get-ha then."

Roan took one of each.

"Don't, please don't," Moya said, but her voice had fallen to a feeble whisper.

The rest of them watched in mute disbelief as Roan and Gifford took each other's hands and waded into the pool. Slowly they began to sink, embracing once more. "Tell Frost and Flood I said goodbye," Roan told Rain in an unsteady voice, then let out a short squeal as the slime surged up to their shoulders. And as the muck reached up to their chins, Gifford and Roan kissed once more, then slipped below the surface.

"Tet! Tet! Tet! TET!" Moya screamed, beating the grass again. She was still on her hands and knees, but her forehead was in the dirt as she struggled to breathe. Moya sobbed horribly, then gasped and sniffled. She looked up and caught sight of Muriel still standing next to the basket. "Sorry. I'm sorry, okay? But I'm really, really unhappy right now."

Muriel said nothing. She had one hand up to her lips, and Moya was surprised to see tears on her cheeks, too. Crying, it appeared, was contagious, and this was one disease the Tetlin Witch wasn't immune to.

"Tet!" Moya slapped the ground with both hands, then got up and began looking around.

"What are you searching for, Moya?" Muriel asked.

"As if you don't know," Moya shot back.

Muriel reached into her basket, plucked out a stone, and handed it to her.

Moya snatched the stone away then looked at Tekchin, finding it hard to believe what she was about to say, knowing he would find it even harder to hear. "Look, you're gonna live another couple of thousand years or so, and I would have died in a measly thirty, give or take, and that's if I was lucky. Wouldn't even be worth the effort, really. If you did stick around, you'd have to watch me get old. And then you'd have to watch me die anyway. You must have thought about that."

"I have," Tekchin said. There was no shock, no concern in his voice. The Galantian didn't even look sad. Everyone else was crying, even Tesh and Rain, but Tekchin was dry as a desert and not the least bit worried. His two-word reply was just as flippant as anything he ever said.

"Okay, then." It hurt her to see Tekchin take it so easily. She'd wanted him to take it well, but there was such a thing as being too brave. "So, you're all set then—with this?"

"I'm going with you."

"Oh—no! No, you are not!" Moya exploded. "That would be so ridiculously stupid. I don't even know how to count all the ways that would be so colossally dumb. Roan could, but since she's dead, there's no one alive that can! It would be a waste. A waste of a very long life. And you have to take the others back."

"I'm going with you," Tekchin repeated casually—no fear, no worry, just that ridiculous Galantian bravado.

"No you're not! Don't you hear me? You're not. You're just not! You have whole centuries left, dozens of lifetimes ahead of you. You don't need to do this."

"But I am. And you will need me when you get to Estramnadon. No one else speaks Fhrey."

"No." Moya came to him, and taking his face in her hands, she cried, "I can't mean that much to you. I can't. I'm just a Rhune. A lousy, loudmouthed Rhune. Most of my own people don't like me. Especially the soldiers. They hate that a woman is Shield to the keenig. Isn't that right, Tesh?"

"I don't hate you," Tesh said. "I've always respected and admired you."

"What the Tet do you know, you culling bastard! Don't listen to him." Moya wiped her eyes with muddy hands, making a mess. "I'm nothing. My own mother didn't love me. And you—you'll live for centuries. You won't even remember my name. I'll be just a tiny fraction of a moment you'll forget. There will be other Rhunes, Fhrey, maybe even a dwarf. Their ladies are actually quite attractive. Did you know that? Of course you do. You must have had hundreds of conquests before me, and you'll have thousands more."

"Nope," he said, encircling her with his arms. "You were my first, and I'm thinking my only."

"What?" Moya's brows came up sharply. "No—that's not possible." She shook her head. "You're lying. There's *no way* you were a virgin when we met."

"Not that." Tekchin shook his head. "You're my first *love*."

Moya continued to stare. She was confused. This wasn't making any sense. She'd lived with the Fhrey for five years and he'd never even said that word. She concluded long ago that it was one of the Rhunic words he'd never learned. Tekchin was an adventurer, a risk-taker, erratic and easily distracted. She was just a plaything to him, something he would eventually become bored with. She wasn't even quite sure why that hadn't happened yet.

"We Fhrey," Tekchin said, "don't stay with one person our whole lives. Maybe because with so much time it gets too boring. I don't know, but we don't feel that deeply for each other. We're taught not to. People go insane that way, too much loss over the centuries. But you're not Fhrey, so you didn't know that people aren't supposed to love each other with such passion. And you—you just threw yourself out there. How could I resist falling in love with that? And you're right. I would have to watch you die. You think that would be bad for someone like Gifford or Roan? How'd you like to be me? Having to live with that pain for centuries? I wouldn't forget you, not ever. And all that heartache, for all those years, would be nothing when compared to even the short time we had together."

She hugged and kissed him, then let go.

Moya took a deep breath then turned and looked sheepishly toward Brin.

"I'm sorry," she whispered as she hugged the Keeper. "Go back. We'll either come out or . . . not. Either way the three of you should go back and let Seph know what happened."

Moya gave the crying young woman a kiss on the forehead, and with a sigh, looked at Tesh. "You take care of her. If I find out you didn't, I will *so* haunt your ass!"

She returned to Tekchin, who waited at the edge of the pool. They checked to make sure they had their stones and feathers. "On the outside chance this works, how do we use this?" She wagged the feather at Muriel.

"It represents the idea of lightness. It should help you rise back up—maybe."

"Maybe?"

"It's not like I've done this before—or anyone else, for that matter. But ideas matter in Phyre. Your will in believing is *everything*."

"Okay, and any pointers on how to navigate through Phyre?"

"Never been, so I don't know, but . . ." Muriel thought a moment. "If Turin wants this, I can't imagine he'll abandon you. I suspect you'll receive help."

"In the afterlife?" Moya said skeptically.

"When it comes to Turin, almost anything is possible. Almost."

"Malcolm," Moya said incredulously, "our little Malcolm, who has trouble putting on his boots, can arrange help for us in Phyre?"

Muriel nodded. "If he wants to, yes."

Moya let out a little laugh. "This is so insane."

"Never a dull moment with you," Tekchin said.

"We're gonna kiss as we drown like Gifford and Roan, right? 'Cause that looked pretty nice."

Tekchin scooped her up and carried her to the edge, where he paused.

"Do it," Moya told him, and in they went.

CHAPTER THIRTY-ONE

Facing the Fane

She was alone, surrounded by enemies, facing torture and death, but she was still Suri, which to the Fhrey must have been as mystifying as planting crops in winter and seeing them sprout.

— THE BOOK OF BRIN

Clank!

Suri opened her eyes just as the rear door to her cage opened. Sun, air, and the promise of liberty flooded in. Fear, desperation, and nausea drained away. The gates of paradise had swung wide; her deliverance was at hand.

Outside, half a dozen soldiers brandished spears, each pointed at her. Stern faces, hateful and cruel, let Suri know they would kill her if she didn't do what they wanted. After her time in the box, what Suri wanted was to kiss them. She didn't act on the impulse. They probably wouldn't have understood. The anxiety she'd harbored at facing the Fhrey in their home city had burned to ash within that crucible of a wagon.

"Thank you," she said with heartfelt sincerity as she emerged from the barred wagon into a dappled patch of sunlight. Suri breathed deep. "Thank you so much."

Those disagreeable faces aiming spears wavered with confusion but weren't daunted. They didn't try to speak to her. Rough jabs ordered Suri to turn and move across the square toward the more elaborate of the two big buildings.

Other soldiers kept the crowd at bay. "Stay back! For your own safety, please keep your distance. Rhunes are unpredictable and can be dangerous, so please stay back and keep the way to the palace clear."

Palace?

She still couldn't use the Art, but free of the cage, Suri could think again.

They're taking me to see the fane.

Suri's joy was short lived as she realized what that meant. So much of the last few days had felt like a fever-induced haze, as if she had been swimming underwater, popping up at intervals to breathe and gain peeks at the world: huge, beautiful trees of a kind she'd never seen, quaint villages built into the sides of hills, delicate homes with high roofs and tall windows, and bright-colored clothes. Suri remembered it all as a jumble of images, sights, and sounds. The veil was now cast back, the fever broken. She observed this new world clearly for the first time.

The spears urged her across paving stones that formed a diamond-shaped plaza, where exquisite statues of stone and elaborately carved fountains depicted flora and fauna. Awnings shaded tables that surrounded the square. Some of them were laden with fruits and vegetables. Others held loaves of bread, baskets, needlework, pottery, and sculpture. One stand displayed a painting, a portrait of a vicious monster in a cage—a slobbering animal with wild eyes and bared teeth gripped the bars.

That's how they see me. Maybe that's how I was. A fine ambassador I've made, but then they haven't been the best of hosts.

As Suri climbed the stairs up the hill to the palace, she glanced back over the heads of her escorts and could see the whole of Estramnadon below. Not so big as she imagined, the Fhrey capital was a masterful work of art. Meticulously kept homes and gardens clustered around the square, surrounded by the opposing hills that acted as pedestals for the two great buildings. The domed one across the way shone as a shaft of sunlight pierced the canopy. The palace before her, an edifice of towers that mimicked the soaring plume of trees, remained in shadow.

She looked back at the wagon in the plaza and heard Arion's words from the past. *You're special, Suri. I can feel it the same way I sense the seasons. It's not merely that you can use the Art. It's you, yourself. I'm certain you're the key to everything. You need to prove to the fane that Rhunes are just as wonderful, as important, and as deserving of life as the Fhrey. If you can do that, they will see their mistake and change their minds. But this can only happen if you accept who you are. Only then can you change the world. All you need is to learn how to fly.*

Suri felt the collar tight on her neck.

How can I do that when they took away my wings?

There were no chairs in the throne room besides the giant one the fane sat on, which wasn't really a chair but rather the conveniently formed roots of several twisted trees. Not that Suri would have sat in one. She found chairs odd things, not unlike shoes and walls. Even after years spent in Dahl Rhen and Alon Rhist, Suri had somehow successfully remained civilized.

Nice room—as far as rooms go.

The ceiling was so high she couldn't see it, and the space felt more like a forest glen preserved inside a cave. The place was dark except for a shaft of light that streamed in from an unseen point and struck the throne where the fane sat. The Fhrey ruler leaned back and to one side, with an elbow propped on the chair's arm and his fingers thoughtfully rubbing his lower lip. He appeared reserved, calm, even bored, but his eyes betrayed a hunger. The soldiers pushed Suri to the center of the room, then retreated, leaving her and the fane alone.

The two watched each other in silence. Suri had never experienced such quiet—no wind or songs of birds, no shuffling feet or murmuring voices. The eyes of the world were on her, waiting to see what would happen.

Was this what you expected, Arion? Suri thought. *Is this where you imagined I would stand? Is this what you wanted me to do? This must finally be that moment.*

"I'm told you were trained to speak our language," the fane said.

Suri nodded.

"That's good because now you will tell me the secret of how to create dragons."

"Why would I do that?"

The fane scowled at her. "Don't you dare speak to me that way!" His voice, amplified by the Art, shook the chamber.

Honestly puzzled, Suri asked, "Higher or lower?"

"What?" the fane snapped.

"How would you prefer that I talk? Higher or lower? Louder perhaps? I can't do a nifty sound weave like you did because of this collar, but I can yell if you're hard of hearing. Or is it that you'd like me to speak in Rhunic? Do you know how to do that?" She shook her head as he stared at her, dumbfounded. "I'm pretty sure it would be best if we stick to Fhrey. Now, I am here as a representative of Keenig Persephone, sent to work out details for a peace between our two—"

"Silence!" the fane shouted, shaking the room again.

Suri wasn't about to be silent. She'd waited and suffered enough. This was the person responsible, the one she'd come to speak to, and she had a great deal to say. "—peoples in the hope of ending this war. So far, I have been assaulted, stripped of my asica, imprisoned in a cage—"

"I said silence!"

"—deprived of food and drink, and humiliated in every village along the way. So before we begin negotiations, I expect an apology."

"You expect—*you expect!*" The fane's eyes bulged, his face flushed, and his hands gripped the arms of his throne. "How dare you! Tell me the secret, or I will have you killed this very minute!"

"Don't you mean—tell you the secret, and *then* you will kill me? That's the truth, isn't it?"

The fane said nothing, but his eyes screamed at her.

Suri nodded. "So let me think . . ." She looked up at the branches overhead and tapped her finger to her lips in false contemplation. "I can give you exactly what you want and then be murdered, or . . . I can insist we work out a plan by which our two cultures can learn to live together in peace—which would absolutely require me staying alive. Let me see . . . hmmm."

"I am the fane of the Fhrey!" He stood up, his golden asica shimmering in the shaft of light. "I was appointed ruler of the world by the Lord God Ferrol. You will kneel and do as instructed!"

"Okay, I've decided." Suri nodded with a pleasant smile. "No, I won't be telling you anything about dragons, and I'm fine with standing, thank you."

The fane formed a weave with his hands. Suri read it as pain, only she didn't feel any. She should have. The way he shaped it, she should have been screaming in excruciating agony. As it was, nothing at all happened.

"It's the collar," she told him. "Some idiot named Jerydd put it on me. If you'd like to take it off, you can try again." She smiled wickedly. "Maybe have your son join us."

"Vasek!" the fane shouted.

The door to the room burst open. A slight female with the eyes of a hawk was the first to enter. She was followed by a giant brute and a handful of soldiers. They looked at Suri, then at the fane, confusion on their faces. The last to enter was a Fhrey wearing a gray cloak with his hood up.

"This Rhune! This—" The fane seethed. He caught his breath, calmed himself a bit, then ordered, "Vasek, take this thing from my sight. I'd give it to Synne, but the collar is a problem. So, you'll get the honors. Take it. Hurt it. Do whatever you have to until it is willing to tell me what I need to know. Do you understand?"

"Yes, my fane," the Fhrey in gray replied.

Vasek gestured to the soldiers, who grabbed Suri by the arms and dragged her out. "I've heard that this Rhune doesn't like small, enclosed spaces. Take it to the Hole," Vasek ordered. "The smallest one. Seal the creature in. No window. No light. No sound. If it doesn't like to be locked up, let's see how much it enjoys an early grave. Bury her."

CHAPTER THIRTY-TWO

The Fate of Fools

I honestly never thought it would end this way. I am guessing those of you reading this did not, either.

— THE BOOK OF BRIN

Brin watched Moya and Tekchin disappear beneath the muck.

This can't be happening. How did it all go so wrong so fast? Brin's mind fought to sort out the events, to make sense of the nonsensical. Tekchin died for Moya. Moya died for Roan and Gifford. Gifford died for Roan, and Roan died for Tressa, but what did Tressa die for? Tressa never did anything for anyone but herself. Why did Tressa go?

As Brin struggled to work out the problem, Rain took a stone and a feather.

No one said a word to him, and true to his quiet nature, he said nothing, either. Rain offered only a firm, resolved nod before entering the pool as if it were a tub and he seeking a bath. Like the others, he was swallowed up in seconds, leaving only Tesh, Brin, and Muriel.

No sense . . . none of this makes any sense! Brin screamed in her head. Why would . . .

Then the answer came to her: Malcolm!

Rain had been in the smithy that night, just like Tressa and Roan. But why would Tressa . . .

Everyone always said that the Fhrey were gods, but we know they aren't. I don't think the same can be said about Malcolm, Tressa had said.

But Malcolm couldn't really be . . .

Her eyes shifted from the pool to the green-and-gray-eyed woman who silently stood there, as if waiting for Brin to make up her mind. Brin thought Muriel would—

Muriel. The name echoed in her mind. It was familiar, of course. Not that Brin had ever known another Muriel, but she'd once read it on—and that's when the circle closed and the last piece of the puzzle fell into place. She realized who Muriel was.

"Is it okay if we stay in your hut tonight?" Tesh asked. His voice was measured and low, a dissociated eulogy. *This is done. It's over,* his soldier's tone declared. Death happened often in his world. *Time to move on,* his eyes said. *Keep moving,* that was Tesh's answer to death. He was so accepting of it, so sober—Brin didn't want to use the word *cold,* even though it fit. "I think it'd be best if we waited until morning before—"

"Tesh, I'm not leaving," Brin said.

"There's no reason to wait here. Brin, they're . . ." He chose not to finish, maybe for her sake or perhaps for his. She wasn't sure which would be better. It didn't matter.

"Not waiting here, either."

Reading the tone of her voice, which was solid and steady, Tesh gave a nervous laugh. "Well, that doesn't make—"

Brin moved to Muriel and took a stone from the basket.

"Oh, no, you're not!" Tesh's tone left no room for argument. He sounded like her father. "You can forget that right now. We're going back. We'll spend the night in Muriel's house and be off at first light."

Brin took a feather as well.

"Brin, do you hear me? Are you listening?"

She stepped toward the pool.

With the speed and agility Brin had only seen him demonstrate in combat, Tesh rushed forward and caught her by the wrist. "I'm not kidding, Brin. I won't let you. You are not going to throw your life away like they did. I'll carry you all the way back if it comes to that."

His face was stern, commanding, an indelible rock.

Brin stayed back at the full extent of her arm, staring at him as his fingers tightened. Tesh had grown in the years she'd known him, in both size and strength. What had started as a nickname had become a title. His entire war band had adopted the name Techylors. His exploits and those of his team in the Harwood had already become legend. Tesh would have no trouble enforcing his threat, but this was too important to give in. She loved him, but that wasn't enough; he had to love her, too. And love had to mean more than just having her.

"You do that"—she shook her head slowly, ominously—"and it will be over between us. I'll never speak to you again. I swear it, Tesh, on my life. I promise you that." She meant every word, and it hurt to say them, to hear them out loud. They sounded like a betrayal, even to herself, as if she were holding a knife to the throat of her own child.

The pain must have shown on her face because at that moment Tesh's stony expression cracked in confusion. "Why?"

"Because it's what Malcolm wants me to do."

"What?" Tesh looked more confused than ever. More than shocked, he was aghast. "Are you insane?"

"You don't understand, Tesh." She was still shaking her head, more in frustration now. She had no idea how to explain. Brin wanted him to understand, needed him to, but knew he couldn't. No words were capable of saying what she felt, what she knew, and how she knew it. To him, to the cold soldier he had become, all of it would sound impossible.

"Don't understand what?"

"That Malcolm is a god."

Tesh rolled his eyes. "Brin, Malcolm was just Raithe's friend. He was a slave of the Fhrey—a slave. If he's a god, how'd that happen, huh? Tell me that?"

"I don't know. I can't explain it, but I believe." She stopped pulling against him and pointed at Muriel with her free hand. "Tesh, her name is Muriel—Muriel, Tesh."

He stared back at her with blank eyes.

"Don't you remember what I told you in Alon Rhist? What I explained about the gods? It was on the Agave tablets. We talked about it the day of our first kiss. Remember? Ferrol, Drome, Mari and Muriel are the four gods born from the same father. She's that Muriel, and if Malcolm really is her father, he'd be a god, too."

Muriel looked at her curiously, but said nothing.

"You aren't thinking clearly," Tesh told her. "Brin, do you hear yourself?"

She paused and nodded. "I do. The question is, do *you* hear me? Tressa was right. Malcolm wanted me to come. He arranged it so I would be here, but I haven't done anything, not yet. Why would Malcolm need me to be included if I have no purpose?" Brin looked at the pool. "My book, Tesh, that's why I'm here, *The Book of Brin*. Malcolm and I talked about it before he left. He told me it would be seen as an authority, like an eyewitness, and it might be the most important thing ever created by mankind. Don't you see?"

He shook his head.

"Malcolm doesn't say anything without a reason, without a purpose. I see that now. He wanted me to be an eyewitness and record what I saw in my book."

"You can't write it if you're dead, Brin!"

She looked up at him. "You don't understand. I'm not supposed to record battles and the names of villages. *The Book of Brin* will be more than that. It'll be the story of . . . of everything. But I can't write it unless I know the truth, and the truth is down there. Everything is. I have so many questions, and I need the answers. It's all part of a plan, Malcolm's plan. All of this is happening for a reason. I have to go. I need to learn the truth of the world, life, and yes, even death. It's all down there, Tesh. Malcolm wants the whole story told, and I'm the only one who can do it."

"You don't know that."

"I do. I do now."

"How? How could you know?"

"I can't put it into words; some things don't work that way. I feel it, Tesh. Like how Gifford talks about the Art. It's as if Elan is speaking to me in this tiny voice. And I know it's true. Tesh, this is why I was born. This is my Gifford's ride." The instant she said it, she felt the turn of her own words.

The answers are waiting. Who I really am, and who I'm meant to be. The very reason why I was created is down there. I don't have to go. Malcolm isn't making me do it, but by doing it . . .

"If I have the courage to go into that pool," Brin said, "then . . ."

"Then what? What?"

"Will you come with me?"

Tesh shook his head, stunned. "Are you crazy? No!"

"It will be all right. I know it will."

"You don't know anything."

"Moya knew less than I do. She didn't believe in Malcolm, and yet she went. Tekchin followed her for no other reason than he loved her."

"No, Brin. That's not fair."

"Why not? I know you love me. I've felt it. You'd die for me, and that's all I'm asking you to do."

"Oh—that's all!"

Tesh looked at the pool with loathing, his lips curling into a sickened frown. "I do love you—I do, and I would die for you, but . . ." The grip on her wrist shifted slightly.

"But what?"

"I can't."

"Why?"

"Because!" He stabbed out with the word, sharp and violent—a tone he'd never used with her.

Brin stared at him, trying to see what was hiding behind his eyes. Tesh wasn't a coward. No one alive could call him that. And she was certain he loved her. She couldn't be that mistaken, could she? Still, she saw it: Anger, fear, hatred all boiled in him at the very thought of—

She sucked in a breath. "Because you're not done."

Tesh said nothing. He refused to look at her.

"It's true, isn't it? Meeks was telling the truth. You killed them. All of them: Sebek, Anwir, and Eres. That's the reason you can't follow me now—there's still one more left. One more Galantian, and you can't die until you've killed him."

"It's more than that," Tesh said. "It's not just one more Galantian. It's the one who ordered it. It wasn't the fane who destroyed Nadak and Dureya. It was Nyphron, him and his band of Galantians. They killed my family and everyone I knew, everyone I loved. And the worst part . . . he did it to use us. He started the war so he could rule the world. Ferrol forbids Fhrey from killing Fhrey, so he slaughtered Rhunes and said it was the fane's doing. He needed us to swing the sword that he can't. Six years of war and his marriage to Persephone has made him respected among our people. They think he's selflessly fighting on their behalf, but he doesn't care about our kind. He only cares about getting what he wants. He's the root of so much death, and none of these people had to die. Not my parents, not Raithe, not your mother and father—none of them. I wanted him to know what it was like to see your whole clan wiped out." Tesh shook his head. "But you know what? He doesn't care. The deaths of others don't matter to him. I think he'll care when he dies, though."

"And that will fix everything, will it?"

With a bitter fold of his lips, Tesh nodded. "It will fix a lot. It will rid the world of a monster."

Brin shook her head. "No, it won't. You'll only be trading one for another."

Tesh's eyes narrowed. "What are you talking about?"

"Revenge. That's what you want, Tesh. And revenge is contagious—evil given for evil received."

"It's not revenge, Brin. It's justice." Tesh looked to Muriel, but while the woman watched them closely, she gave no indication of taking sides.

"And I'm sure that's what Nyphron calls it, too," Brin said. "That's why he wants to conquer his own people. This justice you're after—it's just one more terrible thing someone is doing because something awful was done to them. You aren't fixing anything. You're breaking more things and calling it better! And you aren't freeing the world of a monster, you're taking its place."

"That's not true."

"Nyphron was a legend to his people, a great warrior, and the leader of an elite war band. How many Techylors are there now?"

"It's not the same thing. We are nothing alike!"

"Are you sure? Or are you just refusing to see? Just like Nyphron, you'll do anything to achieve your goal."

"No, I won't."

"Tesh," she said, shocked. "You murdered your own friends. Anwir and Eres liked you. They taught you. They trusted you, and you—"

"They were never my friends! They killed—"

"And now, because I'm standing in your way, you're going to destroy me, too?"

"I would never hurt you."

Brin looked down at his hand on her wrist. "You already are."

Tesh loosened his grip, but he didn't let go. "I don't want to lose you."

She offered him a sad smile. "Tesh, the only way you'll do that is by refusing to let me go."

"That doesn't make sense." His eyes were becoming glassy, tears welling up on his lower lids.

"Sure it does. You just don't want it to."

"Are you honestly asking me to prove my love for you by dying?"

"No." Brin shook her head. "You're right. That wouldn't be fair. And honestly, it wouldn't prove anything." She looked into his eyes. "I'm asking you to prove you love me by letting *me* die."

Through the connection of his hand on her wrist, she felt him stiffen, and she saw the impact.

"If I let go, I'll never see you again."

"Of course you will," she said, her voice softening. "If not in this life, then the next."

"That's not good enough."

"Then come with me now."

"No!" he shouted at her. "I promised. I swore over the bodies of my family."

"Then let me go."

"No!"

"You can't have both, Tesh."

"Why not?" he yelled at her in desperation, jerking her wrist again.

"Because if you drag me away, if you do that, I'll know you just want me and that you don't love me. And knowing that will drive a wedge between us, and I'll hate you for it. But if that's what you want, we both know I can't stop you. So decide, Tesh. Either drag me away, or let me go."

She paused. He said nothing.

"Well? What will it be?" Brin asked. She glanced at his sword. "Why don't you just hit me over the head with the pommel? That'll make it easier, won't it? Then you can just throw me over your shoulder like a stuffed bag, and you won't have to hear me scream. At least not until I wake up." She glared at him. "Go on. Do it! Do it, or let me go."

Tears spilled down his cheeks. Then slowly, gently, his hand opened and released her wrist. His arm fell limply to his side.

Brin offered him a smile, but it did nothing to stem the flow of his tears. "Thank you." She stepped forward and kissed him. "I love you, too."

She turned and walked to the edge of the pool. A thick skin of brown-green slime crusted the top. She half expected Tesh to grab her again, but he didn't.

"You'll be here when I come back, right?" Brin asked Muriel.

"I always am."

"Good. Because I think I'm going to want to have a long talk with you."

"I'll be sure to make cakes to go with the tea."

Brin shuddered as she stood with her toes hanging over the pool's edge. She refused to look back at Tesh. If she did, she might not be able to go through with it. Even with her back to him and after everything she'd just said, she still didn't know if she could go through with it. Brin stood looking into the pool, and every muscle froze. Her heart beat so hard that her body rocked. She couldn't move her legs, couldn't bring herself to take that final step.

I'll see my mother and father. They're down there. They're waiting for me.

That one thought made the difference, and she lifted a foot and shifted her weight forward. As she stepped into the goo, and felt the cold clutch of the muck, she heard the wailing cry of Tesh. She'd never heard him make that sound before. The man screamed in anguish. It hurt her to hear, and at that moment, she reconsidered her decision to leave him.

How can I do this? He really does love me, and he—

It was too late. The pool had her. There was a distinct sucking as she was drawn in, pulled to the center. She could feel it at her feet, a sensation as if she were entering into the throat of a toothless giant. The icy cold— colder than anything she'd ever felt—inched up her legs to her waist. It wasn't liquid, nor mud, but thick, freezing tar that seemed alive. She felt it gripping her, pulling her down as if with hands. She shook, cold and terrified, as inch by inch the muck crept up her chest, forcing the air from her lungs, making it harder to breathe.

Looking up, she saw Muriel watching.

> *And there she sits upon her stool beside the very brink,*
> *And watches as the fated fools down into darkness sink.*

Like the hand of a corpse from a nightmare, the slime slid around her neck. Brin struggled to stretch it higher, tilting her head back the same way the duck had in its desperate effort to draw in that last taste of air.

> *Or you too may find yourself caught up in the mire,*
> *Sinking, screaming uselessly, helpless till you tire.*
> *Then under the muck, under the water, thrashing to and fro,*
> *All of you lost, forever gone, the witch cackling as you go.*

When the slime covered her mouth, when it covered her head, Brin couldn't help it. She began to scream.

Robin and I would like to thank you for reading *Age of Legend*. If you enjoyed the tale, please consider leaving a review on Amazon, Goodreads, Audible, or your favorite online retailer. It's independent feedback by readers like you that gives people the confidence to try the book for themselves. Good, bad, or indifferent, all opinions are welcomed. The only thing we ask is that you leave an honest review.

If you are excited for the next installment, you can sign up at https://michaeljsullivan.survey.fm/age-of-death-notification. This will ensure you're informed about when the next Kickstarter launches so you'll have the best chance at the early-bird specials and other limited-quantity rewards. As always, Kickstarter backers receive the book months before the retail release, so this is the best way to ensure you'll get the book as soon as possible.

In the meantime, if you've not read any of the Riyria books (based in the same world as the Legends of the First Empire series but set three thousand years in the future), please enjoy a sample chapter from *Theft of Swords*, the first book of the Riyria Revelations—an omnibus edition with two full-length novels: *The Crown Conspiracy* and *Avempartha*.

Bonus Chapter

If you enjoyed Age of Legend, *you might also like the author's Riyria books. Here is a sample chapter from* Theft of Swords, *the first book of the Riyria Revelations. This series is set in the same world as the Legends of the First Empire books, but thousands of years in the future. Here's a brief introduction to the book.*

THEY KILLED THE KING. THEY PINNED IT ON TWO MEN. THEY CHOSE POORLY.

There is no ancient evil to defeat or orphan destined for greatness, just unlikely heroes and classic adventure. Royce Melborn, a skilled thief, and his mercenary partner, Hadrian Blackwater, are running for their lives when they're framed for the murder of the king. Trapped in a conspiracy that goes beyond the overthrow of a tiny kingdom, their only hope is unraveling an ancient mystery before it's too late.

Hadrian could see little in the darkness, but he could hear them—the snapping of twigs, the crush of leaves, and the brush of grass. There was more than one, more than three, and they were closing in.

"Don't neither of you move," a harsh voice ordered from out of the shadows. "We've got arrows aimed at your backs, and we'll drop you in your saddles if you try to run." The speaker was still in the dark eaves of the forest, just a vague sense of movement among the naked branches. "We're just gonna lighten your load a bit. No one needs to get hurt. Do as I say and you'll keep your lives. Don't—and we'll take those, too."

Hadrian felt his stomach sink knowing this was his fault. He glanced over at Royce who sat beside him on his dirty gray mare with his hood up, his face hidden. His friend's head was bowed and shook slightly. Hadrian did not need to see his expression to know what it looked like.

"Sorry," he offered.

Royce said nothing and just continued to shake his head.

Before them, stood a wall of fresh cut brush blocking their way. Behind, lay the long moonlit corridor of empty road. Mist pooled in the dips and gullies and somewhere an unseen stream trickled over rocks. They were deep in the forest on the old southern road, engulfed in a long tunnel of oaks and ash whose slender branches reached out over the road quivering and clacking in the cold autumn wind. Almost a day's ride from any town, Hadrian could not recall passing so much as a farmhouse in hours. They were on their own, in the middle of nowhere—the kind of place people never found bodies.

The crush of leaves grew louder until at last the thieves stepped into the narrow band of moonlight. Hadrian counted four men with unshaven faces and drawn swords. They wore rough clothes, leather and wool, stained, worn, and filthy. With them was a girl wielding a bow, an arrow notched and aimed. She was dressed like the rest in pants and boots, her hair a tangled mess. Each was covered in mud, a ground in grime as if the whole lot slept in a dirt burrow.

"They don't look like they got much money," a man with a flat nose said. An inch or two taller than Hadrian he was the largest of the party, a stocky brute with a thick neck and large hands. His lower lip looked to have been split about the same time his nose was broken.

"But they've got bags of gear," the girl said. Her voice surprised him. She was young, and—despite the dirt—cute, and almost childlike, but her tone was aggressive, even vicious. "Look at all this stuff they're carrying. What's with all the rope?"

Hadrian was uncertain if she was asking him or her fellows. Either way, he was not about to answer. He considered making a joke, but she did not look like the type he could charm with a compliment and a smile. On top of that, she was pointing the arrow at him and it looked like her arm might be growing tired.

"I claim the big sword that fella has on his back," flat-nose said. "Looks right about my size."

"I'll take the other two he's carrying." This came from one with a scar that divided his face at a slight angle crossing the bridge of his nose just high enough to save his eye.

The girl aimed the point of her arrow at Royce. "I want the little one's cloak. I'd look good in a fine black hood like that."

With deep-set eyes and sunbaked skin, the man closest to Hadrian appeared to be the oldest. He took a step closer and grabbed hold of Hadrian's horse by the bit. "Be real careful now. We've killed plenty of folks along this road. Stupid folks who didn't listen. You don't want to be stupid, do you?"

Hadrian shook his head.

"Good. Now drop them weapons," the thief said. "And then climb down."

"What do you say, Royce?" Hadrian asked. "We give them a bit of coin so nobody gets hurt."

Royce looked over. Two eyes peered out from the hood with a withering glare.

"I'm just saying, we don't want any trouble, am I right?"

"You don't want my opinion," Royce said.

"So you're going to be stubborn."

Silence.

Hadrian shook his head and sighed. "Why do you have to make everything so difficult? They're probably not bad people—just poor. You know, taking what they need to buy a loaf of bread to feed their family. Can you begrudge them that? Winter is coming and times are hard." He nodded his head in the direction of the thieves. "Right?"

"I ain't got no family," flat-nose replied. "I spend most of my coin on drink."

"You're not helping," Hadrian said.

"I'm not trying to. Either you two do as you're told, or we'll gut you right here." He emphasized this by pulling a long dagger from his belt and scraping it loudly against the blade of his sword.

A cold wind howled through the trees bobbing the branches and stripping away more foliage. Red and gold leaves flew, swirling in circles, buffeted by the gusts along the narrow road. Somewhere in the dark an owl hooted.

"Look, how about we give you half our money? *My half.* That way this won't be a total loss for you."

"We ain't asking for half," the man holding his mount said. "We want it all, right down to these here horses."

"Now wait a second. Our horses? Taking a little coin is fine but horse thieving? If you get caught, you'll hang. And you know we'll report this at the first town we come to."

"You're from up north, ain't you?"

"Yeah, left Medford yesterday."

The man holding his horse nodded and Hadrian noticed a small red tattoo on his neck. "See, that's your problem." His face softened to a sympathetic expression that appeared more threatening by its intimacy. "You're probably on your way to Colnora—nice city. Lots of shops. Lots of fancy rich folk. Lots of trading going on down there, and we get lots of people along this road carrying all kinds of stuff to sell to them fancy folk. But I'm guessing you ain't been south before, have you? Up in Melengar, King Amrath goes to the trouble of having soldiers patrol the roads. But here in Warric, things are done a bit differently."

Flat-nose came closer licking his split lip as he studied the spadone sword on his back.

"Are you saying theft is legal?"

"Naw, but King Ethelred lives in Aquesta and that's awfully far from here."

"And the Earl of Chadwick? Doesn't he administer these lands on the king's behalf?"

"Archie Ballentyne?" The mention of his name brought chuckles from the other thieves.

"Archie don't give a rat's ass what goes on with the common folk. He's too busy picking out what to wear." The man grinned showing yellowed teeth that grew at odd angles. "So now drop them swords and climb down. Afterward, you can walk on up to Ballentyne Castle, knock on old Archie's door, and see what he does." Another round of laughter. "Now unless you think this is the perfect place to die—you're gonna do as I say."

"You were right, Royce," Hadrian said in resignation. He unclasped his cloak and laid it across the rear of his saddle. "We should have left the road, but honestly—I mean we are in the middle of nowhere. What were the odds?"

"Judging from the fact that we're being robbed—pretty good, I think."

"Kinda ironic—Riyria being robbed. Almost funny even."

"It's not funny."

"Did you say Riyria?" The man holding Hadrian's horse asked.

Hadrian nodded and pulled his gloves off tucking them into his belt.

The man let go of his horse and took a step away.

"What's going on, Will?" the girl asked. "What's Riyria?"

"There's a pair of fellas in Melengar that call themselves that." He looked toward the others and lowered his voice a bit. "I got connections up that way, remember? They say two guys calling themselves Riyria work out of Medford and I was told to keep my distance if I was ever to run across them."

"So what you thinking, Will?" scar-face asked.

"I'm thinking maybe we should clear the brush and let them ride through."

"What? Why? There's five of us and just two of them," flat-nose pointed out.

"But they're Riyria."

"So what?"

"So, my *associates* up north—they ain't stupid, and they told everyone never to touch these two. And my associates ain't exactly the squeamish types. If they say to avoid them, there's a good reason."

Flat-nose looked at them again with a critical eye. "Okay, but how do you know these two guys are them? You just gonna take their word for it?"

Will nodded toward Hadrian. "Look at the swords he's carrying. A man wearing one—maybe he knows how to use it, maybe not. A man carries two—he probably don't know nothing about swords, but he wants you to think he does. But a man carrying three swords—that's a lot of weight. No one's gonna haul that much steel around unless he makes a living using them."

Hadrian drew two swords from his sides in a single elegant motion. He flipped one around letting it spin against his palm once. "Need to get a new grip on this one. It's starting to fray again." He looked at Will. "Shall we get on with this? I believe you were about to rob us."

The thieves shot uncertain glances between each other.

"Will?" the girl asked. She was still holding the bow taunt but looked decidedly less confident.

"Let's clear the brush out of their way and let them pass," Will said.

"You sure?" Hadrian asked. "This nice man with the busted nose seems to have his heart set on getting a sword."

"That's okay," flat-nose said, looking up at Hadrian's blades as the moonlight glinted off the mirrored steel.

"Well, if you're sure."

All five nodded and Hadrian sheathed his weapons.

Will planted his sword in the dirt and waved the others over as he hurried to clear the barricade of branches blocking the roadway.

"You know, you're doing this all wrong," Royce told them.

The thieves stopped and looked up concerned.

Royce shook his head. "Not clearing the brush—the robbery. You picked a nice spot. I'll give you that, but you should have come at us from both sides."

"And William—it is William, isn't it?" Hadrian asked.

The man winced and nodded.

"Yeah, William, most people are right-handed so those coming in close should approach from the left. That would've put us at a disadvantage having to swing across our bodies at you. Those with bows should be on our right."

"And why just one bow?" Royce asked. "She could have only hit one of us."

"Couldn't even have done that," Hadrian said. "Did you notice how long she held the bow bent? Either she's incredibly strong—which I doubt—or that's a homemade greenwood bow with barely enough power to toss the arrow a few feet. Her part was just for show. I doubt she's ever launched an arrow."

"Have too," the girl said. "I'm a fine marksman."

Hadrian shook his head at her with a smile. "You had your forefinger on top of the shaft, dear. If you had released, the feathers on the arrow would have brushed your finger and the shot would have gone anywhere but where you wanted it to."

Royce nodded. "Invest in crossbows. Next time stay hidden and just put a couple bolts into each of your target's chests. All this talking is just stupid."

"Royce!" Hadrian admonished.

"What? You're always saying I should be nicer to people. I'm trying to be helpful."

"Don't listen to him. If you do want some advice, try building a better barricade."

"Yeah, drop a tree across the road next time," Royce said. Waving a hand toward the branches, he added, "This is just pathetic. And cover your faces for Maribor's sake. Warric isn't that big of a kingdom and people might remember you. Sure Ballentyne isn't likely to bother tracking you down for a few petty highway robberies, but you're gonna walk into a tavern one day and get a knife in your back." Royce turned to William. "You were in the Crimson Hand, right?"

Will looked startled. "No one said nothing about that." He stopped pulling on the branch he was working on.

"Didn't need to. The Hand requires all guild members to get that stupid tattoo on their necks." Royce turned to Hadrian. "It's supposed to make them look tough, but all it really does is make it easy to identify them as thieves for the rest of their lives. Painting a red hand on everyone is pretty stupid when you think about it."

"That tattoo is supposed to be a hand?" Hadrian asked. "I thought it was a little red chicken. But now that you mention it, a hand does make more sense."

Royce looked back at Will and tilted his head to one side. "Does kinda look like a chicken."

Will clamped a palm over his neck.

After the last of the brush was cleared, William asked, "Who are you, really? What exactly is Riyria? The Hand never told me. They just said to keep clear."

"We're nobody special," Hadrian replied. "Just a couple of travelers enjoying a ride on a cool autumn's night."

"But seriously," Royce said. "You need to listen to us if you're going to keep doing this. After all we're going to take your advice."

"What advice?"

Royce gave a gentle kick to his horse and started forward on the road again. "We're going to visit the Earl of Chadwick, but don't worry we won't mention you."

Afterword

Hey all, Robin here, Michael's wife and helper bee. First, I want to thank all the people who sent in emails saying you've enjoyed my past afterword. It's one of the reasons I'm back again! Michael isn't going to see this afterword until the book is published, so let's chat privately, shall we?

Now, I *think* I know a few things that may be going through your head. The most notable being, *First Minna, then Raithe, and now he "did in" half his cast!* I know. I know. I mentioned he's sadistic in my past afterword, but I hope we've not seen the last of those who have disappeared into the muck. He's evil, but not *that* vile. Right? Right? Michael has always said the series takes a dramatic turn in the last half of the series, and boy, he wasn't kidding! I'm excited to see what we might learn about Phyre, and what lies behind that damn door in Estramnadon's garden. Because they're not all dead. They can't be . . . right?

I'm also sure that as you got closer to the end of this book, you said to yourself, *How is he going to wrap everything up in the few pages left?* And of course, the answer is that he didn't. Neither Michael nor I wanted to end this book on a cliffhanger, but trust me when I say it really was the best approach to tell the tale that's to come. The second half of this series has three major climax points, and this book ends at one of them. Our hope is that once you read the other two books, the method in Michael's madness will make sense. So, while it may be difficult to do, I'm going to ask you to trust Michael's instincts. If you've read his other books, I'm sure you'll know he doesn't disappoint when all is said and done. Finding the Tetlin

Witch was just the first part of the second half, and the good news is you won't have to wait long for the rest of the story. But more on that in just a minute.

And now that the elephants in the room have been addressed, let me turn to the things I liked most about this book. The First Empire series was always meant to be an epic tale, and what could be more ambitious than following in the footsteps of Virgil, Dante, and Milton as we travel into the afterlife? I truly didn't see that coming.

Another thing I love is the way Michael has planted seeds that we are now seeing sprout and grow. In *Age of Myth*, Malcolm said, "Immortal means you can't die . . . even if you want to." I knew that would be important, and we're beginning to see why. I was glad that Malcolm exited at the beginning of this book. We're getting a feel for how powerful he is, and having him around would have made things just a bit too easy. It's also great he didn't know that the Ancient One had escaped from his prison, and we'll soon see how important that is to our mysterious man with the spear named Pointy.

Speaking of *Age of Myth*, it's gratifying to see other little nuggets from that story starting to come to fruition. Some examples include the stone that Raithe puts in his father's hand before burying him, the discussion about how manes haunt those who aren't properly buried, and another little offhand remark from Malcolm when he asks Raithe not to use the Tetlin Witch's name while cursing. Right then, I suspected that Malcolm and the Witch had some *past history*, but I didn't for a minute think that he was her father, or that she was the Muriel that we've heard about from the Riyria stories.

I also like the way Michael keeps switching things up. I never know from book to book who the "real" main character is when I start reading. For this book, it was the most unlikely of characters: Tressa, the ex-wife of Konniger. I never would have suspected this incredibly insignificant (and quite unlikable) side character to come from obscurity and start on a road to redemption that could end up saving humankind in the process. What's more, it's not like she's magically transformed into a good person. She's just as prickly as she's ever been, and I love falling for her even despite her past transgressions.

I'm also fascinated (and worried) about Tesh, whom we've seen transformed into the fighting master we always knew he would be—but we've also seen how the poison of revenge is keeping him from his promise to Raithe and the possibility of a better life. Even more interesting, the cat is out of the bag with regard to Nyphron's involvement in starting the war and Tesh's extermination of the Galantians. If you're like me, you are anxious to see how those two revelations play out.

Okay, what else, what else? Oh! We got to see Persephone come to grips with Raithe as she found the courage to tell him in death what she couldn't in life. It was a touching scene. And the fact that "even now" he still loves her as much as he ever did tore my heart open all over again. It was this scene that kept Michael from "giving in" to me and having the pair meet before Raithe's sacrifice, and once I got to see it, I have to admit, Michael was right for sticking to his guns.

And last, but not least, I *loved* seeing Suri give a verbal smackdown to Lothian. Poor Suri has gone through a lot, and I was worried that all she went through would break her, but it didn't. From time to time I re-read that scene just to assure myself that she's okay.

But even with everything we learned in this book, I'm excited by the fact there is still so much to come. Where is Malcolm, and what will he do next? What is Imaly going to need a second Miralyith for? What part does Raithe (in his gilarabrywn form) still have to play? Will the Fhrey learn how to make dragons? What will our merry band find in the realms of the dead, and will they be in time to save Suri? With each question Michael answers, he presents another two or three for us to think on, and it's that speculation and pondering that makes me love these books so much. Thankfully, he *does* wrap things up neatly when all is said and done, and we are well on the road to finishing out the series. Which brings us to the timing of the other books.

As you might have noticed, the first four books came out at approximately one-year intervals: June 2016 for *Age of Myth*, July 2017 for *Age of Swords*, July 2018 for *Age of War*, and July 2019 for *Age of Legend*. The first three books were released by Del Rey, and they dictated the scheduling of those books. They weren't able to release the rest of the series because a change in corporate policy required them to acquire ebook, print, *and* audio rights. Since we had previously sold the audio rights to the entire series, we were locked out of Del Rey. That put us in search of another publisher, and we were close to signing with two of them. But in both cases, they wanted the series to stay on a book-a-year schedule. Eventually, we turned to Grim Oak Press to act as our distribution partner. It's run by the fabulous Shawn Speakman, and we've got a unique publishing agreement. Basically we are incurring all the costs of production, and he is using his warehousing and distribution resources to get the novels into bookstores and libraries.

One of the advantages of this arrangement is that we'll be able to release the books more quickly. How quickly? I don't have *exact* dates yet. As I write this, it's early April and I have to get this book to press; then I'll be getting the next two installments out to the beta readers (which we plan to do back-to-back). What I am confident about is that those two books will be finished by October 14, as that's when we start recording the audio. If we can get the books released sooner (even if only in ebook), we will. Neither Michael nor I wants to keep you hanging. As with *Age of Legend*, we'll be doing Kickstarters for the last two books, and backers will get their copies much sooner than those buying through the retail chain. If you want early notification of the Kickstarter, you can sign up at https://michaeljsullivan.survey.fm/age-of-death-notification.

Well, that about wraps things up from me. I hope you have enjoyed the travels so far, and are as excited as I am to finish up the series—but to get there I need to get back to work, so I'll offer you my goodbyes and grand tidings. We'll be in touch soon. Oh, and one last thing! Thanks again for your continued support, and feel free to drop Michael a line via email at michael@michaelsullivan-author.com, or you can write to me at robin. sullivan.dc@gmail.com.

Acknowledgments

In many ways, writing is a solitary endeavor. I sit in my office, typing away—just me and the blank page. While I'm there, my task is easy: Write a book I want to read. Doing so is incredibly fulfilling, and more fun than a person ought to have, but it pales in comparison with having others read what I've come up with. When writing for myself, I have a particular bar to clear, but when offering the work to others, I need to up my game considerably. Thankfully, I have assembled a great team over the years, and I'd like to take a moment to introduce you to the people who helped to make this work what it came to be.

First, of course, I'd like to thank my wife, Robin. If you know anything about my background, you are aware that none of my work would have been published without her. But more than that, Robin is the one person who challenges me like no other. She is the ever-vigilant reader advocate, and she keeps my feet to the fire and forces me back to the keyboard when something is good but not "good enough." This book, being the first in the second half of the larger story, had difficulty finding its path. Robin gave me the insight to see where I'd gone astray and provided several fundamental recommendations that made the book what it became. Beyond that, she ran the beta-test process, provided copy- and line editing, took on the heavy lifting of incorporating the professional copyediting, and developed and launched the Kickstarter. If any of you saw even a fraction of what she does, you'd know what I do: The books wouldn't be half as good without her.

Robin and I make a great team, but even our combined efforts aren't enough to get the quality I feel my readers deserve. That's why we bring in others. Some of these people were introduced to me during my traditional releases. Others I discovered on my own and convinced my publishers to make use of their incredible talents. But either way, they've been with me through multiple projects. So, if you liked my books in the past, you'll be glad to hear that they are still with me in the present. If you've read my past acknowledgments, you've seen these names before, and I hope they'll be with me for many years to come. The books just wouldn't be the same without them. For copyediting, we've once more turned to Laura Jorstad and Linda Branam. Their attention to detail and vast knowledge of the written word have saved me from many embarrassments. Thank you, both, for all your hard work. I'm always amazed by your improvements, although by this time I shouldn't be.

Once more the cover artwork was the creation of the incomparable Marc Simonetti—truly a treasure in the fantasy community. I marvel at every creation he produces (whether for me or others). Marc works with some of the biggest names in the industry, including George R. R. Martin, Brandon Sanderson, Patrick Rothfuss, Terry Pratchett, and dozens more. I'm just glad he still makes time for a small fry like me.

For the audiobook version, how could we not have Tim Gerard Reynolds narrate? As I write this, it's mid-March, and we just finished the recording of *Age of Legend,* and yes, we've already booked him for the next two books, which will be recorded in October (the first slot he has available). I'm thrilled Tim has such a long waiting list for his recordings. If my books have done anything to aid in his popularity, well, nothing would make me happier. In addition to Tim, I'd like to include a shout-out to Brooke Magalis (an amazing engineer) who worked with Tim, Robin, and me during the recording. I'd also like to thank the post-production people. Unfortunately, I don't know your names, but that doesn't mean I don't appreciate your hard work. Other people of note at Recorded Books include Troy Juliar, who acquired the title, and Jeff Tabnick, who oversaw all the production tasks.

Having the next books scheduled for recording means the beta readers will soon be busy with the last two installments. For *Age of Legend*, we had both veterans and new recruits. I know how intensive Robin's beta process is, and their hard work paid off as demonstrated by the incorporation of their suggestions. My thanks go out to Jeffrey D. Carr, Beverly Collie, Buffy Curtis, Louise Faering, Cathy Fox, Audrey Hammer, Marty Kagan, Evelyn Keeley, Sarah and Nathaniel Kidd, John Koehler, Joan Labbe, Jonas Lodewyckx, Richard Martin, Jamie McCullough, Melanie, Elizabeth Ocskay, Beth Rosser, Pamela Sanford, Jeffrey Schwarz, and Sarah Webb.

For the last few books, we've also incorporated gamma readers. These are people who get the book just before the presses roll and act as a safety net. Unlike beta readers, who see the book in a somewhat rough state, these people saw a book remarkably similar to the one you now possess. Thankfully, we were able to exterminate the little mistakes they found before the presses rolled. Our thanks go to Sundeep Agarwal, Dee Austring, Tim Cross, Chris Griffin, Audrey Hammer, Stephen Kafkas, Mark Larsen, Alex Makar, Chris McGrath, Doug Schneider, Will Todd, David Walters, and Dick Wilkin.

And that brings us to Shawn Speakman of Grim Oak Press. As some may know, the first three books of this series were produced by Del Rey (an imprint of Penguin Random House), but they were unable to offer a contract for the rest of the series because a corporate policy change requires audio rights, something we sold for the whole series many moons ago. When Shawn found out about this situation, he reached out. I've known Shawn ever since I contributed a short story for his *Unfettered* project. Historically, Shawn has offered signed books, anthologies, and special limited-edition copies by authors such as Terry Brooks, Brandon Sanderson, Raymond E. Feist, Pierce Brown, Naomi Novik, Jacqueline Carey, Jim Butcher, Stephen R. Donaldson, Mark Lawrence, Janny Wurts, Peter Orullian, and many more. Recently, Shawn has started producing mainstream trade publications. Terry Brooks's *Street Freaks* was his first title, and *Age of Legend* will be his second. Shawn and I are trying something unique in the world of publishing, and if it's successful, I hope more authors will take advantage of an imprint that can be flexible and tailor its offerings to the author's needs. Astute readers may notice I also dedicated this book to Shawn. I hope this will be just the first of many projects we can work on together.

Did you know there was a Kickstarter for this project? It's true. With Del Rey out of the picture, we wanted to ensure that every edition in the series looked exactly the same, so we used the same printer, paper, cover stock, and other physical aspects that Del Rey used for their books. Doing so isn't cheap, but thanks to all the patrons of the arts who were willing to pre-order the book through crowdfunding, we made that desire a reality. *Age of Legend* came out in a fantastic hardcover edition thanks to the Kickstarter backers. By the time all was said and done, we had 2,553 backers who pledged almost $111,000 to help bring the project to life. As a backer, they each got to see their name in print. Now, not everyone wanted to be acknowledged publicly, and unfortunately some didn't answer their survey in time, but for those who did, you can find your name in the following pages.

And last, but not least, I want to give a shout-out to all my readers who have read, reviewed, and recommended my books to others. It's because of your amazing support that I get to live the dream of being a full-time author. Not many in this world can earn a living from doing the thing they love the most, but because of your continued support, I'm one of those lucky few. It's a gift I can never fully repay, but I'll do my best by continuing to write stories that I hope will meet with your approval.

Kickstarter Backers

Our eternal thanks go out to the following people (and to those who chose not to be recognized publicly), for being patrons of the arts and making the hardcover edition of this book possible by pre-ordering through our Kickstarter project.

– A –

Colin A. • Sam A. • M. C. Abajian • Chuck Abdella • Aberdwyn • Julian Abernethy • Brian Abrams • Thérèse Abrams • Andrij Abyzov • Iris Achmon • Jen Acunto • Colin Adams • Dr. Andy Adams • Emily Adams • Helen Adams • Josh Adams • Mike Adams • Samantha B. Adams • Michael & Heather Adelson • Daniel Adler • Max Adler • Scott Adley • Lee Adolfson • Natasha Aguiar • Kawika Aguilar • Eddy Aguirre • Donna Ahlrich • Anne Ahonen • Garrett Aikens • Ashley Aleane Akers • Lee Albanese • Alfonso Albarran • Dan Alber • Jeremy Albert • Andrew Alderman • Michael Alerich • Seth Alister-Jones • C. M. Allen • Cody L. Allen • Laura Allen • Jason Almanzar • Sami Almudaris • Nardeen AlSaffar • Olivia Alston • Jesselyn Alvarez • Vijay Anand • Alexander & Matthew Anderson • Andie Anderson • Caroline Anderson • Chris Anderson • Kyle Anderson • Maggie Anderson • Nathan Alan Anderson • Rachael Anderson • Sean Anderson • Sean L. Anderson • David

Andre • Andrea • Rebecca Andreasen • Andrew • Dennis
Andrews • James Andrews • Jocelyn Andruko & Mitchell
Farmer • Andy • Angela & Kevin • Danny Anglen • Jaime
Anglin • Jacek Aninowski • Chrissy Anjewierden • Catrina
Ankarlo • Anoop • Summer Applebaum • David Arcuri • Tamara
Arens • Sue Armitage • Mary Helen Armour • Carl Mya
Armstrong • Matt Armstrong • Cassie Arneson • Aron • Michael
Arsenault • Dyrk Ashton • Bryan Askins • John Fredrik
Asphaug • Austin Atashian • Sam Atherton • The Atkinson
Family • Brent Auble • Jon Auerbach • Samuel August • Carmichael
Aurelio • Devan Ausiello • Matt Avella • Marcus W. Avery • Alice
Aviles • R. J. Ayres • Arya Azarshahy

– B –

Alex B. • Ariane B. • Christophe B. • Dan B. • Donny B. • Elwood
B. • Jaya B. • Richard B. • Nathan Bacon • Bailey • Chris
Bailey • Heidi L. Bailey • Michael B. Bailey • Chris Baima • Olivia
Bak • Balaji • Linda Balder • Steven Read Baldock • G.
Baldwin • Meghan Ball • Nic Baltas • Ben Balzarini • Maciej
Banasiak • Preston Bannard • Joshua Barber • Caldwell
Barefoot • Yasmine Barghouty • Bryan M. Barnard • James R.
Barnes • David Barnett • Christopher Barr • Maura Barrett • Nolan
Barrett • John W. Barron • Rich Barrow • Michael Jonathan
Basaldella•AnnaChristineBassler•DotsyBastes•AaronBatey•Berta
Batzig • Marc Baudry • Darren Baxter • David Bean • Beanie • Tyke
Beard • Abby Beasley • Mark Beaumont • Brian Becker • Christian
& Niquela Becker • Anne Beckmann • Mike Bedan • Danielle
Bednar • Johnny Bedsole • Randall Beem • Alex Beier • Dina
Beinare • Alex Bekerian • James Belcher • Dana Beatty • Dana

Belden • Jessica Bell • Jim "The Destroyer" Bellmore • Ben • Emily Benger • Shane Benich • Michelle Beninati • Travis Benning • Dirk Berger • Larry Berger • Justine Bergman • Michael Bergman • Sara Bergstresser • Ben Berndt • Evy Bernier • Dustin Berry • Peter Bess • Nathan Best • Rati Bhargava • Sanjeev Bhatia • Maria Bianchi • Sara Bickersmith • Ralph Biddle • Justin Biggs • Adam T. Billups • Chris Bilodeau • Miranda Bilodeau • Sarah Birchard • Rochelle Bird • Chris Birkheimer • David Bishop • Jodi Bishop • Josh Bishop • J. Bitterman • Jessica Björklund • Samuel Robin Blackwell • Laly Blasco • Karin & Dietmar Bloech • Jaqui Blue • Ian BossMeng Blum • Owen & Madeline Blumenthal • Tylor Blythe • Angelique M. Keppler Bochnak • Billie Bock • J. Bogzevitz • Cindy Bohn • Nicholas R. Boileau • Zeke Bolce-Schick • Matthew O. Boley • Nancy Bonanno • Megan E. Bonham • Aethon Books • Bookwyrm12 • Jasen Boothe • Tom Borealis • Rikke Borgaard • Becky Bosshart • Brian Boswell • Evan Boucher • Kris Boultbee • Chad Bowden • David Bowden • Jason Bowden • Elise "The Cat" BowerCraft • The Bowersox Family • Robert Bowling • Kayleigh Bowman • Clinton Boxley • Chris Boyd • Christine Boyd • Justin Boyd • McKayla Boyd • Timothy "Doc" Boyd • Michael Boye • Kevin Boyer • R. J. Boyle III • Mac Boyter • Iain Brabant • David Bradley • Orin Brady • Sandy Brady • Andrew Branch • Amanda Brandt • J. Branstrom • Brant • Peter Brass • Daniel Brattabø • Neil Breault • James Stewart Breen • Ethan & Ben Breese • Alexander Brener • Steve Brenneman • Carmen Brenner • Stephanie Bridges • Amy Lesniak Briggs • Michael Broadhead • Julien Brochet • Sébastien Brochet • Rachel C. Brousseau • Austin Brown • Christina & Terry Brown • Christopher R. Brown • Curtis Allan Brown • Forrest D. Brown • Jay Brown • Kevin R. Brown • Michael Brown • Stephen

Brown • Steven Michael Brown • V. Brown • Jordan Brownfield • Jana Broz • Sara Brunson • Michael Jay Brunt • Joshua Brutcher • Suhaib Bseiso • Nathan Buckley • Eftichia Bukas • Scott Burfield-Mills • Micah B. Burke • Robert E. Burke • Jennifer Burns • Tom Burrows • Cassandra Burton • Jenny Busby • S. Busby • Nathan J. Bussey • Megan Butler • Nicholas Buttram • Joris Buys • Korben, Brock & Finn Byars • David Bybee • Kenneth Lawrence Bynon • Nicole Bywater

– C –

Bev C. • Carley C. • Erin C. • Mia C. • Courtney Cabaniss • Josh Cain • Lee Cain • Hilary Caldwell • Joshua Callahan • Callie & Cory • Tatiana Calliham • Clay Calvert • Kyle & Stacie Cambridge • Ross Cameron • Lance C. Campbell • Sarah Cancellieri • Kevin Candiloro • Candy & Justin • Clay Cannon • Sean Cannon • Cantankerous • Bryan Cantor • Terri A.M. Cantrell • Ashley Capes • Brandon Carangi • Pau Carbonell • Alfredo R. Carella • Greg Carey • Ty Carl • Stephanie Carlson • Dane M. Caro • Kyle Čaroban • Alex Carpenter • Jodi Lee Carpenter • Jasun Carr • Carrie • Robin L. Carroll • Alex Carter • Brandon Carter • Mark Allen Carter • Michael Caruso • Kathlyn Carvalho-Silva • Tricia Cascio • Beth Case • Casey • Brian Casey • Amanda Cassuto • Tim Caves • David Lars Chamberlain • Jaime Chan • Kevin Chan • Teik Sim Chan • Tony Chan • Jeffrey Chandler • Paul & Shirley Chandler • Rawee Chanphakdee • Chris Chappell • Susie Chappelle • Jordan Charlton • Chas • Justin Chasteen • Anthony Chatfield • John Chauhan • Jesse Chavez • Brent Chelewski • Yu-Wen Chen • Dr. Peter Shane Cheslock, PhD • Cassandra Chin • Noel Alexander Chin • Charlotte Choo • Chris • Chris & Hema • Megan

Christiansen • Derek Christman • Olivia Christopher • Christy, Jollin & Abby • Vikki Ciaffone • Jasmine Clancy • Brandi Clark • Charles H. Clark • Dave Clark & his five • Jenelle Clark • Justin Clark • Quentin Clauwaert • David Clayton • CleanSprout • Michael Clemens • Joshua Cleveland • Michael Clougherty • Mike Cluff • The Cobos Family • Diane Cobrite • Larry Coker • Ryan Colbeth • Mathew Colburn • Ab Colby • Jenny Colby • Ryan Cole • Etel Colic • Justin Collins • Lawrence Collins • Richard Collins • Todd M. Colucci • Willow E. Colvin • John G. Comas • Nicholas Compton • Susan Contreras • Chris Cook • Elise Cook • Ed Cooke • Christine A. Cooney • Michelle Cooper • Sarah Corbeil • Anke Corbeil • Jonathan Cordell • Jonathan Cormier • Shannon Cornaby • Arletta Kelley Cortright • Kelley Cortright • Leah Corvec • Rin Corvetti • Tyson Y. Cote • Brandon A. Cottrell • Larry Couch • Damon J. Courtney • Stephanie Couturier • Jonathan Cowles • Caitlin Cox & Alex Mellnik • Leo Coyle • Cody Coyote • Brian Crabtree • Daniel F. Craft • Anya Crane • Jeremy Crane • William Crane • Clayton Cravath • Belinda Crawford • Chris Creech • Phil Crimp • Kevin Cronic • Michelle D. Crosby • P. L. Cross • Trevor & Justina Crow • Andrew Cruise • David Crumbley • Aaron Crump • Mark Cummings • Gail L. Cunningham • Tommy Cunningham • Glenn Curry • Andrew Cutler • John Cutright

– D –

Brett D. • Dayve D. • William D. • Giuseppe D'Aristotile • Gail S. D'Silva • Rachel Daeger • Ahmed Daher • Diane Dahl • Daimadoshi • Dani Daly • Elizabeth Daly • Joel Damir • Dana, a writer's friend • Danilo & Trine • Patricio Danos • Isaac "Will It Work" Dansicker • Dara & Maziar • Darryl • Jennifer

Dath • Kevin Davenport-Rackham • Chad Davidson • Boyd H. Davis • Colton M. Davis • Daniel Davis • Ms. Diamond L. Davis • J. Davis & Family • Joanna K. Davis • Leslie Davis • Melissa A. Davis • Nathan Davis • Rocky Davis • Terry Davis • Sophie Dawber • Lilly Dawn • David A. Dawson • Dino Dayao & Morgan Hellar • Chris de Eyre • Marcel "madjo" de Jong • Elodie de Peretti • Wendy de Peuter • Vincent de Rijcke • Guilherme Lira de Sá Garcia • Stuart Deakin • Alex Dean • Joseph Dean • Isak DeFay • Marci DeLeon • Scott Dell'Osso • Rachael DeMaida • Anna Demchy • Diane S. Dempsey • Paul Dennison • Ryan Depuy • Max Dercum • Adam Derda • James M. Derieg • Deryk, Crystal, Sabryn & Seymoure • Eric Devers • Peter Devine & Gina Jiang • Andrew DeVore • Nicholas Francis Diakos • Patricia Diani • Leolani Diaz • Mitchell Diaz • Jeffrey Dick • Simon Dick • Tobias Dickbreder • Arianna DiCostanzo • Ethan Dietz • Bret Dillingham • Crystal Dinh • Lewis Dix • dmsaelee • The Doan Family (Randy, Marla, Colin & Evan) • Andrew Dobry • Bo Dodge • Michael W. Dodge • Christopher Kenneth Doelker • Andrew Doherty • Zoe Dollar • Miguel Domingo • Penny Don • Micheal Donohue • Jackson Donovan • Kevin Donovan • Helene Dooley • Irene Dorau • Calvin Van Dorn • Max Dosser • Kelly Dougherty • Shannon Douglas • Jacob Doukas • Michael Dowds • Chip Downs - CompuChip • Daniel Downton • Alycia & Jesse Doyle • Mary Kate Doyle • E. L. Drayton • Tara Drost • Rachel Drucker • Mengmeng Du • Dilon James Dubyk • Amelia F. Dudley • Lisa M. Dugan • Michelle Puterbaugh Dunaway • David Dunn • Alex Dupuis • Eric Durfee • Brian Dursteler • Vince Dutra • dwsm • Mikey Dysput

— E —

Dain Eaton • Ryan Eaton • Heather Eberhart • Brandy Eckman • Steven Ede • Len Edgerly • Fay Edwards • Liz Egbert • Nathan

Eggleston • Cynthia J. Egli • Ehtasham • Daniel B. Eisen • Evan Eisenberg • Thomas Elfing • Elizabeth • Elldaryck • Trevor Elliott • Jesse L. Ellis • Matt Ellsworth • Bryan Elstad • Johnny Elvers • Sean Ely • Christian Emden • Matt Enberg • Travis Enfield • Angie Engelbert • Alex Engelhardt • Kory Engle • Pierce Erickson • J. L. K. Erso • Gabe Erwin • Joel Espina • David W. Etherington • Elizabeth Etherton • L. Michaela Evans • Joshua Ewer • Morgan B. Ewers

– F –

Maja F. • Olivier Fabre • Magdalena Fabrykowska-Mlotek • Victoria Fair • Anne Falbowski • Urs Falk • M. Falvey • Aunt Fanny • Emma Faubion • Jim Favaron • Michael Fazio • Jeremy Feath • Sherry S. Featherston • Helen Febrie • Carol Feeney • Sander Fekene • Angela Femrite • Natalie S. Fennell • Danny Ferguson • Shani Ferguson • Paula Fernández • Jacob Ferrell • Derek Field • Patricia Field • Andrew Fields • Cari Fifield • Jason Figueroa • Michelle Findlay-Olynyk • Dave & Deb Finn • Shawn P. Finn • Dan Firth • G. Fisher • John Fisher • Brooke Fishman • FitzJuno • Phil Fitzpatrick • Vince Flaxfield • Ryan "Fletch" Fletcher • Chris Floden • J. R. Florek • Jonathan Flores • Manuel Flores • Andy Flowe • S. R. U. Fluhr • Holly Flumerfelt • Anthony Foderaro • Sharon Fodor • Sylvia L. Foil • Gordon & Liza Forbes • Forry • Elizabeth Forsee • Monica Elida Forssell • Hannah Forsyth • Landon Foster • Jeanine K. Fournier • Cathy Fox • Jessica Fox • Foxyvixen • Seth Butler Frampton • Carolyn Frances & Cats • Joanne Francia • Richard Francisco • Miles Frank • George Franke • Karen Franks • Tyler Fredrickson • B. A. Freeman • Spencer Freeman • Randall J. Freitas • Kelly French • Jess Freund • Phil &

Sarah Freund • Åsa Frid • Peet Friedrich • Schuyler Frincke • Helen Froats • Julien Froment • Eric Frost • Michael T. Frost • Connor W. Frye • Fuentez • Daniel Fullem • Melissa Fuller & Will Prier • Don Fulmer • Megan Funk • Danielle Furr • Yurii "Saodhar" Furtat

– G –

Catherine A. G. • Chip & Liz G. • Choko G. • Noah G. • Brian Gacki • A. Gadd • Rakin Gagda • Denis Gagnon • Christina Gale • Ed Galligan • Rumen Ganev • Vitaly Gann • Elora Garbutt • Jonathan Garcia • Amanda Rae Gardner • Christine Gardner • Kelly & Mikel Gardner • Kelly Gardner • Andrew Garinger • Greg & Tess Garrett • Peter Garvey • Cedric Gasser • Brian Gaudet • Lexi & James Gauthier • Sarah Gaxiola • Kenneth Geary • Bryan Geddes • Snævar Geirsson • Bill Genné • Ashley George • Bruno Geraldes • Gerboth • Dr. Heather Germann, MD • Mathieu Gervais • Sheri L. Gestring • Courtney Getty • Hennie Giani • Mark Gibbons • Ian Gibson • Casey Giddens • Alexander S. Gifford • Andrew Gilbert • Cullen Gilchrist • Jeff Gilkison • Claire Gilligan • The Gilpins • Ginger • Richard Glodowski • Ira Gluck • Jeramy Goble • Gargi Godbole & Omkar Kolangade • Kriti Godey • Cary Goggin • Trevor Golden • Emily Gonyer • David Gonzales • Gabriel Paz Gonzalez • Gonzo • Olya Goodrick • Melissa Goodwin-Dikkers • Bhavik Gordhan • Dylan Gordon • Gary Gorman • Joshua Eli Gossett • Michael Gouker • Lisa Gowin • gpkau • Victoria Graca • Robin Graf • Bob Graham • Kris Graham • Ryan Graham • Sven Grams • Michael Graves • Erin M. Gray • Gary Gray • Lauren Gray • Dion F. Graybeal • Bob Green • Gail Goldner Green • Jason "gValo" Green • Layne Greene • Gemma Greet • Lisa Gregory • Garreth Grey • Corey

Grier • Kirk Grier • Tyler Griesinger • Alli K. Griffin • Brian Griffin • Christopher Griffin • R.W. Griggs • Kasper Grøftehauge • Pat Grogan • Grace Gronniger • Katrina van Grouw • Adam & Cortney Grove • Crystal Growe • Steve Gruber • Donald Guerette • Therese Guerette • Andrew Guerra • Ricardo X. Guerra • Kelly Gumpert • Katja Günther • Andreas Gustafsson • Martin Gustafsson • Marce & Allen Guthier • John Tanner Guymon • Michael Guzzo • Noreen Gwilliam

– H –

Andrew H. • Carol H. • J. L. H. • Jeffrey M. H. • Phillip H. • Tyler H. • Kenny Ha • Runar Haaland • Tyler Hackett • Jason K. Hackworth • William Haddock • Justin & Stephanie Hagler • Gary Hake • Jono Hakes • Halcyon • Patrick Haley • Brandon Hall • Emma Hall • Dr. Nathan C. Hall, PhD • Tony Hall • Tim Halsey • Esko Halttunen • Joshua Hamby • Bradley Hamilton • Pamela Hamlet • Audrey Hammer • Steve Hammonds • Mya Hammons • Samuel Hamrin • Kristian Handberg • Gregory Haney • Ben Y. Hannah • Andrew Hansen • Paul Hansen • Tiffany Hansen • Kimberly Hanson • Nichole Haratyk • Earl Harbinger • Matthias Harder • Jordan Harding • LeeAnne Harker • Brandon Harris • Damien Harris • Mary Harris • C.C. Harrison • Chad Harrison • Margaret Harrison • John Ridley Harry Jr. • Anita Harsjoeen • Andrew R.J. Hart • Jacqueline Hart • Jemma Hart • Nicholas Hart • Ryan M. Hart • Michelle Hartline • Justin Hase • Doug Hastings • Rick Hauert • Chris Haught • Martin Haugland • Michael Haure • Sam Haurie • Natalie & Joseph Hawkins • Josh & Meaghan Haxton • Melissa L. Hayden • Matt Hayes • Tim Hayes • Alexis Haymaker • Trevor Hayward • Dan & Rachel Hazlett • Heather • Marc Hecht • Chris Heck • Amy Heffernan • Espen

Agøy Hegge • Matt Heiberger • Nathan Heinrich • Chris Heintz • Kyle V. Helliar • Cole Helms • David Hemmings • Kevin Hempe • Sebastiaan Henau • Jocelyn Henderson • Leah Henry • Scott Henryson • Ulises E. Hernandez • Mitchell Herrera • Frits Van Hertum • Chadrick Hess • Kenneth Hess • Jon Heupel • Hevs & Żmij • Tom Hewitt • Douglas Hickel • Edwin & Ellis Hild • David Hill • Mark Hill • Mark Hindess • Don & Heather Hindle • Daniel Hirsch • Kevin Hjelden • Zuzana Hlisnikovská • Hanh Hoang • Stephen Hobbs • Greg Hoch • Carlissa Hoffman • Christina Hoffman • Douglas Hoffman • Garrett Hoffman • Jeff Hoffman • Andrew Hogg • Linda Hojlund • T. Daniel Holl • Amy Holland • Andrew Holland • Patrick Holland • Simon Hollingsworth • C. Holmes • Corinna Holmes • Lena & William Holmes • Tamara L. Holsclaw • Donald Holsworth • Christian Holt • Robert Holt • Kara Holtzman • Allen Holub • Kristiina Hommik • Wai Chung Hon & Mark Sanasie • Brendan Hong • Francis Hooi • Alex Hoopes • Mike Hopkins • Alysa Hornick • Brian Horstmann • Linda Hosey • Keehn Hosier • Thomas Houseman • Naomi Hovey • S. D. Howarth • Zach Howell • Katherine Howett • Santiago Hoyos • HQ • Tim Hu • Christopher Alan Huddleston • Jonathan Hui & K. K. Miller • Isaac & Joseph Hull • Jeff Hullihen • Mark Humenik • Nathan Hundley • Angela D. Hunt • Rebecca Hunt • Rebel Hunter • Trần Thị Thu Hương • Ethan Hupp • Richard Hurst • April Dawn Hurt • Hamzah Hussain • Jaqueline Huth • Kathryn Hwang • Jeremy Hylen

— I, J —

I love my Lund wife • Susan R. Ichiho • John Idlor • Marcus Ilgner • Mike Ingram • Mandy Ioerger • Andreas Irle • Torian Ironfist • Jeremy

Ironside • Isai & Amy • Isha • Shan Islam • Paul A. G. Ivany • Ciro Izarra • Rima Jabbour • Jacinda & Kaitlyn • Aren Jackson • Martin Jackson • Charlene Jacobs • Catherine Jacqué • Kati James • Victoria Jang • Sally Novak Janin • Jason Janosik • Jeremy Janson • Gisele Jaquenod • Eleazar A. Jarman • Erik Jarvi • Jasmine & Yale • Matt Jefcoats • Jason Jennelle • Jason Jennings • Kooper Jensen • Ashley Jeralds • John Jersey • Lei Jess • Paul Jessee • Jim • Jokito Jo • Kyle Jodrey • Joe & Debbie • Amber L. Johnson • Charles Eric Johnson, Jr. • Charles M. Johnson • Chelsey Johnson • Eleanor Mallory Johnson • Erin & Jerrod Johnson • Fred W. Johnson • Gary W. Johnson • Jason C. Johnson • Jim Johnson • Jonathan Johnson • L. Keith Johnson • Ryan Johnson • Tyler Johnson • Jonas • Andrew Jones • Beau Jones • The Jones Family • Jason Jones • R. Nickolas Jones • Rebecca & Shawn Jones • Jonna, Anthony & DonnaLucia of Aurora, IL • Sreenadh Jonnavithula • David Jordan • Katrina May Jordan • Loretta Joslin • The Jovanovich Clan • Juraj & Andy • Just another fan of MJS • Just Another Paramedic • Justin • Justin & Lisamarie • Matthew Justus

— K —

Brynn K. • Freda K. • Geoffrey K. • Tiffany K. • K* • Marty Kagan • Marise Kahler • Jorah Kai • Joshua Kail • Greg Kajko • Matias Käkelä • Kanab • John Kiwi Kane • Robert Karalash • Eli Karasik • Eliza Karlowska • Simon Karlsson • Jaimison Karp • Richard B. Karsh • Emerson Kasak • Sean Kashino • Anika Kastelic • Christopher "Lobo" Kaster • Athena Kasvikis • Kimberlee Katekaru • Katsza • Alii Katt • Armin Kaweh • Andrew Keane • William G. Keaton • Abigail Keller • Mark Kelley • Michael A. Kelly • Emily Kelsey • Brian Kelso • Jordan

Polly Kemp • Brandon Kennedy • S. Kennedy • Timothy D. Kennelly • Aden Kensington • Kent • Kepi • Mark Kerrigan • Adam Kerstin • Paul Kervin • Melissa Kessel • E. Keswick • Nelli Khamraeva • Tuba Khan • Wahid Khan • Adam Kice • Nancy Kidder • Josh Kilen • Hannah Kim • Lena Kim • Debra King • Ryan King • Shawn T. King • Susan King • Joshua King-Rovenko • Jennifer Kingsbury • Lori Kingston • A. Kipp • Bill & Susan Kirchner • Brad Kirk • Doug Kirkland & Stacey Drohan • R. Kirkpatrick • Alen Kiseljak • Amie Kissel • Justin Kita • Cory Kitchens • Matt Klassen • Matt Klawiter • Evan Klein • Joyce Klein • Krzysztof Klimonda • Jordan J. Klovstad • Matthew Klure • Matt Kluting • J. KluznCannon • Danielle Knight • Michael A. Knight • Knownone • Ko'Ruth, Grenmorian Druid • Matthew & Brittany Kobus • Angella & Matthew Kocian • Matt Koelbl • Jessica Koga • Jeff Kohart • David J. Kohler • Michael S. Kokowicz • Miroslav Kolesár • Andrew Konicki • Kyle Kornic • Zachary Kosarik • Morgan & Rob Kostelnik • Joseph Kotzker • Kevin H. Kramer • Franciscus Leendert Krapels • Jan "Bobisek" Krenek • Virany M. Kreng • Kally Kruchten • Wulf Krueger • Caroline Kruger • Robin Kuckenburg • Nick Kuhn • Aaron Kung • Kimberly Kunker • Larry Kuperman • The Kupferberg Family • Kevin Kurth • Becca Kwiatoski • Kyle The Pike

— L —

David L. • Dora L. • Eric L. • Lillian L. • Mat L. • Sharyl L. • Youko L. • Kyle "Spacecat" Laauser • Mélanie Labarre • Greg LaBerge • Joshua Labonte • Llorente Lacap • Laurie Lachapelle • Sam Lackey • Lady Stormydays • Randall Boone LaGrange • Ronan

Lahar • Calen Lambert • Ryan Lancaster • Eric Lance • Bradley Landress • Landrovan • Richard Langbecker • Jeremy Lange • Dorothy Lannert • Laura LaPenes • Jeffrey Philip LaPlante • Larilyn • A. J. LaRock • Bjarte Larsen • Mark Larsen • Nick Larson • Bryan J. Lash • Scott Latter • André Laude • Kevin Lause • Joel Lavoie • Greg Lawlor • Jason Lawrie • Paul M. Lawson • Shirley Lawson • Debbie Layne • Federico Zona Le Fort • Tony Lea • Justin Leach • Darrell Leadbetter • Michael Leaich • Andreas Leathley • Ben Lederman • Darren Lee • Sandra K. Lee • Jack Leek • Brian Lefebvre • TJ Legge • Scherolyn Leggett • Rainer Lehr • Megan Leifker • Mark T. Lemke • Jerry & Zachary Lencoski • Paul Leonard • Jenna Leonardo • Andrew Leong • Kevin O. Lepard • Jared Lessor • Joshua Lew • Deighton M. Lewis • Lian • Ken Lifland • Elise Lucy Lightbody • Michael Lightbody • Jeffrey P. Limmer • Linas • Chad Cole Lindaman • Thea Lindberg • Adrienne Lindgren • Richard H. Lindhorst • Ewan Lindley • Roxanne Lingenfelter • Brooke R. Lingle • Lisa Link • James Litchfield • Mi Liu • Patricia Liu • Tellina Liu • Whit Lloyd • Dylan Lockwood • Logan • The Lokos Family • Sarah Longlands • Brent Longstaff • Barbara Lookerse • Julia Looney • Kevin Looney • Joe Lott • Nathan Loutrel • Louise Lowenspets • Maja Lozanac • Casey Lozier • Boris Lubarsky • Jonathan Lucina • Lucky Joe • Lucy • Sam Ludford • Lynda Lum • Gabriel Luna • Elena, Deacon & Erik Lundby • Suzanne Lundeen • Lisa Luneva • Angela Maria Lungu • John Lupo • David "Dimsum" Ly • Des Lynch • Duncan Lynch • Jae Lynch • Michael Lynch • Paul Lynch • Steve Lyon • Andrew Lyons • Kristy Kimberly Lyons

— M —

Camille M. • Connor M. • J. M. • Karen M. • Kati M. • Tiffany Ma • Dimitrios, Petra, Erika Angelika & Nikolaos Machikas • Ken

MacLean • Alejandra Madrid • Max Magana • Allie & Ben Mages • Jason Magnan • Jacob Magnusson • Michael Maguire • Steve Maguire • Sarah Mahaley • Maieriesli • Todd Maines • Majecat • Daniel Majors • Chad Makalena • Adrie Mal-Dulin • Malana & Stephanie • Tom Maley • Brendan Mallon • Jonathan Malnati • James Malone • Matthew Manni • Adam Mansell • N. Manzanares • Danielle M. Mar • Yaffa Marcus • Nick Marinos • Sharrie Lee Markin • Michael Markins • Alicia Markle • Tobias Markowitz • Michael Marks • Steven Markulec • Marleigh • Andrew Marmor • Pedro Marroquin • Bradford Marshall • Duke Marshall • Jonathan Marshall • Marco Martagon-Villamil • Brandon Martin • Doug Martin • Jennifer & Mark Martin • Lori & Shannon Martin • Pamela Martin & Royce (the now paid for HRV) • Richard Martin • Jenny J. Martinez • Richard Martinez • Beth Martinson • Aidan Marus • The Marvel Family • Alan Mask • Beth Mason • David K. Mason • Kris Mason • Shaylla Mason-Wright • Amy Mathew • James Matson • Matt • Rebecca Matte • Diana T. Matthews • Jason M. Matthews • Charli Maxwell • Chris Maxwell • Stephanie Maxwell & Richard Terkeurst • Stephen May • Maya & Levi • Lysane Maynard • Scott Maynard • Lindsey Mayoras • Omar Mazin • Lily McAlister • Michael McAulay • David McBride • Nate, Kate, Sarah & Owen McBride • Justin "Hawk" McCall • Kat McCall & John Beutter • Chad McCance • Andrew McCarl • Amanda McClain • Kelly McClenahan • Debbie McCoy • Kyle McCray • Ryan McCredie • Ed McCutchan • Bobby McDaniel • Gerald P. McDaniel • Allison McDonald • Diane McDonald • Mike McDonald • Adam McGee • Mack McGehee • Sean David McGrath • Ryan S. McGuire • John McGuirt • Ian McKee • Patrick McKernan • Jack, Kayleigh & Henry McKinley • Saoirse McLaughlin • Christopher

Bishop McLeod • Terry & Beth McMahon • William J. McMahon IV • Ian McNatt • Laura McNaughton • Katherine A. McPherson • Jen McVey • Monica Medeiros • Abbie Meeks • Renée Meeks • Stephanie Meier • Tanya Meikle • Amber & Brian Melican • The Mellenthien Sisters • Mena • Nikki Menda • John Wendell Mendiola • Marcos Mendonça • Dominic & Sarah Meo • Deanna Mercer • Deb Meyer • MFS • Neighborly Michaela • Miriam Michalak • S. Michener • Mike • Mike • Jerome Mikloucich • Monica Mileti • Neil Millar • Eric M. Miller • Eric Miller • Grant Fitz Miller • J. Lance Miller • Michael Miller • Nathan Miller • Peter C. Miller • Sean Miller • Daniel J. Milligan • Erin Millner • Kendall Mills • Nathan Mills • Elizabeth Todd Milne • Helen Milner • Krisanto Mina • Michelle Mishmash • William Miskovetz • Shruti Misra • Annarose Mitchell • modrukinstealer • Rebekah Moench • Kevin Moeszinger • Kumail Hussain Mohammed • Joseph Mohr • Joe Molnar • Nabeel Moloo • Kyndra Monterastelli & Anthony Tran • Colleen Moore • David W. Moore & Cassie M. Moore • Dustin Moore • Mike Moore • Paul Moore • Serge Mora • Pete Moran • Jasmine Morgado • Marvin D. Morgan Jr. • Michael Morgan • Victor Morgan • Floriana Morina • Stuart Morse • Luka Mosashvili • Mo Moser • Jeremy Moss • Jon Moss • Chad Moulder • Calvin Moy • Juan Daniel Ledezma Moya • Jeff Moyer • Muffin • Sebastian Müller • Alex "Syfer" Muniz • John Murphy • Phil Murphy • Hana Murray • Julie Murray • Tahseen Mushtaque • Anna Mykkeltvedt • Eric Mylius

– N, O –

Axel Nackaerts • nadx • Kate Nagle • Thushrika Naidoo • Angela Naismith • Brett Nance • Nanni • Kristina Napier • Joe

Narcisi • Narrew • Stephen Nash • Natalie • Nate & Neecy • Dwayne & Denise Need • Kapiolani Neely • Kelvin Neely • Ken Neeser • Patrick Neff • Valerie K. Neff • Bev Nelson • Kate Nelson • Samantha Nguyen • Robert E. Nicholson • Sandy Nickell • Erik Nickerson • Joshua Niday • Peter Nierenberger • Jesse Nina • Juliana Nine • Caroline & Isaac Nixon • JP Noble • Patrick Noffke • noj • Øyvind Nordli • Cole Norman • Dr. Charles E. Norton • Dan Norton • Devyn, Anthony & Royce Noto • Benjamin Novo • Dino Nowak • Francisco A. Nunez Sr. • Debra Nussman • Steffen Nyeland • Bryce O'Connor • Jonathan O'Donnell • Neil O'Dwyer • Connor O'Brien • Megan O'Neil • David J. Oberst • Janet L. Oblinger • Oliver Ockenden • Calley Odum • Michael Offutt • Mosby Oliphant • Phillip Olive • Jo Ann Olson • Laurence Olver • Curtis & Tina Olyslager • Þórhanna Inga Ómarsdóttir • Mona Lisa & Michaelangelo Ondevilla • Judah Onefoot • Michael Oney • Linda Opella • N. Opsal • Sam Oquendo • Andrea Orjuela • Tim Ormsby • Jennifer Orton • Troy Osgood • Joshua D. Ostrander • Kirsten Otting • Conny Otto • Lucia Otto • Otus • Annette & Brian Ouellette • Leslie Owens • Katie & Kyle Oxford

– P –

Brad P. • Jackye P. • Jett P. • Patrick P. • Pavel P. • Daniel, Johanna & Ellie Pack • Lea Wallis Padgett • Johannes Paetsch • Christine Palmer • Matthew Paluch • Stefan Panevski • Tony Pantev • Maurice Pantoja • Sotiris Papaefthymiou • Romy Papas • Andrea Pappalardo • Daryl Parat • Scott Pare • Emmanouil Paris • Calvin Park • Mimi Park • Annetta Parke-Houben • Jeremy Parker • Lynn & Jason Parker • Michael S. Parker • Dale Parrott • James F. Parsons • Alexander Pasik • Chirag Patel • Jay Patel • Josh

Patterson • Michelle Patterson • Victor R. Patterson • William Patterson • Nathaniel Patton • Paul-o & Tash-o • Allison Pauli • Pauline • Robert Pavel • Dom Pavlek • Katie Pawlik • Deric Paxson • Paxton, Tatum & Deacon • Micah Payson-Lewis • Joel Pearson • Scott Pearson • Pet Connection • Stephanie Peck • Jakob Pedersen • Joshua Peel • Steven Peiper • Autumn PeLata • Katherine & Kristin Pendleton • Max Peng • Lisa Pennie • Marge Pepe • J. R. Perez • Masón Perino • Taylor Perreault • Scott Perry • Alexander J. Peters • Kessia Petersen • Jay Peterson • Kyle A. Peterson • Jesper Pettersen • Smokey Pettigrew • Justine Phelps • John L. Phillips • Noël Phillips • Bonnie Phlieger • K. Pickett • Jennifer L. Pierce • Matt Pierce • Amy Sachs Pierrottie • Mackenzie D. Pierson • Leslie Pietila • John Pietrzyk • Liam Pietrzyk • Goncalo Pinheiro & Sofia Sousa • Joseph Pisano • David Plaut • B. Plouffe • Carl Plunkett • Suzi Po • Shawn Polka • T. J. Poon • Thomas & Amber Poon • Jen Porn • Calvin Post • Cody Poteet • Shana Potter • Matt Potts • Max Potts • Anders Pousette • Kevin Powell • Ryan Powell • Franklin E. Powers, Jr. • Ryan Powers • Elisa Prada • Craig Prather • Gianna Pratten • Andrew Preece • Benet Press • Edmund Pribitkin • Joseph P. Price • Psiwizard • pTERANadons • Fiama Puccini • Cameron Pugh • Tony Pulickal • Chris Pullman • Matthew Purse • Wendy Putnam

– Q, R –

Jay Quigley • Ben Quinn • Andrea & Brian Quinney • Dr. David A. Quist • Marcus Quoyeser • Pedro R. • Christomir Rackov • Robert Radu • Cindy Radvany • Hali Rae • Christine Ragan • Tristan Ragan • Akilan Rajendran • Slobodan Rakovic • David Ramirez • Marcos Ramirez • Michelle Randolph • Daniel

Ratica • Johnny Ray • Ryan Ray • Mike Raymond • Razzinos • Robert Read • Chad Ream • Keith G. Ream • Jon Reaper • Chris Rees • I. Reid • Espe vom Reihergehölz • Jim & Lórien Reilly • Bradley Reis • Renee Relin • Isadora & Silas Remillard • Kayce Resha • Sarah Retza • Henrik Reuther • Chris Reynolds • Crystal Rhinehart • Rhio • Joel Ribert • Deborah O'Neal Rice • Mike & Tammie Rice • John Riddell • George Ricky Rieckenberg • Cris Mendoza Rielly • Will Rielly • Grant "WereTiger" Rietze • Dana Riggle • Keri L. Riley • Kendra Rindler • Keegan Rinker • Steve Ripley • Casey Rivard • Sonia & Chuck Rivas • Billy Rixham • Brendan Roach • Joel Roath • William Robbins • Edwin Roberson • Derek J. Roberts • Gary Robertson • Greg T. Robertson • Adele Robinson • D. Keith Robinson • Daniel A. Robinson • Monica Rodrigues • Daniel J. Rodriguez II • Lorenzo J. Rodriguez • Miguel Rodriguez • Yuri Melinda Roh • Eduardo Rojas • Jose Rojas • Christopher Roland • Autumn Rolon • Stacey Romeo • Romney, Spencer & Tanner • David Roos • Matt Roos • Charles A. Roque • Rory • Esther Rose • Evan Rose • Jon Rose • Kristen Roskob • Isaac Ross • Thomas M. Ross • Todd Ross • Pål Asmund Røste • Jamin Ruark • Cheryl Ruckel • Amie Rukenstein • Jay Rumple • Conrad Ruppert Jr. • Dale A. Russell • Jen Ruth • Charles Ryan Jr. • Nicholas Ryan • Mladen Ryhard

– S –

Alex S. • Anna S. • Anthony S. • Audrey S. • Denise S. • Divya S. • Garren S. • Mahima M. S. • Ryan & Emilie S. • Sarah S. • Breanna, Matthew & McKinnon Saagman • Arthur Ariel Sabintsev • Gabor Sacharovsky • Kenneth Sadens • Daniel V. Sadler • Sam & Tiffany Sadler • Alex Sakes • Douglas Sakurai • The Salbers • MaryJo

Salva•Catherine Sampson•Matthew Sampson•SnL Sampson•Jason Sandau • Catherine J. Sanders • Alex Sandilands • Shelley Sands • Adriana Sandu • Fernando H. Tanaka Santos • Michael Sargent • Abhilash Sarhadi • Marc Saunders • Glen Sawa • Sax is my Axe • Scarlett pdx • Robert Schaefer • Emily Scharff • David L. Schenberg • Anna Scherer • Marc Schifer • Catherine Schmidt • Douglas Schneider • Tiana Schowe • John Schubert • Roy Schultz • Angela Schwartz • Eric Schwartz • Anna K. Scott • Calvin Scott • Codi Scott • Sam Seah • Travis Seals • Ryan Seaman • F. Sebestyén • Sebideluxe • Nancy Sedwick • Austin Segrave • David R. Seid • Ari Seifter • Suzan Sempels • Sequozu • Gopakumar Sethuraman • Michael Sewell • Chris Seymour • William J. Seymour • Shane • David Shapiro • Scott Shaputis • Brandon Sharp • Tina Marie Sharp • Corey Shaw • David Shaw • Shawn • Bethany Shay • Laura Shea • Fletcher Shedden • Mary Catherine Bernadette Smith Shellnut • Anthony William Shenberger • Catherine Shenoy • Paul Sheppard • Mary Catherine Bernadette Smith Shellnut • Ashley Sherman & Tyler Holmes • John W. Shioli • Keisha Shippy & Kyle Vorderstrasse • Shiro • Shannon & Brandi Shockley • Alex Shull • Heath Shurtleff • Stephen & Bryn Shutt • Laura & Matthew Siadak • Jacob Sicinski • Taha Siddique • Toine Siebelink • Matt Siedman • Brian Sieglaff • Teddy Sigman • Barbara Silcox • The Silsby Family • Pedro Silva • SilverMt • Gregory Silvius • James Simmons • Elaine Simpson • Susan Lee Simpson • Carlee Brooke Sims • David Simser • Kainoe Sinclair • Karen Siu • Jerome Sivesind • Sarah Sjoberg • Kazima Sjøvoll • Mike Skaggs • James Skala Jr. • Birgit Skerjanc • Cheryl Skynar • Eric Slaney • Ella Sloat • Kristine Slot • Aaron Smith • Austin Smith • B. Smith • Carly Smith • Christine L. Smith • Cierra Smith • Elizabeth Smith • Emily Smith • Jeff Smith • Katie Smith • Levi Smith • Michael Smith • Nicole Smith • Ryan

Smith • S. Brian Smith • Scott Smith • Scott Smith • Sharon R. Smith • Shawn Robert Smith • Tiffany Finlynn Smith • Dr. Zachary Smith • Kim Smits • Jonathan Snavely • Emily Snelgrove • Maria Snelgrove • Bruce Snell • Jennifer Grouling Snider • Ashton Sniderman • Kayla Snyder • Tommy L. Snyder • Danny Soares • Mattias Söderholm • Tanja Solaris • Miroslav Sommer • R. Sommerfeld • Robin Sones • Jörg Sonnenberger • Simon Engelbrecht Sørensen • Matthew Sorenson • Jose J. Soriano • Soronir • Patricia Sorrentino • Saverio Sotola • Silke Spiel • Rafi Spitzer • Michael Spredemann • Andrew Sprow • John Squire • Sarita M. Sridharan • Shannon Staff • Steve Stair • Roel Stalman • Stefan Stammler • Mike Stamp • Jackie Standaert • L. J. Stanton • Renee Perlstein Steckl • Brent Steele • Robbie Van Steenburg • Scott "Flying Python" Stefanc • Larson Steffek • Josh Steffens • Jamey Stegmaier • Erik Stegman • Chaim Steinberg • Savannah Kristen Aurora Steinberg • The Stephan Family • Tim Stephens • Mike Stern • Andrii Stetskyi • Duncan Steward • Debra Stewart • Erek Stewart • Joshua Stewart • Matthew Stewart • Michelle Stewart • Theo Steyn • Stilly • Joshua R. Stingl • Andrew Stinson • Sean Stockton • K. Stoker • Elisabeth Jane Stone • Jessica Stormrager • Melicent Stossel • Tim Stotter • Josie Straka • Daniel W. Stratton • Thom Stratton • Eric Streck • Carole Strohm • Jenn Strohschein • Mary Strothenke • Alex Strubel • Stuart & Judith • Corinna Stübing • Geri Studer • Kevin D. Stumpf • Sreevidya Subramanian • Matthew Sugarman • Craig Charles Suiter • Elliot Sullivan • James Sullivan • Kevin Sullivan • Matt Sullivan • Shawn Sullivan • Shawn & Lorrie Sullivan • Stephen Sullivan • Willem J. Sullivan • Ben Summers • Grace Sun • Suragai • Ian Sutherland • Sven • Emily June Swadron • Nate Swalve • Patrick Swanson • Laurie Swensen • Jason Swiger • Saad Syed • Carol Szpara • Mike Szucs

– T –

Alex T. • Amanda T. • Joonas T. • Maria T. • Kristin Taggart • Katarina Takahashi • C. Corbin Talley • Jade Tang • Gowtham Kumar Tangirala • Barry Tangney • Tanith • Josie Tanner • Leslie Tanner • Tash • Andrea J. Tassinari • Lee Tatum • Daryl Tay • Alex Taylor • Clay & Susan Taylor • Deborah Taylor • Michael D. Taylor • Zenobia Taylor • Ayman Teaman • Myles Templin • John Tenison • Bear Terburg • Teresa • Hope Terrell • Jonathan Terrington • Stephanie Tettamanti • Neen Tettenborn • Rachael Thacker • Suwarnan Tharmabalan • David Theis • Peter Thew • Glenn Thomas • Justin Thomas • Terence S. Thomas • Vicky A. Thompson • Dundi Thompson-Hughes • Kaitlin Thorsen • Jacob Thornton & Kiana Burleson • Tiago • Dion Tieman • Tim! • Reyn Time • Mat Timmerman • Scott Timpe • Tina & Marco • Ashli Tingle • Gail Tivendale • TKL • TL4E • Kelton Tobler • Will Todd • togepreee • E. A. Torrie • Matt Townsend • M. J. Tracy • William C. Tracy • Anastasia Trainer • Timothy T. Tran • Patti Trant • Shawna Traver • M. & J. Treeson • Ben Trehet • Toni Trevino • Michael Trick • Rebecca Trieb • Travis M. Triggs • Al Trinidad Jr. • Trish • Jordan Tubman • Evan Charles Tucker • John Tucker • Aaron C. Tufts • Nathan Tullis • Michelle Tumbokon • Tupitza • D. Turnbull • Turned Alchemy • Niki Turner • Tasha Turner • Shannon Tusler • Tycen • Mitchell Tyler • Aris Tzikas

– U, V –

ub3r_n3rd • Cynthia Unwin • Daniela Uslan • Miranda V. • Pete Vagiakos • Teresa & Elizabeth Valcourt • Wesley van de Geer • Harro van der Klauw • Heleen van Hagen • Bryce Van Laningham • Youri Vandevelde • Joshua Vanloan • Gigi Varnum • Alexey Vasyukov • Vegas Shady Lady • Brandon Veltre • Russell Ventimeglia • Sinkleir Vestmann • T. Veto • Matthew Vidalis • Joseph Andrew Viera • vikyle • Isidro "Sid" Villarreal • Bruce Villas • C. Joshua Villines • Chris Vinson • Cheryl L. Vo • David Vo • Greg Vochis • Julie Vohland • Bryce Vollmer • Luca Votipka • Ron Vutpakdi

– W –

Brian W. • Nick W. • Deprice Wade • Laura Waggoner • Johannes "Joe" Wagner • Randal & Lucy Wagner • C. Wags • Kathryn Walker • Allen Wall • Brenna Wallace • Colleen Wallace • Jeremy & Rachel Wallace • Michael D. Wallace • Zoey Leigh Wallace • Jennifer Walsh • Eileen Wang • John K. Wang • William Wang • Carole-Ann Warburton • James Ward • Krissi Ward • Michael L. Ward • Susanne Ward • Simon Warshal • Mack Wartella • Ken Washington • Cameron Watkins • Craig Watkins • Tyler Watkins • Andrew Watson • Ben Watson • Nickolai Damm Watson • Charles Watt • Jeffrey L. Wayman • Matthaeus Wdowiak • Malachi Weaver • Sara Webb • Stephanie Webb • Cyrus Weber • Kevin Wedage • David Weintraub • Eric J. Weis • Luke Weishaar • Andrew & Jon Weiss • Sara Weiss • Seth Weissman • David Welch • Carson Welker • Charles G. Weller III • Susan Wellington • Donald Kerwin Wellman • Amanda Wells • Harald Wenzel • Lee G. Wescott • Beau West • Jeanne Marie West • Z. West • Robert Westgate • Sonora A. Weston • Doug Weyek • Thomas J. Wheatley • Joseph Wheeler • Brian White • Holly White • Jeff & Laurie Whiting • Pam Wickert • Danielle Wiegert • Alex Wieker • Will Wight • Anissa Wiley • Kelley

Wilkens • Dick Wilkin • Pieter Willems • Stephen Willems • Tim Willemstein • Brandon Willey • Bryan M. Williams • Jessica Williams • Jim Williams • K. H. Williams • Kambrie Williams • Matt & Becca Williams • Scott M. Williams • David L. Williamson • Rachel Kaleonani Williamson • Jeanne Marie Willis • Scott Willis • L. Wills • Monique Willshire • Chuck Wilscam • Mark Wilson • Marshan Wilson • Michael "V.B." Wilson • Murray Wilson • Stuart Wilson • B. Win • David Winter • Ian Winter • Lauren & Eric Winter • Nicholle Winters • Matt Winton • Max Wirtschoreck • David Wirtz • Clarissa Witherly • Holly Wittsack • Steven, Ben & Zach Witzel • Scott Witzeling • Jessica Wolfram • Mirjam Wolfsbergen • Mitchell Y. Wong • Jason C. Wood • D. P. Woolliscroft • John Woosley • Michael Workman • Rebekah Wortman • Andrew Wright • Charles & Christine Wright • Jake Wright • Jeannette Wright • WRN • Ronja Wulfkuhle • Kristy Van Wyhe

— X, Y, Z —

Xuul • Valerie Y. • Yogesh Yagnik • Susan Yamamoto • Jimmy Yang • Lemuel Yap • Keith Yarborough • Gail Yates • Kyle A. Yawn • Yolanda & Kevin • Benjamin Charles York • Daniel Young • Deanna Young • Ryan Young • Teresa Yvonne • Peter Z. • Allie Zaenger • Robert Zangari • Brandon Zarzyczny • Roger Zemann • Seán Zephyr • Jehnytssa Zetino • Lisa Zidar • Perrin Zideos • Alyssa Ziegenhorn • Sandra Zielinger • Chad Zilla • Glenn Zink • Mike Ziska • Jill Zofchak • Kálnoky Mátyás Zsigmond

Glossary of Terms and Names

AGAVE: The prison of the Ancient One, which is deep in the heart of Elan and was discovered by the dwarfs when excavating Neith. During Persephone's trek to find and destroy Balgargarath, the Agave was rediscovered, but its prisoner had escaped.

AGAVE TABLETS: Written by the Ancient One, these tablets detail the creation of the world, the secrets of various metallurgy techniques (such as how to make bronze and iron), and the weaves (spells) used to manifest the Art into an immortal creature after making a crucial sacrifice.

AIRENTHENON: The domed and pillared structure where the Aquila holds meetings. Although the Forest Throne and the Door predate it, the Airenthenon is the oldest building in Estramnadon. It was nearly destroyed during the Gray Cloak Rebellion, saved only by the efforts of Prince Mawyndulë.

ALON RHIST: The chief outpost on the border between Rhulyn and Avrlyn. For centuries it was staffed by the Instarya, and provided a bulwark that prevented the Rhunes from crossing into the Fhrey lands. It was named after the fourth fane of the Fhrey, who died during the Dherg War. After the death of Zephyron, rule of the Rhist was granted to Petragar, who lost control of the fortress when Nyphron returned with the Rhune horde. It was destroyed by Fane Lothian's forces during the Battle of Grandford.

ALYSIN: One of the three realms of the afterlife. A paradise where brave warriors go after death.

ANCIENT ONE: Also known as The Three or the Old One, the Ancient One is a being whom the Dherg claimed predates the gods of Elan. He was locked deep underground in the Agave, where he wrote a number of tablets about his existence and the origin of Elan. After being ill used, he escaped, leaving behind a demon to bar the Dherg from their homeland.

ANWIR (Fhrey, Asendwayr): Quiet and reserved, he is the only non-Instarya Fhrey member of Nyphron's Galantians. He has a penchant for knots and uses a sling for a weapon.

ANYVAL (Fhrey, Umalyn): Healer of Alon Rhist who treated Persephone after a raow attack left her severely injured during the Battle of Grandford.

AQUILA: Literally "the place of choosing." Originally created as a formalization and public recognition of the group of Fhrey who had been assisting Gylindora Fane for more than a century. Leaders of each tribe act as general counsels, making suggestions and assisting in the overall administration of the empire. Senior council members are elected by their tribes or appointed by the fane. Junior members are chosen by the senior. The Aquila holds no direct power, as the fane's authority is as absolute as Ferrol Himself. However, the Aquila does wield great influence over the succession of power. It is the Curator and Conservator who determine who has access to the Horn of Gylindora.

ARIA (Rhune, Rhen): Mother of Gifford. She had been told by the mystic Tura that she would die giving birth to her son, who would become the fastest man alive and save humankind. She did indeed die, and while her crippled son seemed an unlikely hero, he ultimately fulfilled the prophecy.

ARION (Fhrey, Miralyith): Also known as Cenzlyor. The former tutor to Prince Mawyndulë and onetime student of Fenelyus. Arion was sent to Rhulyn to bring the outlaw Nyphron to justice and was injured when Malcolm hit her on the head with a rock. After partially recovering from her wounds, she fought Gryndal, a fellow Miralyith, when he threatened to destroy Dahl Rhen and kill all its residents. She took up residence with the Rhunes in the hope of finding a peaceful end to the conflict between Rhunes and Fhrey. During Persephone's trek to Neith, Arion was critically injured. When she recovered, she came to Alon Rhist to help the Rhunes defend against Fane Lothian's attack. She was killed by Mawyndulë during the Battle of Grandford.

ART, THE: Magic that allows the caster to tap the forces of nature. In Fhrey society, it's practiced by members of the Miralyith tribe. Goblins who wield this power are referred to as oberdaza. Only two Rhunes are known to possess any Artistic ability: the mystic Suri, who is extremely accomplished, and Gifford, who is still very much a novice.

ARTIST: A practitioner of the Art.

ASENDWAYR: The Fhrey tribe whose members specialize in hunting. A few were stationed on the frontier to provide meat for the Instarya.

ASICA: A one-piece robe-like garment worn by Fhrey in various configurations. Those without ties are commonly used by the Miralyith.

ATLATL: A device used to extend the distance a spear can be thrown.

AUDREY: Moya's bow, named after her mother.

AVEMPARTHA: The Fhrey tower created by Fenelyus atop a great waterfall on the Nidwalden River. It can tap the force of rushing water to amplify the use of the Art. Kel Jerydd is the head Miralyith stationed at the tower.

AVRLYN: "Land of Green," the Fhrey frontier bordered on the north by Hentlyn and by Belgreig to the south. Avrlyn is separated from Rhulyn by the east and south branches of the Bern River.

BALGARGARATH: A creature created by the Ancient One in retribution for his mistreatment by the Dherg. It rendered the homeland of the dwarfs uninhabitable. Created by an incredibly powerful weave, it is the Art manifested into corporeal form, and as such, it can't be harmed by any use of magic. It was destroyed by Persephone's party unraveling its spell after penetration of a weapon that contained its name.

BATTLE OF GRANDFORD: The first official battle in the Great War between Rhunes and Fhrey. While each opponent held the upper hand at various stages of the battle, ultimately the forces of Fane Lothian were routed mainly because of the emergence of an unstoppable dragon and the addition of the Gula horde, which had been summoned to the battlefield after Gifford's ride to Perdif. Despite the Rhunes' victory, Alon Rhist was predominantly destroyed during the multiday siege.

BATTLE OF MADOR: During the Belgric War, the battle between the Fhrey and Dherg where Fenelyus first used the Art, crushing the Tenth and Twelfth Dherg legions under a pile of rock that formed Mount Mador. The battle turned the tide of the war by stopping the Dherg advance.

BELGREIG: The continent to the far south of Elan where the Dherg people reside.

BELGRIC WAR: A war between the Fhrey and Dherg. Also referred to as the Dherg War or the War of Elven Aggression. Ultimately the Fhrey won and sent the Dherg into exile.

BELGRICLUNGREIANS: The term Dherg use to refer to themselves and their kind.

BERN: A river that runs north–south and delineates the border between Rhulyn and Avrlyn. Historically, Rhunes were forbidden from crossing to the west side of this river, but once Nyphron joined the Rhunes in a war against Fane Lothian, that restriction ended.

BLACK BRONZE: A metal alloy whose recipe—known only to the Dherg— utilizes gold, silver, and copper. It's especially important in the making of sculptures. It was the metal used to make a sword with Raithe's true name inscribed upon the blade, making it the only weapon capable of vanquishing the gilarabrywn he eventually became.

BOOK OF BRIN: The first known written work chronicling the history of the Rhunes. It dates back to the time of the first war between Rhunes and Fhrey.

BRECKON MOR: The feminine version of the leigh mor. A versatile piece of patterned cloth that can be wrapped in a number of ways.

BRIN (Rhune, Rhen): Keeper of Ways for Dahl Rhen and author of the famed *Book of Brin*. During the giant attack on Dahl Rhen, Brin's parents, Sarah and Delwin, were killed. Brin accompanied Persephone to Neith, where she found and translated a number of tablets left in the Agave by the Ancient One.

CARATACUS (Fhrey, no tribe affiliation): A legendary wizard who created the Forest Throne using magic that predated the Art. He is also the one who delivered the horn to Gylindora, along with instructions on how to choose successors.

CENZLYOR: In the Fhrey language, the term means "swift of mind." A title of endearment bestowed by Fane Fenelyus onto Arion, indicating her proficiency in the Art.

CHIEFTAIN: Traditionally, the leader of a given clan of Rhunes. During the rule of a keenig, chieftains' power diminish, as the keenig rules over all Rhunic people.

CONSERVATOR OF THE AQUILA: The keeper of the Horn of Gylindora and, along with the Curator, one of the two Fhrey most responsible for administering the process of succession. The Conservator is also responsible for picking a new Curator when needed. The current Conservator is the Umalyn high priest Volhoric.

CRESCENT FOREST: A large forest that forms a half circle around Dahl Rhen.

CRIMBAL: A fairy creature that lives in the land of Nog. Crimbals travel to the world of Elan through doors in the trunks of trees. They are known to steal children and host elaborate banquets.

CURATOR: The vice fane who presides over the six councilors of the Aquila, elected by a vote of senior members. The Curator leads meetings of the Aquila in the absence of the fane, and chairs the Challenge Council, which decides who has the right to blow the Horn of Gylindora. Together, the Conservator and the Curator are the Fhrey most responsible for determining the succession of power and administering the Uli Vermar challenge process. The current Curator is Imaly.

DAHL (hill or mound): A Rhune settlement that is the capital city of a given clan and is characterized by its position on top of a man-made hill. Dahls are usually surrounded by some form of wall or fortification. Each has a central lodge where the clan's chieftain lives as well as a series of roundhouses that provide shelter for the other villagers. Originally there were seven Rhulyn-Rhune dahls and three Gula-Rhune settlements, but two (Nadak and Dureya) were destroyed by Nyphron and his Galantians and one (Rhen) was destroyed by giants working with Fane Lothian.

DELWIN (Rhune, Rhen): A sheep farmer who was the husband of Sarah and father of Brin. He was killed by the giant attack that destroyed Dahl Rhen.

DHERG: One of the five humanoid races of Elan. Skilled craftsmen, they have been all but banned from most places except Belgreig after losing the War of Elven Aggression. They are exceptional builders and weaponsmiths. The name is a pejorative Fhrey word meaning "vile mole." The Dherg refer to themselves as Belgriclungreians.

DOME MOUNTAIN: Raised peak above the city of Neith, brought down by Suri and sealing the entrance to the dwarven homeland.

DOOR, THE: A portal in the Garden of Estramnadon that legend holds is the gateway to the afterlife and the place where the First Tree grows. It is thought to be impenetrable.

DROME: The god of the Dherg.

DRUMINDOR: A Dherg-built fortress located on an active volcano at the entrance to a large strategic bay on the Blue Sea. Two massive towers provide protection from any invasion via water.

DUREYA: A barren highland in the north of Rhulyn, home to the Rhune clan of the same name. The entire region and all the clan members were destroyed by Nyphron and his Galantians. Before their destruction, they were the most powerful warrior clan of the Rhulyn-Rhunes. Only two Dureyans were known to survive: Raithe (now deceased) and Tesh.

DURYNGON: A prison under the Verenthenon at Alon Rhist used to house prisoners and exotic animals that are studied to determine how best to defeat them.

DWARF: Any flora or fauna of diminutive stature (as in dwarf wheat or dwarf rabbits). Also, the name Persephone gives to the residents of

Belgreig, which is easier to pronounce than Belgriclungreians and not as insulting as Dherg.

EILYWIN: Fhrey architects and craftsmen who design and create buildings.

ELAN: The Grand Mother of All. God of the land.

ELF: Mispronunciation of the Fhrey word *ylfe,* meaning "nightmare," and a derogatory term used by the Dherg to insult the Fhrey people. Tesh and other fighters often refer to Fhrey by this pejorative.

ELYSAN (Fhrey, Instarya): Close friend and adviser to Zephyron.

EREBUS: Father of all gods, as discovered by Brin in the Agave tablets.

ERES (Fhrey, Instarya): A member of Nyphron's Galantians. His main prowess is with spears and javelins.

ERIVAN: Homeland of the Fhrey.

ESTRAMNADON: The capital city of the Fhrey, located in the forests of Erivan.

ESTRAMNADON ACADEMY: Also known as the Academy of the Art. The school where Miralyith are trained in the ways of magic. Entrance to it requires passage of the Sharhasa, an aptitude test. It was formed by Fane Lothian's first son, Pyridian, who later died. Lothian's second son, Mawyndulë, initially failed the Sharhasa.

ETON: God of the sky.

FANE: The ruler of the Fhrey, whose term of office extends to death or until three thousand years after ascension, whichever comes first. The current leader is Fane Lothian, son of Fenelyus.

FENELYUS (Fhrey, Miralyith): The fifth fane of the Fhrey and first of the Miralyith. She saved the Fhrey from annihilation during the Belgric War by creating Mount Mador and crushing thousands beneath it. While she could have easily destroyed the Dherg civilization, she ended the war instead. The reason for her change of mind remains a mystery.

FERROL: The god of the Fhrey.

FERROL'S LAW: Also known as Law of Ferrol, it's the irrefutable prohibition against Fhrey killing other Fhrey. In extreme situations, a fane can make an exception for cause, or can designate a person as exempt. Breaking Ferrol's Law will eject a Fhrey from society and bar the perpetrator from the afterlife. Since it is the Fhrey's god who will pass judgment, no one can circumvent Ferrol's Law by committing murder in secret or without witnesses.

FHREY: One of the five major races of Elan. Fhrey are long-lived, technologically advanced, and organized into tribes based on profession.

FIRST CHAIR AND SECOND CHAIR: Honorific for the chieftain of a dahl and their spouse. Its origin comes from actual chairs that are placed on a dais in a dahl's lodge.

FIRST MINISTER: The third most important person in Fhrey society (following the fane and the Curator). The primary task is the day-to-day administration of the Talwara. The present First Minister is Metis, who replaced Gryndal.

FIRST TREE: Fruit from this tree is believed to grant immortality, and it's rumored to lie behind the Door in Estramnadon. The Belgric War was fought largely because of the dwarfs' belief that this treasure was being kept from them.

FIVE MAJOR RACES OF ELAN: Rhunes, Fhrey, Dherg, ghazel, and Grenmorians.

FLOOD (Dherg): A builder, Frost's brother, and one of three Dherg responsible for unleashing Balgargarath from a complex series of noise-creating traps. To save him from execution, Persephone takes the three dwarfs back to Tirre after Gronbach's broken promises. He was one of the people in the smithy the night Suri transformed Raithe into a gilarabrywn.

FOREST THRONE: The seat of the fane, located in the Talwara in the capital city of Estramnadon. Created by Caratacus, who intertwined six trees as symbols of the (then) six tribes of the Fhrey.

FROST (Dherg): A builder, Flood's brother, and one of three Dherg responsible for unleashing Balgargarath from a complex series of noise-creating traps. To save him from execution, Persephone takes the three dwarfs back to Tirre after Gronbach's broken promises. He was one of the people in the smithy the night Suri transformed Raithe into a gilarabrywn.

FURGENROK (Grenmorian): Leader of the Grenmorians, the giants of Elan. He was employed by the Fhrey to attack Dahl Rhen. While many were killed and the dahl was destroyed, the ultimate goal of killing Raithe, Arion, and Nyphron failed.

GALANTIANS: The Instarya party led by Nyphron and famed for legendary exploits of fighting prowess. While it is believed that they were exiled from Alon Rhist for disobeying orders to destroy Rhune villages, Tesh knows they were actually responsible for the destructions of those dahls, a ploy by Nyphron to start a war between Rhunes and the leadership of the Fhrey people. The Galantians returned to Alon Rhist just prior to the Battle of Grandford and have been instrumental in training the Rhune horde to fight Fane Lothian's army.

GARDEN, THE: One of the most sacred places in Fhrey society, used for meditation and reflection. The Garden is in the center of Estramnadon and surrounds the Door, the Fhrey's most sacred relic.

GATH (Rhune): The first keenig, who united all the human clans during the Great Flood.

GELSTON (Rhune, Rhen): The shepherd who was hit by lightning during the giant attack on Dahl Rhen; uncle to Brin. He's been enfeebled since the attack, and his care has largely been performed by Tressa.

GIFFORD (Rhune, Rhen): The incredibly talented potter of Dahl Rhen, whose mother died during his birth. Because of extensive deformities, he wasn't expected to live more than a few years. Gifford is a fledgling Rhune Artist and instrumental in saving Alon Rhist thanks to his late-night ride to Perdif.

GIFFORD'S RIDE: During the Battle of Grandford, Gifford became the first Rhune to ride a horse, and he did so through the heart of Fane Lothian's forces as they lay siege to Alon Rhist. Against all odds, this late-night ride brought him to Perdif, where, using the Art, he lit a signal fire that brought the Gula-Rhune horde to the aid of the embattled Rhune forces.

GILARABRYWN: A dragon-like creature Suri created by sacrificing her best friends: first Minna and later Raithe. A gilarabrywn is created using a spell found on the Agave tablets in Neith, which manifests the Art in corporeal form. The first gilarabrywn was crucial to the survival of Persephone's party, and it was ultimately destroyed by Suri when it was discovered it couldn't leave the confines of Neith. The second one was responsible for saving Alon Rhist during Fane Lothian's siege, and it has yet to be destroyed.

GOBLINS: A grotesque race feared and shunned by all in Elan, known to be fierce warriors. The most dangerous of their kind are oberdaza, who can harness the power of elements through magic. In the Dherg language, they are known as:

Ran Ghazel (Forgotten Ones of the Sea)

Fen Ran Ghazel (Forgotten Ones of the Swamps)

Fir Ran Ghazel (Forgotten Ones of the Forest)

Durat Ran Ghazel (Forgotten Ones of the Mountains)

GOD KILLER: A moniker given to Raithe of Dureya, who was the first known Rhune to kill a Fhrey (Shegon of the Asendwayr tribe). While staying in Dahl Rhen, he killed another Fhrey (Gryndal of the Miralyith).

GRAND MOTHER OF ALL: Another name for the goddess Elan (the world).

GRANDFORD: The location of a great bridge that allows crossing of the Bern river. It marks the boundary between the Fhrey-held fortress of Alon Rhist and the Rhune plains of Dureya. It is the site of the first substantial battle of the Fhrey–Rhune war.

GRAY CLOAKS: A secret society of Miralyith who attempted to overthrow Fane Lothian because he wasn't doing enough to elevate the position of Miralyith over other tribes in the Fhrey society. Principal members include Aiden, the group's leader, and Makareta, who manipulated Mawyndulë to help them discover weaknesses in the fane's defenses.

GRAY CLOAK REBELLION: A failed attempt by the Gray Cloaks to kill Fane Lothian and instate Mawyndulë as the new ruler of the Fhrey. All members (except Makareta) either died during the insurrection or were put to death by Fane Lothian in public executions.

GREAT WAR: The first war between the Fhrey people and the Rhunes.

GRENMORIAN: The race of giants who live in Hentlyn in northern Elan.

GRIN THE BROWN: A ferocious bear who was responsible for the deaths of many residents of Dahl Rhen, including Mahn, Persephone and Reglan's eldest son; Konniger, former chieftain; and Maeve, the dahl's Keeper of Ways. The beast was eventually killed by Persephone.

GRONBACH (Dherg): The mayor of Caric and Master Crafter of that city. He deceived and tricked Persephone into ridding Neith of Balgargarath and failed to uphold his promise to provide weapons to the Rhunes to fight the Fhrey. His treachery led to the eventual destruction of Neith by Suri. Brin's outrage with the dwarf makes him a central villain in her famed *Book of Brin*.

GRYGOR (Grenmorian): A member of Nyphron's famed Galantians and the only giant of the group. Known for his love of cooking and use of spices. This fondness for the culinary arts has fostered a friendship between him and Padera, Dahl Rhen's oldest member. He died while defending Keenig Persephone when Fane Lothian's forces made their final assault on Alon Rhist.

GRYNDAL (Fhrey, Miralyith): The former First Minister to Fane Lothian. Respected as one of the most skilled practitioners of the Art, Gryndal was killed in Dahl Rhen by Raithe after the Miralyith attempted to destroy the dahl and all its residents.

GULA-RHUNES: A northern alliance of three Rhune clans (Dunn, Strom, and Erling) that had a long-standing feud with the seven southern Rhulyn-Rhune clans. Historically, the Fhrey have pitted these two sides against each other and fostered their mutual animosity. As conflict with the Fhrey intensified, the Gula- and Rhulyn-Rhunes joined forces, all serving Keenig Persephone.

GWYDRY: One of the seven tribes of Fhrey. This one is for the farmers and laborers who are responsible for raising crops and livestock.

GYLINDORA FANE (Fhrey, Nilyndd): The first leader of the Fhrey. Her name became synonymous with *ruler.*

HABET (Rhune, Rhen): The Keeper of the Eternal Flame, responsible for ensuring that the braziers and the lodge's fire pit remain lit.

HAWTHORN GLEN: Home to Suri and Tura.

HENTLYN (land of mountains): An area to the north of Avrlyn, generally inhabited by Grenmorians.

HERKIMER (Rhune, Dureya): The father of Raithe and a skilled warrior known as Coppersword. He was killed by Shegon.

HIGH SPEAR VALLEY: Grassy plain just south of the High Spear Branch of the Bern River. Home to the three clans of the Gula-Rhunes.

HOPELESS HOUSE: Alon Rhist residence of Gifford, Habet, Mathias, and Gelston. So named because it housed the most unworthy of Dahl Rhen's remaining people. While not a resident (because of her gender), Tressa spent much of her time there as an honorary member.

HORN OF GYLINDORA: A ceremonial horn kept by the Conservator that was originally bestowed on Gylindora Fane by the legendary Caratacus. The horn is used to challenge for leadership of the Fhrey. It can only be blown during an Uli Vermar (upon the death of a fane or every three thousand years). When blown at the death of a fane, it's the fane's heir who is challenged. If the fane has no heir or if it is blown after three thousand years of reign, the horn can be blown twice, providing for two contestants.

IMALY (Fhrey, Nilyndd): A descendant of Gylindora Fane, leader of the Nilyndd tribe, and Curator of the Aquila. She's been providing refuge to Makareta since the Gray Cloak Rebellion.

INSTARYA: One of the seven tribes of the Fhrey. Instarya are the warriors who have been stationed on the frontier in outposts along the Avrlyn border since the Belgreig War.

JERYDD (Fhrey, Miralyith): The kel of Avempartha. He led the attack on Dahl Rhen, which destroyed the village but failed to kill Arion, Nyphron, or Raithe.

KASIMER (Fhrey, Miralyith): Leader of the newly re-formed Spider Corps, a group of Artists who can combine their power for coordinated attacks. He died during the Battle of Grandford.

KEENIG: A single person who rules over the united Rhune clans in times of trouble. Until the appointment of Persephone during the Fhrey war, there hadn't been more than a few appointed since the days of Gath, who saved humankind during the Great Flood.

KEEPER OF WAYS: The person who learns the customs, traditions, and general memories of a community and is the authority in such matters. Keepers pass down their knowledge through oral tradition. The most famous Keeper is Brin from Dahl Rhen, who created the renowned *Book of Brin.*

KEL: The administrator of a prestigious institution such as Avempartha or the Academy of the Art.

KNOTS: Known to disrupt the natural flow of the Art, knots often create difficulty in communication and prevent consensus building. Once a knot is unraveled, so, too, are arguments unknotted, leading to eventual agreement. The knot that holds together a being created from the Art (such as Balgargarath or a gilarabrywn) is loosed by piercing the creature with its true name.

KONNIGER (Rhune, Rhen): Shield to Chieftain Reglan of Dahl Rhen and husband of Tressa. Konniger ruled Rhen for a short period of time between the reigns of Reglan and Persephone after assassinating the former. He also tried to kill Persephone and was inadvertently killed by Grin the Brown.

LANGUAGE OF CREATION: The root language of the gods and every living thing in Elan. The chords plucked while performing Artistic weaves tap into the language of creation, the building blocks of all living things.

LEIGH MOR: Great cloak. A versatile piece of fabric used by Rhune men that can be draped in a number of ways, usually belted. A leigh mor can also be used as a sling to carry items or as a blanket. Usually, they're woven with the pattern of a particular clan. The female version, known as a breckon mor, is longer, with an angled cut.

LINDEN LOTT: The chief Dherg city after the fall of Neith. It holds an annual contest to determine the best in various endeavors valued by the Dherg people, such as building, forging weapons, and digging.

LIPIT (Rhune, Tirre): The chieftain of Dahl Tirre who was killed during the Battle of Grandford.

LITTLE RHEN: The area of Alon Rhist that mainly houses Rhunes displaced from the destroyed Dahl Rhen. The original Fhrey inhabitants left that area after the Rhunes took over the fortress.

LOTHIAN, FANE (Fhrey, Miralyith): The supreme ruler of the Fhrey, father to Mawyndulë, son of Fenelyus. He came into power after an unusually gruesome challenge in which he defeated Zephyron of the Instarya in a humiliating and cruel display of power. He led the Fhrey advance on Alon Rhist during the Battle of Grandford and fled in disgrace.

MAEVE (Rhune, Rhen): The former Keeper of Ways for Dahl Rhen and mother of Suri; she was killed by Grin the Brown.

MAGDA: The oldest tree in the Crescent Forest; an ancient oak known to offer sage advice, including information that was instrumental in saving the village of Dahl Rhen when it was targeted by First Minister Gryndal of the Miralyith. She was killed during the Grenmorian attack on Dahl Rhen.

MAHN (Rhune, Rhen): The son of Persephone and Reglan. He was killed by a ferocious bear known as The Brown.

MAKARETA (Fhrey, Miralyith): A member of the Gray Cloaks and the object of Mawyndulë's first romantic crush. After the rebellion, she took up residence with Imaly.

MALCOLM (unknown): The ex-slave of Zephyron, former resident of Alon Rhist, and best friend of Raithe. He's attacked two Fhrey with rocks: Shegon and Arion. He has also been providing counsel to Nyphron and was instrumental in getting Suri to sacrifice Raithe in order to create a gilarabrywn to defeat Fane Lothian's forces.

MARI: The patron god of Dahl Rhen.

MASTER OF SECRETS: The adviser to the fane who is responsible for Talwara security. Vasek is the current holder of that title.

MAWYNDULË (Fhrey, Miralyith): Prince of the Fhrey realm; the son of Lothian, grandson of Fenelyus, and former student of Arion and Gryndal. He was present at Dahl Rhen when Raithe killed Gryndal. For a short time, he represented the Miralyith in the Aquila as the junior councilor and later as the senior. He was duped by the Gray Cloaks into providing them aid, but was not involved in the rebellion.

His action to save himself ended up saving the life of Imaly and several other Fhrey when he held the Airenthenon together. During the Battle of Grandford, he killed Arion.

MEDAK: A Galantian who was killed by Gryndal during Gryndal's attack on Alon Rhist. Younger brother to Eres.

MELEN: A Rhulyn clan known for its poets and musicians, ruled by Chieftain Harkon.

MENAHAN: The richest of the seven Rhulyn clans. Known for its wool and great sheep flocks. It's ruled by Krugen.

MERREDYDD: One of the four Fhrey outposts manned by the Instarya to protect the frontier. It is the one farthest south.

METIS, MINISTER (Fhrey, Nilyndd): Highest-ranking member of the Nilyndd tribe, responsible for creating weapons and armor. Also the current First Minister who obtained the position after the death of Gryndal.

MINNA: A wolf and the best friend of Suri, who dubbed the animal the wisest wolf in the world. Minna was sacrificed by Suri and turned into a gilarabrywn that fought Balgargarath and saved Persephone's party. When it was discovered she couldn't leave the city of Neith, she was killed using a sword bearing her name.

MIRALYITH: The Fhrey tribe of Artists—people who use the Art to channel natural forces to work magic. Their tribe is currently in power, and because of their skill with the Art, this is not likely to change in the coming future. Many members of this tribe have begun to think of themselves as gods, or at least at a higher level than other Fhrey tribes, as evidenced by the recent Gray Cloak uprising.

MOUNT MADOR: A mountain conjured by Fane Fenelyus during the Belgreig War, killing tens of thousands of Dherg.

MOYA (Rhune, Rhen): Shield to Keenig Persephone, Moya killed Udgar (chieftain of Gula-Rhune Clan Erling). She's the first person to use bows and arrows and was the one who shot and destroyed Balgargarath. She is romantically linked to Tekchin, one of the Fhrey Galantians.

MURIEL: Daughter of Erebus, as discovered by Brin in the Agave tablets.

MYSTIC: An individual capable of tapping into the essence of the natural world and understanding the will of gods and spirits. Both Tura and Suri are mystics from the Hawthorn Glen.

NADAK: A region in the north of Rhulyn that is home to the Rhune clan of the same name. It was destroyed by the Fhrey Instarya, and most of its residents were slaughtered.

NARASPUR: The horse that Arion rode from Estramnadon to Alon Rhist. She left it at the fortress after a fall during her debut trip. Later, Gifford used Naraspur on his late-night ride to Perdif to alert the Gula soldiers to come to the defense of Alon Rhist.

NARSIRABAD: A large spear from the lodge of Dahl Rhen used by Malcolm. Its name is Fhrey for "pointy."

NEITH: The original home of the Dherg in Belgreig. It was an underground city and the most revered place in the Dherg culture. For thousands of years, the Dherg were denied use of Neith by the Ancient One, who in revenge created Balgargarath to kill any who entered the city. Neith was later destroyed, buried by Suri during an emotional outburst.

NIDWALDEN: A mighty river that separates Erivan (the land of the Fhrey) from Rhulyn (the land of the Rhunes). The tower Avempartha sits in the middle of it at the Parthaloren Falls.

NIFREL: Below Rel. The most dismal and unpleasant of the three regions of the afterlife.

NILYNDD: The Fhrey tribe of craftsmen.

NYPHRON (Fhrey, Instarya): The son of Zephyron and leader of the famed Galantians. After attacking the new leader of Alon Rhist, he was declared an outlaw. He and his Galantians found refuge in the Rhune village of Dahl Rhen. His bid to become the Rhune keenig failed since only humans can rise to that position. During the Battle of Grandford, he made a pledge to Malcolm for a favor to be fulfilled at a later date.

ORINFAR: Ancient Dherg runes that can prevent the use of the Art.

PADERA (Rhune, Rhen): A farmer's wife and the oldest resident of Dahl Rhen, she is known for her excellent cooking ability and for being the best healer in the dahl.

PARTHALOREN FALLS: The massive set of waterfalls that Avempartha resides on. The rushing water provides an enormous power source to channel the Art.

PERSEPHONE, KEENIG (Rhune, Rhen): Ruler of all Rhunes, former chieftain of Dahl Rhen, and widow of Reglan. She killed Grin the Brown and led a party to Neith to kill Balgargarath. When Gronbach failed to provide promised iron weapons, she tricked him into revealing the manufacturing process to Roan, who took this knowledge to the Rhune people. She was severely injured by a raow during the Battle of Grandford. She has been wooed by both Raithe and Nyphron (who did so at Malcolm's prodding).

PHYRE: The afterlife, which is divided into three sections: Rel, Nifrel, and Alysin.

PLYMERATH (Fhrey, Instarya): The gate guard who was on duty the night the fane's army arrived at the outskirts of Alon Rhist.

PRYMUS: The military commander of a large unit of men within a legion.

PYRIDIAN (Fhrey, Miralyith): First son of Lothian, brother to Mawyndulë, and founder of the Estramnadon Academy of the Art, now deceased.

RAIN (Dherg): Perhaps the best digger of his people, he was one of three Dherg responsible for unleashing Balgargarath from a complex series of noise-creating traps. To save him from execution, Persephone took the three dwarfs back to Tirre after Gronbach's broken promises. He was a grand-prize winner at the Linden Lott competition and one of the people in the smithy the night Suri transformed Raithe into a gilarabrywn.

RAITHE (Rhune, Dureya): The son of Herkimer; also known as the God Killer. He killed Shegon (a Fhrey Asendwayr) in retribution for his father's death, and Gryndal (a Fhrey Miralyith) when he threatened the people of Dahl Rhen. He refused the position of keenig because he felt war with the Fhrey was impossible. He is in love with Persephone, but she does not reciprocate. He was the first person to train Tesh in combat skills. He was transformed into a gilarabrywn by Suri and was instrumental in routing fane Lothian and his forces.

RAOW: A feared predator that eats its prey starting with the face. Raow sleep on a bed of bones and must add another set before going to sleep. A single raow can devastate an entire region. Persephone and Sebek were wounded by one that was sent to assassinate her and Nyphron.

REGLAN (Rhune, Rhen): The former chieftain of Dahl Rhen and husband to Persephone. Killed by Konniger in an attempt to usurp his power.

REL: One of the three regions in the afterlife, the place where most people who are neither heroes nor villains go when they die.

RHEN: A wooded region in the west of Rhulyn that is home to the Rhune clan of the same name. It was formerly ruled by Reglan and later his wife, Persephone. Dahl Rhen was destroyed by a Grenmorian attack initiated by Fane Lothian for harboring Nyphron of the Instarya and killing First Minister Gryndal. It was abandoned when the surviving residents moved to Alon Rhist.

RHIST: A shortened name for Alon Rhist, the Fhrey outpost.

RHULYN: The "land of the Rhunes," bordered by the Fhrey's native Erivan to the east and the Fhrey outposts in Avrlyn to the west.

RHULYN-RHUNES: The southern clans of Rhunes: Nadak, Dureya, Rhen, Warric, Tirre, Melen, and Menahan. The Rhulyn-Rhunes have been in constant conflict with the northern tribes of the Gula-Rhunes.

RHUNE: One of the five major races of Elan, the race of humans. The word is Fhrey for "primitive," and for some, it is seen as derogatory. This race is technologically challenged, superstitious, and polytheistic. They live in clusters of small villages, and each clan is governed by a chieftain. There are two major groups of Rhunes, the Gula-Rhune from the north and the southern Rhulyn-Rhunes. The two factions have warred for centuries.

RHUNIC: The language spoken by the humans who live in Rhulyn.

ROAN (Rhune, Rhen): An ex-slave and incredibly talented and emotionally scarred inventor. With the help of the Dherg, she perfected wheels and carts. She adapted the javelin and the device used to start fires to invent the bow and arrow. Thanks to Persephone, she was able to observe the Dherg process of making iron swords. She was a member of the party that accompanied Persephone to Neith, and one of the people in the smithy the night Suri transformed Raithe into a gilarabrywn.

ROUNDHOUSE: A typical Rhune dwelling consisting of a single circular room with a cone-shaped roof, usually covered in thatch.

SARAH (Rhune, Rhen): Mother of Brin, wife of Delwin, best friend of Persephone, widely known as the best weaver in Dahl Rhen. She was killed by the giant attack that destroyed Dahl Rhen.

Sebek (Fhrey, Instarya): The best warrior of the Galantians. He used two cleve blades named Thunder and Lightning. Sebek was Tesh's first Fhrey fighting instructor. Tesh killed Sebek while the Fhrey lay in his sickbed after being injured by a raow during the Battle of Grandford.

Shahdi: The non-Instarya military group charged with maintaining order in Greater Erivan. These were the main troops used by Fane Lothian during the Battle of Grandford.

Shegon (Fhrey, Asendwayr): A hunter stationed at Alon Rhist to provide the warrior tribe with fresh meat. He was killed by Raithe after Shegon killed Herkimer (Raithe's father).

Shield: Also known as Shield to the chieftain or chieftain's Shield. The chieftain's personal bodyguard, and generally the finest warrior of a given clan.

Sile (Fhrey, Asendwayr): Employed after the Gray Cloak Rebellion, he is one of two bodyguards who never leave the side of Fane Lothian. His size indicates he may have Grenmorian blood.

Spider Corps: A group of Miralyith specially trained in coordinated attacks in which one Artist directs the combined power of the others in the group.

Strom: One of the three Gula-Rhune clans. The other two are Dunn and Erling.

Suri (Rhune, Rhen): The illegitimate child of Reglan, who had an affair with Maeve (Dahl Rhen's Keeper of Ways). She was left to die in the forest but was saved and raised by a mystic named Tura. She is one of two Rhunes known to possess the ability to use the Art. Her best friend, a white wolf named Minna, was turned into a gilarabrywn in the Agave of Neith. Later, Suri destroyed the entrance of Neith during an emotional outburst. During the Battle of Grandford, she transformed Raithe into another gilarabrywn—an act that was instrumental in turning the tide of that battle and forcing Fane Lothian to retreat. Arion of the Miralyith believes Suri is the key to peace between Fhrey and Rhunes.

SYNNE (Fhrey, Miralyith): Employed after the Gray Cloak Rebellion, she is one of two bodyguards who never leave the side of Fane Lothian. Renowned for her quick reflexes.

TALWARA: The official name of the Fhrey palace where the fane resides and rules.

TECHLYOR: In the Fhrey language, the term means "swift of hand." Sebek was the first one to use Techylor when referring to Tesh, who later used the term for the specially trained men under his command.

TEKCHIN (Fhrey, Instarya): One of Nyphron's band of outlaw Galantians, Tekchin is a rough, outspoken warrior whose preferred weapon is a thin, narrow-bladed sword. He is romantically linked to Moya, Shield of Persephone.

TEN CLANS: The entirety of the Rhune nation, comprising seven Rhulyn clans and three Gula clans.

TESH: The orphan boy who, along with Raithe, is all that remains of the Dureyan clan. His hatred of the Fhrey has driven his intensive training.

Tet: A curse word derived from the Tetlin Witch.

Tetlin Witch: The universally hated immortal being thought to be the source of all disease, pestilence, and evil in the world.

Tirre: Clan of Rhulyn-Rhunes. Its dahl is located in the south of Rhulyn on the Blue Sea, and is known for salt production and trade with the Dherg. Their last chieftain was Lipit.

Traitor, The: The moniker Mawyndulë bestowed on Arion for her part in First Minister Gryndal's death while aiding the Rhunes of Dahl Rhen.

Tressa (Rhune, Rhen): Widow of Konniger, who was the ex-chieftain of Dahl Rhen. She is generally despised and shunned by those who know her. She was one of the people in the smithy the night Suri transformed Raithe into a gilarabrywn.

Treya (Fhrey, Gwydry): Personal servant of Prince Mawyndulë.

Trilos (Fhrey, unknown tribal affiliation): A mysterious person obsessed with the Door in the Garden.

Tura (Rhune, no clan affiliation): Mentor to Suri and an ancient mystic who lived in the Hawthorn Glen near Dahl Rhen. She was most noted for her ability to predict the future.

Uberlin: Mythical source of all wickedness in Elan, believed to be the father of the Tetlin Witch.

Udgar: The former chieftain of Clan Erling of the Gula who challenged Persephone for the position of the keenig. He was defeated in one-on-one combat by Moya.

ULI VERMAR (the reign of a fane): An event that occurs three thousand years after the crowning of a fane or upon his death, when other Fhrey can challenge to rule. This is done by petitioning the Aquila and being presented with the Horn of Gylindora.

UMALYN: The Fhrey tribe of priests and priestesses who concern themselves with spiritual matters and the worship of Ferrol.

URUM RIVER: A north–south Avrlyn river west of the Bern, and the place where Raithe would like to make a new start.

VASEK (Fhrey, Asendwayr): The Master of Secrets.

VELLUM: Fine parchment perfected by the Dherg for drawing maps, made from the skins of young animals.

VERENTHENON: The huge domed meeting room of Alon Rhist used for official meetings and the dissemination of orders. It was collapsed by the Miralyith during the Battle of Grandford.

VIDAR (Fhrey, Miralyith): The senior councilor of the Aquila representing the Miralyith tribe. He made Prince Mawyndulë the junior councilor. He was framed by the Gray Cloaks and removed from his position by Fane Lothian.

VOLHORIC (Fhrey, Umalyn): The senior councilor of the Aquila representing the Umalyn tribe. He also holds the position of Conservator of the Aquila.

VORATH (Fhrey, Instarya): A member of Nyphron's Galantians. He has taken to the Rhune custom of wearing a beard. His weapon of choice is a pair of spiked-balled maces.

WOLF'S HEAD: A high outcropping of rock rising above the Dureyan plain. During the Battle of Grandford, Moya's archery corps devastated Lothian's Miralyith who were attacking from that position. After the battle, it became the resting place of the gilarabrywn that Suri created from Raithe.

ZEPHYRON (Fhrey, Instarya): The father of Nyphron, killed by Lothian during the challenge for fane upon Fenelyus's death. Zephyron died in an unusually gruesome fashion to make a point about Miralyith superiority and the folly of challenging their rule.

About the Author

Michael J. Sullivan is a *New York Times* and *Washington Post* bestselling author who has been nominated for seven Goodreads Choice Awards. His first novel, *The Crown Conspiracy,* was released by Aspirations Media Inc. in October 2008. From 2009 through 2010, he self-published five of the six books of the Riyria Revelations, which were later sold and re-released by Hachette Book Group's Orbit imprint as three two-book omnibus editions (*Theft of Swords, Rise of Empire, Heir of Novron*).

Michael's Riyria Chronicles series (a prequel to Riyria Revelations) has been both traditionally and self-published. The first two books were released by Orbit, and the next two by his own imprint, Riyria Enterprises, LLC. A fifth Riyria Chronicle, titled *Drumindor,* will be self-published in the near future.

For Penguin Random House's Del Rey imprint, Michael has published the first three books of the Legends of the First Empire: *Age of Myth, Age of Swords,* and *Age of War.* The last three books of the series will be distributed by Grim Oak Press and are titled *Age of Legend, Age of Death,* and *Age of Empyre.*

Michael is now writing The Rise and the Fall Trilogy. These three books are based in his fictional world Elan two thousand years after the events of Legends of the First Empire and one thousand years before the Riyria novels.

You can email Michael at michael@michaelsullivan-author.com.

About the Type

This book was set in Fournier, a typeface named for Pierre Simon Fournier (1712–1768), the youngest son of a French printing family. He started out engraving woodblocks and large capitals, then moved on to fonts of type. In 1736, he began his own foundry and made several important contributions in the field of type design; he is said to have cut 147 alphabets of his own creation. Fournier is probably best remembered as the designer of St. Augustine Ordinaire, a face that served as the model for the Monotype Corporation's Fournier, which was released in 1925.

3-5-26
5-28-22
12